Praise for *Kamika[ze Lust]*
(Winner of a 200[...])

"Great courage must account for such complete disregard of political correctness, and great sensitivity for such sadness."
—Amanda Filipacchi, author of *Vapor* and *Nude Men*

"Like an official conducting an all-out strip search, first-time novelist Lauren Sanders plucks and probes her characters' minds and bodies to reveal their hidden lusts, and when all is said and done, nary a body cavity is spared."
—*Time Out New York*

"*Kamikaze Lust* makes a connection between unrealized lives, sexual repression, and the fear of death. In Sanders' hands, what is usually clichéd or gratuitous is hot."
—Amy Ray of the Indigo Girls

"*Kamikaze Lust* puts a snappy spin on a traditional theme—young woman in search of herself—and stands it on its head. In a crackling, rapid-fire voice studded with deadpan one-liners and evocative descriptions, Rachel Silver takes us to such far-flung places as a pompous charity benefit, the set of an 'art porn' movie, her best friend's body, Las Vegas casinos, and the psyche of her own porn-star alter ego, Silver Ray, all knit together by the unspoken question: who am I, anyway? And as Rachel tells it, asking the question is more fun than knowing for sure could ever be."
—Kate Christensen, author of *In the Drink*

"This sexy little novel isn't afraid to be steamy—but it isn't too jaded for romance either."
—*The Advocate*

"Lauren Sanders is a writer of extraordinary skill."
—*Bay Area Reporter*

"The fact that Sanders can so overtly take on sex and death, write almost exclusively of their relationship to each other and their effects on a developing personality, and not sound clichéd, is a monumental achievement in itself."
—*Toronto Star*

"Sanders zips and zooms through Rachel's overturned life with prose as sharp, quick, and deadly as any suicide mission."

—*Out Magazine*

"In *Kamikaze Lust*, Lauren Sanders manages her own later-day book of changes. We follow the plight of a city reporter in hot pursuit of a controversial story, but when her newspaper union suddenly strikes, she finds herself in need of carryover cash. She becomes a ghost writer for a porn diva—and the story follows the transfiguration of her sexual and literary pursuits. From Bay Ridge to Vegas—with a memorable supporting cast—dysfunctional family members and porn stars—this high-paced novel gracefully covers ground. By the touching conclusion, Sanders has investigated the age-old questions that bookend life: sex and death."

—Arthur Nersesian, author of *The Fuck-Up*

"Without wit or heart, this much sex would be unsexy, particularly if the author were using the titillation factor as mere bait for jacket blurbs. Instead, it serves a broader purpose, illustrating that the boundaries we use to demarcate civilized society are largely an illusion, and that labels like 'porn star,' 'cancer patient,' and 'lesbian' are meant to signify—falsely—'people nothing like us.' Here sex bleeds so naturally into life, and life into sex, that books that shy from this human realm begin to seem prissy and suspect."

—*City Pages* (Minneapolis/St. Paul)

"*Kamikaze Lust* is a whirl of New York neurotic fast-quipping with a line or two courtesy of Miss Sandra Bernhardt, but who better to borrow from than the Princess of Pith?"

—*Time Out London*

WITH OR WITHOUT YOU

WITH OR WITHOUT YOU

a novel by

LAUREN SANDERS

Akashic Books
New York

Published by Akashic Books
©2005 Lauren Sanders

Author photo on back cover by Lisa Ross

ISBN: 1-888451-69-6
Library of Congress Control Number: 2004106243
All rights reserved
First printing
Printed in Canada

Akashic Books
PO Box 1456
New York, NY 10009
Akashic7@aol.com
www.akashicbooks.com

for RoRo

Acknowledgments

Many thanks to the following people who in one way or another have helped me through the long journey of this book: Kim Bernstein, Nina Chaudry, Rory Devine, Elena Georgiou, Angela Himsel, Mark Leydorf, Brenda McClain, Mary McGrail, Thais Morales, Eileen Myles, Jaymie Ridless, Aaron Zimmerman, my parents, and the rest of my friends and comrades. Big-time thanks to J.T. Rogers for sharing his wisdom and insight and for the early morning wake-up calls; to Johnny Temple and Johanna Ingalls for running the classiest literary shop in town; and to Gerry Gomez Pearlberg (and Mao, Otto, and Gumdrop) for being so darn wonderful to come home to.

JULY 2, 1987: THE MORNING AFTER

BECAUSE I'M WEARING ALL MY CLOTHES, and because the bay is choppy, I pretend I'm trapped in a giant washing machine. Sun pecks the back of my neck, warming me through the glass. My legs bob up and down. It's a light spin cycle, the setting for silk blouses, lacy underwear, or, if you're my mother, an endless string of sheer pantyhose, the kind I don't mind on other girls but hate wearing myself. Gentlemen prefer them, too. Ask my father. He and his pal Gustave shoot the most popular hosiery commercials in town.

You were wearing black hose when I left you. Maybe it was a different brand, but the sparkle in the crisscrossed fibers gave your shins the look of one of their spots. Edgy but sophisticated. And no blood on them, attached to your two black boots pointing skyward, forecasting the journey. If you believe in that kind of crap.

I swim out a few feet where the waves are calmer, turn over on my back, and float. In camp they called this the dead man's float. But I've never felt more alive. Too alive for a murderer. Though I'm not any normal murderer, and you're no ordinary victim.

Just a few days ago, I thought about picking you up outside the theatre and taking you to a fancy restaurant. Maybe bringing you to my summer house once my family cleared out. You were so tired and needed a break. Even with all the makeup caked into your cheeks I could tell—particularly that day I found you sitting in the stairwell, your legs triangled and head resting between them. You were pulling the blond hairs from your scalp one at a time. It must have been tough keeping up with your *World* scenes and being in a play at the same time. But you told *Soap Opera Weekly* it was a nice break from Los Angeles. Not that you didn't like L.A. You had an apartment somewhere in Hollywood, a little red car and big sloppy dog, a personal fitness trainer. You said it was the only city where you ever felt comfortable.

I'd considered applying to art school out there before my parents decided Syracuse was the place for me. I think I told you in one of my letters how my father knew some guy at the school there. Jack promised he'd help fund the media literacy center if they'd overlook my lame SAT scores and enter me in the class of '91. Nancy helped me complete the application, constructing the essay in a way that made me sound conventional. Just a slaphappy girl from the suburbs, my teenage years spent cheering football players from the bleachers and playing in the band. When we finished the draft, I asked, "Who's this?"

"Exactly who they're looking for," she said, and I knew she'd done her research. She always did. It was how she made a fortune selling houses to other people just like herself. She said there was no way I would ruin the opportunity at Syracuse the way I'd sabotaged their attempts to send me to dance class—getting expelled for, quote, "negligent uncoordination." And all of those camps. When I was booted from the last one for hitchhiking, Nancy called me an ingrate. A couple years later she was even more pissed I refused the nose job that was supposed to be my birthday present.

You had a perfect nose. Small and buttonlike. If your nostrils were any bigger, they would have been piggish, a distraction from those clear blue eyes. So reflective I could see myself in them, a shadow, the outline of my knuckles on the cool metal. Eyes corkscrewed and pleading . . . *Why?*

I skim my right hand along the gray-blue water. When it dips below the surface, it grows purplish white and humongous. No longer my hand at all. I can't stand it. So I go down, fighting the weight of my parachute pants. They seem to have inflated. I touch my sneakers to the bottom and it feels turbulent. This is where the delicates give way to chain-gang fabrics, the denim and cotton and flannel.

Underwater my ears rumble like a distant subway car and I'm

freaking. Can you hear the palpitations in my chest? Stay down, I tell myself. It's only fair. Beams of light split the oily water. It's not the celestial strobe near-death freaks talk about but more like the headlights from Jack's BMW. Bright white circles illuminating this undersea world: moss, gnarled seaweed, silt. I try digging my feet into the bottom but it's too rocky. What feels like slippery crepe paper wraps around my neck and I flinch, kicking off my sneakers. My lungs fill with water and I force myself up. Hacking but alive. Forget what anyone says, it's hard to drown when you know how to swim. I am for one moment happy. My breathing turns to laughter and I dolphin-flip forward, wondering what I'll do today, a bike ride, sit by the pool . . . it's summer. Then I spot the motor boat coming toward me and remember where I am, what I've done.

I lean my head back into the water. Chickenshit. The boat rocks to the side of me. Aboard are two men in khaki pants, green shirts, and sunglasses, one by the steering wheel, the other leaning his thick leg on a bench and chewing a toothpick. Their patches say Shelter Island Police Department.

"This is a no-swimming zone," says the cop behind the wheel.

"I'm not swimming."

"Sure looks like it."

"Can't you see I'm trying to kill myself?"

I regret that the moment I say it. Mostly because they laugh at me. Ridiculous creature. Out here in the bay on a blinding summer day, wearing all my clothes, telling them I want to kill myself when I don't. I was never good at suicide. Not for any throbbing love of life but a total lack of nerve. I just couldn't do it. And, like most things in life, you don't get many points for your failures.

But now I am a celebrity murderer. A murderer soon to be a celebrity. I deserve a little respect from a couple of bumble-fuck cops. The talky one backs away from the steering wheel and throws out a rope ladder. History warns, climb aboard or they'll shoot. And they should, if justice is anything like the Bible says. An eye for an eye, tit for tat. But because like my father I'm an atheist, I grab the ladder and with wrinkled fingers hoist myself aboard. Sun smacks the left side of my body. My skin is always quick to burn. A splotched face'll ruin the perp walk. I'll look pathetic on the news.

"Got any sunscreen?" I ask.

The silent cop hands me a tube of lotion. Taking it from him, I notice a piece of egg or muffin trapped in the thick strands of his moustache. The hairs remind me of a straw broom. I imagine them pricking the lips of a girl and know even with a mouth so creepy he can get it whenever he wants. Bastard.

I squeeze a few drops of coconut lotion into my palms and rub them together before bringing my hands to my face. The lotion, too greasy under normal circumstances, loosens the salt-water mask on my cheeks. Then I do my arms. When I'm finished, I hold out my fists. "You can cuff me now."

Silent cop smiles, the dirty straws above his lips expanding as he surveys my waterlogged Syracuse sweatshirt and parachute pants. Talking cop says, "I think we better get you home. You on-island for the summer?"

"No."

"Then where do you live?"

I try to remember the address of my summer house but draw a blank. They're questioning me like I'm any other suicide teen. I probably seem young. When my hair's wet you can't see the shock of white on the left side. Makes people think I'm older than I am. I've got ancient hair and two webbed toes on each foot.

Talking cop is trying to be nice, smiling as he says they can't take me home if they don't know where I live. "I'm telling you, arrest me!" I shout at him. "Read me my rights . . . I have the right to remain silent, the right to an attorney, c'mon."

"You watch too much TV."

"You really don't get it."

"No, *you* don't get it," silent cop says. It's the first time he speaks and I don't like it. "We got better things to do than play idiot games all morning. So tell us where you live or we'll dump you back in the bay."

"Go ahead," I say, sick of their small-time attitude. They have no idea who they're dealing with. "I killed someone big last night," I say, and they both burst out laughing. "Hey, jerk, if you don't believe me, call New York. Ask them about Brooke Harrison. I'm about to make you very famous."

Saying the words I am for a few seconds tough like the baddest motherfucker in the world. Bad like Al Cappone, Michael Jackson. *Badder than old King Kong, meaner than a junkyard dog.* Then I see your face and know you're watching.

The cops look back and forth between each other and me. They must have seen the news and are trying to decide if I'm actually . . . my temples pound. I said I killed somebody. And told them your name. Anything I say can and will be held against me. *I said I killed somebody!*

I want to drop to my knees and beg their forgiveness, beg for a lawyer, but something tells me stay tough. I lean back on my hands and stare off into the blues of summer. A sea gull caws overhead. The ocean glimmers in the distance like a flattened disco ball; up close you can see the hypodermic needles, beer cans, and plastic bags floating nowhere.

Suddenly, I know what to do: I jump overboard.

The water is colder, more intimidating. Breathing in, I swallow all the water I can this time. Something hard and fleshy pulls across my stomach, and I feel my body being lifted up and thrown over the boat. Shoving me to the floor, the silent cop puts a black boot on my stomach. We are both dripping wet and hyperventilating.

"Give me the cuffs," he says.

"Don't got 'em," the other says.

"What?"

"Last night . . . at the school."

"So?"

"I think we left them in the car."

"Fuckin' idiot! Get the wheel!" the silent cop screams, pressing his foot down against my stomach. I'm going to puke. He lifts a soiled towel from the floor, pulls me up, and turns me around. Now he's got his foot on my back and he's squeezing the towel around my wrists behind me.

My face splashes against the fiberglass, the sun caressing the right side of my face this time. I hear the motor crank, feel the waves beneath my stomach. Then the voice rings faintly in my ear. "Listen up, sweetheart, here comes Mr. Miranda . . ."

GIRLS, GIRLS, GIRLS

I AM QUIET IN MY CELL.

I read a lot in my cell. I lie on my bed a lot talking to you.

Those jokes about women behind bars—they're all true. Jail is crawling with dykes, although most of them would never use that word. Not too different from what I found outside. But here they're big into role-playing. For the girls who like to be manly, the kind who scare the pants off me they're so real, so much the better. They rule with their heavy boots and bad haircuts, their chests puffed out like drug lords.

If a girl's strong enough or the opposite, there's more sex in here than you can imagine. Most do it for power, some to connect. Others want to feel anything at all. These are the women who let Mimi zap them with her vibrating needle. Ink siphoned from a ballpoint pen. She's been after me since the day I arrived and asked her how she made the needle move. She lifted her transistor radio. There was a wire attached to a small motor in the back, but I still didn't get it. She said I would know it all one day, when I let her tattoo me. I smiled but no way was I letting her brand me.

As the days go on, I want to give in. I like her silky green-black etchings and know she could copy one of my drawings, although I haven't drawn anything in the month and a half I've been in here. My fingers won't connect to my brain. So I pretend not to know anything about art and artists, pretend I never earned the praise of my painting teachers or interned at the advertising agency, pretend I never even owned a sketchbook, all for the sake of Mimi, who's convinced she's schooling me in the creative process. She's the toughest of the tough girls and all the protection I have inside. The trick is I have to please her, if you know what I mean, which is much better than the other way, getting pleased, though she's schooling me a bit there, too. I wonder if I'm still a virgin.

Mimi likes my doing but won't say so. Even after she gets off a few times then throws me off, making what we are together worse than what got either one of us in here in the first place. "I'm going to tattoo the word on your stomach," she says, and runs her hand along the haphazard hairs beneath my belly button. She tries to yank at one, but it slips between her fingers. "Right here, it's gonna say *pata.*"

"Why does it have to be in Spanish?"

"Because it's happy."

I smile because *happy* is as good as anything gets for Mimi. She uses the word the way other people say *cool* or *excellent*. It rolls from her tongue, sweet like strawberry margaritas, like her Spanish phrases I can understand thanks to Long Island's exceptional public schools. In seventh grade, we were forced to check a box for either French or Spanish. Having no preference, I shut my eyes and dropped my index finger on the paper. It fell closest to Spanish.

Mimi's got a guy and a couple of kids outside. They all do; gay for the stay is how they put it, and I get the feeling it's not something they talk about otherwise. It's hard to imagine most of them wiping dirty faces and throwing dinner on the table. I get the feeling women have been through a lot of shit in their lives before ending up here. You can see it in their eyes like smudged nickels, their sandpaper skin, no matter what color. Faces blend into one another after a while. But not Mimi's. She's got the look, and that dusky aura like the ring around Saturn. It takes my built-in 3-D glasses to see it.

This time, Mimi's waiting trial on four counts of armed robbery and reckless endangerment. She shot the owner of an appliance store as she and a friend were loading her station wagon with television sets and videocassette recorders. She says the shooting was an accident and I believe her. She does not use drugs. She is an artist. She sounds like you.

The handsome attorney my father hired says I shouldn't talk about you. He's convinced I didn't do it, although I confessed to those moron cops, and the evidence against me is mounting. But when the bottom of the Hudson spit up what they thought was my gun, it had no fingerprints and didn't match the deadly bullet. My lawyer had the cojones to claim my gun never existed. There is somebody else who's seen it, I warn him, not to mention one house missing a .38 Special and blue Tiffany bag full of bullets. But so far he's managed to talk our way around that, too. Still, the D.A. postponed my bail hearing, railing to the papers, "We're going to prosecute this case to the fullest extent of the law!"

So I'm stuck at Women's House. Sounds like a safe space: some warm and cuddly hippie commune. But let me tell you, I'm scared. There are gangs in here who kill people in other gangs 'cause they look funny, women who gouge out eyeballs with their fingers or pound in heads with a padlock wrapped in a sweat sock. At first my lawyer tried to get the case moved to juvie, but since I'd just turned eighteen and the crime was getting so much press, the D.A. said I would be treated as an adult. And adults without bail end up here, waiting to be shipped Upstate, where most of the big prisons are—literally, up the river. When I'm in a funny mood, I tell myself it's like being sent off to college, but usually I hate myself too much to joke. I wish I lived in California where they have the death penalty. I would be gassed for sure because it's a television culture out there.

In some ways, death would be easy. A quick electronic current or snap of the spine and it's over. I've been having nightmares about dying—always violently. I've been nailed to a cross and stoned, shot by firing squad, had my limbs severed by the Long Island Rail Road. Dreams so vivid I wake up sweating and shaking, my body twisted in pain. So I try to stay awake, each night playing back your death in my head.

I messed up, I tell Jack and Nancy when they come to visit. They ignore my sloppy confessions. Jack wrings his fingers together.

Nancy stares at the couple making out by the front windows. In her eyes, a wandering glow. Hands on the table, the guard shouts. Jack asks if I'm eating right, if I'm talking to the shrink. Before they leave, he gives me ballpoint pens and yellow legal pads. Between reading up on my case and apprenticing with Mimi, I'm trying to write my story. One of the reporters asked for it, but I don't give a shit about him. If I don't tell it like it is, somebody else is going to get it out there first. I hear your mother's been talking to some people. I guess she's got a right.

The problem is I spend a lot of time scribbling notes and shredding the pages. I feel guilty because paper can be hard to come by, but not for me because I'm a famous prisoner. Because my daddy's rich and my lawyer's good-looking.

So hush, little darling.

Don't you cry.

I DON'T REMEMBER THE WOMB or coming out or any of the other stuff that happens when you're really young. Without the baby book Nancy kept my first couple of years or my grandmother in the desert, I might never have known it took me only eight months to pull myself up off the floor or that the white streak in my hair had sprouted from a bald spot, that I was a most verbal child, though I made up my own names for everything, and that it was me who'd started calling my parents by their first names, actually one name: *Jackanan,* short for Jack and Nancy, says my grandmother.

I spent a lot of time with her early on and then we moved out of the city and then my grandparents moved across the country and I hardly ever saw them. There were a few more houses and schools and summer camps before we landed on the northern tip of Long Island the day the president was shot. The day I met Blair.

I was eleven years old. You were fifteen. We didn't know each other yet, but later I discovered it was a special day for you, too: the day you got into the summer program at the American

Academy of Dramatic Arts. "I was opening the letter when I heard the news," you would later say. "I thought it was weird I could be so lucky when there was so much violence and sadness in the world. I sat down and cried and cried and cried."

Was it as bruised and foggy on that day where you lived? The weathermen in New York all predicted rain. April showers had come early, and Nancy wasn't happy. The land was more tender where we were going. "The last thing I need is everyone tracking mud all over my new floors," she said. "You hear me, Lily? No running around!"

"But what if it doesn't rain?"

"Don't get cute with me, just watch your feet."

I stared down at my black high-tops, red laces strangling the tongue, and imagined they were stuffed with dynamite. One wrong move and I'd destroy the world. Was it better to hop and take fewer steps or glide on the tips of my toes? The fate of mankind rested in my feet. Go lightly, I decided, like walking on thumbtacks. I wanted to scream, "Look, Nancy, I'm watching my feet!" But she'd gone back inside.

I crumpled into my father's car and took out a small spiral notebook from my back pocket, sketching the moving truck in soft pencil lines. Nancy promised this move would be the last. She finally found the perfect house, she'd said, and Jack and I rolled our eyes. She had a way of getting lost in her own sales. But when Jack had gone with her a week later, he came back gushing over the views of the city and a backyard that folded onto the beach. He was a salesman, too. He said I'd practically have my own wing, and I imagined a house like a bald eagle soaring over the shore.

Our new house was made of wood. And cinder blocks. And had all these curves and odd-shaped windows and a totally flat roof. It looked like a science lab nestled in the pine trees, a place where pro-nukers hatched plans to destroy the human race. Jack said the house was created in the sixties by an architect who worked with shorelines. We'd had the windows open on the drive out, and as we came closer, I could smell the beach. Slivers of muddy gray waves crashed behind the trees, growing bigger and bigger as we turned into the driveway.

"Isn't it amazing?" Jack said.

I shrugged. "It doesn't look like a house."

"Ahh! That's the beauty of it. Who says a house has to be something you'd draw in second grade? Huh . . . who? It's almost the twenty-first century for Christ's sake and we're still living like farmers. Why go back when you can go forward? Be of the time . . . you hear me?"

"Where's the front door?"

"Wait'll you see . . ."

Jack led me up a path to what looked like a long cylinder. Hidden on the other side was the door. We stepped through, and the Long Island Sound spread out in front of us. The space was huge and open, with different levels and lots of sliding glass. Dipping down a couple of steps, we came closer to the view: big, watery, and expansive. Between the clouds lay bits of Manhattan. On a clear day, Jack promised, I'd be able to see the skyline.

He cracked open a cardboard box that said Stereo. "First things first," he winked at Nancy, who was trailing behind a man carrying a couple of chairs.

"Jack, I need you," she said.

"It'll just take a sec."

She grimaced.

"Come on, baby, we can't unpack without music."

"You're impossible." She walked over to him, messed up his hair like he was a puppy. She never touched my head. My hair was knotty and I hated brushing. Only my grandmother ever noticed. She thought I was trying to hide the white streak in front. It meant I was wise, she told me. Some day I'd appreciate it. "Wait, wait, halt!" Nancy grabbed a mover by the arm. "That's a picnic table. It goes in the yard."

"You said garage." The mover sighed.

"No, I didn't. I wouldn't say that. Anyway, let's go, move it outside . . . you're causing gridlock in here."

He hurled the picnic table higher over his head and shuffled off. Jack watched him, smiling. "Poor guys have no idea who they're dealing with."

Nancy was *impossible*. The movers cowered before her, thick sweaty men reduced to gurgling infants whenever she lifted her clipboard or pointed a finger. Carting the stuff is only half the job, she said. They were supposed to put everything in the right place, and only she knew where that place was. They worked for her, remember. She'd made them lay plastic over her wood floors, and it still wasn't raining.

Hooking up the stereo took longer than Jack had planned. The wiring and all. I watched him for a while, then sat down on a folding chair in front of the sliding-glass doors. The waves looked icy. Someone had opened one of the doors, leaving only a screen, and I was freezing. I put on my down jacket but felt silly. Most of the movers were wearing T-shirts. Red. With the name of the company written across the chest. They spoke to each other in another language, and there was a sped-up, silent-movie rhythm to the way they moved, like the colonies of ants in the sidewalk cracks at our old house, rushing in and out of their sandy little hills with sticks and grass and other bugs for dinner. The movers carried furniture wrapped in waffled blankets and tossed box cutters back and forth to snip off the tape. They had their own cooler.

A static blast rocked the half-empty house. Crazy echoes. Everything stopped, even the mover-ants. Jack shouted, threw his hands over his head, and did his Mets dance to a jingle for a bank. "Whoo-hoo! How do you like that?" he shouted. "I'm the music man!" I giggled. A couple of movers smiled, then went back to their lifting and circling. Jack bent over, turned down the commercial, and started thumbing through the channels . . . an old Elvis song . . . more fuzz . . . stock market numbers . . . then the voice: ". . . No word yet on the president, who according to reports is currently undergoing open-heart surgery at a local hospital after a shooting outside the Washington Hilton this morning . . ."

"Holy shit!" said my father. A couple of movers locked to a couch stopped dead in their tracks. Some shouted in their language. A few more gathered around, all ant eyes and wide-open mouths. Their world shut down.

"Nance!" Jack screamed. The movers whispered, so sad and serious I wished I could understand them, wished I had someone to whisper with. Jack looked too weird. He called Nancy's name a few more times, tried to find a new radio station. Nancy appeared on the balcony above. "Somebody got Reagan," Jack said. "They shot him."

"What? Who?"

"I don't know . . . it's impossible to get any goddamn information on the radio. I should've hooked up the TV first."

Nancy stepped down the staircase, her long curls bouncing against her shoulders like she was walking into a ballroom, and joined us around the stereo. Jack found a station with less screaming and commercials. The announcer said the president was in surgery (this one didn't say anything about his heart). A witness said he'd heard a sound. *Like flashcubes going off.* Then there was a big commotion. Shouting. The Secret Service tackled the president and shoved him into his limo. Three other people were left lying on the sidewalk. The president walked into the hospital himself, smiling, strong. He was a cowboy. Or he'd played one in a movie. Now he was ruler of the free world. Bullets didn't scare him. Police had arrested a young man at the scene. An assassination attempt for sure.

"Not again," Jack said, and turned down the radio. I thought he'd be happier. He hated the president. Last fall, when there was still hope, he'd tacked a bumper sticker to the refrigerator that said, Anybody but Reagan.

"This is different." Nancy touched his arm, and I knew they were talking about John Lennon, who'd been killed a few months earlier. Jack and Nancy had been playing Beatles albums nonstop. Kids at my old school said it was Yoko's fault for breaking up the Beatles. But they'd also said the white streak in my hair meant I was retarded. Jack said Yoko was good for John. She helped release his genius.

"Jesus, Lily, I was just about your age," Jack said.

"What do you mean?"

"The last time."

"With John Lennon?"

"John Fitzgerald Kennedy," Jack said, drawing out every sylla-ble. Same name as his own: John-but-everyone-calls-me-Jack. "Didn't I ever tell you about the day Kennedy was shot?"

"Only a million times," Nancy cut him off, then glanced at the movers who'd gathered in a tight circle, a hand on a back, arm wrapped around another neck. A colony. Jack followed her gaze. I wanted him back.

"Let's hear it again," I begged my father. "Please . . ."

"Later, Lily," said my mother.

"Come on."

"She's right, you've heard it a gazillion times," Jack said. His eyes dropped, and I knew he was remembering how he'd come home from school to find his neighborhood spilling into the streets, people crying and praying and hugging each other, like the mover-ants, others walking around with transistor radios plastered to their ears. It was an Irish-Catholic neighborhood. Jack Kennedy was their guy. So, earlier, they'd gathered in front of tiny black-and-white TV sets, congregated at Kelsey's, or stood before the window at Sears, proud to see their guy and his beautiful wife parading through Dallas. And then . . .

This is the part where my father always got teary, especially if he had a few drinks in him. He even spoke kindly of his mother who'd let him spend the night at his cousins' watching replays of the grainy loop since they didn't have a TV set at home. My other grandmother—the dead one—thought television was the devil's tool. But on that day the devil himself had come to America in the body of man called Lee Harvey Oswald. TV didn't seem so bad.

Jack was right; we could have used the TV. To see the shot. *Like flashcubes going off.* Watch the Secret Service tackle the president.

"Okay, look, there's no use sitting around," Nancy said, and I thought she was talking to me. But she stood with the movers. "He could be in surgery for hours, and we've got half the truck to unload. Come on, let's go!" She clapped her hands. A couple of movers looked shocked. Rolling deep-brown eyeballs. They hated Nancy. I hated her for making them hate her. "You are bosslady," one smiled, then called out to the others in mover-words. He had big ringlets of brown hair and talked with his hands. He must have been the leader. Jack patted his shoulder. "It's all right, man, I'll let you guys know if anything happens."

"He is a strong man, this president." The leader-ant made a fist with his right hand. "He will live."

"That's what I'm afraid of." Jack flashed his JFK smile and the leader-ant's face softened. They laughed together. When you had his attention, Jack could make you feel like there was nothing or nobody else in the world. You wanted to keep him happy, even if you thought he was full of it. The leader-ant guided his men back to work. Walking toward us Nancy whispered, "Ever think you'd see a bunch of illegal immigrants crying over a Republican?"

"Doesn't matter what he was," Jack said. "Now he's gonna be a hero."

"I'm telling you, this is different, we don't even know him," Nancy said, and stalked off.

"Are you kidding?" Jack popped up after her. "He rides horses. He got the hostages out. He's a movie star for Christ's sake; even Kennedy only looked like a movie star . . ." His words fizzled out. Left was the faint voice of a deejay. Clouds rumbling outside the sliding-glass doors. The waves, though small, were violent and white, thousands of hands shaking up the underworld. Confusion down there, too.

I slid open a door and slipped outside. A deck led down to our own little beach. One side was fenced in, the other had a few bushes and barky trees. The air smelled sappy, salty. Wind slammed into my face, nonstop stereophonic blasts of static, under a sky so blank and low you couldn't really make out the horizon. Everything was gray. I walked a few feet to a big rock, climbed up, and stared out at the water. A light drizzle came. More of a mist really. Then a figure emerged through the fog, like it had popped straight out of the underworld. A mermaid or different kind of mover-ant, one that lived in the sea. But the closer it came the more womanlike it was. She wore a tight gray raincoat.

Stopping a few feet away, she smiled, and I turned my head,

thinking one of my parents must have snaked up from behind. People never smiled at me. But it was just the two of us, almost the same height with me on the rock. "Nice day for a walk," she said.

Her voice was hard and soft at the same time, and I felt like I'd seen her somewhere before. She said days like this she loved the beach. "The sky, the water, everything's bursting at the seams."

That's what I was thinking. About her.

"You live here?" she said, raising her chin toward our house, her eyes all squinty, like she knew how way past ugly it was.

"Yeah, but I didn't pick it out," I nodded.

"I should think not," she smiled again. "What's your name?"

"Lillian G. Speck."

"Well, hello, Lillian G. Speck. I'm Blair." She pointed a long red fingernail through the fog. "I live over there."

"In the water!"

"Next to it. In a little cottage."

"Cool."

"Want to see? I have tea and cookies. We can be neighbors."

I followed her along the beach and around the back of our trees. Right there was a little white house with a normal roof, two front windows with bunched-up curtains behind them and green shutters outside. It was closer to our place than to the mansion on the other side, but it looked like a key-chain version of the bigger house. Blair said the cottage was originally a guesthouse; now the people in the mansion rented it out. She said she liked listening to the waves before she fell asleep, and it was close to the airport. "Unless I'm flying overseas, but lord knows I try to avoid that. Long flights make my skin flake." She bent down at the front door and lifted a mat that said, Ring My Bell. Underneath was a shiny gold key. She picked it up and stuck it in the keyhole. "I never take it unless I absolutely have to," she smiled. "Now you know my secret. Promise you won't tell."

"I promise."

I stepped inside behind her. Heat pumped loudly, and everything smelled perfumed. To the right was a tiny kitchen, to the left what looked like a living room. Before I could take it all in, two hairy white cats rushed to the door, sniffing and pushing their faces into my shins. Blair bent down and pet their heads, same as my mother had touched my father. Like she owned him. Staring up at me, she said, "These are my girls, Grace and Marilyn. Yes, you . . ." She nuzzled her lips against theirs for kisses. Rubbed behind their ears. "Such gentle babies . . . yes . . ." She looked up at me. "Maybe you'll take care of them when I'm away. They haven't been doing well at the kennel. Do you like cats?"

I nodded yes, though I had no idea.

"Then it's settled," Blair smiled, stood up. She unbuttoned her coat and hung it in the front closet. "May I take yours?" she asked, and I wriggled out of my down jacket. We were both wearing sweatshirts. Mine was plain and bulky, hers cut off at the waist, just below the Delta Airlines logo. When she stretched up I could see her belly button. An inny.

She told me to have a seat on the couch, while she went to the kitchen, filled a kettle with water, and set it on the stove to boil. The couch was white and slippery. I had to plant myself all the way back so my feet barely touched the floor. Grace and Marilyn jumped up with me, fluffy little armrests. I couldn't tell which was which. Blair brought over a tin with pictures of butter cookies on the cover—the same one my grandmother kept on top of her refrigerator in the desert—then returned to the kitchen. The house was so small I could see everything. She poured steaming water into two mugs, dropped in tea bags, then set them on a tray with a few packets of Sweet'N Low, tiny containers of nondairy creamer, and napkins that said Delta Airlines. She'd taken them from work. She was a stewardess.

"Wow!" I said. I'd never met a stewardess. At least not outside of a plane.

Filling our cups with water, Blair apologized for not having real milk. "I can't keep it in the house with the girls around," she said.

"It's okay." I dumped a couple of creams or whatever into my cup. The steam rising from it felt good after being outside, but it started my nose running. I covered one nostril with my finger and sucked up the other, no use: A few seconds later the runoff was back. Blair didn't seem to notice.

She kept on talking about the cats and milk. "They love it but it makes them vomit. People think milk is so good for cats . . . I don't know where that comes from. Anyway, I feel too guilty drinking it around them . . ."

I tried to nod, but felt the snot escaping and tilted my head back. A glob of it landed in the back of my throat. I reached for my cup and choked on a mouthful of steam. Blair smiled. I took a deep breath, relaxed. Then this small cough ballooned into a fit, with so much spunk to it I slid forward, forcing the cats away. I couldn't stop hacking.

"Easy there," Blair said. She reached over and grabbed my cup. Pulled me back up. I was still coughing and smoldering with embarrassment. Feeling like a two-year-old with her hand rubbing my back, her hair so close I smelled the burnt-vanilla scent of the dye. Same as Nancy's. "I'm sorry," she said. "It's too hot. Here . . ." She handed me a napkin. "Blow your nose. Sometimes that helps."

I blew so hard my eyes watered. I was all liquidy, but she didn't care. Guess it wasn't as bad as milky cat vomit. Everyone should have to have pets. I let the coughing go until there was nothing left in me. Blair gave my arm a quick squeeze. "All better, little flower?" she said, her smile so cozy it was worth the goopy mess. I slid back closer to her. Neither one of us said anything for a few minutes as we drank our tea and the cats came back and she turned on the TV and there was the news about the president. Blair shouted, "Good God!" She had no idea, she said, and if she'd known . . . Wasn't it just so dreadful? Who would do such a thing? She looked grave. Like stewardesses in airport movies. I wanted to say something, but couldn't think of anything nice about the president and remembered a teacher or counselor or somebody telling a group of kids who'd been calling me skunk puddle that if they didn't have anything nice to say they should keep their mouths shut, and I couldn't believe people actually said that kind of stuff in real life, not just on after-school specials. I decided to zip it. Blair stood up and paced, making me nervous, and I wished she'd never turned on the damn TV.

She stopped in front of it and bent down. On the shelf below were a few bottles that clanked between her fingers. "He's a movie star and he freed the hostages," I blurted out, thinking of what my father had said, only making it sound better. "He's going to live."

Blair lifted a bottle that looked like a genie could make a nice home of it. "Oh, let's hope so, Lillian," she said, and popped the cork. The booze rushing into her teacup smelled sweeter than Nancy's gin. Stronger, too. After a few sips Blair's face untangled, her smile veering upwards as if someone had attached a line to the corner of her lip and lightly tugged. She leaned her body into mine, everything more rubbery. I liked her like that.

Watching the news we learned the guy who'd shot the movie-star president had been planning it for weeks, to win the love of a pretty blond actress. It was a Hollywood thing. But an outsider, one of the president's men, who'd never been in the movies, took the worst of the bullets. They weren't sure whether he'd make it. Meantime, the president would be out of surgery shortly. The news people said he was expected to make a full recovery. They talked about his strength and good nature. When they brought him in he joked about forgetting to duck, they chuckled. At one point, I looked over at Blair and, seeing her close to tears, wondered why she was so upset about a Republican. Maybe she was an illegal immigrant.

The more she drank the more teary she became. Like my father when he talked about John Kennedy, but Ronald Reagan . . . It's not like he was a real politician. Or a rock star. Blair was quiet and breathy, her shoulders rising into hiccups. She kept saying it was awful, just awful . . .

"Are you a Republican?" I asked.

"Me?" She crossed her hands over her chest. "I don't even vote."

"Then—"

"It's just too much. All of these, these guns . . . and . . . Any loser can pick up a gun and . . . I was in the city right after Lennon."

"John Lennon!" I shouted. It was like she'd read my mind.

"Such a tragedy."

"I thought about him, too."

Blair turned toward me, eyes focusing through her rubbery mask. "I'm so depressed," she said. "Lillian, will you stay?"

I SIT CROSS-LEGGED ON THE BED in my cell with a brand-new legal pad and write your name: Brooke Kelsey Harrison. You never used your middle name. I didn't even know you had one until that last night out on the Island, when stumbling through a fiery afterglow, I discovered an old-fashioned drugstore and jumped ten feet upon opening the door and hearing the bells announce my arrival. A couple of people looked up. Heart beating wildly in my chest, I lifted a pack of bright orange peanut butter crackers. Overhead light made the plastic glimmer, the squares a radioactive orange, salt chips like diamonds, and to think I'd never noticed how beautiful they were when I used to steal them from the deli, all cotton mouth and craving, and suddenly I wished more achingly than a stoned-out longing for salt and sweet to go back and undo it all, when the words burst through the TV set behind the cash register: *Brooke Kelsey Harrison died at St. Vincent's Hospital in New York. She was twenty-one years old and star of the popular daytime drama* World Without End.

I saw my face on a Wanted poster. Walls closing in, heat fizzling under my sweatshirt, I bolted from the store back to the beach and threw myself down on the sand. KELSEY!? The name hung between the blackening clouds, mocking me. Like an echoed scream on a basketball court . . . *Kelsey . . . elsey . . . else . . .* Everywhere I turned was that name and cantaloupe-orange crackers, and my throat lumped up realizing how much of the world I'd barely registered before smearing my shit all over it.

I throw the pad against the cinder blocks. My heart pounds and I'm wheezing. If only my breath would stop. But whenever I try and hold it I end up coughing worse than that day at Blair's—I'm a total wimp. I pick up the pad and tear at the pages. Somebody shouts, "Shut the fuck up, psycho!" I fall back onto the bed and dig my fingers into my wrist, my nails wrapping around that vein I know won't burst without major assistance. Like I said, I never had the guts, not even . . . What was I supposed to do? Huh? You tell me. After you'd broken the covenant, burned me . . . literally. I was just trying to help. That play was attracting the wrong kind of people, those who'd heard you took off your shirt and wanted to see Brooke *Kelsey* Harrison's tits. Guys, of course. Girls were more interested in the real you. There I go generalizing, but I can because I've never felt like a guy or a girl.

And I don't give a damn about politics. I would never shoot the president or any other politician. Dead or alive, they become heroes too easily. My father was right. Ronald Reagan was more popular after the assassination attempt, and the actress wrote a magazine article. I am not making this up. It's how things go in America. Scratch that. My lawyer says I'm not supposed to talk about America, says it makes me sound fanatical. I know the difference between love and fanaticism, I tell him. I know I never really dated you, that you weren't my actual girlfriend. He says I'm not supposed to mention you, remember.

So I keep it in, like always. We never needed words, it was deeper with us anyway: the kind of bond most people only dreamed about, like something out of a buddy movie. I didn't have to tell you what I was thinking, you just knew, and maybe you weren't my girlfriend, but you could have been once you got rid of that idiot boyfriend and we . . . I don't care what they say, you knew why I'd come. You had the look, the dusky glow I'd first seen in Blair. It starts in the eyes, the way a girl holds a stare too long before her face lights up, how she's not afraid to get her lips wet when she speaks.

This is different from the women who write me letters. It's crazy how they want to claim me only to pounce all over me. I never said I was part of their group; never took any oath or entrance exam. They talk about visibility, saying if "we" were seen as normal I might have been less ashamed and found better girlfriends. They tell me I am self-hating. If so, it's got nothing to do with girls, it's because of you, Brooke; you who died by the bullet though you visited children's hospitals and raised money for leukemia research and went on the Jerry Lewis Telethon and talked to every single person waiting in line for an autograph at the mall. That's what the world saw. What the world needs now.

Heroes and villains.

Want to know who's who? See how many women in here become your biggest fan when I'm around. They sneak up on me in the shower, or when I'm alone in my cell and can't scream for Mimi.

If I bleed enough afterwards I can go to the infirmary, where the doctor winces, unable to hold back his disgust. I see myself through his eyes, only a kid. A white girl at that. Privileged. *It's a damn shame.* I want to break through the wrist guards and smack his face, left right left, shouting, "That's the point, you racist motherfucker!" But instead I look down and count the specks. Sad, there's so many of them. Count the Lillian Ginger Speck, the John Homer Speck, the Nancy formerly Cooperstein never had a real middle name maybe that's why she's so fucked up Speck . . .

I see the three of us smiling on a Christmas card.

> *Wishing you happiness*
> *and love,*
> *The Specks*

If I'm lucky the doctor turns away long enough for me to grab a handful of tattoo needles. Mimi says we can't reuse them because of the virus. Mimi has a strong name: Miriam Adorno Colon. She says her family was royalty back in Puerto Rico.

Sometimes I don't know why she bothers with me, why she slipped into my cell those first weeks they had me on suicide watch and told me she was going to take care of me. It was her job, she said, and I wondered if she'd been assigned to me the way they'd given her the mop and pail before I arrived. "*Muñeca*," she named me, early on. "You know what it is, *muñeca?*"

I nodded no. The word had never come up in Spanish class.

"It means baby-doll, and that's what you are now, my little *muñeca*." She held open her mouth on the *ca*, the closest she ever got to smiling, and I was touched. For some reason this tall, muscular woman with sleeves rolled up over her biceps and hair held back with scotch tape had taken a liking to me, even after everything she must have heard. Or maybe because of it. Whatever her reason, I vowed not to let anything slip by me this time.

I WAS WALKING HOME, NOT UNHAPPY, when Blair found me. It was late afternoon, the sun still alive. Summer. I heard the hum of her 280Z before she idled up and slid down the window, slowly revealing herself: blond hair, sunglasses, bright red lips, stewardess' uniform. "Hello, little flower," she said, and I felt her Blairy warmness. Nobody had ever called me anything but my own name. She asked where I was coming from.

"Camp. The bus just dropped me off."

"And where are you off to now?"

"Home, I guess."

"Me too! I was in Houston and Chicago this morning."

Yawning, she stretched her arms up and out. Her right palm landed on the stick shift. Blair loved her stick. It was why she'd plucked the 280Z from the used car lot in Bayside. That and the color. White. Like the crests of waves spilling off the Long Island Sound and always wet-looking. Cruising, the wheels even swished. Inside vinyl seats sparkled. White teacups. Blair wiped them down every morning with window cleaner. I could see her driveway from my bedroom window. I got up every morning that summer to watch. Blair. In her uniform or cutoffs. Bent over the front seat, caressing it with a clean white handkerchief, her thighs bumping back and forth as she hummed along with the girls on the radio.

Someone was singing now. About a man with a slow hand. Easy. Like the words added up to something. Sexy. But I didn't know that word yet. I thought of the magazines delivered in brown paper packages to my parents. There was always a hose and sudsy water and, sometimes, a stewardess.

Blair turned to me, lifting her glasses. "Let's go check on the girls."

The lock clicked open. I rubbed my muddy high-tops against the curb. Didn't want to offend her car. Her. Everything about her was so clean and perfumed. Like my mother. But with Blair it didn't bother me so much.

Sunglasses back in place, she pushed the stick into first. The car jumped. "I was going to ask you to feed them," she said. The stick went down. Her left knee extended. "Then I figured I'd be gone less than twenty-four hours so why bother you."

"I love those cats."

She smiled and shifted into third. I wished I could see under her sunglasses. She had great eyes: big and sweet and always reminding me of the day she'd come up from the underworld and given me tea. Her grip tightened around the stick and she pushed down, all knuckle, strong. We jolted back a second. Suspended in time. I stared at her legs, so close her knees touched when she shifted. She made the most boring stuff look like fun.

We swished down the road. Blair turned up the radio and swayed. Every so often she sang out a line. Opening my window, I felt the warm air. Smelled the salt and pines. I loved how spread apart the houses were here, the cover of trees. "Mmmm, aren't those pines heavenly!" Blair shouted, and it amazed me how she always knew what I was thinking, how great it was that we'd moved in right next door, how she always seemed to find me on the nights Jack and Nancy were in the city, like we'd had an invisible, unspoken plan.

Downshifting, she turned onto our street. "You want to stop off at home?" she asked, slowing up a bit.

"Nope."

Blair pushed her left leg down, her palm on the stick, and shifted back into third. And music pumped from the radio. Her knees grazed each other. And her shoulders rocked as she sang about turning upside down and round and round, and I watched her body go up on the inhale and down on the exhale. Blair was movement, and you couldn't get that from a magazine, no matter how you twisted and turned the pages.

The car hiked forward, and I startled.

"Why are we—?"

"Look." My mother was backing out of the driveway. Blair honked, waved. Like it was all part of the song. The muffler in my stomach buckled. I didn't want Nancy anywhere near Blair. She was mine.

Nancy backed up behind us, then inched forward and slid down her window. She was dressed all sparkly, wearing tinted driving glasses. Blair turned down the radio. The two cars growled at each other, sides almost touching. Nancy's was bigger.

"Hi!" Blair said. "I found this one meandering along the yellow brick road."

"She's quite good at that."

"What?" I said.

"Meandering."

"Aren't we all," said Blair. So on my side. "But don't you look phenomenal, Nancy! Big plans tonight?"

"Just dinner." Nancy looked right over Blair to me, which was odd. When it came to talking, particularly about food and restaurants, Nancy was expert. She always said, "You know me, I can do twenty minutes making dinner reservations!" But that day there was no gloss, no cover. "How was camp?" she asked, sarcastic-like, as if she already knew the answer. We'd been waging silent war since the letter from my counselors had come. They said I refused to integrate with the group. Nancy'd shoved the letter in front of me the other night while I was eating cold pizza. "What is it with you?" she said finally. "What's your problem?" Heat like an electric blanket shrouded me.

That day I'd waited as two boys and two girls picked teams for a tetherball tournament, and every time someone called a name that wasn't mine, I stared at the counselors smacking that dumb yellow ball back and forth, dust spreading from their cool leather sneakers and landing in the back of my throat. It was the easiest game, you wrapped a ball on a string around a pole, but my grandmother said those were the best kind. She and her brother had grown up playing kick-the-can and tag. They couldn't believe it when they'd gotten a ball. Two generations later someone had attached it to a stick.

We always wanted more. But there was a rush to the winning whack—that point where speed and strength combined and you slammed the ball over your opponent's head, sending it coiling around the pole so you barely had to tap it when it came your way again. The laws of brute force were on your side. Like magic. Someone called my name and I jumped up but was shoved aside by another girl who whooped over and high-fived her friends, I think her name was Lydia, and I stood paralyzed like that damn pole, the string coiling around my neck as every last girl, even those with long fingernails and those who forfeited turns for their boyfriends and those who always missed the ball but jumped so high their asses leaked out of their shorts—even they were all chosen before me. Finally a counselor steered me toward team four. "Aw! We didn't pick *IT!*" said a boy with a baseball hat turned backwards. My captain. "This isn't a democracy," the counselor smiled, and walked away. The boy glared at me. "Mess up and your ass is grass."

"More like a whole field," said a stickish-thin girl, and they both laughed.

I felt exposed, as if the whole vaporous memory had material-ized on a screen in front of Nancy. But when I looked up from the letter she was gone. A couple of days later I'd heard her laughing into the phone, "Of course we'll be there, unless Lily manages to get herself thrown out of another camp."

No way would I give her the satisfaction, even though I hated this camp more than the last. I told her it was great.

"Really?" said my mother, her nose scrunched up, eyebrows floating above her glasses. Gold dots in the frame. Her initials.

Before I could tell her how we'd done archery and I'd hit the bull's-eye and only once had (accidentally, I swear) skimmed the shirt of the skinny girl, Blair broke in. "You heading into the city, Nancy? It's a fantastic night for it. Just perfect for walking around the seaport or downtown."

"We'll be on the east side," said my mother. A chill wind brushed through the car, raising the hair on my arms, and I wished I could climb under a thick comforter and shut my eyes. I was so sleepy. The engines hummed even louder. Purring. Like the girls when you touched behind their ears.

"Well," Nancy cleared her throat. "I guess I'll be off . . . I have to catch the 6:10. Lily, there's some chicken in the refrigerator. We'll be home late."

"She can eat with me," Blair said.

"Really, don't feel obligated."

"Not at all."

"She's good on her own."

"It's my way of saying thanks." Blair turned from Nancy to me and tapped my thigh. "For me and the girls . . ." She kept her hand there a few seconds and when she lifted, it felt cool. Right through my jeans. They were cutoffs like she wore on her days off. Mine fell below the knee. Nancy hated them. She never wore jeans, even if they had somebody's name on the back pocket.

"Well, then . . ." Nancy said. "I guess we'll see you later."

I nodded, said bye. Blair said have fun and tilted her stick into first, second. I looked in the rearview mirror as Nancy signaled left and out of sight, and my stomach slowly released. We rumbled past my house into Blair's driveway, this time sliding into neutral. She shut off the engine. My ears adjusted to the wind, the waves, the cry of a sea gull. "Ready?" Blair smiled. Then popped open her door.

Outside the air felt heavier. Cooler. Summer nights had the damp chill of clothes pulled too soon from the dryer. We lingered a bit before heading inside. Blair put on the kettle and went to change out of her uniform. I heard the closet slide open, a drawer pull, her feet creaking across the wooden planks, cat claws clicking like high heels behind her. "Lillian," she called to me. "You can put on some music if you want . . . or the TV." She glided into the bathroom, and I heard water splashing in the sink. She always left the door open, even when she peed. Scanning her albums I found mostly disco music. Girls with one name and tons of hair: Donna, Diana, Barbra—the guys at camp said disco sucks but they'd never seen Blair swing her hands above her head as she danced around the kitchen counter, like she felt each beat in a different part of her body.

The kettle screeched, and I jerked forward. My hands landed in the white shag. I steadied myself on all fours and like a cat leaned into the wall. Blair came out in faded jeans and a pink V-neck. All soft and powdery. Walking by she rubbed the back of my neck and I said, "Meow!"

She couldn't hear me over the wailing kettle. "I swear it used to whistle and then one day it became a foghorn!" she shouted, and with her hands covering her ears rushed over to turn it off. I pushed myself up onto the couch.

Blair brought over the Delta tray with steaming cups of tea, Sweet'N Low, and those tiny containers of creamer. "Let's relax a bit, then we'll see about food," she said. "Are you terribly hungry?"

"Not really."

"Me neither." She pulled out the tea bag with her spoon and curled the string round and round. Once I'd tried that at home, but Nancy said it was bad for you. You ended up drinking chemicals from the bag and they caused cancer. I didn't mention this to Blair, who was still wrapping and wringing to get out every last drop. Imagine if I picked up a tetherball and simply walked the ball around the pole, pulling tighter and tighter as I circled, so tight the ball eventually popped like a dandelion head from the string or the pole bent forward—that's what she liked to do to her tea bags. Squeeze 'em with a slow-mo kind of force. Like what happens when you wrap a thread around your finger. Tension makes it stronger than the skin beneath it. Squeeze hard enough and eventually it'll slice right through the skin. That's the thing about slow-mo force: it can be just as deadly, as brute, and even more insidious. You really have to work it. Blair's tea bag puffed out between the lines. Like a purplish finger, or my stomach around my mother. And then it happened. The string broke through. Little leaves showered over her cup. "Dammit!" she said, and looked close to tears. "My nerves are shot. I need something better than tea." She stood up and grabbed the genie bottle from the shelf. The label said V.S.O.P. I remembered Jack once telling me it meant Very Special Old Product. It was the only alcohol Blair kept in the house. She took down a fat glass and looked inside. I wanted one, too. And asked.

"I don't know," Blair hesitated.

"Jack lets me drink from his wine glass," I said. Not a lie.

Gustave had told him it was what kids did in France. What I
didn't say was I'd been sneaking sips from Nancy's gin glasses for
years. She left them half full around the house, like she left her
half-smoked cigarettes, an offering to some invisible god or
ghost. Sometimes I smoked the ends, trying to determine where
my mother'd just been by the freshness of a lipstick stain, the size
of a remaining ash, the lingering scent of her perfume, and
through this put together a life in pencil drawings: Nancy talks
on the phone, Nancy watches TV, Nancy supervises the cleaning
lady, Nancy touches up her eyebrows, Nancy hangs out in the
hot tub.

Blair tilted her head toward the ceiling, then picked up
another glass. "You're sure?"

"Totally."

"Well, why not?"

She set down the two glasses on the coffee table, poured one
half full, the other less so. She handed me the emptier glass.
"*Prost!*" she said in a funny accent. "That's 'cheers' in German. I
do JFK-Munich sometimes, and let me tell you, you've never seen
such a clean city. It sparkles like Oz. You're supposed to sip now."

"Huh?"

"After the toast."

"Oh, okay."

I did. It tasted like cough medicine only it made me cough.
"Slowly," Blair said, and I sipped again, this time feeling the liquid warm the back of my throat. "Very good, Lillian," she said,
and the way she pronounced my name was so feathery, like everything in that house of grays and pinks and whites. I turned my
head and came face to face with a poster of an old cruise ship. I
was so right: Blair was motion.

We played a game. I pointed to cities in her Delta book with
a ballpoint pen, the kind that clicked into action. Then she took
the pen and wrote down words about the city I'd chosen . . . *clean,
dirty, small streets, big buildings, museums, cafés, cemeteries.* Under
her thumb, the pen clicked maniacally and sounded like Morse
code. I used to bang out Morse code on empty Coke cans with
some kids on another block. All I remembered was S.O.S. I

wanted to tap out V.S.O.P. Blair was my very own very special old product.

She high-fived me whenever I chose Paris or Nashville, her two favorite cities, and I thought, this is what it's like to be picked first. A warm drizzle of tea leaves. Blair refilled our glasses. She told stories about traveling. She didn't sound like anyone else I knew, even when her words slurred. I thought it was because she traveled to other countries. After a while, tired from the game, we leaned back and looked at the faces on television. They seemed smaller than normal, but I could understand them better. My body felt warm and tingly and I couldn't stop laughing. And the brandy'd started tasting really good.

"Oh no!" Blair said. "I forgot about dinner."

"Are you hungry?"

"No. But I promised your mother."

"She'll never know."

Blair pushed herself straight up and yawned so big I could see all of her teeth. "Excuse me!" she said. One of the girls—Marilyn, maybe, Grace had the bigger ears—meowed and jumped from the couch. "Then I guess we'd better get you home. Your parents'll be back soon."

"I doubt it."

Blair's eyes sunk.

"They stay out really late when Jack's got clients. They go dancing and stuff."

"And they always leave you alone?"

I nodded. "When I was really young I stayed with my grand-parents, but they moved to Arizona. Sometimes they let me stay at Gustave's—that's Jack's partner, he shoots the commercials but Jack's the one who makes everything happen. My grandmother says he could sell oil to an Arab."

Blair stared at me, biting her lower lip to hold back the tears. I liked that she was sort of a crybaby. In commercials stewardesses always smiled, in movies they had stone faces. Blair was the real deal. I could imagine her going out of her way to find a passenger an extra pillow, track down a special meal, sneak a kitten on board.

"It's not right," she said. "You're eleven years old."

"Twelve. My birthday was June third. I'm a Gemini."

"I'm Scorpio," she said, then stood up and held out her hand. "Come . . . you can stay here tonight."

I followed her into the bedroom, faking a yawn, though I was anything but tired. Blair gave me a T-shirt that said Delta Softball and went into the bathroom to pee. "If that doesn't fit there's plenty more," she said. I'd already taken off my other shirt and slipped Blair's over my head. I turned and saw her sitting on the toilet. "This is okay . . ." I stammered. She stood, and before pulling up her pants I caught a look at her bush, which like Nancy's had all of this stringy hair—Nancy liked to walk around naked after her shower. Air-drying. I didn't have any hair and decided I wouldn't. Wasn't that kind of girl. Blair flushed, splashed a little water on her face, then shut off the light. The bedroom went dark, except for the dim shadow of her Statue of Liberty night-light.

"You look adorable," she said and tickled my side. "Now let's get you into bed."

She tucked me underneath her bleachy white sheets with the big cotton comforter we sometimes dragged out when we watched TV, and I remembered earlier in her car, how I'd gotten so sleepy and imagined a blanket settling on top of me. It was a vision, the way I'd first seen her come up from the sea. Grace and Marilyn jumped up on the bed, sniffing around me as Blair slipped out of her jeans and V-neck, stopping every few minutes to sip from the brandy bottle. *What happened to her glass?* I lifted a cat and she purred. An electric powder puff, cooing . . . *V.S.O.P. . . . V.S.O.P. . . .*

Peeking through her white fluff, I watched Blair. Body like a brandy bottle, lips mumbling a song about angels, doing a slow-mo kind of dance. She slipped on a silky white nightie. Everything in the bedroom was white and pillowy. Heaven. I laughed. "What?" she said.

"Nothing."

"You're scared of me, aren't you?"

She was standing there in a short terry cloth bathrobe looking like she was born for those airline commercials. *Hi, my name is Blair and I'm gonna fly you like you've never been flown before.*

"Well, let me tell you, there's nothing to be afraid of."

"I'm not."

"Good, 'cause you're safe here . . ." her voice cracked, "and ya know, I dunno . . . you just shouldn't be alone like that." She took a long sip from her bottle and sat down next to me. I was, in fact, terrified. I'd never been in bed with another person. You didn't get into a bed with someone unless you were married or . . . maybe Blair and I were going to get married. Stretching out one leg at a time, she leaned up against her elbow so her boobs were almost popping out of her nightie. "Lillian G. Speck," she said.

"Yeah?"

She stared at me for a minute, then rolled her head back, laughing hysterically. When she came back up her eyes were all teary. "Do you have any idea how much I hate flying?"

"Huh?"

"Never mind." She sipped from her bottle. "I'm sorry, did you want some?"

"No thanks."

"Okay, then, it's bedtime." She put down the bottle and snuggled under the sheets. One of the girls lay between us. "*Meow*," said the cat, and Blair rubbed behind her ears. "Yes, my good girl . . ."

"Meow!" I said, and Blair smiled.

"Are you my good girl, too?" I fluttered my lips, purring. She stroked the back of my neck. I folded into her body and put my arms around her. She held me tight around my waist, moved her legs against mine, and there was her smell—the brandy, the hair dye, the powder—and there were her hands rubbing my back beneath the Delta T-shirt, her silk nightie soft against my cheek, and the motion, the rocking together as she hummed the angel song softly and wrapped me up slow-mo, tight as that string around her tea bag, and I had a vision or memory, I couldn't tell the difference sometimes . . . my parents, naked, with another woman in their bed and they're touching her body and licking her titties. There's soft music and Jack's insect eyes. He smiles, *Go to bed, Lily.* And they all laugh.

But that was years ago, before I'd made it into a bed of my own. Blair's.

She held me a little longer, then slackened her arms and whispered, "Good night, little flower." My head drifted into the crook of her elbow. Like this we fell asleep.

JACK COMES TO SEE ME WITHOUT NANCY. He says she's gone away for a while, gone to a place where famous people go to have breakdowns. Jack thought he was famous long before I made us all infamous. It was the business that swelled him, all of the restaurants and wrap parties, the drinking and dancing and drugs. Same shit that did in Nancy.

Not that my own past is clean. When the lawyers scratch the surface, they find the usual stuff: pot, coke, speed, tranqs, pills I knew only by color, shape, or size, but never heroin. None had come my way. By now, thanks to the witness—the one who claims to have seen the gun—the entire world knows I lifted quite a bit of contraband. Everything from my parents' scrips to the gun that allegedly killed you. The gun the cops can't seem to find. My lawyer says the witness is jealous and delusional and would give anything to be involved in such a high-profile murder. Better hope that gun doesn't turn up, I warn my lawyer. I'm getting wary of his tactics, and my father knows it.

"I saw the rabbi yesterday," I goad Jack. I've been seeing the rabbi since the priest started bumming me out. All his talk about confessing and following Jesus really meant I had to stop doing Mimi and keep my hands off myself, too. I like the rabbi better. He says I'll find forgiveness through hard work, discipline, and prayer.

"We talked about evil."

"Oh, that's good," Jack says. "You want a soda or something? I got all these quarters today." He taps his fingers on the table and looks over at the woman next to us. She's squeezing the bones out of her two young children. I imagine the guards prying them apart with a big wrench.

"He says I should plead guilty."

"Who?"

"The rabbi."

The way Jack stares we could be sitting in a ski lodge or at the cafeteria at the Museum of Natural History and about to go home together. I never thought I would see him like this: speechless. He retreats behind his black-Irish eyes, the circles beneath them a deeper purple than the week before.

"Did you hear me?"

More silence.

"It's what he thinks—and I want to, too."

Almost religious, my father's wordlessness. A droplet forms in the corner of his right eye.

"We can get this over with, maybe. Move things along. Know what I'm saying, Jack? Jack?"

Droplets called back: false alarm: his face ices over.

"Come on, you don't understand what—"

"Stop it, okay, just shut up!" he shouts, and I can't remember ever hearing such pain in his voice. Around us women talk, smiling when they touch their people. Some couples grope furiously. They should be home on their couches, not sitting in folding chairs, one dressed, the other in green pajamas. Keeps us all equal inside but nobody's really the same. There's a hierarchy, a social ladder not too different from on the outside, how pretty girls got picked first for tetherball and my mother always thought she was better than everyone 'cause she drove a fancy car. In here I'm on the high end because of Mimi and because I'm a tabloid prisoner. I get the TV people, the journalists, the famous shrinks and experts in youth crime, even a renowned feminist. Makes me pretty well hated by a lot of girls in green pajamas. I want to explain this to somebody, but the only one here is Jack and he's in no mood.

I need a visitor who's not family, not a professional or parasite. In biology we learned about parasites—most of the time they cause diseases in their host. I want a different kind of parasite, a new disease. I wish I had a boyfriend to slobber over while everyone tries not to look. It's all boys out here, no girls together, and that's strange considering how much of it goes on inside. Here it's about a quick kiss, hands fiddling with zippers underneath the table. Cock. I've never seen Mimi with her man. That would piss me off royally and we are trying to control my anger. The rabbi says anger is our way of acting out our mortal fury, the fear we're going to die expressed as rage at the almighty. I don't believe in any god, I tell him, and he says this itself is a form of anger.

My father taught me to be an atheist. He hates religion.

His mother had believed in the Son of God. She hung his picture in every room and near her bed raised a statue of his dying body. When she passed, she kissed her fingertips then let them graze against his smooth little arms. She believed in his power to drive away demons and heal the sick. To save her people from their sins. She knew what he might say in any situation. He was inside her always. Kind of like you and me, but I wouldn't say that to anyone.

The first bell sounds, and I am relieved. No more avoiding my father's face. Guards start breaking up couples. This is when the tears come, but not mine. Jack stands to leave. "Listen," I say. "Would you just think about it, okay? I'm going crazy in here."

"I'm sorry, but it's better this way."

"Better for who?"

"That's what Brickman says."

"I don't trust him. I think I need another lawyer—there's this woman."

"Forget it." He sighs, runs a hand through his hair, and a few black satin strands fall forward. For one second I hate myself for turning his life upside down, making everything unfamiliar to him. Me in here, and Nancy gone, too.

"Look, Brickman's your hire," I say. "He doesn't know anything about me, he doesn't want to hear it."

"So what? It's not like your marrying the guy. He's being paid to get you out of here, not listen to your problems."

"My problems are his problems. The other lawyer says—"

"Oh for Christ's sake, stop it! I've got problems, too, you know. You think this guy comes easy—he's the best there is and he bills more per hour than Jesus, so I don't want to hear it, okay? This is your lawyer—Jonathan Brickman—and you're gonna listen to what he says and stop talking to the fucking rabbi!"

The second bell rings. Jack puffs out his cheeks, flutters his lips. "Look, I'm—"

A guard taps his shoulder. "Let's go, pal. Save it for next week."

Jack nods. Opening his arms, he turns toward me. I reach out and hug him around his stomach, hating myself. When I let go, he tries giving me his J.F.K. but is waylaid by droplets. I watch him angle his broad shoulders past the guard and hop into the elevator.

After he leaves, I have someone take me to the library. I check our clippings almost every day as I sit by the window near the case law books. There are a few new articles, some stuff about all the journalists swarming around your family. If she does tell their story, your mother says in *Time,* it won't be sensational, and I know it's a jab at me. Like anything I do'll be *sensational.* I shove the magazines off the table and look out the window at the tomato plants. Though it's late in the season, they're exploding in red and orange. A girl in green pajamas digs her fingers into the soil and that's the job I want. They're almost ready to let me work, my lawyer says. I'm no longer dangerous to myself and others.

For a while, I watch that girl dig and pick and point to where she wants a guard to cut back the leafy vines. I imagine kidnapping her and filling the position. I grow the fattest tomatoes of the season. They feed the entire city. And win prizes. I end up on television, this time for the right thing.

I was supposed to be helping Mimi with Angel's tattoo. A devil with a pitchfork, which Mimi says is *happy* since her name is Angel. Angel's not much older than me, but she's been schooled on the system, in and out of detention centers and jails for drugs, stealing, cutting people up, troubles that began when she was twelve. She says she used to have sex with other girls' boyfriends just so they'd fight her. Once she participated in a human autopsy. "You know what that is, Long Island?" she asked, and I could only guess. "It's when you cut somebody from their neck down to their private parts and they're still alive, you know? You pull 'em open and poke around with their organs."

It was straight out of a horror movie, what I might have fantasized when I was really mad, but there is a big jump from saying I'm gonna rip your guts out and actually doing it. It makes pulling a trigger seem chicken-shit. Angel's one of the toughest girls I've ever met. I almost can't believe she's got two kids, would have had three if she didn't miscarry after a fight last year. Now she's pregnant again.

Sometimes she lets me put my hand on her stomach and feel the baby. "You have to talk to her," she says. Her *her* sounds so much like *huh* it reminds me of the girls in my high school. They'd all drop their Gucci purses at the sight of Angel with her scarred neck and arms, the extra piece of skin hanging over her right eye.

"What should I say?"

"I dunno, anything. Sing something," she nods, her hand on mine on her stomach. "Sing to my baby, Long Island."

Like I'm going to say no to her. So even though I'm tone-deaf and can only remember the tune to the theme from *World Without End,* I hum to Angel's stomach. She loves the song and asks me to do it whenever I see her. That's another reason I'm hiding out in the library—afraid of messing up the baby's karma humming the theme to a show forced to change more than a few story lines after I murdered its star. Instead, I watch the lucky girl clip tomato vines and try to remember your *un*sensational face.

NANCY'D PLANNED A PARTY for my thirteenth birthday and told me to invite some friends. Nothing big, she said, just a cookout. She had the food delivered from the supermarket. Around noon Jack rolled the grill out of the garage and puffed two yellow umbrellas over the picnic table. Nancy brought out the good plates and napkins and silverware. From my bedroom window, I watched the back-and-forth, excited. Blair was coming at two.

Gustave and Pamela arrived first—they always came for parties—Gustave in one of his baseball hats and dark sunglasses, Pamela in a bright dress and high heels, her thick brown hair styled differently every time. She was Gustave's second wife and younger than the rest of them. She had been studying photography at a university in France when they met, love at first look for Gustave. She called him a romantic boy. They were full of champagne bottles and gulpy laughs and loved parties. For my birthday they gave me a little white box with layers of tissue paper and, underneath, a silver necklace in the shape of a thick bubbly L. I said thanks and kissed them on both cheeks the way Gustave had taught me. For years I'd thought this was a French kiss, until I overheard a couple of girls at camp saying, did he French you? did he use his tongue? and knew it had to be more. The rest I learned from movies. Nancy brought out a pitcher of gin & tonics and eyed the necklace. "It's positively gorgeous," she said. "Put it on."

I did, even though I hated things hanging from my body. "That looks great," Nancy said. "Doesn't it?"

"Fantastic, I'm so glad we went for the silver," said Pamela, who was wearing quite a bit of it herself. She was born in Morocco where her father had been a jewelry maker.

"Yep," shouted Jack, over his shoulder. He was at the grill. "The thing about silver is you can wear it with anything."

Talk about the necklace went on for some time. How I was going to love it, could even wear it with jeans, blah blah, meow meow. They were so loud, their gestures exaggerated. Like I was deaf or something. I couldn't care less about jewelry or my parents or Gustave and Pamela, all I knew was Blair hadn't arrived. I walked over to the side table where Nancy'd set up hors d'oeuvres, ate a few chunks of bread loaded with brie and pâté, some olives and chips, then poured a g & t and headed to the beach. It was almost three and I was getting worried. What if she'd gotten stuck in another city? Or one of the cats was sick? But she would have called. But she never called. I just went over, mostly at night, and we played the traveling game before squeezing with the girls into bed.

A few times there was someone else in the bed. I watched from my window as she stepped out of a car that wasn't her own and a shadowy figure followed her inside. Much as it killed me, I knew I wasn't supposed to go over. Maybe whoever was there now, but not in the daytime. That's when I'd go over, boil water for tea, and carry the Delta tray to bed, where she lay with a washcloth over her forehead. "You're my savior," she'd smile, and I felt important. We had to get her ready for work. It was tough when she had a transatlantic flight. She was terrified of sailing over oceans.

But she wasn't flying, and I'd told her three times about the party.

Jack called out, "Hey, birthday girl! It's chow time."

I climbed up on my rock and stared at the Sound, its still blue cover a torment. Blair only came out in the mist. I picked up a stick and tried to sketch her in the sand. Maybe whoever in the dark car had taken her into the city for lunch. She loved the seaport. And whoever would want to make her happy, she was so great, who wouldn't want to make her happy? Thousands of strings clenched around my stomach. I hated Blair.

"These burgers are raring to go!" Jack said again.

I hurled the stick out to sea and decided to go find her. Halfway to her house she appeared through the trees, practically glowing in a white sundress and hat that looked like Saturn. She held a package wrapped with a shiny silver ribbon.

"Didn't you hear me!" Jack was pissed. "We're almost ready up there. What are you doing?"

I suppose it looked funny. Me, standing in the pines with— she was gone! I swallowed and said nothing, I was doing nothing, then crunched over the fallen pine needles behind my father in his chef's hat. Gustave had taken over at the grill, where he stood pressing a couple of hamburgers with a spatula, charcoal clouds rising above him. "Whoa, Gus!" Jack said. "You're searing too heavy, the outsides'll burn."

"It's the way the hamburger should be enjoyed."

"But keep mine raw inside!" Nancy called out from the end of the table, where she and Pamela huddled together smoking cigarettes.

"You are some kind of wild animal or something," Gustave growled.

I sat down a few places away from my mother and noticed all

the settings around the table. Slow-mo strings worked deep into my stomach. Gustave dropped a burger on my mother's plate and she nudged it open with her fork. It was pink and slimy but the meaty smell cut a trail to my nostrils. I wanted to sink my teeth into the flesh, feel the juices running down my chin. I was starving AND I felt like throwing up. If I could get away now, I thought, I'd be fine. Escape to my room and watch TV until the sun set and Gustave and Pamela returned to the city and I could get over to Blair's. "Okay, Lily G-for-genius . . ." said my father, for a moment taking a break from emptying the grill, though still holding a pair of tongs and brushing the back of his hand against his forehead. Weary. Steamed out. "I burned these babies just the way you like 'em."

"I forgot to call back Grandma!" I blurted out. "To thank her for the check."

"You can do that later," Jack said, and plucked those remaining hot dogs, blackened for me. But I was too queasy.

"I want to do it now."

"What's your problem?" Nancy said.

Gustave brought over the platter full of hamburgers and hot dogs. "It is finished," he said, and sat down next to Pamela.

"No problem, it's just I don't want to forget is all."

"I'll remind you . . . later. And where are all your friends? You did tell them it was an afternoon thing, right? I am not going to start feeding people all over again in a few hours."

Nancy stared, slow-mo turning brute, and the tea bag burst. "You don't have to feed anybody, okay?" I snapped.

"I don't—"

"Nobody's coming!"

"Nobody? What happened to—"

"Leave me alone!" I shouted. "I just want to go to my room!"

"Your room! Why!?"

"Let her go . . ." said my father as I stalked inside.

Wind carried their voices upstairs over the clatter of silverware, ice cubes shifting in tall glasses, the smell of graying barbecue coals giving way to coffee, cigarettes, and a thicker, sweeter kind of smoke. Summertime. I sat at the window, listening. At first they talked about it, Nancy saying she was at the end of her rope with me, and Pamela comforting, "They're all sulky at that age," and they both laughed, which raged me up. I wanted to scream, "I am not sulky! I'm like Gustave: a romantic boy," but soon they moved on to other things and hummed along with my father's jazzy records and carried the pitcher of gin & tonics over to the hot tub before the birds, tired of competing with sad songs, settled in for the evening, and the floodlights shot on . . . *like flashcubes going off.* A picture: two loud couples in a hot tub at dusk. There's nothing more depressing.

When their voices melted into the clanking of plates and turning of car engines, I knew the coast was clear. I went downstairs, sipped from a few half-drunk glasses on the counter, licked their powdered leftovers off a portable mirror, and opened the refrigerator. Inside was my untouched birthday cake. White with blue flowers and lettering: Happy Birthday Lily. I took the box and went over to Blair's. She opened the door in her bathrobe. "Do you hate me?" she said, so soft and crybabyish I couldn't stay mad at her. She let me in, poured us a couple of glasses of brandy, and explained that she'd been home all day, something had gotten into her. "I just couldn't get out of bed," she said.

"But I saw you."

"What?"

"Outside. This afternoon."

"Oh, honey, I am so sorry," she said, and put her arms around me. I hugged her back, forgiving her for running off and missing my party. It was okay, I said, all I'd wanted was to be with her, and look where you are, she said. Now, did I want my birthday present? She handed it to me and I didn't question why it was different from the box she had earlier. This one was in a plastic bag from the art store. I pulled out a gigantic black book and my chest swelled. "For your drawings," she said. "Now you can keep them all in one place."

"It's amazing."

"And whenever you draw you'll think of me."

"I think about you all the time."

"That's very sweet." She stroked my cheek, then looked away. She was sadder than usual and could barely keep her eyes open. "Should we have some cake then?" she smiled, and I nodded, thankful a bit of the Blairyness had returned.

She put on the soundtrack to *A Star Is Born* and brought over the cake. For good luck I smeared my name with my pinkie and cut us each a big square. We washed it down with brandy, listening to the record. Blair cried when Barbra Streisand sang at Kris Kristofferson's funeral. "It's so sad. He turned her into the person he wanted, made her this big fantastic star, and then hated her for it," she heaved, and I sat there not knowing what I was supposed to do. She took a gurgly breath. "Come and give us a hug." She held open her arms. I hugged her and it was the longest I'd ever held anyone, the two of us in that little cottage, candles burning, three-quarters of a birthday cake and a bottle of brandy in front of us. Surfacing, her eyes tinted pink, she said, "Oh, don't mind me, I've been going all day."

"What's the matter?"

"Nothing." She rubbed my arm, then bit her lower lip. "And everything . . . it's just . . ."

"What?"

She shut her eyes and took a deep breath. "You know that I tried, right? I really really tried, but I can't be your mother." A thousand floodlights beamed in my face. I was red-hot, exposed, and felt like I was being slowly strangled. I didn't want her to be my mother—who would want to be someone's *mother*? If I could've I would've stuffed that word back behind her faded red lipstick. But it hung between us like a rain cloud. "It's okay," she continued, "you're very smart, you'll figure it out someday, and they won't have me to kick around anymore."

"What do you mean? Who's kicking you? Why are you talking like that?"

She laughed, then her eyes pooled again.

"Are you okay?"

Big sigh, head thrown back, she said, "Be a stewardess, they told me. You're the perfect height for it. A lot of women are too short or too tall, did you know that? There's a perfect height and a perfect weight." She'd told me this before, all the rules. Everything down to the color of lipstick she was supposed to wear. "Half the people I know eat laxatives for days before, but I never had a problem with that. It was the flying that got me, Lillian. How's that for irony? Nobody ever said anything about what happens to your brain when it's stuck up in the air day after day. Everything's got something hidden in it . . . there's a lesson for you. I can still teach you things, even if . . ." She was tearing too much to speak. I put one hand on her shoulder, the other on her arm, and managed to get her standing, thinking how weird we'd look if anyone saw us, but that was the beauty of it: it was just between us. We needed each other. I took her into the bedroom and helped her kick off her jeans. "Thank you, darling," she said, and sat me down on the bed, taking my hands in hers. "When you remember me, Lillian—" she paused for a long breath, "and you will . . . please be kind."

The next morning she flew to Paris. Not long after that she was gone. No note, no forwarding address, nothing. It had been days since I'd seen her, so I went over to her place. Shutters closed up the windows, and when I lifted the mat, the key was gone. I walked around to the bedroom window and through a crack saw the empty white walls. "Blair?" I said, tentatively at first, then screamed and banged on the front door until a man came out of the mansion.

"What's going on?" he said.

"Where is she?"

"Beats me," he said. "She never told me where she was going." She'd left the key in his mailbox a few days ago. At first he was upset she didn't give notice but after thinking it over he and his wife decided to trash the place and build a swimming pool. I could use it if I wanted, he said, and disappeared up the slate pathway to his house.

I walked to the beach, sat down on my rock, and stared out at the water without really looking. Afternoon became evening and I knew she'd gotten lost somewhere and couldn't come home or didn't want to. I'd driven her away.

My house was dark and emptier than ever. I went upstairs but turned toward my parents' bedroom instead of mine. Opening the top drawer of Jack's dresser, I found the cigar box where he kept his pot under a cover of bunched-up pairs of thin black socks. I rolled a joint and sat back on the steely gray sheets and smoked. This bed was bigger than Blair's. King-sized, my father had said, and it could have held the entire royal family, even with the pretty new princess, or two parents who entertained after dark, or me and Blair and the girls. I couldn't imagine sleeping alone every night, never again hearing her whisper, "Give us a hug," then clamp around me like an octopus. It wasn't fair. I went into the bathroom and ran burning hot water in the sink and shower. Steam fogged the mirror, condensing on the pale green tiles and black window. Lights dim, my face a skeleton, I punched the mirror until my knuckles stung and little knives shot up my arm. The face was still there, mocking me. *Guess she didn't really need you after all . . .* I picked up Nancy's round, plastic razor and rubbed the blade against the purple veins in my wrist, watching as a few dots of blood rose along the frayed skin. I cut deeper . . . and deeper . . . until I should have felt it. In the mirror, the face: *That's not a kill-yourself kind of razor, shithead.*

There was blood all over the sink; I was numb. I stuck my wrists under the scalding hot water and screamed.

THE LITTLEST DIVA

MILDRED HARRISON OFTEN TOLD THE STORY of her older daughter's first performance. It was back in 1970 when, at the tenacious age of five, Brooke was cast as the youngest daughter in the town's production of *The Sound of Music* and, as they say in the business, ended up stealing the show. Said piracy occurred during the "So Long, Farewell" number. Some claimed the move was a ruse, calling the girl a little schemer; others chalked it up to sheer stage presence. Either way, the fact remains that after singing her final lines and being scooped up in Mr. Von Trapp's brawny arms, instead of resting her head on his shoulder as Mildred had seen her do in rehearsals, Brooke beamed a half-toothed grin and winked at the crowd, breaking the time-honored wall between actor and audience. It was an inclusive gesture, generous, and hardly conscious of its cheeky colonization, for it seemed as if that flash of gum and brand-new pearlies had been part of the original script, perhaps a move left behind in the hills of Bavaria to be resurrected when the audience was ready. And that night in Blue Bell, Pennsylvania, they were ready.

There came a sudden burst of laughter, then a round of extended guffaws prompting all present to rise one by one until the entire auditorium was swept up in the beneficent cacophony of a standing ovation. Mildred herself never having been on the receiving end of such public idolatry tried to imagine the power of those hundreds of hands working in unison. If the clamoring palms could speak, she mused, they might have said, "Enough already, my fingers are numb!" Or perhaps: "Watch your elbow on the negative swing, sir." Yet for the person on stage—her child, who'd barely lost her baby teeth—the sound of those arms thundering against each other bellowed like an edict from Mount Sinai: *We love you, We adore you, We're crazy about you!*

It's fair to say that by the time Mildred and Tom Harrison carted their young starlet out of the Blue Bell Recreation Center, Brooke was the cynosure of the night. Half the cast followed the Harrisons to Friendly's, where Brooke ordered a banana boat and stared out the front window at the stream of station wagons pulling into the parking lot, the green grass and tall trees lit up in the spiral glow of their headlights. Brooke did seem rather taken with the lights, Mildred thought, watching as her daughter's attention returned to the table, where they were joined by the head of the rec center. "I knew you had it in you," he said, reaching across Mildred to squeeze Brooke's nose the way that had always made her giggle during rehearsals. Just then, Ed Barclay, who'd played Mr. Von Trapp, entered the restaurant and smiled warmly, though Mildred wondered if he resented Brooke for running off with the show as his six children watched from the audience. If there'd been any ill will on the kids' part it was buried in their caroming about the restaurant with toy guns and bandannas and GI Joe dolls, even the two girls, and Mildred silently thanked herself for talking Tom out of having a third child although he'd really wanted a boy. After two you seemed to lose track.

Brooke waved to Ed Princess-Grace style, a subtle pivoting that reminded Mildred of her grandmother, who'd been something of a small legend on the local Pennsylvania stages back in the twenties. "Maybe it's genetic," Mildred said, wiping a drop of chocolate syrup from Brooke's chin.

"What is?" Tom said.

"Her. Tonight. All of this."

"Whatever it is, she's got it. You've got it," the director cooed, again reaching for Brooke's nose. This time she flicked a spoonful of vanilla ice cream at his chest.

"Brooke!" Tom tried to sound disciplinary but couldn't contain his laughter. Neither could Mildred.

Even the director had to smile, though the ice cream had left a wet spot on the lapel of his brown leather jacket. "Oh, she's a little star all right," he said, taking pains to keep his hands folded in front of him until he stood to leave.

Later that night as they lay in bed, Mildred and Tom decided they would enroll Brooke in acting classes and find her an agent. It was an idea they usually laughed off when someone told them, and someone was always telling them, that Brooke should go into modeling, perhaps do commercials. She had that penetrating yet comfortable gleam in her eyes. A friendly, middle-American smile that said, I am just like you but cute. What Tom and Mildred hadn't been aware of—though now that they thought about it, they really should have seen—was Brooke's knack for performance. Back and forth the eager parents volleyed, prompting each other with examples of their child's singular talent. There was the way she sat with her face pushed up to the TV set, lip-synching to, say, Mary Tyler Moore and reciting the lines at dinner as if she were taping the next day. Then, every morning, she would descend upon Mildred's makeup mirror, instructing her mother to comb her natural blond hair into pigtails, though the style of the day was either scrappy waves or harsh picture-frame cuts. Brooke, too, always made certain the marble balls of her hair bands matched her outfit, a perplexing goal, or so it seemed to Mildred who'd never thought much about linking the tans and grays and blues she favored and kept her hair pulled back with utilitarian metal barrettes. But Mildred and Tom had unearthed the motive for Brooke's fashion regimen at back-to-school night when they learned that Brooke had waltzed into her kindergarten class demanding that she read the daily weather reports their teacher scrawled across the blackboard. It was with great pride that they envisioned their daughter standing at the front of the room: "Good morning, classmates . . . today is Tuesday . . . the sky is overcast . . ."

A weather girl did have to look her best, so Mildred and Tom had decided that Brooke would model her outfits for them and two-and-a-half-year-old Cynthia. Mildred thought they should try and incorporate Cynthia into Brooke's life since the little girl already spent most of her time shadowing Brooke up and down the stairs of their turn-of-the-century farmhouse. For her part, Brooke treated her younger sister as a doll, mute and malleable. And Cynthia played the part. "Head down!" Brooke would say, and Cynthia pretended to sleep. "Eat!" and she opened her mouth for Brooke to stuff with canned corn, raspberries, or bittersweet chocolate chips. "Play dog!" and she curled up in the basket their golden retriever pup had outgrown soon after they'd bought him. Brooke also liked to roll a blanket around her sister's body so only her head and feet were visible, turning her into a cocktail frank.

Once Mildred found Cynthia hot-dogged in the linen closet. "Come on, honey," Mildred said, tugging at the blanket.

"Nooooooo!"

"Cynthia!"

"Book! Book! Book!" Cynthia wailed.

Finally, Brooke appeared. She was in her cowgirl pajamas and biting into a big green apple. She towered over her tightly wrapped sister. "It's just like a cartoon!" Brooke giggled.

"Book!"

"Brooke!"

"Book!" Cynthia's tears fell even heavier, saliva dripping from her nose onto the yellow blanket.

Brooke reached down and with her appleless hand patted Cynthia's head. "There, there, hot-dog girl, there's no need to yell. Nobody's gonna eat you. Didn't we talk about sacrifice?"

"Will you please unwrap her," Mildred requested of her firstborn, although her distressed tone seemed to give Brooke a feeling of power, as if Mildred were asking her daughter's permission instead of commanding her. And the way Cynthia quieted down under Brooke's palm was astounding, the two of them locked in a graceful staring contest.

"I'm losing patience," Mildred said.

"This is for her own good."

"Oh, for the love of God, Brooke."

"Mother, I'm warning you, just let her finish the activity. She's got to learn things for herself." Brooke batted her glassy blue eyes and took a crispy bite of her apple before tramping back downstairs. Mildred watched her little head descend then turned back to Cynthia who looked more comfortable than ever, rolled up in her pink baby blanket on the floor of the linen closet. She sat down in the hallway beside the closet, and after hearing a few tiny snores, unraveled her daughter and carried her to bed.

The following weekend, Cynthia opened the front door to Mildred's parents and ran through the house shouting: "Book, Book, your grandparents are here!"

That was weeks ago, when Brooke was merely the core of the Harrison household. Now that she'd become Blue Bell's favorite daughter, Mildred thought of Cynthia and felt a heavy weight on her heart. She reached beneath the covers for Tom's hand and tucked it in the cavern between her breasts, her favorite spot. In their first blurry weeks of marriage, after they'd moved in and started working on the farmhouse, it wasn't all the decorating and household budgeting, nor was it the dinners with new neighbors and Sunday morning church services, the way she'd learned how to sign a check, "Mrs. Tom Harrison," or even their lovemaking, which always left Mildred feeling a bit illicit, for it wasn't anything like she'd imagined, and it had been difficult keeping still underneath Tom the way her mother had instructed was essential for impregnation (luckily all that business was over now and they were none the worse for it), but rather, from the beginning, it was the heat of Tom's hand nestled close to her heart as they fell asleep—a gesture as simple as flashing a cherubic grin—that made Mildred Harrison feel married, and that feeling made all the difference. Whatever happened with their daughters would be all right as long as she and Tom stayed connected, Mildred told herself, although on that cool summer night after witnessing Brooke's Gretl, even Tom's cornerstone gesture and all that it implied wasn't working its magic. They were going to have to watch the girls more carefully from that day forward.

REFLECTIONS IN RED GELATIN

YOU WERE THE NEW GIRL ON THE SHOW. In the middle of the night a group of rebels had come, blindfolded you, tied your hands behind your back. You woke up in a bed covered by mosquito netting, confused. Pulling back the net, you saw the large flowering cactus scaling the cement wall, guard and protector. You touched the petals, poked your forefinger against a spike, and there it was: a tiny dot of bright red blood, more beautiful than any drippings that ever popped through my own veins. Which were throbbing. You pounded your fists against the door until your knuckles turned pink, then collapsed against the prickly tentacles. I was ambushed by your tears. Pale blue eyes. The desert sky. My stomach clenched and the room started spinning and I was glad I was sitting on my grandmother's couch but wished she'd go away. She talked loudly during commercials.

They brought you water, a hard roll, thin slices of meat. They wore party masks and beards like Castro's. Strapped machine guns to their tan fatigues. You asked, "Where am I? Why am I here?" So small next to them, but defiant. Your cheeks fire-brushed. I couldn't believe how much you reminded me of Blair, not your face really but the aching, the reaching behind your eyes. Since she left I'd looked all over for that.

One of the rebels leaned in close. "It won't be much longer," he said in a bizarre accent, breath shifting his beard to the left. Behind him, the deep whine of an organ. "We've contacted your *real* father."

Your face torched, totally Blair—the look, of course, but I didn't know it yet.

Imagine you're not who you think you are. That when someone, say, a masked rebel, says your father, he's talking about a different person from the man you've always called Dad. I thought about this a lot the day after your kidnapping, the day I started seeing again. I was staying at my grandparents' condo in Arizona, banished for being kicked out of the final camp, waiting for the man I'd never once called Dad to join us on the weekend. It wasn't looking good. He was busy, and Nancy had a cold. She'd been getting sick a lot. I pretended I had another father, with a different (dead) wife. A multimillionaire who thought I'd died at birth until he was contacted by the rebels, and when they told him his daughter was still alive, switched at birth, he knew it was true, he'd always known, and set off for the dunes.

I asked my grandmother if maybe I was adopted. Her hand a soft mitt on my cheek, she said, "Don't be silly. You're the spitting image of your father."

Was, I thought. Was . . .

My grandfather and I set out for the mall in his olive-green Cadillac. I adjusted my thighs on the hot vinyl seat, eager for the air-conditioning to get going. It was almost midday in Scottsdale and sunny. Heat pounded the windows of the old Caddy, gravel snapping beneath its wheels. Back in the Bronx this car was classy, here it seemed rundown, a level up from the metal carcasses left alongside the highway. It roared through the streets, straining to pump cold air through the vents inside while coughing up black fumes outside, the seats covered with silver duct tape to keep the hard yellowed foam from cracking through the vinyl. Worst of all, the Cadillac symbol on the hood was gone, the result of an accident last year. Grandpa swore he'd seen the pole in front of him and then somehow had forgotten it. He was starting to forget stuff—closing the refrigerator door, his favorite radio show, where he'd left his flip-flops. Grandma said he was getting more and more like the president. He even wore cowboy hats.

I pulled my seat belt across my lap and Grandpa sighed. In

profile he looked like Einstein, bushy white hair and eyebrows, thick black glasses, droopy doglike eyes. I wanted to tell him I still trusted his memory, but my gesture had been anything but innocent. There was talk about selling the Caddy, which made me mad. What was he supposed to do, ride horses?

We drove through the blond mountains, cutting across the highway. Grandpa wanted to visit Radio Shack to pick up a new antenna for the television set. I said I'd go along, not out of camaraderie, but because I'd woken up with brownish stains on the rolled-up toilet paper between my legs and needed something stronger. It was no sweat losing the old guy and slipping off to the drugstore. I found a small box of pads, the kind I'd been taking one by one from the machine in the girls' bathroom since the bitch had come. My earlobes pricked as I put the box on the counter. It was the first I'd ever bought; didn't want any evidence in the house. The saleslady lifted the box, holding it above her head for the whole store to see, like she was *trying* to get it higher than even her stubby arms would allow. I started to sweat. She lifted her glasses, turning the box, mumbling, "Kotex, Kotex . . ." It sounded like a missile or fighter plane, blasting smoky cunt farts through the sky. The prickling moved down my neck. I thought, Hurry up, lady! I thought, You wrinkled-up idiot! Zeroing in on the price tag, she lifted her glasses, half-glasses really, attached to a chain around her neck. "It's hard to see the numbers sometimes," she said, and all the burned-up hatred since the bitch had come sizzled inside me like a well-done hamburger. Stupid bitch!

I grabbed the box out of her hand and pointed to the price tag. "It's two forty-nine," I said.

"Why you—" She glared at me.

"Two forty-nine."

"I can read."

"Then ring it up. What are you waiting for?"

She shook her head, mumbling to herself, "I just can't see the same as always is all . . ." as she slowly punched the numbers on her register, dragging it out on purpose. I dug into my pocket and tossed three one-dollar bills on the counter.

"Keep the change."

She didn't look up. A few steps away I realized I was walking in public with a gigantic box of Kotex under my arm. People were staring. I ran back for a bag and hoped to find another cashier but that woman in her dumb jean shirt with the rhinestones along the collar was the only one. I imagined her picking out the shirt at the store across the way, maybe a friend telling her how adorable she looked, though her hair was thin and greasy, her face like a walnut, and she had a tick in her left eye—way past even normal-looking. And she still bought the sparkliest shirt. If I kept thinking about it I'd start bawling, and I wasn't like that. I shoved the Kotex under my shirt and found a clothing store. In the dressing room, I broke into the box and stuck a pad in the crotch of my underwear, lining the others around my waistband like a rebel packing wads of hundreds.

There was no garbage bin, so I left the box and skated across the mall. My grandfather was still testing antennas. He was a good tester, an electronics guy by trade. Since he retired, Radio Shack had become his second home. All the salesmen knew him by name and encouraged his experimentation. They got a kick out of him, this old man who talked like a New Yorker but called everyone "partner," like he'd learned it in the movies.

"Ready for lunch, little buckaroo?" Grandpa said, and we returned to the sweltering Caddy, on our own since Grandma ate lunch at the clubhouse on golf days. I wanted to go home and unload my ammo but kept quiet as we passed Palm Court and continued on a few blocks to the Old West village, an amusement park where everyone dressed like they hadn't changed their clothes in a hundred years. You could see the outline of the Ferris wheel from the pool at Palm Court, cars decorated like covered wagons, but it was a much longer walk than it seemed. You couldn't get anywhere around here without a car.

At the gate, the attendant dressed like a cowboy smiled at Grandpa. "How's it going, Mr. Cooperstein?" he asked.

"Mighty fine, mighty fine. This here's my kinfolk, my grand-daughter. Take off your hat, Lily."

"Why?" I said.

"Because you're in the presence of a gentleman."

I took off my Mets cap and the fake cowboy bowed. "Pleased to meet you, ma'am."

"Me too," I said, though I didn't mean it. The gatekeeper was gross, full of acne worse than mine, which tended to bunch around my nose, chin, and forehead. His tongue sloshed around his lips like a cow's, but he let us into the park for free. Grandpa tapped his back a few times, said he was a fine young partner, and we headed for the saloon.

Saddles and stirrups clung to the walls and there was a mechanical bull in the corner. A sign above it said no rides before five p.m. Behind a glass counter, smoke rose from the grill, spitting up grease and meaty air globules. Signs on old parchment advertised menu items: tortillas, burgers, chili, corn chowder, root beer. Grandpa ordered a bowl of chili; I got a chili burger with thick fries, and we took our trays to the woman dressed like an Indian who sat behind an antique cash register. She was odd-looking for an Indian. Her shiny black hair was molded into two long, thick braids, but her skin was pasty white, her nose tiny and thin. When she looked up to give us our total her eyes glimmered bright green. The costume made her seem less of an Indian and more an advertisement for interracial marriage, but I wasn't sure if Indians qualified as a race. Some people said Jews did. And there was a Puerto Rican kid at school. What about him? It was all so confusing.

"What kind of Indian are you?" I asked her.

She raised her shoulders and smiled. "Navajo."

"Cool."

"We're peaceful. We live on the reservation."

Grandpa fidgeted next to me, frantically checking his pockets.

"Are you okay, Mr. Cooperstein?" the green-eyed Navajo said.

"I can't find my wallet."

She stared at him, cockeyed now. Grandpa apologized, said he'd had it with him just a few minutes earlier at Radio Shack. "Oh horses! I must have left it at the store. And it's almost high noon!"

"I have money, Grandpa," I said. I always had money; my allowance was fifty a week.

"Now, little lass, you stay out of this."

"Not again, Mr. Cooperstein."

"Where is that doggoned wallet?"

Grandpa looked distraught. He kept slapping his hands against his body hoping the wallet might appear. "It's okay, Grandpa, I can pay," I said. "We'll get your wallet after lunch." I dug the money roll out of my pocket, peeled off a ten, and handed it to the Indian. Grandpa's eyes sunk lower than I'd ever seen. He leaned back against the counter while I collected the change. The fake Navajo said have a nice day, and we walked outside to the picnic tables.

"How could this have happened?" Grandpa said, and stared at his bowl of chili. Not knowing what to say, I bit into my burger. Chili plunked from the patty to the wax paper covering my plate. Another bite and my fingers were bathing in it. I went to get more napkins from the counter, where a few tourists in street clothes were ordering food. Others mingled about with the Old West people.

I asked a cowboy how long he'd been in town and he said he came with the miners after the Civil War. They'd been battling the Apaches and the outlaws ever since. In fact, he said, there was a bad guy on the loose right now, the outlaw Edmond Cleve. I said I'd look out for him. "You do that, son," he said, "but you'd do better to trade in that cap of yours for a real cowboy hat."

My hat confused the Old West people. Cutoffs frayed just below my knees, leather high-tops, and the large, baggy T-shirt didn't help, but my baseball cap with its perfectly worn-in arch and faded orange lettering closed the deal. In the 1800s the men wore one kind of hat, the women another, although even now people thought I was a boy whenever I wore the Mets cap Jack had bought me. We used to go to games together when I was really young. My favorite player was Tom Seaver, with his iron arm and dusty knees. The greatest pitcher ever. I had his number on my Slugger pajamas.

Back at our table, a woman in a flowery bonnet and dress that hooped out at her ankles came by with a basket full of rock candy. "It's from the mines—diamonds," she said. I took a piece, Grandpa didn't. He looked like he was going to cry.

Suddenly (I don't like the word *suddenly*, by the way, and have been skeptical of it since my eleventh-grade English teacher, Mr. Belgrave, criticized it in an essay of mine—one that I'd actually written myself—saying, "Nothing happens *suddenly!*" but sometimes things do occur without warning, right away, quick as wink, as these Old West imposters might say and thus) shots pealed through the air and everyone jumped out of their seats, crowding the dirt road in front of the saloon. A few women in fancy dresses shrieked and fainted. "High noon, Lil!" Grandpa shouted. "It's high noon!"

We crammed in next to an old shopkeeper in a white apron. "It's Edmond Cleve!" he shouted. "The outlaw Edmond Cleve."

Cleve galloped in, a black figure on a black horse, even the dusty bandanna across his nose and mouth was black. He turned every so often to fire at the sheriff who trailed a few feet behind him. The sheriff let go of the reins with his right hand and scooped up his lasso. Spiraling above the sheriff's head, a braided cotton halo, the rope took on a life of its own. It leaped in Cleve's direction and caught his gun. The crowd cheered. The cowboy I'd spoken to earlier stepped closer to Cleve's horse and forced him down. Cleve turned toward the sheriff, right hand on his holster. The two were headed for a shoot-out.

"So we meet again, Cleve," the sheriff said. "This time I'm going to run you out of town for good."

"We'll see about that, sheriff."

"This is your last chance," the sheriff said, and I noticed my grandfather mumbling his lines with him. "You've got ten seconds to turn and walk on out of here or I'll blow your head off."

"Not if I get you first!" Cleve drew his remaining gun and fired, but the sheriff ducked and grabbed his weapon. Shots flew; we all shouted. The woman with the rock candy dropped her basket. Cleve and the sheriff missed each other, dragging out the duel until, finally, the sheriff hit Cleve. Blood exploded in his chest, he tripped backwards. The sheriff shot him again and this time he went down in a flurry of cheers.

A saloon girl dressed in a snug, frilly bodysuit with a tiny silver gun tucked into the red satin ring holding up her stockings kissed the sheriff on the cheek, leaving a red lip print on his face. Then she turned to the crowd. "Give it up for the sheriff, isn't he just scrumptious?" The sheriff bowed. "And how about a cheer for the nastiest outlaw in the land, Edmond Cleve!" The woman sauntered over to him and, eyebrows fluttering, offered him her hand. Accepting it, he bounced up, bloodied neck and all. Back from the dead. He pulled the saloon girl into a serious kiss. People clapped and whistled. He was much cooler than the sheriff. Bad guys always are.

"She looks like Mae West!" Grandpa said, smiling, and though I didn't know Mae West, that underwear said everything. Sexy. Like Blair in her uniform. Kiss finished, Cleve and the woman raised their hands in the air. For a minute you couldn't tell the tourists from the actors, there was so much commotion. Grandpa whooped and hollered, "Bravo! Bravo!" He loved the whole song and dance; everyone did. But it was weird imitating people from another time. This gone world resurrected. I felt like an intruder, phonier than the Indian girl with her sparkling green eyes—alive at their expense. Palm Court with its shiny white walls and tennis courts was ages away.

Grandpa stayed in a good mood as we set off for Radio Shack to retrieve his wallet. It was a short drive but felt like a trek, especially since we'd made it a few blocks from the Old West town before realizing he didn't have his glasses. I ran back and found them on the table where we'd been sitting and returned hyperventilating. The sun was too strong, the air dry and dizzying. I was starting to think we'd never make it back to Palm Court and wondered if that was what Grandpa feared. That one day he'd forget himself and be the man who never returned. There was a song he loved by the Kingston Trio about the man who never returned. One day he gets stuck on the MTA when a fare strike hits and can't get off the train. He spends his days riding back and forth along the suburban lines and every day his wife comes by and chucks him a sandwich. That made no sense, I told Grandpa. Why didn't she just give him a nickel so he could get off the train? Grandpa said he wouldn't have taken it because that would mean he'd accepted the fare hike and it was a protest song like songs in the sixties but it came earlier on. When workers were the thing.

Hours later, it seemed, we returned the Caddy to its spot and walked through the pool area, where Grandma sat with her girl-friends underneath a large tent. As soon as she saw us, she checked her watch and stretched up out of her chair like a cat. A very tan woman wearing a sun visor and matching yellow tennis outfit caught her. "Cocktail time?" she said, and Grandma nodded. Every day, like high noon in the Old West town, Grandma and Grandpa marched inside for drinks at three. Occasionally people joined them, but Grandma hated entertaining and liked watching her soap while she sipped her bourbon.

"You ready, Hog?" Grandma said.

"At your service, my dear." Grandpa winked, and all the ladies by the pool said, "Ahhh."

The walk inside took forever. I was lightheaded and bloated, and no matter how deeply I inhaled I couldn't fill my lungs. Like I imagined you in your compound.

I went directly to the bathroom and stuck on a new pad, rolling the other one the way a girl at camp had demonstrated for another one. Roll it like a big fat joint, she'd said. I hid the bloody wad in my beach bag, along with the clean ones I'd liberated from my waistband. Later, after they'd gone to bed, I'd toss the dirties in the garbage outside. Nobody'd ever know.

I found my grandparents in the kitchen preparing the cocktail cart. Grandma opened a Tupperware container full of peanuts in the shell and poured them into a bowl, then lifted a Ziploc bag of pretzels from the cabinet next to the sink. "Ew!" she shrieked. "Termites!"

"Let me see." Grandpa left the freezer where he'd been filling an ice bucket. I followed him. "Those aren't termites, they're ants," he said.

"Everyone's been talking about the termites."

"Have you ever seen a termite? They're straight and narrow. An ant's got a figure like the gal outside the saloon. Remember, Lil?" He moved his hands in the shape of an hourglass.

"Mae West."

"Look, look at those curves. What you've got here, Rosie, are good old-fashioned ants."

"So do something!" Grandma said.

"I will," he replied, and we stood waiting. "Go and watch your show, go on. I can't work with you looking at me."

Grandma and I paraded into the living room. She turned on the TV set, adjusting the antenna to temper the static. "Saul!" she shouted. "What about that new antenna?" He called out a few garbled words from the kitchen, the ant-slayer. Even bugs were straight or curvy. I'd rather be a termite, tough as steel. Eat through wood like a professional wrestler. But I'd started anting out long before the bitch, just like the stupid movie in health class said I would. The film was grainy black and white, and full of cartoon diagrams of the reproductive system. The narrator said *virgina*, sneaking the word *virgin* into *vagina* on purpose. Jack would have loved that, but I was too grossed out to mention it.

Grandpa wheeled out the cart with bottles of alcohol and soda, an ice bucket, the peanuts and pretzels. He mixed a drink for Grandma, then one for himself, clinging to the formality though the nuts were stale and his fingers shook around the glass. Grandma stuck her hand in the peanuts and, without looking up from the TV, cracked one open with her fingernails. "What are you drinking, Lil?" Grandpa asked. "Ginger ale? Coke? Or I could make you an egg cream?"

"Okay."

He dangled his fingers in my face. "Poof, you're an egg cream."

"Very funny."

Grandma shushed us from the couch. The *World Without End* theme song was playing. Grandpa trod into the kitchen and returned with a glass of milk. A glob of chocolate layered the bottom like a sand sculpture. He unscrewed the bottle of seltzer and poured. In the Bronx, the beverage man delivered crystal fire extinguishers that squirted soda in laserlike streams. Jack and I once had a seltzer fight, dousing each other in the front yard. You couldn't do that with a screw-off bottle, and the egg creams in flat Arizona were never as foamy as I remembered them.

Grandpa handed me my egg cream, picked up his cowboy hat, and walked through the sliding-glass doors to the terrace. He liked to sit in his ratty reclining chair and listen to talk radio, the horizon set out in front of him, a never-ending canvas. Within minutes, he would slide the hat down over his nose and fall asleep. Grandma and I settled in to wait for you.

But the rebels came first. They asked for ten million dollars to help fund their maneuvers. We saw them circling in the sand, fingers worrying their beardless chins. It didn't matter if we saw their faces. They were hiding from you.

The one who'd spoken to you pulled another one aside, closer to us. "What if he doesn't come?"

"Oh, he'll come," said the other, both of their accents gone. "Life has been good to him, but he's been marked by sorrow. He never had another child. Never remarried. Everyone thought his wife was crazy, but he believed her when she said it wasn't their baby, that their child was out there somewhere. He kept on believing it even after she poisoned herself."

"But the money . . . it's a lot of money to ask for."

"This man owns three diamond mines! He has ten houses, a fleet of jet planes. The only thing he doesn't have is his child . . ." This smarter, taller, tidier rebel put his hand on his partner's shoulder. "Never underestimate what a father will do for his daughter."

"I know," said the darker, long-haired, more muscular one. "But what if he doesn't believe us . . . or . . . he's trying to trick us. Anything can happen, and the girl, you see . . ." His voice trailed off.

"Oh my god, you've fallen in love!"

The two men stared at each other. One angry, the other exposed. My heart was in my throat.

"Have some peanuts." Grandma pushed the bowl in front of me, but I waved it away. Not hungry. Of course the fake rebel was in love. Grandma said that's why he joined their plotting in the first place, and she would know. She'd been watching the show for years and could tell you the history of every character. I've since learned that female elephants absorb massive amounts of information during their lifetime, remembering grazing locations, enemy territory, dead relatives. I'm not sure how researchers figured this out—I mean, you can't really ask an elephant what she remembers—but they swear that's the way it is, the great matriarch a memory keeper for the entire tribe. I like seeing my grandmother this way.

"Don't tell me you're on a diet." Grandma held out a peanut for me. "Your mother's always on a diet, trying to get rid of those curves. But some girls just got 'em. That's the way it is. We used to be so ashamed to be thin, it meant you were poor. You sure you don't want this?" I took the peanut, which looked like an ant or Mae West or you in your torn kidnapped jeans. Curves everywhere, in everything, bombarding my frontal lobe like the word *virgina*.

"Why don't you take your hat off?" Grandma said, cracking into a busty shell and munching on the peanuts inside. She was working for the ant people, trying to get me to be a "lady," although her own curves were exiled to frayed black-and-white photos. I envied her. No more worries about ants or termites, no more stinking pads, she could just be herself. I stuck the hat in my back pocket. "There, that's it," Grandma said. "You have such beautiful hair." She patted my knotty head and it felt almost as good as Blair's comforter wrapping around me as we stared at the TV screen with its stormy lines.

Out of the static came a Gustave Monde spot I'd seen them film. It had one of those jingles you couldn't stop singing even though it sucked. "That's one of Jack's commercials," I said, and Grandma and I watched the brunette on screen grab a subway pole, looking so tall and carefree. Grandma was shocked when I said she'd bawled her eyes out in between takes, who knows what about.

On TV the jazzy voice behind her sang:

So very sexy, sophisticated.
Anything goes.
From your hips down to your toes.

"Sexy toes?" Grandma said. "Who ever heard of such a thing? She probably has athlete's foot."

I laughed but thought of my father and how he'd followed that brunette with the eyes of a lovesick rebel. You were the sexiest thing I'd ever seen.

MIMI SITS ON MY BED, watching me finish the tattoo I'm engraving on a lemon. I'd been carrying the piece of fruit around for three days trying to decide what to do with it. Mimi's instructions were to pretend it's a person. "If it was somebody, like somebody who was really muscular with a bald head and always wearing tank tops and big gold chains, think what kind of picture does it make? Maybe a bull or a lion. Animals are very good. Most people, they like some kind of animal."

"Then what about Angel's devil?"

"With her it was different. We needed an opposite. Sometimes it's just that way. Feel it out, *chica*. You'll know what's right."

Easy for her to say. She's been tattooing for years. Easier, too, when your subject talks. I've spent too many hours feeling out this lemon.

Mimi's so close I can feel her breath against my shoulder. Her watching makes me insecure about my design. At first I thought of doing a face, a silhouette, Mimi's profile, but as I squeezed that lemon in my palm thinking about its destiny I became convinced it was like everything else here, captive. I started drawing chains, not the industrial kind, but more like something you'd find in the display case at Macy's: S chains, box chains, beads, ropes, and her-ringbone gold. What made it to the lemon resembles a string of pinto beans beginning at the stump on top and winding its way along the bumpy yellow road.

A final wipe with a tissue and I'm ready to pass it off to Mimi. I am excited, proud, and a little bit scared. Mimi sits down on my bed for her inspection. I don't want to look nervous so I commit my cramped, ink-stained fingers to picking through the mail. As usual, there's quite a bit of it. People telling me they hate me, calling me a monster. Nancy apologizing for not being around after school, never meeting with my teachers, and for ignoring me the day I'd come home and declared I was going to marry Blair. I didn't think she remembered the way she'd laughed, "You sure about that?"

"We don't need a big wedding or anything," I said, having somehow decided that Jack and Nancy should pay for it. Their house was much bigger than Blair's, it was the least they could do.

"Help me zip up," Nancy tapped her shoulder, then lifted her hair into a ponytail. "Jack's bringing home some people."

She sucked in her stomach, which made her more fidgety. The freckles on her back bounced up and down. I pulled the sides of her cocktail dress together and started zipping. "Then it's okay?" I asked.

"Okay?"

"You'll do it."

"Do what?"

"Have the wedding."

"Sure, whatever . . . Oh shit, it's late." She'd turned her attention to the thick gold watch on her wrist. "Lily, do me a favor. Go down and take out the mozzarella salad. The basil's gotta breathe."

I watched her sit down in front of the makeup mirror and adjust the rows of lights on both sides so her face looked peachy. Her eyes were wide and dark like mirrors. Cocaine eyes. When she was drunk her eyelids slid down like Levolors, her hips swaying back and forth the way Blair danced to disco songs, her laughter loud and wet. Like her lips. On coke, those same lips were chapped and dry. Kissing her must have been like sucking on a cactus.

That day she puckered up to the mirror, layering her desert lips with Vaseline and amber lipstick. I couldn't tell if she looked beautiful or like a clown. She must have thought it looked okay, if in her rose-tinted reflection she saw anything at all.

Two months later, Blair was gone and nobody ever mentioned her. But sometimes when we drove past her house I'd catch Nancy staring, waiting for me to confess I'd driven her off and she'd left a hole so deep inside me I'm not sure it ever closed. Maybe those holes never do. We just find new places to drill inside ourselves.

Every day my mother's letters get fatter. She's got lots to apologize for. I write her back and say it's okay, everything's A-okay.

Odd, how I'm taking care of people outside, when in here I can barely look out for myself. I need Mimi, but I'll never let her know how much—I learned that from Nancy, too.

The shrink says my mother felt like she sacrificed her life giving birth to me. I was not planned, never supposed to be there. Some people die a little bit when they have a child and can't get themselves back. Nancy even had her tubes shut down to prove it. No more babies. Everything about her said Dead End. Except when she was high. I don't tell my mother what this shrink says. I don't mention Mimi or the tattooing. I tell her I am reading spy novels in between all of the legal books and that I am going to grow tomatoes.

Mimi holds the lemon between her fingers, squinting like her eye's some kind of decoder. I want to yell out, "Tell me, tell me already!" But then I'd pay. A big envelope from my lawyer breaks away from the pack. Opening it I find my mental status examinations.

"My psycho tests are here," I say out loud. Mimi looks up for a second, then gets back to studying my lemon. The citrus scent reminds me of blond girls seducing the sun down by the beach. Once I'd tried it, figuring the blond highlights would help my white hairs blend in, but my sticky lemonhead only attracted swarms of yellow jackets and made my forehead itch. Nancy laughed, asked why didn't I just open a bottle and dye it the normal way. She thought I was such a freak.

This I remember from my baby book: *Lily has peculiar habits. She likes to stick her hands in her diaper and play with the contents. Sometimes she rubs it on the wall. S says encourage experimentation, so we've covered her bedroom with tack paper.*

Nancy'd be surprised to see how sane I come off in my MSEs—a bit bored and condescending, but smart. Now maybe the media will stop comparing me to Hinckley and Chapman, although I see the similarities. We were all lonely, all too much in love, but that's the extent of it. And to the moron reporter who said we'd all been inspired by *The Catcher in the Rye:* I never read the book. The cover was so boring.

What they don't say is that you answered two of my letters, each time telling me to follow my dreams, and even though your letters were typed, yes, typed with eight-by-ten glossies attached, I knew you'd really signed them because the guy at the copy shop in town had explained how to decipher a real signature from a copy under a magnifying glass. I imagine your thin fingers holding a silver pen with your initials engraved on the side, when the words come: *Dream, Lillian! Follow your dreams.* Your face melts behind my eyes.

To get back to Mimi, back into the moment, I start reading my mental tests out loud:

—Who is the president of the United States?

—Ronald Wilson Reagan.

—Who is the vice president?

—George Herbert Walker Bush. The United States senators from New York are Alfonse D'Amato and Daniel Patrick Moynihan. The mayor is Edward I. Koch, governor Mario Cuomo.

—Okay, okay, that's sufficient. Do you know who Brooke Harrison is?

—I refuse to answer that question.

—Where are you?

—Bellevue. Manhattan. State of New York. America. Western Hemisphere. Earth.

—Do you know why you're here?

—I have no idea why any of us are here.

—In Bellevue. What are you doing in Bellevue?

—I'm accused of murder and being tested to see if I'm a loon.

—Did you know Brooke Harrison?

—Once again, I refuse to answer that question or talk about her on the grounds that it might incriminate me.

—Lillian, your lawyer hired me, I can't incriminate you.

—You mean you work for me?

—In a manner of speaking, yes.

—Then stop asking questions you know I can't answer or you're fired.

—Fine. May we continue?

—Go for it.

*—Okay, I want you to start with the number one hundred
and subtract seven. Then keep subtracting seven until you get
as close as you can to zero.*
*—The other shrink did this with threes yesterday. Why aren't
we doing threes?*
—Just do sevens please.

I'm reading my calculations when Mimi breaks in. "It's fantastic," she says.

"Would you believe I got Cs in math? Except for geometry."

"You made a lemon chain." Beaming, she dangles the oblong ball in front of me. She's hyped my design resembles a string of tiny lemons, the fruit kept down by her own people. I'm not kidding, she really says that, and with so much pride I pretend her interpretation had been my intention. You can do that with art. Mimi lifts my shirt and rolls the tattooed lemon around my stomach, kneading harder and harder, like she's pummeling dough for bread, though I can't imagine she's much of a cook. Just as I have trouble picturing her sitting down to dinner with her husband and kids in their kitchen filled with curios. The Virgin Mary and friends. "I had a feeling about you, *muñeca*," she hums, so close to my ear it tingles all over. I'm not used to being touched like this, I wish she'd hit me or pull my hair. If I turn my head I can still read my psycho test.

—How long has it been that you've liked girls?
—That's a stupid question.
—Well, when did you know you were a lesbian?
*—Who said I was a lesbian? I never said that. I'm not into
labels. Besides, I sometimes like boys. There was this boy, in
my senior year—*

Mimi's hand clamps down on my arms. She shoves the test to the corner of the bed, then sits down on my stomach, holding my arms above my head. "You're not paying attention."

"Yes I am."

"Then what did I just say?" She tightens her grip around my wrists.

I worm beneath her. "The lemon's down by her own people."

She bursts out laughing, throwing her head back, then comes up and smacks my cheek. It's a different kind of tingling, one I can deal with. "That was maybe three sentences ago. You don't listen too good. When are you going to learn?"

She ties my hands above my head with a T-shirt. I don't resist. Out of the corner of my eye, I spot a couple of women standing outside my cell, watching. I'm strangely impressed with myself, having always been afraid to change pads or take a shit if anyone was within earshot. Being shy requires freedom and I have none. Mimi unzips my pants, pulls everything down. A few wiry black hairs peek over my stomach. She rubs the lemon back and forth over my pubes so hard it burns.

I kick my legs up behind her, flipping like a caught fish.

She slaps me, then grabs my chin. "You want to play rough?" she says. Slowly, not removing her eyes from mine, she moves the lemon to my hole, pushing to where it pains a bit, then taking it away. My stomach muscles contract. "You goin' weak on me now?" She pushes a bit farther this time, then pulls it back. Pushes and pulls so I'm dying for the whole thing.

Outside they whoop and holler, someone says, "Tastes like Sprite!" and they all crack up.

Mimi's face looms smugly. She rolls the lemon up my stomach and I nod my head, no. "You want it?" she says, and I bite my lip. I won't say so.

She shoves the lemon up my cunt so hard I gasp. Fucks me royally, and their watching only makes it easier. The lemon half in, half out, she digs her fingernails into my stomach and I scream. Those nails've been sharpened into triangles. If I were tattooing her, I'd draw a tiger. She grazes lightly up the sides of my body, under my arms where it tickles, but I don't dare move or she'll stick me again. The lemon pops out and I'm fired, afraid she'll notice and give it to me harder, more afraid she'll get disgusted and walk away.

She unties my hands, leans back, and pulls me down on top of her. Taking my hands in hers, she slides them underneath her shirt. I pinch around her nipples. She yanks my head down between them, and I sigh like I'm finally home, though it's a place I've never been. A *tit*-bit from my baby book: I was raised on plastic nips and fake milk and maybe that's why it feels so good. I suck like I'm pulling from an ultralight. Hard. "*Chica*," Mimi whispers, and I know what's coming next, one of the first things she'd ever said to me, the thing that no matter how many times she says it never fails to send tiny needles down the back of my legs: "I know exactly what you want."

WHAT I REMEMBER MOST about that summer in Scottsdale is you. Not the star you would soon become, but the girl I discovered those afternoons in my grandparents' condo. You were part of the whole cocktail routine, the everyday drink and settling in. Grandma swore it would help her live to be a hundred. "A drink a day keeps the doctor away," she said. "What? That's how they do it in Europe. Ask your friend Mister Monde." And every day the ladies down by the pool chuckled as Grandpa and I followed her upstairs, passing the glowing red digital clock that said 15:00. Military time. Fifteen hundred hours at base camp meant you were just minutes away.

Getting there was grueling. I walked back and forth down the long carpeted halls of Palm Court, where the air never changed. It was cold and brittle and smelled antiseptic, cleaned out of everything that actually made it air. What was air anyway? Nitrogen, oxygen, a little carbon dioxide. We'd studied this in science class. I should have paid attention. I wanted to know why the air inside the condo was so different from the air outside. Maybe they'd messed with the elements, mixed in a few chemicals so it was freshened but not fresh, like the air inside a plane. I hated planes.

I tried holding my breath and got headspins. Goosebumps stretched up my arms and legs. My long shorts did nothing to ward off the cold and made me look like a troll, but a cool one. Leader of the trolls on a troll-filled planet. I proclaimed myself ruler of the hallway.

At all costs I avoided swimming, which was a shame because I was good at it, but even without teen-girl diapers I hated wearing a bathing suit and girls weren't allowed to swim in shorts. Out by the pool, I watched some of the other kids, visitors like me, a few I remembered from earlier trips. A girl on the diving board sneered before launching herself into the water, Olympic-like. She was popular at Palm Court. The year before, she'd held hands with a boy near the tennis courts and one afternoon in the game room told me to scram while the rest of them huddled silently. The same kids who jumped in and out of the water.

The girl's grandmother stood next to the lifeguard, practically licking his ear. "Richie," she said, "Richie, are you watching her? I'm talking to you, Richie. Can you hear me?"

He laughed, said yes. "Of course he's watching her, he can't take his eyes off her," another girl said. Richie ignored her. Only a few years older than us, he had an important job, guarding the kiddie cargo shipped to Grandma's for the summer. He wore a cowboy hat and Speedo bathing suit. White cream covered his nose. He smiled as the stuck-up diver hoisted herself out of the pool by her palms. Dripping wet, hair plastered against her face, she was all eyelashes. She skipped back to the board. A few kids egged her on from the water. Richie *watched*. I wanted her to miss. Trip over the board. Crack up.

It was better in the hallway. I owned the hallway.

And I liked the art room. Early in the trip I'd set up an easel outside on the terrace. The lady who monitored the room thought I was odd. None of the other kids painted in the daytime, they were all out by the pool. And most never used watercolors. They liked the plaster sculptures, she said. Prefabricated ashtrays, napkin holders, plaques, animal heads, soldiers—anything they could slobber with tempera paint. Watercolors were more subtle. Better for the oldies, easier on their eyes. Where did I learn to paint?

I'd been messing with art stuff since forever but had no idea what I was doing. Pretending, I squeezed brushes in between my teeth, splashed diluted colors across the thick paper. My thumbprints dotted the foreground, imitating the desert landscape, craggy sand and far-off mountains, rugged like the surface of the moon but tinted reddish brown, the side that never came out in public. Sometimes the moon got tired of being a black-light poster.

I met a man named Mickey who painted in oils and wore a smock covered with pineapples, bananas, and mangoes. On top of his easel was a photograph of his grandchildren, two young boys who between them craved more than a few teeth, like the idiot from *MAD* magazine. Mickey had outlined the photograph on his canvas in pencil and was painting it section by section. He was the most patient person I'd ever met. Every day he tackled another sliver of canvas, a few strands of hair, an eye, the rounded collar of a shirt. I couldn't get anywhere with my watercolors. It was tough drawing the nubby cactuses and thorns, plateaus adrift in a pale blue sky. Everything I did looked like a bad version of the print by a famous artist we had hanging at home in the den. I think she lived in New Mexico. I used to look into the fossils and sand and think New Mexico was as foreign as China. That was before my grandparents moved to Arizona. Now the desert was familiar. I understood its muted colors and canyons, the big irrigation systems, wells like monsters, wires crisscrossed above everything. Grandpa said it took years to tap enough water to build Palm Court.

And someday maybe there'd be a tourist attraction like the one down the road—the new Old West. Instead of the sheriff and the outlaw Edmond Cleve, it'd be filled with imitations of people like my grandparents and the ladies at the pool. Luckily, the oldies kept coming; there would be no shortage of actors. Someone goofy would play Mickey with his fruited smock. He was helping me get an oil palette together and lecturing on color but nothing helped.

Eventually I would give up and stomp into the game room. A couple of kids were always playing Ping-Pong. Old men sat around dark wooden tables flipping decks of cards between stacks of red, white, and blue poker chips. They smoked fat, smelly cigars. I imagined the smoke being sucked up through the vents and pulled into a monstrous air machine for purification. Snuffed out with carbon dioxide. Re-freshened.

Back in the art room, Mickey would still be at it. Working on cheeks one day, he showed me the colors he'd blended to make skin. I asked how he did the shadows and he cupped his hand around his ear, the one with the hearing aid trapped beneath a horseshoe of white hairs. He did this whenever I spoke to him. It looked so funny I tried it and was amazed by the acoustics. Like talking underwater. We were a couple of deep-sea dwellers stuck in the freshened-air colony of Palm Court.

One afternoon, Grandma caught us talking with our hands over our ears and rushed me out of the art room. It was three o'clock. Upstairs, she said I shouldn't joke around like that. "The man's lost his wife, now his hearing's going, poor thing," she said. We were in the kitchen with Grandpa preparing for cocktail hour. "I know you think it's funny but that's his only way of hanging on."

"We're just having fun."

"You're having fun, this is his life," she said, and looked over at Grandpa who was whistling as he smashed a tray of cubes into the ice bucket. So much like Mickey, like the old lady in the drugstore, hanging on to whatever's left . . . I wanted to crawl into the closet and roll around in the moth balls, fumigate my brain. Refreshen it. Instead I went to the bathroom, stuffed a towel in my mouth, and screamed.

When I came out, the *World Without End* theme had already played and Grandpa was sitting on the terrace, his cowboy hat hanging over his face. "You missed the beginning," Grandma said. "Alex is on the verge of finding Jaymie Jo. He's talking to the Latin police."

I sat down next to my grandmother beneath the quilt and within seconds forgot how bad I was feeling, completely absorbed in Alex's search to find Jaymie Jo, his long-lost daughter. "Poor Alex," Grandma said, "all that money and he's seen nothing but tragedy." So when the rebels had contacted him and said you'd been switched at birth and demanded ransom, Alex Rheinhart knew it had to be true and set off for the jungle. Meanwhile, you waited in your cell not knowing any of this, until the rebel who'd fallen in love betrayed the group and told you that you had a different father, a very rich father, and when you expressed concern he wouldn't come, the rebel comforted, "Don't worry, he'll be here very soon," and looked so sad I almost felt bad for him. I knew exactly how he felt, not wanting to give you up.

Your face had become more familiar than the desert. People were like that. They were supposed to grow on you, not slam into you like an eighteen-wheeler, a long-lost father. I felt sorry for you missing all those years with your father. You said you'd always known something was off, always felt so lost, so alone, and I understood. My father hadn't made it out all summer. Yours had planned a few maneuvers of his own. He was the King of Diamonds, after all. He had his own private army. But at the last minute he was jumped by the kidnappers and dragged to another room, not knowing you were right next door with a giant cactus and mosquito netting, waiting for the father you'd never known.

My grandmother turned off the TV. The room went quiet except for the bumpbumpbumping of my heart. "Maybe we'll sit together by the pool this weekend," Grandma said, and I nodded. But I knew I was going to go crazy two whole days without you.

All I had was the hallway, and Mickey, and Grandma said we could go to the mall. Grandpa needed a part for an old radio. But I wanted the grandmother who stood in the kitchen complaining about termites that were really ants as she spilled peanuts into a bowl, Grandpa mixing me an egg cream before slinking out to the terrace for a nap. The television screen a comfort, like streaming seltzer water from a twist-off bottle. Different than the Bronx but it worked in the New West with air so thin and dry we were lucky to get any bubbles at all. What was the chemical property of bubbles, I wondered. How did they make H_2O fizzle? Air, of course. Like I used to blow air bubbles in the pool, back when I could still wear a bathing suit. I imagined a factory of troll people blowing bubbles into vats of seltzer water with long plastic straws as simply as Grandma and I settled in beneath the patchwork quilt on the couch.

By the end of the summer I'd memorized the lines on your face and could have mixed the glimmering tan of your skin. I asked Mickey to show me how. We spent three days mixing color, and at the end of the week, he invited me to have lunch with him in the dining room for oldies who didn't cook. Grandma said I could go, although she disliked the place herself. She said it was like eating in a gymnasium. Mickey ate there all the time. Since he lost his wife, he hated eating alone. If it weren't for the dining room he probably wouldn't eat at all, he said. We had cream of mushroom soup and tuna salad sandwiches smothered with tangy mayonnaise. I drank apple juice and Mickey had coffee. Dessert was red Jell-O squares topped with whipped cream, what they'd given us at camp, and later, at school, and even later . . . well, let's pretend, for a moment, there is no even later. For Mickey's sake. He was such a sweet old man.

The thing is, once the whipped cream's gone you can see yourself in the squares. The reflective power of red gelatin is amazing. The day I looked into my dish with Mickey I saw my face shriveled up like a raisin. The oldies were rubbing off on me.

Mickey took out his wallet and showed me a plastic accordion of pictures of his family, explaining their stories the way Grandma told me about the characters on *World Without End,* everyone connected to someone else. I listened even when it got boring. Nobody in his family was as exciting as you were. No one had ever been kidnapped or long-lost or dealt diamonds. I also fought to ignore the group of kids who hung out by the pool now eating lunch together. I could hear their laughter, make out a few words . . . "He likes you, Amy," "Shut up!" "I'm serious . . . *Amy and Richie sitting in a tree . . .*"

I asked Mickey why he painted from a picture. He cupped his hand against his ear and asked me to repeat the question. "Aren't you supposed to paint what's not already there, but the stuff inside?" I asked. "Isn't that what art is?"

"I don't know the first thing about art, my young friend. I only paint the things I love."

He said it didn't have to be people, but he liked that best. It was a way of keeping them with you even when they went away. And hearing those simple words I knew why I'd been struggling for three days to mix the browns and yellows and whites of your skin, knew I'd finally found a use for that sketchbook Blair had given me just before she left. Now both of you would be with me always.

Mickey and I finished our lunch and walked up our trays. Again, it was a lot like camp. We dumped out the leftovers and handed the trays to a man who stood behind a window. I peeked into the kitchen and saw a few giant silver pots hanging from the ceiling, a stove in the middle of the room, chrome sinks stuffed with more greasy pans from the meal. A couple of guys about Richie's age stood over the sink. Dark-skinned, black hair— Indians or Mexicans. Most of the workers were Mexican. In the new Old West town, phony Mexicans with twinkling green eyes will wash dishes while the oldies lounge by the pool, play golf, drive to Radio Shack, paint pictures of the things they love, everyone gulping molecules of air beneath the desert sun.

IT'S HOLY HOT THE FIRST TIME the metal doors close behind me. I look up and see one milky window sealed shut. A couple of women circle me like cats, one wears a blue bandanna tied around her head, the other has no teeth in front and big white freckles, definitely the softer one. I'll stick with her. Heat burns out my eyes, ears, nose, and the room stinks of chemicals. Like the hydrochloric acid we'd burned in test tubes, long ago. I read somewhere that smells tap the first level of memory. The primal stuff. I used to go to school. I never studied and did okay. Inside we sent up flames in test tubes, outside, in big houses, kids burned white rocks in glass pipes and it smelled the same. Just like this laundry room.

"If you need the bathroom, ring." The guard yanks a thick rope, and a gong sounds. "No stopping for anything else. This is an important job. I don't need to tell you how dirty laundry breaks down the system."

I nod. They always use the word *system*. I have no understanding of systems, communities. That's how I ended up here.

The guard smiles. Jack used to smile whenever he tried to talk serious. He never could get the words out. Instead, we'd eat cereal together.

"You're one lucky girl," says the guard, and my coworkers stare.

The job erases everything. Takes on its own rhythm. A mini-system. By the second time the room smells only like itself. Detergent, bleach, the sour static of the dryer. I never knew air could smell this bad, much worse than Palm Court, but only for a few seconds. You have to catch the memories quick: I never saw Nancy open the dryer. Someone else, usually someone dark-skinned, did our laundry. Then the smell goes. Humans are so adaptable. But we're still breathing crack air, shuffling it through our own private systems, everything recycled into everything else. At night I taste dirty socks in the back of my throat. They say we carry all the elements of the universe within us. Maybe we store air from all the places we've been, too. Maybe that's memory.

Chandon is the toothless, freckled woman. Every morning she and Stella with the bandanna are there first, the washing machines and dryers already rumbling. Chandon sits on the card table, one foot touching the floor, her fingers wrapped around a paperback without a cover. "Another day, another dollar," she winks. I walk over to the pyramid of canvas bags, spill out the contents of one, and start sorting the whites and darks. Everything has a number on it. Indelible ink. Like my mother used to tag my clothes whenever I left home. She ordered iron-on name labels through the mail, and the dry-cleaner steamed them on. Here I'm a number: 5248.

"Wha'cha doin'?" Stella's voice jabs, makes me hotter than I already am. "That's my job. You're here for the folding."

"But I thought—"

"Don't think," she nods, "just do what you're told."

I make a spitting sound, tough. "Nobody told me anything."

"I'm telling you, you're a folder."

A few days later I see her in the TV room, the "fishbowl." She stands in front of the old set. There's a yellow tint to the glass and dirt caked into the buttons and in the middle of the screen a chip the size of a marble. The worst is you don't know whose dirt it is. I picture thousands of troll hands as Stella clicks the knob, flicking through the soaps, videos, reruns, *The People's Court.* Another woman says, Stop. She wants to see her *People's,* she loves her

People's. "Shut up!" Stella says and continues flipping. I move further from the group.

When I walked in, they all stared. I haven't been in here too often. Movement is systematic, too. Took me a couple months to earn it. Now I have a job. I can walk without a guard into the fishbowl and watch television.

"Would ya pick a channel already?" says another woman. She is big and white and lumpy, brown hair cropped around her face.

"When I'm good and ready," Stella says.

The *People's* woman says: "I want my *People's!*"

"Anything worth watchin' these days is on cable," says the big white woman. "Why you even bothering with regular channels? All you got this time a day is soaps. I hate fuckin' soaps."

Stella ignores her, cruising through the soaps just to get the white woman's goat, although they're allies. Who else could get away with that kind of backtalk? The clock on the wall says half past three. I think of my grandmother and my heart feels twenty thousand pounds. On TV flash hospitals and waterfront scenes, every soap opera town has a waterfront, then the monastery and that same bad priest and . . . you? Blood draining out of me, I stumble backwards. Stella stops the dial. The white woman says, "Oh, come on, what is this shit? I just said I can't stand this show."

"You got taste up your ass," Stella says, then shouts over a few bodies, focusing her eyes on me. "Don't you think, folder?"

I can't speak I'm so frazzled. They were supposed to write off your character. Jaymie Jo Rheinhart is dead.

"Hey, I'm talking to you," Stella says, those I'm-telling-you eyes, that don't-mess-with-me voice stealing me from the screen. Conscious of the sharpened bedspring taped under my arm, I stare her down. Her brown face is scarred from knife fights and she's full of muscle. I don't care. One slip and I'll slice her the way Angel's been teaching me.

"She asked you a question," the white woman edges closer to me. "Do you like the show or not? You're the tiebreaker."

Do they think I'll cave that easily? "It's a good show," I say, careful not to move anything but my lower lip. My tone is flat. Emotionless. Like I killed once and will do it again if I have to.

Crazy, I'm in for a momentary flicker of violence and learning to be more violent than ever.

"You think it's a good show?" Stella walks toward me. "Well, I don't agree. I'd say it used to be a good show, before you got to fucking with it—you lucky I don't put your head through the glass," she huffs. "Shit. That was my show."

A couple of women gather closer and I know what's coming. First they corner you, throw a towel or jacket over your head, then do whatever. That tiny piece of metal in my armpit's not worth a damn.

Stella puts her face up against mine so I can't see the TV, can't see if it's really you or my mind's playing tricks. On TV, the priest is talking, saying something about his feelings. On soaps people always talk about their feelings. Even guys. "I been watching since I was a kid!" Stella shouts over him. "For a while, it was the only show that got any black people. But what you know about that? Huh? What the fuck you know about anything?"

I don't answer. What's there to say? I spy a woman reaching behind her, another one moving around the circle toward me. I'm going down. I lean into the few strips of sun stretching through the bars. Then the volume dims. "What the . . . ?" Stella turns around. I shuffle forward and see Mimi standing by the TV set, her right hand on the filthy knob, and Chandon next to her. I had no idea they knew each other, but maybe I'd sensed it, maybe that's why I liked her that first day in the laundry. Jail is like junior high. It's less about who people are, more who they hang with. Their reputation. Mimi's people are mostly Spanish; Stella's black. They do not like each other.

"What the fuck you doing?" Stella says.

"Turning down the volume," Mimi says.

"Nobody said turn it down." She brushes past Mimi and ups it even louder. For one second, everyone is drawn to the screen, where the evil priest talks to the girl who's not you, though she looks so much like you I want to scream. Are they fucking insane? My grandmother is watching this! It was her show, too. Twenty thousand pounds of heart cut through my spin cycle. I want to cry. Shutting my eyes I see you in your leather miniskirt and psychedelic pink stockings . . . I miss you so much.

"You little bitch!" Stella shouts, coming toward me. Mimi steps in between us. Stella pushes her aside, picks up a folding chair, and hurls it at me, but I duck. It bounces off the wall. I slide my right hand under my shirt going for the thin cut of spring.

"You throw like my great-grandmother," Chandon says to Stella, and a few people laugh. A couple more chairs fly. These coming from the back. Stella's girls. Chandon takes down one of them. From out of nowhere, Mimi barrels in and bumps Stella backwards.

"That was my show," Stella says.

"Figures."

"Bitch got no right messing with my show."

Mimi snorts: "Too late."

No comeback, Stella's madder than ever. She reaches down and pulls a piece of glass from her sock. "You stupid spic!" she says to Mimi, but slams glass in my direction. Wind sweeps across my chin, but she misses. Mimi grabs her arm and wrestles her to the ground, stepping on her hand until she drops the glass.

One of Stella's girls throws herself on top of Mimi, so I take my spring and stick her in the back. Her skin feels like putty. I can't get my spring out. My head fogs; I'm a palpitating mess. The girl flips on her side, screams, "Fucking stalker bitch!"

I shove my fingers in her face and calmly say, "Get off her or I'll poke your eyes out," but it's not my voice I hear. It's not my fingers set to gouge her eyes out. I shove her off of Mimi, who grabs Stella's glass but stays on top of her.

"I'm gonna get you, bitch!" Stella shouts over Mimi at me. "That was my show!"

Without turning her head, Mimi says, "Go, *chica*, get out of here," but I don't want to be a coward, not about you. "Go'wan, go! We got this covered," Mimi says, and I know she's right. Another chair crashes. I see Chandon brushing off her green pajamas.

On TV the priest says: "Delilah, let the Holy Father show you the way." She turns. She's not even Jaymie Jo.

I mope back to my cell. Angel's stretched across my bed, hands folded behind her back. Mobility is a strange thing. People just show up whenever they want. Keeps it interesting. A dim shadow on the wall makes it look like Angel's got a basketball in her stomach. I imagine pressing down so hard the ball shoots out of her and think of the circus lady shot from a cannon, only here Angel's the cannon. Like the Oriental women in my parents' tapes who shot Ping-Pong balls, darts, tiny pieces of candy, which must take more skill than dropping a baby. I don't like that Angel's pregnant, don't like pregnant women. But I like Angel.

"Whassup, Long Island?" Angel says. Her accent reminds me how we called it *the guyland*. But I've had enough of memory lane today.

"I can't sing the song right now," I blurt out, still in shock from my encounter with Stella and that priest. What kind of sadists run a story line at the expense of a dead star? Have they no respect for your memory? As soon as my hands stop shaking, I'll write the network.

Angel hoists herself up on her side. I drag over a metal chair, the same ones they have in the fishbowl. "You seen a ghost or something?" she says. "You whiter than the walls."

I sit, run my hand through my hair, wet with sweat. A chill rushes through me. I'm hunched like the oldest of the oldies with my arms and legs crossed. It's easy to feel old when you wear the same clothes every day. Angel pulls a cigarette from the pack in her bra and lights it for me. The first drag makes me lightheaded, after the second I want to cry. I keep my head down, watching my sneaker tap against the floor. It doesn't belong to me, the same way the angry voice and fingers weren't mine. Angel touches my head. I want to speak, but nothing comes out. I can't even smoke. I just hold the damn thing so close to my face it singes a couple of bangs the way it used to happen with bong hits. Outside. The year I had a friend . . . and look where that got me.

"That shit smells nasty." Angel takes the cigarette from my hand and brushes off my bangs. She strokes my hair, a touch like my grandmother's mitten—not the least bit tainted. "You gotta hang in, know what I'm saying? No, you don't know what I'm saying, you don't know, you think somebody holding a knife to your throat's gonna say, 'Tell me what's George Washington's birthday or I'll kill you. Tell me the capital of New Hampshire.' All that shit's a distraction, just forget you ever knew it. Being street smart's all that counts now, especially when you get around a bunch a niggas." The N word shocks me every time, I'd been so scared away from it. When I was in first grade, my parents sold one of our early houses to a black family, and all the kids at school called me nigger lover. A teacher overhearing them scolded, "Don't you ever, ever, ever use that word!" It was the worst word. But it's all you hear inside. The minute anything breaks it goes racial. Angel lifts my chin, grabs a piece of skin next to my ear. "Next time you cut from here"—she drags her fist across my mouth up to the other ear—"to here. Then you pull down the tongue like this." Pretending to yank my tongue, she warns it won't work if you don't cut the face right. She calls this a Colombian necktie.

My shoulders cave inward. I'm not street smart AND I can't think of a single city in New Hampshire. "Man, we gotta school you better, get you *happy*." Angel smiles because *happy* is Mimi's word and we don't really talk about Mimi. Again, she pets my head, and it seems fucked-up this woman who's sliced up people's faces and ripped out their body parts and uses the N word can be so gentle. I'm glad it's her and not Mimi here now. Too much sex makes me weary.

But even Angel's magic palms can't realign the fire in me. The shrink says I've walked the world with eighteen years of it bottled up inside. Whenever she says this I think of that TV show *I Dream of Jeannie.* J.R. Ewing in his first life, before he got fat and rich and rode horses, releases the beautiful Jeannie from her bottle, but she's really the side of himself the young J.R. had hidden away, the playful, devious, wild person he'd be if he didn't have to show up for work every day in a uniform. Uniforms do funny things to people. But the second he opens that bottle his life changes, and believe me, anybody's life can change in a few seconds.

Angel must feel my muscles contracting, see my sneakers tapping faster. She takes her hand away, leans back on her elbow, and I'm smothered in guilt. I can't figure out why this stuff comes when people are nice. I don't think like this with Mimi. I never want to yell at her or scratch her eyes out until she goes away.

I drag my chair back to the desk and take out a legal pad.

Angel asks if she can listen to my Walkman, the one Mimi's been eyeing for a new tattoo gun. I toss it to Angel, who slips the headphones over her ears and folds her hands on top of her stomach. She hums along with the radio, *happy.* So happy I'm giving her the damn thing.

REAL DIVAS DON'T CRY (UNLESS THEY'RE ASKED)

W*OEFUL* WAS A WORD not used much in the Harrison household. Mildred herself couldn't remember ever speaking such a sentiment out loud, yet if anyone had asked what she was feeling that October morning when she and Brooke boarded the silver Amtrak car in Philadelphia for the *World Without End* audition in Manhattan, she might have said woeful. In fact, the self-proclaimed throwback who wore her monochromatic skirts below the knee and dragged Tom swing dancing some Saturdays, longed to roll down the window of the train and regale those gathered on the platform with a heart-wrenching, "Woe is me!"

But of course the windows on the modern locomotive were sealed shut, the platform was empty, and back then people weren't yet in the habit of questioning Mildred Harrison. A good thing for Brooke, who didn't need the added burden of her mother's nerves; Mildred knew Brooke probably had her own fears about auditioning for the "high-school-aged" Jaymie Jo, though she'd just turned seventeen a few weeks earlier and her agent, Kenny Zeller, kept telling her she was made for the role. He'd even put in a furtive call to Mildred, saying they had it "hook, line, and sinker." Kenny and Tom had once discussed trout fishing and since then the agent always tried to work in an out-doorsy metaphor or two. "Listen," he told Mildred. "This is something I wouldn't usually tell somebody's mother, but I think you'll understand. They're looking for someone real, someone who looks like a regular teenager, but with major-babe potential. Who better, huh?"

Who better? Mildred asked herself as the train snaked up through the factories and fields of southern New Jersey. True, Brooke seemed a shoe-in, but what mother wouldn't feel uneasy about accepting her daughter's major-babe potential? And film was such a fickle medium. Off the top of her head, Mildred could recite the list of pilots, commercials, and industrial videos Brooke hadn't clinched, each rejection sending Mildred into a cauldron of fear and insecurity. The stages in and around Blue Bell, even in Philly, were one thing, but Mildred knew that out there in the world of television were hundreds of Brookes, all vying for a few precious spots in the public's imagination, and while the who-better question was paramount, she couldn't zap the imperialistic cry of its number one competitor: Why her? Brooke wasn't that special really, just another pretty girl with a good memory for dialogue. Constantly Mildred found herself wondering whether they'd made the right decision in pulling her from public school, sending her to New York for training, letting her travel for summer stock productions. Well, Kenny Zeller thought them right, and, forgetting his ten percent interest in every job, Mildred tried to believe him. She listened when he explained that Brooke's time had come. Maybe she would never be the proverbial child star, but weren't most of them dead, in rehab, or washed up by eighteen? Brooke, on the other hand, had enough regional spots and theatrical performances for directors to take seriously, but she was still fresh. New blood. And she radiated a kind of poise and self-possession rare among young people.

So stalwart and tenacious was Brooke that Kenny would joke that she and Mildred had reversed roles, Brooke becoming the stage mother to her mother, for it was Mildred who bit her fingernails down to the cuticles on those nights before auditions, while Brooke boiled water for chamomile tea and made certain Mildred packed her spongy globe that looked like a blue baseball with green continents instead of seams. Mildred liked to squeeze it in her palm as they awaited Brooke's call. "It's going to happen, Mom, if not this time then the next. Everything's leading up to it," Brooke often said, words offering slight assurance to Mildred, who was convinced her daughter had to be in denial. It wasn't right the way she never cried after a rejection.

Meanwhile at night, after Mildred and Tom made love and he rested his hand between her breasts for a few minutes before swinging his legs over to his side of the bed and shutting his eyes, Mildred would slip into the bathroom, sit down on the toilet, and cry big tears that sometimes left her breathless for hours. Had Tom ever discovered his wife and asked what was the matter, she wouldn't have known how to respond, her feelings being all tangled up like the knots in her favorite gold necklace, and she'd never had much patience for dwelling on the negative. Instead she kept her feelings from everyone: Tom, Brooke, Kenny, their parents and friends, and especially from Cynthia, who was becoming an odd sort of teenager. Mildred never knew what to make of the way her youngest daughter's eyes watered every night during the six o'clock news, nor how she couldn't sit through an entire war movie. Yet recently, Cynthia had spearheaded her own tactical maneuver, breaking into the junior high school science lab and emptying from their formaldehyde baths those frogs awaiting the procession of shaky X-Acto knives later that week. The girl made no attempt to hide her crime, even left a note saying, "WE WILL NOT DIE FOR YOUR SINS . . . thanks for the proper burial, Cynthia! (P.S. Stop Animal Testing)." The next day she was suspended for three days, a punishment Mildred thought excessive though she wouldn't interfere in school affairs. Privately, however, she applauded her daughter's spirit, just as she'd cheered silently when Cynthia painted her walls and ceiling black, then pasted up hundreds of glow-in-the-dark stars and solar systems and relinquished her four-poster bed for an air mattress, which she said gave her the feeling of sleeping outside. It was refreshing to see the girl developing tastes and opinions of her own, although the reference to animal testing did seem a direct jab at Tom, whose work at Paxton sometimes involved rats or tiny monkeys, a small price given the outcome: new and better drugs. One day he might help to cure cancer or discover a way to halt his father's diabetes. While she would never argue that the end always justified the means, Mildred had to come down on the side of science, although she did recognize the ethical complexities of the situation. Cynthia, on the other hand, at the dawn of her teenage years was typical in one way: She saw the world in absolutes. You were either right or wrong, and more often than not, Mildred and Tom were flat-out wrong.

Brooke, however, was always right, and the two girls had bonded deeply over the years, something Mildred and Tom couldn't have arranged any better if they'd tried. Recently Brooke had been taking her sleeping bag into Cynthia's room and spending the night in her sister's pin-up planetarium. "She's built a whole world in there," Brooke told Mildred. "It's so incredible. You know, I've been thinking . . . she's the real artist in the family." And if this realization prompted any sort of anxiety in Brooke, she followed her mother's example of swallowing it and wholeheartedly embraced her sister, always, always lobbying for Cynthia to join them on shoots and auditions. "You've got your squishy ball, I've got Cyn. She's my good luck charm," Brooke had said a few nights earlier; she'd wanted Cynthia to come to New York. But Mildred put her foot down.

"She can't miss any more school," Mildred said. "She's already fallen behind."

"So what? She's smarter than everyone in her class. She doesn't need school. She's going to do something really great someday and none of this is going to matter. Please let her skip school tomorrow, please let her come."

"No."

"But—"

"I mean it, Brooke. No."

Mildred couldn't afford the added stress of carting along another daughter. She was already beside herself. This was Brooke's biggest audition yet, a high-profile spot on a major daytime soap, and when ingénues were the biggest stars in the game. Already a few had become household names and were now making movies. Mildred sensed that Brooke was thinking that far ahead, believing Kenny when he told her she practically had this part without an audition and from it would stem many others. Although the role sounded demanding; Kenny had done some digging and discovered that within the year this character would suffer a kidnapping, reunite with the father she never knew, and become romantically linked with a young black man—that is, if the story line made it past the more conservative sponsors. But Kenny had a good feeling. He explained to Mildred that soaps could get away with that sort of thing: Who was going to raise a fuss about an interracial relationship when characters were routinely enduring brain transplants, torture chambers, multifaceted infidelities, maybe a return from the dead? Heck, there was even a bunch of villains trying to control the weather . . . the weather! Kenny said it was positively mythological. No, he told Mildred not to worry about a few I.R.K.'s ("interracial kisses," he'd translated over the telephone, and Mildred could see him curling his fingers into quote marks), and despite the rise of political conservatism, she knew that people were curious about such matters.

That the couple were teenagers on the show made the situation more palatable to Mildred who didn't know many black people herself. There was one family who lived a couple of roads away, and Mildred would always wave when she saw them out in the yard or say a few words if she ran into the woman at the A&P. It was the decent thing to do. But every so often when Mildred drove by their adorable A-frame and saw it covered with toilet paper and signs telling them to go back where they came from, she was besieged by the overt animosity of the act and disgraced by her own tacit complicity in not making sure the family was invited to the block parties, the duplicate bridge games, the winter festivals she always attended. No, she never gave the injustice, the indignity, a second thought until she drove by the house desecrated and imagined a brood of penetrating eyes peering out from behind the curtains with their index fingers pointing: shame on you. She could barely catch her breath, and perhaps if she'd been a different person, more like her younger daughter in her quest for right and wrong, Mildred might have lingered with this feeling, no matter how discomfiting, but instead she let it disintegrate as quickly as the A-frame in her rearview mirror. Only now she found herself wondering if they, too, might suffer should Brooke get the role. Blue Bell had already shown its true colors, so to speak, and hadn't the silent majority just a couple of years ago voted the conservative Ronald Reagan into office? Even Tom had become a neocon, jumping parties to align himself with the former Hollywood star. For weeks after the election Cynthia called her father Mr. Harrison, while Brooke accompanied him to a screening of *Bedtime for Bonzo* at the rec center. Yes, there was potential for trouble in the family, in their community, not to mention in the rest of the country, but Mildred pushed all of that aside as Brooke excitedly pointed out the Empire State Building almost directly in front of them and they sunk underground toward the great city of New York.

As the train crept into Penn Station, Brooke plowed her arms through the sleeves of her suitably monikered denim jacket, then yanked her knapsack down from the shelf. "Let's go," she said, removing her sunglasses from her breast pocket and fitting them above her forehead, a second set of eyes. Mildred couldn't help staring. Her daughter was a "major babe" all right: so blond, so expressive, her eyes a metallic blue and shiny like the brand-new graffiti-resistant subway cars, her lips naturally rosy just like Tom's. That was Mildred's favorite thing about her husband.

"Come on, Mom, it's gonna be wicked hard getting a cab," Brooke said, her whiny tone reminding Mildred that she was indeed a regular teenager as well.

"All right, all right," Mildred said, and though the train hadn't stopped completely, she grabbed her purse from the empty seat next to her and joined Brooke to wait for the doors to open.

They were the first people off the train, Mildred following Brooke down the escalator and up the steps to Eighth Avenue where it was wicked easy finding a cab, actually, but Mildred didn't dare joke before an audition. They made it to the network offices half an hour before Brooke's call, finding Kenny Zeller already settled in the waiting room. His hair was buzzed short in the back with wispy bangs in front and black as the T-shirt he wore beneath his oversized gray blazer. A bit odd, his appearance, though Mildred knew it was what men on television looked like. When her lips brushed against his smooth cheek in greeting, Mildred embraced the smell of verbena, maybe, or pine, and wondered if Tom might agree to using a little cologne. He certainly wouldn't be caught anywhere in Blue Bell wearing a T-shirt and suit jacket.

Kenny led Mildred to a leather armchair, then took Brooke's hand and sat down next to her on the couch. "Okay, here's the deal," he said. "I'm hearing they haven't liked anyone yet, so it's practically yours. Remember what we said."

"Nothing fancy, just be myself."

"Right. You've got what they want. No need to embellish."

"Aren't you gonna say carpe diem? You always say carpe diem," Brooke smiled, her tongue jutting over perfectly curved lips, a studied twinkle in her eyes.

"Better than that," Kenny pointed his forefinger at Brooke. "It's carpe ano now. Carpe decade. Carpe, carpe, carpe."

Brooke grabbed his finger, smiling, and it seemed they'd come out from the same distant land only to find each other in the great diaspora of New York City. With them Mildred felt like the outsider. That sinking feeling in her stomach returned, accompanied by a frightening premonition. Brooke was going to get the part.

Minutes later, out came a woman about Kenny's age, a young thirtyish, wearing the same kind of oversized suit, only hers was black with a silky camisole under the jacket. The hallowed trinity of mother-ingénue-agent stood to attention, and after a round of obligatory handshakes, it was time for Brooke to audition. "Should I come with?" Kenny asked, and the woman responded no. Brooke winked at Mildred: Kenny always asked and they always said no. It was their private joke. Then, calmly, as if she were walking into the kitchen for a snack, Brooke collected her things and followed the woman to the white door. Before going in, she stopped and dug Mildred's globe out of her bag. "Squishy ball," she said, tossing it to her mother.

Mildred pressed her fingers into the rubber, feeling comforted for the first time since they'd boarded the train that morning. It wasn't the ball, but the fact that Brooke had remembered it. She knew her priorities, and she was so confident. She's ready, Mildred thought, though years later that moment would come to haunt her: Perhaps she should have stuffed the squishy ball down Brooke's throat and dragged her back to Blue Bell. What were they thinking? She was only a child. But on that dazzling fall day Mildred was obscured by the glamour, the intensity, the prospects of it all, if not totally without guidance, for Mildred Harrison, after watching her daughter walk off with the woman in the suit, did something she hadn't done on her own in years: She prayed.

She did not speak very loud. Nor did she kneel, preferring instead to invoke God from the security of her leather armchair. It was a short prayer, a few simple words asking God for an end to his putting them through the ringer, the echo of a recent service, her vague requisition a deliberate nod to the unknown forces that might lie ahead. When she finished Mildred felt inexplicably jubilant and wondered if the Almighty had pumped her with laughing gas. Her giggles would have graduated to all-out laughter had she not been shushed by Kenny Zeller who was standing with his face pressed into the doorjamb. He was spying on Brooke's audition.

Protective antennae on high, Mildred bolted up out of her seat and whispered, "Get away from there!"

But Kenny turned his head and, with his forefinger on his lips, said, "Shhh!"

Then, with the very same finger, he motioned for Mildred to join him. A quick glance between them passed before Kenny took a couple of steps back, making room for Mildred. She bent her knees, leaning into the crack of light coming from the audition room, and as her eyes adjusted she saw Brooke standing with her hand on her hip, listening to the voice of a man whom Mildred could not see. He was saying that because *World Without End* was a soap, Jaymie Jo would be seen every day in many different situations, so they needed to see whether Brooke was a versatile actress. A versatile actress? Only weeks earlier she had been earning raves from her teachers in this very city. Hadn't they read her résumé? For the first time since Brooke started acting, Mildred had to fight the stage mother's urge to burst through the door screaming: "She's the best. Simply the best!"

But being so new, this desire quickly fled. Mildred took a deep breath and crushed the squishy globe in her right hand as her daughter fell into the scene. The setup: Jaymie

Jo has just learned that a friend was killed in a car accident. Her father (the invisible male voice) comforts her with truisms Mildred found a bit overblown. But the heck with him, she couldn't believe the array of expressions dancing so effortlessly, so elegantly across her daughter's face. Who was this young woman emoting in front of her? Is it possible that Mildred had never looked beyond her removed posturing? Or was Brooke the best actress she'd ever seen?

What happened next was even more shocking, as Brooke burst into an aria of heart-stopping sobs, the likes of which Mildred hadn't seen since her daughter was a young child, but in that one moment behind the white door, for the benefit of the director and producers, Brooke had managed to cough up all of the pain, all of the rejection, all of the frustration of the last few years, and it was perfect. Just perfect. In fact, Mildred herself was so absorbed in the moment, she bounced to her feet and this time would have screamed an ecstatic "Yes!" had Kenny not stretched his hand out from behind and covered her mouth. Mildred slipped backwards, but Kenny kept her standing. With his free hand he lifted Mildred's wrist as if he were conferring a title on a professional boxer, the globe rising like a thick glove above their heads. And despite the obviousness of the pun, Mildred Harrison did at that moment feel like she had the whole world in her hands.

LIFE EXPERIENCE

Y OUR FATHER IS SUCH A BABE," said my friend Edie. Of everything in the living room—two giant TV sets, at least four videocassette recorders, camera and tripod, a rack of blinking stereo components, paintings signed by famous artists, leather couch and chairs from Italy, heated slate floor, and that amazing view—she'd zeroed in on a shelf with a couple of framed photographs. It was her first time at my house, and I told her she was going to hate it. But she said it was kind of cool. She liked the flat roof and openness. It reminded her of houses she'd seen in magazines. I was glad she'd invited herself over.

She had appeared one day in homeroom, not long after you'd collected your first Daytime Emmy for playing Jaymie Jo Rheinhart. You'd gotten so big so fast. One day you were the new girl in Foxboro and the next you'd hogged the cover of every soap magazine in America. I was happy I'd been there from the beginning and had started clipping articles. Some I hung on my bulletin board or taped to the walls, others I carried in my sketchbook, practicing what Mickey'd taught me about art. In colored pencils I kept you with me always, taking any free moment to draft the outline of your face, a new outfit, or that boyfriend of yours who presented new color possibilities. It was important work, you told a reporter from *Soap Opera Digest,* and I pledged to support you even though the producers had received a bunch of angry letters, and my grandmother called from Arizona to tell me you didn't look like the kind of girl who would date a *schvartza,* and something about the way she said the word made me shiver and like her a little bit less. People were always chipping away at themselves, little by little making it more difficult to love them. You understood this. In the same *Digest* interview you said it was hard to trust people since you'd become famous. You could relate to your character coming into a whole new life. You'd had to leave your entire family on the other side of the country, having landed a role on one of the only soaps that didn't shoot in New York, and making friends was never easy for you. "I understand what it's like to feel all alone in the world," you said. "I'm kind of an outsider."

I clipped that quote and taped it into the sketchbook Blair had given me. You and me, we were both outsiders, both alone in the world. We could tell each other things. There was (and still is) a way we communicated that went beyond time and space.

And you were opening up to me. I knew you liked McDonald's hamburgers, preferred Pepsi to Coke, though your favorite drink was Orange Crush. You went to church on Sundays whenever you were home in Blue Bell, Pennsylvania, with your family. You had your hair trimmed and highlighted once a month, your legs and bikini line waxed every three weeks, which was sort of upsetting. You couldn't have been that hairy, you were a natural blonde, and I wondered whether you'd think I was too hairy, but I was terrified of hot wax and razors and usually made a mess of stuff that came easy to other girls. I'm telling you, my genes and chromosomes had crossed wires somewhere along the way. One night I dreamed I was in the desert apartment with my grandmother. She pulled me out on the terrace and beneath the rhinestone stars asked if I knew anything about hermaphrodites.

"They have both sex organs, like the earthworm," I said, psyched to display my knowledge. Earlier that week in biology we'd pinned rubbery earthworms to blocks and sliced them down the center.

"Good, then you'll understand," Grandma said, and gave me the face she'd used when she thought I was making fun of old Mickey.

"Understand?"

Her face stretched from grave to ghastly. "That's what happened to you!"

I bolted up in bed. My sheets were soaked and I could barely breathe. I pulled my hands behind my hot, sweaty neck. It wasn't true, I told myself, it was only a dream, only a dream . . . I was overwhelmed by the thumping of my heart, my soothing words, but when I turned my head toward the glass I swear it was you speaking, not me.

You were the first person since Blair who really knew my mind. But you were having a tough time in Hollywood and just like Blair you needed someone to look out for you: I was up for the job. The first step was getting to know each other privately, until I could leave home and become famous. We needed to be on equal footing in the outside world.

My immediate world was high school, with the same kids from junior high. Edie was the new girl. Just like you. But in a way, she was your exact opposite. You were so light and clean-looking, eyes as clear as the Pacific; Edie had the darkest black hair I'd ever seen, wore ripped T-shirts and fishnets. Up close her skin was like milky cellophane and her eyes, once you got past the raccoon makeup, flashed a purplish blue—a young punked-out Liz Taylor. You visited animal shelters and said people's hearts should be filled with love not hate. Edie was a flesh-and-bone hypodermic of hatred and contempt. In the lunchroom, I'd overheard people say she was a witch, a devil worshipper, a cokehead, a pot dealer; she'd had an abortion (which was why she had to leave Ohio where she'd been living with her father), French-kissed her older brother, sucked off the bass player in a heavy metal band from the south shore; guys kept roaches from the joints she'd smoked in their wallets. I often caught myself staring at her, wondering if she knew what people said, what it felt like to be so talked about.

Then one strangely warm winter afternoon during lunch, I sat in the dried-up grass near the steps by the gym (smokers' corner) trying not to listen to a group of girls nearby. They talked about the dumbest things. A shadow loomed in. I looked up expecting a cloud but instead saw Edie standing over me. "You shouldn't smoke cigarettes," she said, but before I could think of a response she sat down next to me and continued talking. "They're totally useless, you know? They don't even get you high."

"It's not about that."

She took out a lighter and plastic stick with a metal tip that looked like a tiny baseball bat. "Oh yeah? Then what's it about?" She put the bat in her mouth, flicked the lighter in front of the metal, and inhaled. Her chest puffed up with smoke, the smell unmistakable. Jack's.

"I don't know, smoking keeps me mellow," I said. "Gives me something to do."

She burst out laughing. Tiny gray clouds staggered from her mouth. "Okay, that's good, that's honest, that's cool, I believe you. There is absolutely nothing to do around here. See, I have this theory that's kind of based on science . . ." She stopped for a second to grab another hit from the bat. Then she handed it to me. "Go ahead. I packed that baby good this morning. It's Peruvian Gold. It'll blast your boobs off." She laughed and I lit up, though I'd never got stoned in school before (never got stoned outside of my own house). And we were right on the front lawn. "Look at them," Edie pointed to the girls in smokers' corner. "Have you ever seen people who look so much like each other? And talk so much like each other? They probably do it the same way, too."

I laughed. "Yeah, it's kind of scary."

"Did you ever have this? You're sitting in class and all of a sudden everybody's voices become echoes?"

"Like an echo chamber," I said, leaning back on my hands to count the clouds rolling in.

"An echo chamber?"

"It's like a mirrored room, only the walls are cushions instead of glass. You make a noise and it bounces back in a million different ways. They use them for sound effects on TV."

"That's exactly my point! Everything in this school, in this town, on this whole planet, you know . . . so much of it's meaningless sound." Edie took a sudden pivot and grabbed my arm. "Did you ever listen to the Butthole Surfers?" No, I hadn't ever. Her eyes exploded. "Oh my god, they're the best. The only good music these days is coming from the other coast. I'll play you the Buttholes sometime. You're gonna love them . . . I have to tell you, those are really cool pants"—they were camouflage—"I've got a halter top the same. And those sneakers, okay, where'd you get them?"

"In the city."

"I knew it! You don't look like everyone else around here."

"Neither do you."

She let go of me and slipped the bat into the chest pocket of her jean jacket. Then she glanced left and right as if somebody was watching us. "Okay, are you ready for this?"

"Your theory?"

"Theory?"

"Before. You said something about science."

"Science?"

"Yeah, science."

Edie's eyes crossed and she knocked her palm against her forehead. "Oh my god, I forgot!" She giggled and I giggled and before I knew it we were both rolling in the prickly grass, laughing our heads off. We breathed heavily, sighed, then Edie sat up and said she had to see a guy called the Ayatollah over by the junior high. "Got a business meeting." She tapped the pocket above her chest where the bat was and winked. "But first I have to know, have you always been here?"

"Since I was about twelve."

"That's exactly when I came down!"

"But you just got here from Ohio."

"That's where I landed, poor me . . . talk about the soundless masses. I'm really from the planet Andromeda," she said, and I giggled, but she didn't join me. "Don't tell me you're a nonbeliever! I'm so disappointed." She raised her hands to the sky and shouted, "Darvon, must I take them all under my wing!"

For one second all the girls in smokers' corner turned toward us. I could hear my heartbeat, feel my brow heat up though the sky had chilled over. I liked talking to Edie but she was really weird. Hovering over me, her purple eyes shooting through their heavy black frames and violet lips glowing, she looked like some kind of hybrid, a girl-monster. All the rumors I'd heard about her flashed like billboards across my cerebral cortex. Maybe she was from another planet. Maybe she was just trouble. There was a recklessness to her, like she could do something really bad. One of the smoking girls said, "What a slut!" and they laughed as their soundtrack quickened over the wind.

"USE-LESS!" Edie shouted at them, then turned to me. "Open yourself up a little," she said. "Things are never just what they seem." She walked away, jet-black hair swinging against her faded jean jacket. I watched her disappear into the naked brown trees.

A couple months later she was in my house. "What's his name?" she asked, fingering that picture of my father in his bathing suit. It was covered with one-dollar bills.

"Jack."

"Jack," she nodded. "I like it."

As if he might have had to change it if she didn't. She was that sure of her opinions. She put down the photograph and said we should listen to some music. Behind my eyes came a dull throbbing. I wasn't supposed to touch Jack's stereo. And all *my* music was upstairs, including some CDs. I loved the little plastic jackets, those sparkling discs with their rainbow beams, the crisp scratchless sound. It was like stealing a piece of the future. Jack had CDs but kept all of his albums, too. Edie was skipping through them, saying what a massive collection, too bad there was so much hippie music, my parents must have been hippies. "Not really," I said. "They were too busy."

Edie nodded. "Mine too. You were born in '69, right?"

"Uh-huh."

"Me too. And I even have an older brother. My parents spent the sixties changing diapers."

"Mine were in school. College was, like, such a big deal for them. Now it's, like, who cares?"

Edie laughed. "I know, totally. Training camp for zombies."

"You look at most famous people today, and they never went to college."

"That's my point exactly. Nobody around here's going to teach you anything important. It's all about life experience. Can we smoke in here?"

"Sure," I smiled. "But hold on a sec, okay? I'll be right back."

Edie said fine, she'd pick out a record. I went upstairs to Jack's drawer, detached a bright green bud from his stash, and was crossing the balcony from my parents' wing to mine when I heard a crash of drums and guitar and looking down saw Edie standing in front of Jack's stereo banging her head from left to right and back again. If Jack found out he'd be royally pissed, but what could I do? I stood for a couple of minutes watching Edie bounce up and down, pumping her fists in front of her, and I thought, I could never walk into someone's house, put on the stereo, and dance alone. *Who did she think she was?* I crushed the bud in my hand. At that very moment, Edie looked up and saw me standing on the balcony. "Hey!" she shouted. "What are you doing up there?"

I said, just wait, she'd know soon enough, and she shrugged, then swung her arms up over her head and continued dancing. I stopped off in my room to turn on the VCR. (A few months later I would know how to set the timer.) It was almost three and I didn't want to miss *World*. My favorite thing about videotape: you could be in two places at once. I hit Play and Record just as the theme song was coming on and then hopped downstairs. Edie was still swinging her body in front of the stereo when I returned with the crushed-up bud. She stopped and took it in her hand. "Holy shit!" she shouted, breathing heavily. "Where'd you get this? Have you been seeing the Ayatollah? No, this doesn't even look like his shit, doesn't look like anybody's I've ever seen. I know practically everyone, and why's it so crumbly? . . . You gotta learn how to take better care of your pot. Something like this should really go in the refrigerator."

"Yeah, right next to the milk and OJ. Maybe in the butter dish."

"All right, smarty pants, but you can be more clever about it. I keep mine in one of those ham tins underneath my bed. At the very least you should isolate a cool, dark place. Trust me, I know about these things."

"I'll see what I can do."

"So, come on, what gives? Where'd you get it?" She looked at me hard. In the background a woman wailed about a river. Edie bounced over to the stereo and turned it down. "Ike and

Tina, baby! One of the least corny albums I could find. Now, come on, tell me everything. I haven't seen dope this green since Andy—that's my brother, he's at UCSD but he's not, like, a jughead. He plays football and grows pot in his backyard and has a band . . . they're called Black Box and they're excellent and they once played in the same club as the Buttholes. You'd really like him, Lil . . ."

Two things: (1) Nobody but my grandfather ever called me Lil. I hated it. But in Edie's mouth the name seemed reborn. Cool even. (2) Her brother sounded like a jerk, but who wasn't?

I nodded and said nothing. She kept on nudging about where I got the pot, and finally I said, "Jack."

"Your father gets you pot?"

"No, no, it's not like that. He doesn't *know* about it, or if he does, we've got, like, what they said in social studies: a de facto understanding."

"You liar! Your parents are such hippies! I'm okay with it, don't worry. I mean, I know the deal. Anyway, all those bands at Woodstock are all playing in football stadiums now. They're corporations. Oh yeah, I know all about hippies giving it up for the big bucks, you don't have to be embarrassed."

"I'm telling you, they're not hippies. They never went to Woodstock or anything. Jack's in advertising. They have to do a lot of schmoozing and partying."

"Yeah, sure, Lil, whatever you say."

"I'm serious."

Edie shook her head back and forth, smiling. "So, come on, what are you waiting for? Flare up Jack's dope."

We smoked, and Edie talked about how great it was and asked if I could get more and I told her only if we kept within the rules: one medium-sized bud per month. Any more and Jack might have to say something, although he'd probably go after the cleaning lady first. They'd blamed the last one for money I lifted from Nancy's wallet. It was right after Blair left, and I was still saving up to go and find her. Jack said if Linnelle was taking the money she must really need it. Maybe they weren't paying her enough. They gave her a raise. And congratulated themselves on their problem-solving skills. A few years later, Linnelle was gone and a woman named Sema took her place. No one ever said why.

"Hello!" Edie snapped her fingers in front of me. "This is a no-zoning area. I had enough of that back in Ohio. Nobody says anything out there, but it's different from Andromeda. We read each other's brain waves."

"That sounds awful. I wouldn't want everyone knowing what I think."

"It's not like that. You have your private mind that people can't access, unless you want them to. The thing is, you're in control. You can make the information public, or transmit to one or two other people. Your choice."

It sounded familiar. The way you and I communicated. Edie said all the electrical wires and satellites and TV antennas on earth made it harder to read people here. Too many signals jumbled together. Still, she was more psychic than most people. "I bet I can read you," she said, slipping forward on the couch and beaming her purple eyes into mine. "Let's start with something easy. What kind of guys are you into?"

"Um—"

"Don't answer! The point is, I have to guess." She put two fingers on the side of each one of my eyes and hummed. Up close she smelled like pot and candied lip gloss. "Okay, I'm getting a signal . . . Wow, you're an open book." I squirmed a bit. What if it was everyone? Not just you and Blair. What if my brain was wired all wrong and anyone could see it? I felt myself heating up. "Here we go," Edie said, her fingers massaging my temples, our knees touching. It felt good. "Okay, you like the depressed intellectual type, a lot of dark clothes and facial hair, right? Come on, am I right?" I smiled. She was so not from another planet. I could read people better than that, even through TV screens. "Hah!" Edie shouted. "I knew it. That's totally not what I'm into. I like 'em big and sexy, with tight, round football-player butts and really big dicks. Not too thick though. Nice and long and thin."

She dragged out her words so I could see those dicks. I had a few visuals stocked from my parents' porno tapes. Dicks resting in hairy palms, bouncing between scrawny white legs, making tents of their tight white underwear. I liked watching them grow under the cotton and sometimes in class imagined all the penises simmering beneath those wooden desks, aching to bust through their dungaree shields like the fire-breathing dragons on black concert T-shirts. I liked this immediacy, their need to be tended and tamed. Guys were always raising their hands to be excused and running off to the bathroom. All kinds of jerk-off sessions must have gone on in there. I said this to Edie, who moved in closer and pulled us down to the floor. "Holy fuck! It's so hot!" I smiled and told her it was heated. She stretched out on the fiery slate and said, "Nice. Really fucking nice." I wanted to lie down next to her but stayed cross-legged. I was sort of dizzy. "Okay, Lil, you're really gonna like this," she said in a deep, low voice. "Damon—he's one of my boyfriends. I've got another one: Bobby. But he's a little scary. He drives a beat-up old Chevy and has the coolest little flask that fits in his bomber jacket. We haven't done it yet or anything. I just got in his car and we kissed a little. I have no idea where he lives even. Everything about him's a total mystery. But, anyway, Damon . . ." she smiled, and between her lips that name became full of secret messages and meanings. "He starts off so small I can put the whole thing in my mouth and in, like, just a few seconds he gets so big I swear I'm gonna choke. I'm telling you, it's the coolest thing."

"That's wild," I said, and tried to ignore the pins and needles in my legs. I couldn't stretch them forward without hitting Edie, and my back was wedged against the couch. My jeans felt like plaster casts and my butt was burning off.

"Wild? That's nothing. Sometimes when we're on the bus together I put my head in his lap, and oh my god, he gets so hard! Once—" She put her hand on my thigh without looking up. It threw a weird tingling into the mix. She continued talking, lying there like the slate floor was her own private beach. "I can't believe I'm telling you this, you're so easy to talk to, Lil. Anyway, a couple of months ago we were on the bus and it was so hot and stuffy and Damon took off his jacket and put it over us and he got hard in like a second and you know . . ." She fluttered her eyes, and my cheeks flushed. I could feel how hot it was on that damn bus.

Could see his head thrown back, her arms moving under the coat. It was like I'd walked into one of my parents' videotapes. I could barely breathe but managed to say, "Go on." Edie took her hand off my leg and sat up. She glanced over my shoulder, where the Long Island Sound was rumbling away outside the windows. Waves crashing like the roar of a bus in motion. Edie in the backseat, hand pumping a long, thin dick. She turned back to me, eyes like glimmering headlights. "I made him come, Lil. Right there on the fucking M34 or whatever. It was such a rush, even better than getting stoned. I keep playing it over and over in my head."

She looked off into the water again. For the first time in days the sun peeked through the clouds, throwing a steamy pinkish glaze over the tiny beach. "Hey, I've got an idea," Edie said. "Let's go see Damon!"

"Now?"

"Yeah, he works at the mall. We can take the bus from town."

"It takes like an hour to get into town," I protested. The thought of walking all that way felt like trudging through the desert on a hot summer day. The only place I wanted to go was into the kitchen for a grilled cheese sandwich, then up to my bedroom to watch *World*. I was sort of hoping I could get Edie to watch with me.

"Wow," she said, "you've really got a lot to learn. You're gonna be so happy you met me. It's ten minutes in a cab."

"We're going to take a cab to the bus?"

She stared at me like that was the stupidest question she'd heard in days, like there was nothing I could do to protest without sounding even stupider. Edie and I were going to the mall to meet Damon. You and the rest of the world would have to wait.

LAST WEEK THE SHIT HIT THE FAN. This according to my lawyer, Jonathan Brickman. He asks if I know what happens when the shit hits the fan: Everyone gets splattered.

Brickman gives me the quick coverage: Gustave Monde collapsed the company he and Jack had launched fifteen years ago and joined a Hollywood stable with big-time movie and music video connections. It was written up in the trades, Brickman says. Huge news. Not that anyone was surprised. Jack hadn't been bringing in much work these past few months, and Gustave needed work, didn't he? A writer can write in solitude. A painter can paint. But a director, very much like a monarch, is nothing without his subjects. Since I'd been inside, the question wasn't whether Gustave would leave, but where he might end up. "Nonetheless, it's a slap in the face," Brickman says, shaking his head ominously, and I feel like I've eaten a cup of laundry powder. When I'd seen Jack over the weekend, I bugged him again about getting a new lawyer. He was sullen and withdrawn. Could barely bring himself to argue. He curled his fingers into fists, took deep breaths, clicked his lips together, kept checking his watch. Whenever I said something, he answered, "That's nice." It was like talking to a piece of cardboard.

"He wanted to tell you," Brickman says, "he just didn't know how."

"That's lame." I remember the call I'd made from the Shelter Island police station: "Jack, I'm going to need a lawyer . . ." It's not like I knew what to do. And this is what my father came up with.

"It's a tough blow, Lily," says the lawyer Jack hired. "He's not himself. Which is all the more reason we have to stay on track here. The more holes we can plug in their case, the easier it'll be for everyone."

"I want to change my plea," I say.

"What are you talking about?"

"Let me plead guilty, bargain for a lesser charge, get out of here at least."

"Were you listening to anything I just said? Your father is suffering. Suffering worse than you can imagine. Didn't you hear me when I said the shit hit the fan?" He slams his fist down on the metal table, his thick ring reverberating like a gunshot. I am stunned to attention. He sits down across from me. I can smell his cologne or aftershave. It reeks of sailboats and split-level houses, designer suits and weekends in Paris. Everything about him says "I'm loaded." He moves his high-priced face in close, almost whispering. "Do you know where that saying comes from, Lily? The shit hit the fan. Let me tell you where it comes from. It's an old vaudeville joke. A guy's having stomach pains and knows he's about to have diarrhea. He walks into a crowded bar so pained by this point it's amazing he's made it so far, and yet somehow he manages to ask where the toilet is. The bartender points up a flight of stairs. At the top there are two doors. The guy's about to lose it, mind you, when he opens the first one and sees a hole in the floor. 'Primitive,' he might have thought if he'd had any time to think, but you know how these things go, right? So he squats down over the hole and lets it loose, every last drop, then sighs a happy little sigh and walks downstairs to find everyone in the bar's disappeared, and the place is covered with smelly, brown soot. 'Where'd everyone go?' he asks, innocently. The bartender looks at him and says, *'Where were you when the shit hit the fan?!'"* Smiling ear to ear, his face is the perfect outline for a Colombian necktie. Then his brow clouds over: "Do you see what I'm saying, Lily? You've got to look underneath your own shithole here. It's not just Gus I'm talking about. Things have gotten worse than you can imagine. Much, much worse . . ." He tells me again how Jack is suffering. Between my legal fees and Nancy's rehab, he's going broke. He's sold a couple of cars, taken out a second mortgage on the house, put the summer place on the market, and his career's stalled out on both coasts. He's a salesman, remember, and his number one product has just jumped ship: Imagine if Colgate lost its patent for toothpaste. Everything is more . . . *tenebrous,* I think Brickman says, more tenebrous than ever with the media trailing him, and now the crash. His investments are worth less than they were a week ago. "See, Lily, he's got to believe this'll end. He's got to trust that I'm going to get you out of here. It's the only thing giving him any hope."

What he really means is Jack needs to believe I'm innocent. That he had no part in birthing a monster. It's the only way he can get on with his life, save face. And in walks the attorney singing sweet alibis.

For the next couple of days I am haunted by Brickman's words. I look up *tenebrous* in the dictionary and it says *dark and gloomy,* like Jack's face whenever he comes to see me. I imagine him day after day sitting in his office with the door closed and blinds down; lights dimmed to nothing, he wades through it. Shit. Splashed across his windows the way I used to finger-paint it, piled steaming high on his desk, caked into the grooves of his oak floor, nothing escapes. Even his neat black furniture used to be a pat on the back, now it's cold, sinister, angry as the telephone blasting his heart to the moon when it rings. On the other end it's nothing but shit.

My father used to love his job. He saw it as a public service. Once he told me, "Some people build buildings, some sew shirts, some make milk cartons, others run the farms that make the milk . . . The point is, everybody's selling something. Gus and me, we're selling lifestyles. We give people stories, these tight little nuggets of life, and they go, 'Hey, I want that, that'll make me happy.' Maybe they never even thought of it before, it doesn't matter. We tell them what they want, how to make their dreams."

This was a man who'd built his own. After his father'd died young—some kind of liver trouble—it was just Jack and his mother. Their house was modest, they never owned a car or even a radio. Jack was enlisted by the woman as a young boy to deliver tiny decorative pillows to their neighbors. Each pillow had a saying sewn on top, something his mother had dug up from the Bible and stitched with her Singer: "Love thy neighbor as thyself"; "If thou have ears, listen"; "Whom the Lord loves He disciplines." Jack loved going out on pillow runs. He was invited into people's homes, given food, Coca-Cola, was introduced to television. He watched shows with cowboys, listened to crooners, saw people become millionaires, but it was the sponsors he loved most. How they set out a world of endless possibility. Creation. You didn't have to be who your family was.

And so in those grainy black-and-white images my father saw what his mother had failed to show him: He saw his future.

I call Gustave Monde collect at his home in L.A., and he picks up. It's very early in the morning out there. "Well, hello, Lily! Hello!" he says. "What a surprise! . . . Very well, it's good to hear you. We've been thinking, eh . . . Pamela did write a letter, I think."

"I got it. And I wrote her back. Listen—"

"But tell me, what is it like there? Are you doing okay with yourself? Sometimes I read things that are not so fantastic. But the media is terrible. They make it like everything is a film. A bad film."

"It *is* like a bad film," I say, thinking, Actually, it's more like TV and I'm trapped inside. Nobody ever turns off the set and says it's time to go to bed.

"And how is the food?"

"Not too bad, really, but I want to talk to you about Jack."

Through the phone I hear him take a deep breath. "I am very sad about this," he says. "Very, very sad."

"Can't you help him out?"

"It's terrible. The whole situation just stinks."

"There's got to be something you can do."

"I'm sorry, Lily, but really there is nothing . . . nothing."

Dramatic, his words resonate like the bang from Brickman's ring. What a fucking liar. "Oh, come on," I say, "you're Mr. Hollywood. I saw your name in *Variety*. Don't tell me this."

"We are out now on the coast all the time—there is nothing left in New York. Nothing. Jack, he knows this too but he's stuck. He can't leave in the middle of . . . in the middle of everything. This is not his fault, I know, but neither is it mine. You don't know the pressure there is with these things. Please understand, I'm not saying you are . . . you did . . . it's just that there's too much publicity, and I am working harder than ever—in fact, I must now go and prepare for work. I can't hold on the telephone. But please, you'll call again?"

"I don't believe this. Jesus, you're supposed to be, like, my godfather!" I say, blood crawling up my neck.

"No, not officially. There was never a ceremony."

"But he didn't do anything," I plead, about to crack.

"I wish I could help, you don't know how much, but—"

"Bullshit!" I bang my fist against the side of the phone. Needles fly up my elbow, everything throbbing. I hit again . . . and again, biting my tongue to keep from screaming.

"I feel terrible about—"

"No you don't. You're a fucking asshole!"

"It's not my—"

"ASSHOLE! ASSHOLE!" I slam down the phone with my good hand. *What an asshole!* Sinking against the wall, wishing it would grow a pair of arms and take me in, everything throbs. A guard comes and lifts me up. My pinkie hangs low, like it's stupidly splintered from the rest of the group. The guard touches it lightly with her fingertips and I flinch, "Ahhhh!" Feels like she's trying to break it off. I squeeze my elbows into my sides, clench my teeth together, as she whisks me off to the infirmary, where like something out of a dream the white coats wrap me up and pop me with codeine before sending me back to my cell. Mimi slips by, dragging her mop and aluminum pail behind her. They let her in even though they're not supposed to.

As the guard unlocks, she stares at the white bandage on my hand. "Oh, *chica,*" she says, and leans her mop against the wall. I could vomit from the bleach and ammonia clinging to the invisible ring she carries everywhere. Like an earthly saint with dishpan hands, stinking worse than the chemicals on her rubber gloves, she can still get me with the look. Makes me stir where I don't necessarily want to, not with my hand injured and head clogged. She's directly in front of me now, long brown hair swept behind her back and she's so tall, almost six feet. From where I sit, I'm looking straight at her stomach. She sits down next to me, grazes her middle finger against my splint, looking at me with those deep brown eyes like Jack's. So dark I'm afraid of falling inside and never coming out. Tenebrous eyes.

"Angel's having the baby," she says finally. My throat clamps shut. Nothing in, nothing out, not even the stinking air. Already lightheaded from the drugs, I fall back against the cement. *Ow!* It's my head this time. Pounding so hard I feel like smashing it harder. I feel like screaming, "Gustave Monde is a fucking asshole!" but I can't even raise my head. Mimi crosses herself and takes my good hand, kneeling me down with her in front of the bed. "My little *muñeca,*" she says, "let's say something together. Let's pray for Angel."

And because part of my blood belongs to the grandmother I saw only three times alive and once in her coffin, the one who claimed a personal relationship with Jesus, maybe he'll listen to me, if it isn't all a bunch of crap like Jack always said. Imitating Mimi, I press my hands together, careful not to disturb the white coils around my pinkie. Mimi's Spanish tickles the insides of my eardrums, though it's hard to figure out exactly what she's saying besides Jesus and Angel. *Hey-zeus* and *Ahn-hel.* I want to say something for Angel's sake, but I'm not sure how it works. I envision Angel's face, beads of sweat falling as she pushes cannonlike. An eerie feeling sweeps up through my knees, then come the pins and needles. "Please let Angel be okay," I murmur.

Mimi takes the back of my bandaged hand and kisses it lightly. Still speaking her language, she tells me not to worry, tells me she'll take care of me, tells me she loves me, and when I ask what she means she calls me a *happy* girl, *locacita.* "Don't all mothers love their daughters?" she says. Then we commit incest.

EDIE SAID BOBBY DAVIS HAD A VELVET PENIS. And that wasn't his best quality. She liked his ringlets of white-blond hair, the way his faded Levi's hugged his tight ass, how he stuffed the lining of his bomber jacket with bags of sticky green pot and drove a monster Chevy with souped-up wheels, so different from the sleek foreign cars that filled the parking lot at school. But Bobby didn't go to school. He mixed cement for his uncle's construction company in Queens. I think that was where he lived. He just came around to buy pot from the Ayatollah and flirt with Edie. They'd hooked up over the summer just before she'd gone off on a teen tour and met a bunch of guys whose names sounded like those foreign cars. Edie'd rated them all on a scale of one to ten for looks, personality, bod. Sergio was her favorite, she'd said. An eight-ten-seven: European guys were skinny and they hardly ever showered. "Here's the main difference between European and American guys," Edie'd told me. "European guys smell funkier and their hair gets really greasy, but you'll never find shit stains in their underwear. They scrub their assholes three times a day. Put that in your book."

I'd been jotting down "life experience" phrases in my sketch-book. Edie said they'd come in handy when I stopped scribbling pictures of soap stars and got out into the real world. She had some kind of beef against you from the beginning, only I never realized how bad it was until it was way too late.

On the show, you and Max were engaged to be married, and the whole town of Foxboro was jazzed up about interracial mar-riage. This was big stuff. And in your personal life, you were col-lecting money at shopping malls to help feed the hungry kids they showed on TV. Lots of people were doing it. Just before Thanksgiving you took a trip to Africa with a couple of rock stars to help deliver the food, and at the Emmy's (your second win) you had tears in your eyes. "We're gonna keep going until every child on earth has enough food to eat and a warm bed to sleep in," you said, in your sparkling black dress and high heels. I'd videotaped the whole thing and had been pausing the tape to draw you from stills, even though Edie said you were a hypocrite. Most celebrities were. It was no sweat raising money for starving kids in Africa without thinking twice about starving kids right here at home. But our kids weren't running around naked with pregnant-woman stomachs and white paste around their lips. I thought you were noble and asked Nancy to write you a check. A few weeks later, you sent a thank-you note that hung next to a few Emmy sketches on my wall.

Edie said my room was starting to look like an Egyptian tomb, every bit of space covered in words and pictures, whole sto-ries written on the walls. She said it was weird, but that was before she started watching *World,* too. We spent a lot of time in my room looking at TV and getting high and talking about guys. At the moment we were working on what Edie called my virginity problem. She had me make rating lists of guys in my sketchbook and lectured me on finding opportunity like it was the most important thing in the world. Not that I didn't want to lose it, I just didn't want anyone touching me. In pornos it looked so grubby, and I really didn't see the point. At camp a girl had said orthodox Jews did it through sheets. That sounded okay but I never mentioned it to Edie. She was on a mission.

Then one cold Saturday night Bobby Davis called and invited her to a party in one of the big mansions by the Sound. He said he would bring a friend for me. Edie was psyched. She was sleeping over, and I didn't have a curfew. But we had a few days' worth of *World* to watch.

"I've got the tapes all ready," I sighed.

"So fucking what," she said, "they're not going anywhere."

"But we had a plan."

"Jesus Christ, Lil, you can always watch TV. This is reality. This is a gift. An *opportunity*. God, can't you see . . ." she huffed and threw her head back. "You know, anybody else would have given up on you by now."

My throat tightened. I looked up at the glossy black window, which at night reflected my walls. You floated kaleidoscopically, from all angles, begging me not to go. Edie caught me staring. "Are you even listening to me?" she said. "You know, most people wouldn't give a damn about *your* life experience. And tell me, if it wasn't for me, who else would devote even five minutes to your virginity? Tell me, who?"

"I don't know."

Drooping shoulders, a high-pitched whine, she imitated me: *"I don't know* . . . When are you going to take some responsibility for your own experience? Do you want to stay a virgin forever or what?"

"It's not that, it's just . . ." I stopped myself. How was I supposed to tell her you were more important than anything I'd find outside? Even a de-virginizer. Someone I'd never even met. Our philosophies were totally opposed.

"What?" she pressed.

"Huh?"

"Come on, what's your excuse this time?"

"I have an English paper due Monday."

"Is that what you're worried about?" Edie laughed.

"I haven't even read the book."

"Oh my god, Lil, you putz . . . why didn't you say something? I can take care of that. Let me take care of that. We're going to the party! Yeah!" She threw her arms in the air, then picked up the phone again and asked information for somebody named Jerome Finkelstein. "Toss me a pen," she said. I did, and she jotted down a number on her palm, then dialed again. "What's the book?" she said.

"*Brave New World.*"

"Science fiction. That's cool, that's my kind of thing, although it's not really a classic, might be tough—hey, is Susan there?" she spoke into the phone. I walked closer to the closet where she was standing in front of the full-length mirror rubbing purple lipstick from the corners of her mouth as she waited, then perked up. "Hey, Susan, it's Edie, how's it going?" she said. "I'm cool. Totally cool . . . well, except for a little problem I heard you can help me out with . . ." Laughing, she explained the situation, systematically checking her makeup, running chipped fingernails through her hair, straightening her velvety green skirt over ripped fishnets. Was it a joke, her wearing velvet? Or a reminder? Every time she grazed herself she thought of him. A few minutes later, she hung up the phone. "You've got your paper. It's on the book's view of sex and reproduction. Sounds cool, right? I almost want to read it myself. She says it hasn't been used since 1981 and it's only forty bucks."

"Forty dollars?"

"Well, what did you expect? This is contraband. This is underground economy. Susan Finkelstein is the Ayatollah of term papers. Now, let's get you dressed."

I had on a black turtleneck and khaki safari pants—I looked fine. Edie disagreed. Sizing me up, she said I should at least find a tighter shirt and put on a little mascara, but I refused. Adamantly. She accused me of fighting opportunity before it began, and I said just let me try it my way tonight, if it doesn't work I'll reconsider. "Okay . . . under one condition," she smiled—I knew what she wanted: Jack's pot.

I led her into my parents' bedroom, and together we opened Jack's sock drawer, took out his leather cigar box, and sat down on my parents' bed. Inside the box was a bigger bag than ever and something else: a tiny orange vial filled with white powder. "Holy shit!" Edie said. "Your parents are so cool." The last time we'd found a matchbook from a club called Symposium. Edie said it was a sex club. She'd read an article about it in the *Village Voice*. It said couples went together and traded partners. Some did it in groups. But most men didn't go with other men, afraid it would make them gay. Women were different, more experimental. They could go back and forth more easily. Edie said that made sense. She said she was going to have sex with a girl someday, and my body temperature jolted. I grimaced and said . . . I can't remember what I said, my blood was pumping like molten lava, and then she said something like everyone should have that experience at least once and I felt like she was stripping layers off my skin and she must have sensed something because she added this (and I remember it clearly): "Not that I'm advocating it tonight or anything." And then I felt really bad for a while and it was that badness swelling back as we argued about Jack's coke. I thought we should leave it alone. A couple of buds were one thing; cocaine was expensive. But Edie thought otherwise. "Go and get your book," she said.

"No way!" I didn't trust her alone with that stuff for a minute.

"Then listen to me and listen good: Jack wanted us to find this."

I laughed. "Oh yeah?"

"It's in his underwear drawer!"

"Socks."

"Same difference. It's like the first rule of being a parent. If you want to communicate with your child, you check out his underwear drawer because that's where he's leaving anything he wants you to find. Everyone knows that's the first place people look." My brain was spinning and we hadn't even smoked. If everyone knew the sock/underwear drawer wasn't a real hiding spot, then what could looking really tell you about your kid? And Jack . . . what did it matter? This was his house. Nobody was checking up on him. But Edie said things were different around here. "Your parents don't act like parents and you're no normal kid. No offense. I mean, who wants to be normal, but my point is, everything around here works in reverse. Trust me, Jack's a smart guy. He knows you've been looking in that drawer and he still leaves all his shit in there. That's practically an invitation."

Mostly to shut her up, I said okay and cut a few thick lines on one of Jack's marble book ends. We snorted them with a rolled-up twenty. Edie fell back on my parents' steely gray sheets and said, "Fucking A!" Her tits, covered in fraying white words—*Talking Heads*—bobbed up and down. I chewed my lip, but couldn't really feel it, couldn't feel anything inside my mouth, and imagined my slack jaw unable to form words, sentences, and why the fuck were we going to a party with demented faces? That's it, I thought, I'm staying home. I'd lose Edie downstairs, somewhere between the den and front door. It was a big house. As if she'd read my mind, she bounded up and ricocheted from room to room, practically dragging me by the collar. My nose twitched and I couldn't swallow, but Edie said that would stop as soon as we had a few drinks and helped me put my arms through my coat, saying, "Oh, man, this is good shit, this is really good!" She paced. I followed, and when she turned we collided. "Jesus, Lil! Don't walk so close."

"Everything's so tight in here."

"Let's wait out front."

Outside, my breath fogged in the crisp black night, but I didn't feel cold. I was riled inside. Felt like jumping out of my skin. I wanted to run down to the beach, run past the swimming pool that used to be Blair's house, although everything about it was fading. I couldn't remember where the front door was, how I'd reach under the mat for the key and let myself in. Everything was a big Blairy blur.

In the distance came the clink of a low-hanging carburetor, followed by a few shouts. Headlights rolled toward us. Edie grabbed my upper arms. "Okay, you ready?" she said, and I nodded. "Trust me, it's gonna be okay. Just follow my lead, you can do that, you're a fast learner. And remember, Lil, this could be your lucky night." She let go of me and waved her arms in the air. Her down jacket rose up over her hips. "Whoooo! Bobby!" she shouted. "Over here!" An old Chevy with dark windows screeched in front of us. Bobby Davis and his velvet penis had arrived.

We—me, Edie, Bobby Davis, and his six-foot-two, two-hundred-fifty-pound friend, Noz—pasted ourselves behind a group of girls who'd been dropped off in a Rolls Royce and slipped inside the huge Colonial house. Market value: a couple million, easily. Nancy would have wet her lips at the prospect of that commission. The foyer had marble floors, life-sized statues, and antique-looking paintings in thick gold frames. Opposite the double front doors was a wide staircase like something out of an old horror movie. A boy I recognized from chemistry class was leaning on the banister, talking to a few people gathered on the steps, the faint echo of a Phil Collins song spilling from a lighted room in the distance. As we passed, a couple of spokes in the banister cracked beneath him, and the boy slipped back. Bobby reached out and pulled him up. Red-faced, he brushed himself off and sneered at Bobby. "You're welcome, Prince Charles," Bobby said. The boy kicked another spoke until it broke through the middle like a chipped tooth.

"Asshole!" Noz said. "I hate these motherfuckers. What the fuck are we doing here?"

"It's a party," Bobby said, and steered us toward the brightly lit room. A giant chandelier hung sloppily from the ceiling and heavy curtains with velvety swirls covered part of the windows, exposing patches of the black night like illicit skin. It made me think of my mother, how she'd always leave the outdoor shower in the Hamptons before realizing her towel was too small. Edie pulled me further into the room, where some girls from school huddled in tiny cocktail dresses, a mushroom cloud of cigarette smoke rising above them, and it looked like something I'd seen on TV, one of those parties you were always showing up at, even though you preferred staying home. This was good practice for me. Phil Collins repeated the same line over and over again. You had to be really famous to get away with that kind of crap. One of the anorexia girls dropped a cigarette butt and crushed it underneath the heel of her shiny leather shoe. It smelled funky, like burning hair. Looking down, I noticed the carpet was covered with cigarette burns.

"We need those drinks," Edie said, and pointed to a few people sipping green liquid out of long glass goblets and munching on what looked like pieces of sushi.

"And sushi," I said, entranced, mouth watering. "I love sushi!"

Grabbing me by the elbow, Edie counseled: "Never eat at parties. It makes you look desperate."

"What?"

"Trust me."

We left the ballroom for a dark cavern with leather couches and walls smothered in books. A group of guys wearing dinner jackets and loaded with gold jewelry sat around a table playing poker like the old men at Palm Court. One of them smoked a cigar, a rich-boy gangster type. "Welcome, ladies," another one said. I think he was in my math class. "Are you the hookers?"

"In your dreams," Edie shot back, and we quickly left, continuing on into a huge open space off the kitchen where we found the food and drinks and Noz stuffing pieces of sushi down his thick throat like Godzilla swallowing an entire town.

I pointed at him. "He's eating."

"It's different for guys."

"Yo E-D rhymes with V-D!" Noz shouted across the table. "B-D's been looking for you. Says we're supposed to meet him upstairs in the executive suite, whatever the fuck that is. You want some raw fish?" He dangled a piece of tuna in front of her face and it looked like a tongue, his tongue, only thinner. Sniffing it, he said, "Smells like—"

"Hmmm, let me guess . . . pussy?" Edie grabbed the piece of fish and flung it in the air. It stuck to the ceiling, then plopped onto a girl's bare shoulder. She flicked it like a fallen leaf, a bug, a minor nuisance that barely interfered with her monologue.

Noz smiled. "Hooo-sah!"

Edie reached into the punch bowl and filled a couple of goblets with green liquid. While her back was turned, I sneaked a piece of salmon from the table, dropped it in my mouth, and swallowed before she finished pouring and handed me a glass. "What is it?" I asked.

"Who cares?" She chugged hers, then waited for me to do the same. We refilled and drank a few more glasses with Noz, before following him through the kitchen, where a couple of people held pieces of sushi over the blue flames of a gas stove, toasting the rectangles of fish, rice and all, like marshmallows. The smell was worse than the burning rug, but they glowed beautifully. Little electric rainbows. I wanted to hold one in my hand, feel it ride down the back of my throat, hot. How was Edie not hungry? We hadn't eaten in hours. A clock on the microwave said five, another one on the wall said nine, and I wondered if either hour was correct and which would get us out of there faster. But we descended further inside, climbing a steep staircase off the kitchen and making our way down a long, dark hallway, floorboards creaking beneath our feet, toward an echo of music and laughter, golden triangles of light. Edie called it the VIP room, and I imagined you and me being ushered into a Hollywood club together. People turned their heads, shouted your name, grabbed at our clothes. You took my hand. *Stay with me, Lillian.*

Hundreds of candles burned around gigantic pillows spread out on the thick carpet and soft velour couches, all bursting with faces that made me think of that people-are-strange song, but the B-52s blared from speakers on the ceiling, a fire simmered beneath a brick mantel covered with soot and candle wax, and in the middle of the room, a door with a full-length mirror nailed into it was propped up on two footstools covered in fur, deer probably, with hooves attached to the bottom. In the smoke and candles the door looked rubbery, bending like a worm above its furry feet, trying to slither back over to its hinges off the blue-tile bathroom where a group of girls danced in ballet costumes or I was really wasted and seeing things and felt a leaf? a bug? crawl up my arm and flicked it like the girl who'd flipped the tuna from her shoulder but instead of coming off it yanked me to the floor: Edie's arm. You were lost in the fog. Edie and I sat down in front of the door. Bobby Davis loomed over it, his pink face blown up in the mirror, octopus-like, with huge dilated eyes and nostrils engorged. He was a rock lobster. A silver tube connected his nose to the mirror, the thickest lines of coke I'd ever seen laid out in front of him. Next to him was the Ayatollah. Edie'd finally introduced me to him a few weeks earlier when I put a cork on Jack's stash. He sold us an eighth of reddish buds from Hawaii, almost as good as Jack's.

The Ayatollah filled a glass pipe with a chip of something that looked like rock candy and handed it to Edie. Giggling, she put her lips to the glass. The Ayatollah flipped open a metal lighter and brought down the flame. Curls of smoke fluttered through the pipe, the smell chemical but sweet, sugar melting over a Bunsen burner. Watching her, the Ayatollah's eyes sparkled. He was so gorgeous. Long black hair flowing down his back, smooth caramel skin, brown eyes, a straight elegant nose that made him seem ancient and foreign, which he was. What I liked best was if you looked too quickly you might have thought he was a girl.

He dropped another diamond chip into the pipe and held it out to me. Inflated in the mirror it looked like a neon test tube. This guy in his white tank top and drawstring pants was some kind of rad scientist. "Go ahead," Edie said, dreamily. "It's not like the shit you get on the street. This is *sweet*."

Sweet as sugar, I thought, easy to smoke sugar. I reached for the pipe.

"The only difference is what you call it," Bobby said.

"This is not true," said the Ayatollah. He grabbed his lighter, but before bending to fire me up, he said everything he presented was uncut, pristine, and pure. He said his connection was only once-removed from Peru. He used his Bic like a pointer.

"Whatever," Bobby said. "Expensive crack is still crack."

"You are mistaken, my friend. This is not crack."

"Crack is whack!" Edie said, and burst out laughing. She rolled her head against Bobby's lap. I'd never seen her so silly.

The girl in the tutu—which I now realized wasn't a tutu but a short frilly skirt—leaped out of the pale blue light and spinning toward the stereo announced that she would never smoke crack, or do any drug besides pot. "I want normal kids," she said, and in the mirror I saw the blown-up pipe glowing in my hand, radioactive, toxic, terrifying. I didn't want kids, I hated kids, but the thought that I was doing something to mess up my chances of having them felt dangerous . . . and not in a bad way. A frustrated Ayatollah repeated that this was not crack, he would never sell crack . . . I didn't care what it was, I wanted it more than anything. The music scratched off and the room vibrated with Edie's mantra . . . *crack is whack!* . . . *crack is whack!* It made the Ayatollah laugh.

Suddenly (I can't help it, I need this word) all six-foot-two,

two-hundred-fifty pounds of Noz slammed down next to me and tried to wrestle the pipe from my hand. "Wait your turn," I said.

"You're my date, right?"

"I guess."

"So I go first." He pushed his mouth inside my arm toward the pipe and looked up at the Ayatollah. "Light, faggot."

"What did you call me?"

Noz stared at him. "Faggot, you know, like a bunch of sticks. I need fire."

In the corner, the girl in the mock tutu pressed buttons on the CD player and the soundtrack from *The Rocky Horror Picture Show* began. Slow-mo wheels in gear. A lot of weird staring. Out of the corner of my eye, I saw the Ayatollah. He looked scared, even prettier than before. Level, my face fell upon Noz's tattoo, a fleet of Budweiser horses carting a keg around his upper arm. To the right the girl by the stereo whooped and pirouetted in front of the CD player. Noz shoved his slimy head further inside my arms. Sweat covered the back of his neck, making spikes of the bottom of his hair. He smelled like fish and BO and was shoving his hip against me. I tried to dislodge him with my foot. The music jumped abruptly, and the tutu girl threw her arms in the air, shouting: "Let's do the Time Warp! Let's do the Time Warp!" More girls rushed from the bathroom and formed a line, screaming the words to the song in high-pitched voices.

"You shit," Noz said to me. "You're making me hard!" His dick grew through his jeans just like I'd imagined it—fire-breathing dragon on a concert T-shirt, mini-Godzilla drenched in scaly pond scum. No velvet in sight.

Bobby put his hand on Noz's shoulder. "Chill out a second, man."

"Get off me!" Noz looked up at him, sweating. His salty wetness seeped through my sleeves and I wondered if this would go into my book as a prelude to opportunity. Around me voices pealed:

> . . . *It's just a jump to the left . . . and then a step to the ri-i-i-ight . . .*

"What's his problem?" Edie kicked Noz's thigh.

"It's his mother's birthday," Bobby said, and held out the silver tube to him. "Here, man. Do another line."

"He doesn't like birthdays?"

"He doesn't like his mother."

Bobby dislodged Noz's arms from mine and my heart beat faster than those girls doing the Time Warp. Noz leaned over the table—bigger, fatter, and even more disgusting, but I couldn't stop thinking about his dick against my thigh, what I'd done to him. Didn't think I could do that to anyone. This was going okay. As long as he didn't start thinking he was my boyfriend or anything. You were my first priority. The Ayatollah flicked his Bic, rolled his eyebrows. Sugar time. I put the pipe to my lips. He leaned over from where he'd been huddled with Edie and lit me up. Smoke caked my throat, not sugary at all, it tasted like baby powder. Cold bubbles rushed my head and I felt like a commercial . . . *plop plop, fizz fizz* . . . Daddy's little girl. My legs started to tremble, my jaw tightening, as all the forces in the room converged in the Time Warp. I wanted to dance but my legs were gelatinized, swishing like the rubbery door. How could I trust them? I drummed my hands against my thighs and swayed. Edie picked up a roach clip from the mirror and made it talk. "I want to bite you, baby," it said.

Finished with his lines, Noz wedged in next to me and leaned his arm on my shoulder . . . *plop plop, fizz fizz* . . .

My toes tingled and my head bounced to the song on repeat cycle, I think. I could have sworn we'd come to the end and all the girls had collapsed on the floor like they do in the movie then bounced up again. We were all stuck in the Time Warp. I gnawed the inside of my cheek, darted my eyes back and forth. There was movement next to me, a few words brewing between the Ayatollah and Noz, Edie chewing the roach clip into Bobby's face, and I imagined her munching on velvet which couldn't have been as cottony as my mouth felt just then. The girls were still doing the Time Warp, a line of slimebag Rockettes making lasers out of their arms and legs. The Ayatollah lit a joint and handed it to Edie, who smiled and took a deep drag.

"If she was my girl, I'd watch out," Noz said to Bobby. "I heard she's a nigger lover. Hoo-sah!"

"Don't fucking *hoo-sah!* me," Bobby said. "You fucking moron."

"I'm serious, man. You don't know how they are with chicks."

Edie stared at the roach clip. "Hello, Mr. Alligator, I'd rather talk to you than anybody else here. You're not prejudiced, you're just a reptile. Green. And we all know it's not easy being green . . ."

"Alls I'm saying is the nigga's got eyes on her." Noz glared at the Ayatollah.

"Who are you calling nigger?" the Ayatollah said. Edie undid the first few buttons of her shirt and peeled back her bra.

"What are you doing?" I stammered. She ignored me.

"Nigger, A-rab, same difference," Noz, my date, was saying. "You're all nothing but a bunch'a criminals and terrorists. Every time I turn around one of you's hijacking a plane or pushing some old guy off a boat."

"Listen, man," Bobby moved behind him. "He's not a terrorist, that's why he's living here. And in case you forgot, it's his shit you've been scarfing all night, so chill the fuck out."

"You just don't get it, man. Guys like him, they're ruining our fucking country!" Noz said, his eyes gnarled and bloodshot, sweat collecting in his sideburns. "My father fought like a crazy son of a bitch for this country, he died in the fucking war, and for what? So *he* can come in from Saudi Arabia and take all our jobs away?"

"I'm from Iran, asshole." The Ayatollah moved closer to Noz. Bobby stepped between them, lightly pressing his palm on the Ayatollah's chest.

Beneath them on the floor, Edie circled her left hand around her tit, revealing a hard pink nipple. Little bumps crawled around it, like tiny growths on a twig. The dancers contorted their bodies . . . *Then it's a pelvic thrust—ooh-ah—that really drives you insa-a-a-a-ane* . . . Everything was happening at once, a split screen, surround-sound. The Ayatollah and Noz stood eye to eye, or more correctly the Ayatollah's eyes to Noz's chin, Bobby still wedged between them. Had to admire the Ayatollah, trying to ward off Godzilla. Edie opened the roach clip with her right hand. It said, "You look good enough to eat," then bit her nipple. "Whoa!" she bounded up between the three guys. "Look at my tit! Look at my tit!"

Bobby and the Ayatollah looked. "Holy shit, Edie!" Bobby said.

"Whoa! Edie number one! Edie fucking rocks!" She screamed and threw her hands in the air, bouncing back into the Time Warp girls.

"Fuck that! I'm saying something important here," Noz said.

"Nothing you say is important, you are too stupid for anything important," the Ayatollah said, and Noz's face froze.

Noz slung back his hand and punched, time slowing to nanoseconds, as the Ayatollah ducked and Noz's hand slammed into the wall behind him, cracking through layers of plaster. "AAAAHHHHHHHHHHHHHH!" he screamed, louder than Edie number one, louder than the girls doing the Time Warp again and again and again.

"Now, look what you've done," the Ayatollah said. "You've put a hole in the wall. I'm sure Felicia will send you the bill."

"Are you kidding me?" Bobby said. "This whole house is falling apart."

"That's what these houses are like, high-class slums," Edie said. "Everything's cracked and peeling. Nothing ever works. Did you see my tit?"

"Yes, it's quite impressive," said the Ayatollah.

"ARRRRRRRRRRRRGH!!!!" shouted Noz, his fist crammed into his balls, and I wondered if he was still hard.

"Okay, shit-brain," Bobby took him by his good arm, "let's get you to the hospital."

It wasn't as bad as it could have been. They could have not admitted Noz right away; they could have not wrapped his swollen, black-and-blue hand in plaster strips as we sat in the white light of the emergency room tapping our feet against the floor, grinding our teeth, taking turns pacing to the water fountain; they could have not written down his name and address and promised to bill his mother; they could have not handed him an envelope full of codeine pills, which we shared in the parking lot before Bobby decided we'd better get Noz home. He'd already passed out next to me in the backseat. Minutes later, we were cruising through the knotted trees and dark clouds, the stars and slight hook of moon having gone into hiding while we were at the hospital, driving toward Queens. The world seemed more desolate than ever. Tiny black streets with row houses and sagging traffic lights. Big empty boulevards lit up by gas stations. Only our presence gave the streets any purpose, and it depressed me being in a place where a few fucked-up teenagers in an old Chevy were the extent of any "scene" once the movie theatres and shopping malls and diners had shut down for the night. You were probably just heading out with your famous friends. Famous people always hung around other famous people. It didn't matter whether they really knew you or not.

Bobby crossed over the train tracks to a few blocks of small one-level houses, many of them flashing with Christmas lights. A few had 3-D manger scenes, Jesus all grown-up and glowing, even Santa himself tore across a couple of tiny lawns, reindeer ahead of him like the horses galloping around Noz's biceps. I'd forgotten that part of Christmas. The lights and stuff. Practically everyone in my town was Jewish, and the most anyone did for the season was plug in a boring electric menorah. These homes with their flickering rainbow lights were so beautiful. So alive. We pulled up in front of a house covered with cracked brown shingles. In the window, a Christmas tree smeared in multicolored bulbs with a shiny gold star on top was shoved in front of a curtain. Bobby turned off the car and jumped out to get Noz, who didn't want to move and begged Bobby to let him sleep in the car. He was practically screaming when the front door opened and a ghostly figure in a long nightgown and green army cap with flaps covering her ears appeared behind the outer door. She propped it open and wagged a fist in the air. "Nelson Kenridge, you get in here!" she shouted, and I felt like I was seeing something I shouldn't be seeing.

"Aw, why'd you have to bring me here?" Noz asked. Bobby shrugged and hiked him up against his shoulder.

"Nelson Kenridge, I'm gonna whoop your ass 'round your

head!" his mother shouted, and it was hard not to laugh, she looked so silly.

Noz pleaded with Bobby, "Can't I go to your house, man?"

"Sorry, man, you know the deal."

Bobby carried him to the front door where the mother he didn't like waited in her soldier hat to whoop his ass. She tugged him inside by his bad arm. He shouted, "Get the fuck off me, you crazy bitch!" as the door closed behind them. Bobby turned on the ignition, and we drove off in silence. I kept seeing Noz's mother shaking her fist in the air.

In the blink of a heavily drugged eye we were out of Queens and rolling through winding roads and temples and houses so huge compared to Noz's it was sickening. I almost wished we'd taken him with us, but what would we have done with him? My opportunity was gone. Bobby stopped in front of my house and he and Edie smiled at each other like I was supposed to leave, but when I opened the door they followed me out. "He's only gonna stay a few minutes, okay?" Edie asked, as if I had a choice. I nodded and told her they could hang out in Jack's office next to the TV room. Edie grabbed my cheeks in between her hands and pecked me on the lips. "You're the best, Lil."

I smiled, and my cheeks felt hot though it was so damn cold outside. I led us inside, showed them Jack's office, and ducked into the TV room. There, I shacked up on the couch watching a *Ben Casey* rerun and every so often staring at my uncracked copy of *Brave New World.* The next day I would have my essay on sex and reproduction in that new world, which I imagined wasn't much different from this old world, where Edie removed her green velvet skirt and combat boots for a guy with untied sneakers on the floor of my father's office. A part of me hated that she could give it up so easily. But I had to admit I was curious about her, what she smelled like, if she kissed with her tongue, the kind of sounds she made. I muted the TV to see if I could hear her.

. . . please!

She moaned so loud I could have been in the room with them. I rose from the couch and inched closer, noticing she'd left the door open, and it was like something placed in an underwear drawer: She wanted me in the room with them, the way you drew me into your world at night. Edie was on top of him, her head illuminated slightly by a streetlight not far from the window. Hair smothered her face as she bounced up and down, the roach clip still clawing her nipple, Bobby's velvet penis inside her. "I'm the best," she heaved. "I'm number one."

"Yeah . . . you're number one," he said, and reached up for her head. He pulled her down and they kissed in the dim shadows. I leaned against the wall, watching their tongues touch, the insides of my legs sweating in my khakis.

Edie broke from Bobby's lips, threw her fists in the air, and shouted: "Whoa! I'm the best fucker in the whole wide world!" She glanced forward and I thought she saw me. My heart jumped.

"Yeah, you're the best," Bobby said, and she smiled down at him.

"The best what?"

"The best fucker . . ."

"In . . ."

"The whole wide world," they said together, slowly. Then Edie threw her head back, and their bouncing resumed.

Quietly, I returned to the couch and tried squeezing my legs together but couldn't catch the seam between my legs, that place where all the stitching met in a bump. Edie'd called it the jean clitoris. I felt inside my pants, but only for a few seconds before it didn't seem right . . . them in there, me out here. And I was usually in my room . . . with you. This was sort of perverted. I pounded my fist against my crotch until it stung. Edie shrieked and my thighs caved inward. I couldn't resist.

As my normal breathing resurfaced, I pumped up the volume on *Ben Casey* and kicked back, elbows folded behind my head. Tiny snowflakes danced outside the window, the sky so black and heavy you couldn't see the water. I watched the white pellets for a while before Edie and Bobby stepped out of Jack's office and walked to the front door. The care Edie took not to make any noise as she tiptoed back through the living room touched me, only I didn't want to hear one word about Bobby Davis or velvet. I turned my knees into the couch and pretended I was sleeping.

Edie shook my arm and whispered my name a couple of times. I didn't budge. She shut off the TV, pulled the afghan from the back of the couch, and blanketed my body before spooning in behind me with her arm around my waist. She smelled sort of musty, like she'd been in a sauna, but her body felt warm against my back. I'd never slept that tangled up in anyone before, not even Blair who couldn't fall asleep unless she was flat on her stomach, so I was surprised when I drifted off and woke up hours later with four inches of snow in the backyard and Edie's arms around me.

I AM SUPPOSED TO GROW TOMATOES. Big red bulbs that make the community famous. Instead I spend my mornings pulling uniforms, underwear, socks and sheets and linens and towels from the dryer and shaking them out the way I've been taught. One clean crack before sliding them under the massive iron cylinder. You almost can't believe a machine like this exists outside of someone's imagination. So big it could steamroll, say, Stella, who's never without one eye on me as she moves the wrung-out laundry from washer to dryer, and leave her flat as a character in a Saturday morning cartoon; so hot the stuff falling off the other end needs a few minutes to cool before folding. A steak shoved under the barrel would brown, one side at a time, although it'd be paper thin and carry the taste of metal and fabric softener.

Chandon catches the linens on the other side and puts them in a pile. She is a folder, too. When the load is through I come around and help her. She doesn't look up. "My window was all fogged this morning," she says.

"It's almost Thanksgiving."

"Maybe we should cook up a turkey."

"We can brown it on the iron."

"It'll stick like crazy to that thing," Chandon laughs.

"Spray some Pam, add vegetables. So they'll be a little flat."

She smiles and grabs a starchy white sheet by the corners. I take the other side and together we fold it over once, pulling tightly to smooth the creases. We fold again, moving a couple steps toward each other, the sheet drooping between us like the diagram of fallopian tubes I remember from health class. Angel's baby never screamed when they sliced him out of her stomach. She said she couldn't push anymore so they had to do a cesarean. Then they stapled her skin back together like a term paper. Before they carried off the silent child she named him Alejandro.

Chandon grabs my ends, I take the bottom, and we step again. It's a good method, ours, and in the last few weeks we've narrowed it down to a science. Apart from the heat and skanky air, working in the laundry's not so bad. The machines are noisy, but in a strange way it's peaceful down here. We're the inner sanctum. Clothes come in dirty and leave clean, like blood circulating through the heart, but not in Angel's baby because his heart has the virus.

"You seen her yesterday?" Chandon breaks a few minutes of silence. I nod yes and hope that's all to the conversation. She senses my discomfort. "She don't look so good's all I'm saying."

I nod again. "Yeah, I know."

We finish the last sheet and move on to the pillowcases, each of us standing at one side of the table. At home Nancy had king-sized pillowcases. Blair's were silk. By the end of the night my cheek had always slipped down to the very edge.

"You scared?" Chandon says, without looking up.

"Scared?"

"She got it, you know."

"Maybe she's just the carrier. It can happen like that."

"She knew all the time."

"It takes two, it could have been the father."

"Sorry, Long Island." She finally looks up, her eyes injected with sadness. "That just ain't the way it goes with this thing."

Our faces lock a second, long enough to feel the weight of Angel's destiny, and then, quietly, we return to the folding. The way Chandon works her fingertips over the pillowcases they could be bound for the fanciest hotel in the world. Bedding so crisp and pure I want to mess it up the way somebody messed up Angel with a contaminated prick or needle.

But I can't think about that now. Not when I have pillowcases to fold. A job to do. At home I never had chores. Jack was against them on principle. He'd grown up helping out his mother and hating every minute of it. As soon as they could, he and Nancy paid people to do the laundry, mow the lawn, clean the cars, put the right amount of chlorine in the pool at our summer house. Everything always sparkled. Not an item out of place. The couches and chairs looked like people never sat in them. Another memory: After Blair left, I'd begged and begged for a cat, and Nancy said, "Where did you get that idea? This isn't that kind of house. A cat would be miserable here." I took my case to Jack who said cats gave him hives but it was up to my mother. I asked one more time, promising to feed it and let it out to pee, the way Blair had done it with the girls. But Nancy wouldn't budge. "Do you have any idea what cats do to couches?" she said, and I remembered the frayed coverings on Blair's bed, the pulls in her rug, those scratches on the coffee table. Cats'll mess up anything, they don't care. It was my mother who would have been miserable.

I grab a pile of towels and white socks with black numbers scrawled on the side in indelible ink, numbers Chandon and I match together in the final stage. Folding is an orderly business. We do one section at a time; first linens, then clothing, and everything matches up in the end. Even when we lose a sock, we know who's missing it by the number left over. I had no idea I would thrive on this kind of order, just as I never realized the necessity of keeping my space neat. Outside I never even made my bed. As long as I kept the door shut, Nancy didn't care. I could shut myself off from the rest of the house. In here I'm on display, cleanliness a reflection of my character. I bribe a guard for bleach to scrub my toilet every other day. The first time he handed me the paper cup covered with saran wrap I opened it and took a whiff. A sourness crept up my nostrils and made me think of Mimi. Bleach was all hers. Laundry detergent and scrap metal belong to Chandon. When we break we smoke cigarettes away from the chemicals. She's afraid we might torch the place. I think it's impossible. Or somebody would have done it already.

Chandon sits sideways on the windowsill, smoking, her other hand curled around a jaundiced paperback. The cover's turned back so I can't see the title. I could have brought something to read, I'm a big reader, anyone'll tell you. But this is supposed to be our time together. My neck flushes, the taste of hot metal on my tongue. I move closer to Chandon to see what's more interesting than me. She turns her shoulder further into the window. I stab my cigarette next to her on the wall, squirming behind her to get a look at the author and title on top of the frayed pages. Can't see. Tight brown hairs pull her scalp into a part. It's the color of those big white freckles on her face and arms. I like that she's both light and dark. I am the same wishy-washy yellow all over. "You coulda just asked." Chandon swings around, and I startle backwards.

She holds out the book, her forefinger planted inside to save her place. It's *The Autobiography of Malcolm X*. A popular book in here, mostly with black girls. I sometimes forget Chandon's black since she hangs with Mimi and Angel. She says she's from the West Indies so she understands Puerto Ricans, but at heart she's as black as Stella. "This thing with Angel's too deep," she says. "I need something to grab onto, some direction, know what I'm saying?"

I nod, I do. I really do.

Chandon tells me she's been talking to the Muslims for a while. This doesn't mean much. In here everyone's always talking to somebody or reading something that's supposed to have all the answers. Prison is a philosophical supermarket. Not too different from college, I suppose. Only you don't want to be putting Rikers on your resume. Chandon says Malcolm converted to Islam in the white man's prison. "No offense, Long Island," she says, "but white people got blood on their hands."

I nod again, although I can't figure out what that's got to do with Angel.

"See, what I'm saying is, you got to believe there's some order to it," she continues, "some kind of rules guiding us. Shit, if you don't, might as well sign on here for good."

Her eyes wander toward Stella, who sits by the radio eating a Hershey's bar. Privileges. "She on her way Upstate again," Chandon says. "I heard her mother's inside, too. Big reunion coming."

"Can't say I'm sad to see her go."

"Why? Somebody else just gonna take her place. They come and go. You know Mimi been in three times in five years."

Now she's got my full attention.

"Think about it: On the outside, what she got? A coupla kids and some sorry-ass motherfucker draining every last cent of the white man's handouts, when he ain't disappeared himself. Here she got her people. She got everything taken care of, don't gotta worry about nothing 'cept her enemies, but her people be watching her back. What she don't know is it's exactly what they want."

"What who wants?"

"The system."

"I don't understand."

"It's complicated," Chandon says, and taps her paperback against her other outstretched palm. "You gotta read the book."

I nod, say maybe I will. Chandon smiles and shakes her head like she does whenever I make a joke, but I'm not kidding. I want to understand the system and say so. "Guess it can't hurt," she says, then shoves Malcolm into the back of her pant seam. I follow her to the pile of clothes we'd left before the break. Blue shirts stacked by number. Matching pants. "Executive wear," Chandon jokes, as we fold and laugh together, but that book hangs between us like a drooping sheet, one we can't sort by number and tuck away.

Angel's got the virus. No matter what kind of prophets we summon, no matter how perfectly we match the numbers or how neat we keep our cells, there's no order in the universe that can knock the bad blood out of her.

THAT PAPER I BOUGHT FROM SUSAN FINKELSTEIN earned me an A and more attention from Mr. Belgrave, who grilled me in class like I ought to know things; so I had to keep up with *The Canterbury Tales,* even when I was wasted and couldn't understand the tangled writing and was convinced Belgrave was testing me to see if I was really Finkelstein-smart or if that paper had been a fake. I'd re-typed it before turning it in to cover my tracks. Consistency was the key to deception. Learned that earlier in the year when I'd stupidly turned in an absence note from Nancy after forging a few of my own. They called me down to the office and accused me of penning it, but when the assistant dean phoned Nancy and she said no, it was really hers, what could they do? People are such morons. I would have hauled Nancy in and demanded she account for all the previous notes, but that's me and I don't trust anybody.

The hippies used to say don't trust anyone over thirty. Makes sense, although that was almost two decades earlier which meant even the youngest hippies had hit thirty by the time I was in eleventh grade and were all walking around not trusting each other. If you ask me, that's how Ronald Reagan became president and how former hippie Ted Belgrave with his corduroy jeans and turquoise pinkie ring ended up teaching Chaucer to a group of kids who without him might have thought Chaucer was a type of sneaker or sports car. None of us paid much attention to the book, though I did like the idea of having these different people telling their tales and together they made a village, kind of like how it happened on *World*. People were always repeating their own little histories and connections.

Of course I hadn't read "The Wife of Bath's Tale" on that numb Tuesday in January and knew Belgrave was on to me. There was an undercurrent beneath his words, warnings transmitted from his brain to mine. Like you, he knew how to speak with his eyes. Looking at him almost hurt. I tried staring out the window but that only made things worse. It was one of those blistering sunny days that looked like winter on television, the entire world glossed to make even my faded army coat seem the most vibrant green. Or maybe that was the ganja I'd bought from the Ayatollah.

No matter how sunny it was, Belgrave never pulled down the shades. He liked playing the shadow man, dodging streams of sun as he paced up and down the aisles. I had to tilt my head back to see him. In the sun you could make out the gray hairs around his temples, the thick lines in his forehead, and the beanbag eyes bulging into his cheeks. He must have been about Jack's age but he looked a lot older. Sadder, too. The radiator squealed. As if it had to pump harder to keep up with the killer-hot sun outside and wasn't thrilled about it. I wondered if Belgrave had been any happier when he was a hippie, wearing tie-dyed shirts, brown curls rolling down his shoulders.

A few sunbeams stabbed my eyes, and my neck collapsed. I leaned against my right arm, let my hair flop over my face. School was worthless. In a couple of months I was going to the Garden to a world hunger concert, even if Edie wouldn't come with me. I'd ordered two tickets on my credit card. You might show up, you'd mentioned it in your newsletter, *Babbling 'Bout Brooke.* It was our responsibility to help feed the world, you said a few weeks later at a press conference with one of the guys from Crosby, Stills & Nash. You were going to perform with them. It would be historic. Nobody knew you could sing.

Long as you didn't make a record. I hated when famous people thought they could do everything. But you were made for the stage. You would wear white sailor pants, cowboy boots, a sparkly halter top, hold the microphone close to your lips as the crowd called out your name . . . *Brooke, Brooke, Brooke!*

"Lillian!" Belgrave's voice jolted me upright, sun jammed between my eyes. I think I said, "Huh?" The class laughed.

"Okay, settle down. I don't hear any of you racing to tell me what the Wife of Bath sets up in her prologue. What is it? Is it Chaucer? You don't like Chaucer? He too boring for your excitable, modern minds?"

Silence from the class. Belgrave shuffled out of the sun, moving even closer to my desk. The radiator was going haywire, hissing and squalling like a trapped animal. My stomach dropped to my knees: Something bad was about to happen, I could feel it.

"Well, let me tell you, Chaucer is not boring. There's more farting, burping, drinking, and screwing in here than in . . ." Belgrave's voice floated into the whining radiator. Every so often I picked up a phrase . . . *post-industrial complex . . . too much television . . . the warfare of stupidity* . . . words I probably would have agreed with if I could have followed them. There was too much going on in the room with the radiator and sun at war, and all of us on edge, and Belgrave talking about the Wife of Bath like she was his favorite character on *World*. He said somebody had to say something or we would all have to write five pages about her that evening. "I can't believe there's not one person in this room who's going to try and save you all from an essay," he said. "Nobody? Not even you, Lillian? I thought this would be right up your alley. Come on, help out your classmates, give us something, anything, about the Wife of Bath."

He stared down at me, clasping his paperback copy of *The Canterbury Tales* to his chest, holylike. The sun shifted once more, turning its beams on the stuffy oxygen particles, and I thought I was going to pass out for lack of hydrogen, nitrogen, and whatever else freshened the air inside at my grandparents' condo. It was missing here, in the heat. My armpits got hot. We were in for it. Belgrave was about to speak again, when a man burst into the room. "Ted! Get your class, come quick! The space shuttle blew up!"

"What!?" Belgrave jumped. A few people gasped, whispered.

"Just after the launch, they were, like, two thousand feet into the air and the thing exploded." The man—a physics guy named Erlichman—circled his arms out above his head.

"Oh my god! How?"

"Nobody knows. They've got the TVs on in the auditorium. Get your class, let's go!"

"All right, everyone take your stuff and follow me," Belgrave said, his face bleeding pure jaw-dropping horror, so exaggerated he seemed like a mannequin posed in shock: weak, defeated, and confused. Erlichman looked the same. It was weird being sixteen and feeling more stable than most adults. Not that I had any recycled claims about not trusting anyone over thirty; more often I felt sorry for them. Big deal. It was just another spaceship. But I had forgotten one thing: the teacher in space. A high school teacher from Concord, New Hampshire.

Weeks later, the cleanup still in high gear, her lesson plans for space would be found floating in the Atlantic Ocean. The crew compartment would reveal that some of the astronauts had been alive during the three- to four-minute fall to sea. By then we would also know the accident had been caused by a routine booster failure and could have been prevented, which made people very mad at NASA. But on the day the space shuttle exploded there was wholesale grief and confusion as Ted Belgrave pushed open the door to the auditorium, his fingers still gripped to that copy of *The Canterbury Tales*.

I ducked out of the harmonic grieving session soon after Belgrave and a few other weepy teachers took to the podium. Belgrave had said it was okay for us to mourn as we watched the shuttle burst over and over again with the sound muted, leaving commentary to the adults. A total mistake. They were wrapped up in the mythology of outer space. Ships with romantic names like Apollo, Viking, and Venus. Guys in space suits giant-stepping with the American flag long before the man on the moon became the MTV logo. The space race might have ended a decade ago, but today, if you believed the teachers, marked the end of an era. A teacher! How could NASA blow up a teacher?

When I was a kid I'd told my third-grade class my father was an astronaut. Every morning I watched him board the silver cars of the Long Island Rail Road and pretended he was plunging into the solar system, off to explore worlds unknown. I had the coolest father in my class. Then one Saturday at the supermarket, Jack and I ran into my teacher. He said it was an honor meeting an astronaut and wondered if Jack would come and talk to the class. Stroking back a few strands of shiny black hair, his eyes like sparklers, Jack said thanks but he didn't like public speaking, just the thought of it sent him into a cold sweat, he didn't know how teachers did it. My teacher smiled. Flattery was Jack's business. Later he told Nancy the story, and she laughed. My father could barely ride a bicycle without dosing himself on Dramamine. "I really like those silver suits, though," Jack said to my mother, and she smiled, and my lie had become something funny between them. I told people he quit the space program.

Seventy-three minutes after takeoff, the space shuttle Challenger had flamed into the most beautiful stream of white smoke, and mission control shouted, "THERE'S OBVIOUSLY A MAJOR MALFUNCTION!!" and the town of Concord, New Hampshire, cried.

Outside by the gym, people huddled smoking cigarettes in the shifting rays of sun, pretending it was a normal day, only we'd gotten out a little early. The steps were crowded. I found Edie high on top, sitting next to the Ayatollah. He held a ledger book in one hand and punched numbers into a calculator with the other. Every so often he stopped and blew into his bare hands. It was freezing out.

I wedged myself in front of them and lit a cigarette. Edie rolled her eyes, stomped her purple boots on the cement. "You're killing yourself," she said.

"This is smokers' corner. Don't tread on me."

"It's a free country."

"Not really," muttered the Ayatollah, still engrossed in his calculations.

A jappy guy from my social studies class shoved his way through the crowd and stood over us, casting a shadow like a giant robot. He slipped a black leather wallet from the inside pocket of his ski jacket. It had a European name stitched into the arm. The Ayatollah looked up, shielding his eyes with his right hand. "The usual," he said, and the guy nodded. He leaned closer to the Ayatollah, slipped him a few bills, then backed away.

"You inside before?" the guy asked.

"For a little while."

"It looked like a video game."

"More like skywriting," Edie said.

"Yes, skywriting," the Ayatollah nodded. He scribbled into his book, then closed it and handed it to Edie. "A message from the CIA, no doubt."

The jappy guy burst out laughing. "You're paranoid, dude."

"Oh, I am paranoid. You Americans are really something. You never see the connectedness of things, you don't want to believe that your government can betray you. You think because you elect these people they will do exactly what you tell them and only what you tell them. That's so naïve. Have you read the newspaper lately? Central America has been contaminated by the CIA."

"So they blew up the space shuttle?"

"I have no conclusive evidence, but the timing is suspicious. This thing is so big. It's a global disaster. Everyone is involved—

Russia, the Middle East, everyone, and it's all going down in these little countries where people are so poor they don't know any better. Do you have any idea how many lives this country is responsible for? How much blood has been shed already?"

The jappy guy backed up a step, nodded. He was either frightened or bored. "Hey, don't look at me, dude. I'm antiwar."

"What war? There is no war. This is not Vietnam. We're talking about global terrorism, about total U.S. domination. The information is there if you want it, but you don't. You come to me, smack my hand, *'Hey, dude, I'm antiwar.'* You don't know the first thing about war. None of you do."

Edie put her hand on the Ayatollah's thigh. "Relax, baby," she said, "it's not Nathan's fault if the CIA blew up the space shuttle."

Baby! She called the Ayatollah *baby,* her fingers digging into his leg like it was her turf, she'd been there before . . . when? A couple of weeks ago, she'd said he was too girly; I was the one who told her he was cute. And he had tons of coke. My throat contracted. I took a deep pull of nicotine and exhaled close to Edie's face.

"Ugh—Lil!" she flagged her hand in front of me. "How many times do I have to tell you, keep that shit away from me!"

She barely looked at me, concentrating on the Ayatollah and Nathan who were patching it up. "No, dude, you've actually given me something to think about," Nathan said, holding out his hand to the Ayatollah who took it and clasped it in between his palms.

"Don't think, do," said the dealer, as if he were a prophet and not just a foreigner with major connections and long eyelashes. He let go of Nathan's hand. I took a final drag of my cigarette and exhaled a stream of smoke so straight and white it hypnotized me.

"Fuckin' A!" Nathan said, and everyone stared at the smoke as it splintered into a big white Y across the baby-blue expanse as if the letter had been carved by a skywriter to follow the path of the space shuttle.

We were all transfixed, even the Ayatollah. Here was something the CIA couldn't have planted. A natural phenomenon. We watched the smoke fizzle into a grayish haze, and I wondered if it had been that way with the shuttle, whether it simply withered away or the people standing at the base of Cape Canaveral had to run for cover under pieces of scrap metal and spaceship debris. It didn't seem right how some things shot up into the sky and came crashing down while others arched as perfectly as a flipped cigarette.

I was overrun by a chill so deep I thought I had pneumonia. Nathan bounced off the steps, his robotic arms slipping out into the afternoon, everything preprogrammed. The Ayatollah put his arm around Edie's shoulder, this time like *he'd* been there before, and I could have kicked myself for not seeing it coming. They all became her boyfriends after a while. She barely said goodbye before they walked off arm in arm, and a few minutes later I saw the Ayatollah's Jaguar take off down the street. I smoked a couple more cigarettes in the brutal cold, listening to the bells ringing at the junior high as the younger kids flocked outside, screaming and laughing and bouncing up and down like they hadn't heard about the national disaster. Or didn't care.

Finally, I stood up and balanced myself against the cement wall. I was about to leave when Belgrave found me and asked for a cigarette. Eyeing him curiously—he was a teacher and all—I flipped open my box of Marlboros and we shared my last two cigarettes, the sky wisping into its deep-winter palette—azure, cyan, indigo, Air Force blue, space shuttle silver. Like names on pastel crayons. Gray-blue smoke rose above our heads. It was weird smoking with a teacher; if anyone saw me I would have been laughed out of smokers' corner, and even weirder, Belgrave wasn't saying anything. I kept expecting him to nail me for not reading "The Wife of Bath's Tale," but he just smoked and tipped his head toward the spiraling blues above us. "My brother is a physicist," he said, after he'd taken his last drag and crushed the butt with his penny loafer. "I have no idea what he does, really. Something about splitting molecules. He's always telling me he's on to something revolutionary about negative space. Do you have any idea what that means? Negative space?"

I nodded no. In chemistry, we'd learned that negative ions were attracted to positive electrodes. In algebra, negative numbers plotted less than zero but they didn't really exist. You couldn't have negative two cigarettes. When they were gone they were gone. I looked down at the crumpled-up Marlboro box in my hand, thinking, I have no cigarettes. A negative statement. What was the equivalent for space? In painting, it was the part you left blank. I said this to Belgrave, and he borrowed my curious eye.

"And if you cover the whole canvas," he said, "what then?"

I shrugged. "It's all positive?"

A full pack of cigarettes.

"Hmmm . . ." He nestled his chin with his thumb and forefinger, then summoned the sky once more. "And up there? Is that positive or negative?"

"I guess it depends where you're looking from," I said, thinking of Edie and her claims to be from the planet Andromeda. She liked looking down on the stars.

Belgrave turned to me, nodding his head up and down, *affirmative*. I was almost sorry when he thanked me for the cigarette and told me I'd been good therapy for him before wandering back through the gym. I rushed to the late bus. It was full of kids from the basketball and swim teams. Nobody would let me share a seat. They laughed, whispering to each other, and occasionally I saw a spitball loop overhead. They'd be sorry one day when I was a famous painter. I was going to draw negative space. It would be a major development in the world of art, explosive in a good way. I would be interviewed by *People* magazine. You always thanked your first drama teacher at the Blue Bell Recreation Center. I would thank Belgrave. He wasn't an art teacher, but he had this theory of negative space . . .

The bus pulled in to the last stop, and the few of us still remaining walked off into the clear, dark night—hyacinthine, purple-ebony, shiny-combat-boot black with glowing white stars. Like Blair's fake diamond earrings. A longing to go by the swimming pool passed quickly this time. I took a final look at the night sky, shook a few spitballs from my hair, and headed inside, where I knew I'd find you waiting at my window.

LUCKY LITTLE LADY IN THE CITY OF LIGHT

MILDRED HARRISON FLEW TO LOS ANGELES. Despite the smooth skies and half-empty rows of seats, she spent much of the flight gnawing her fingernails and nursing the straw of the one Bloody Mary she allowed herself, habits she hadn't been able to shake since Brooke had gone Hollywood. It was her most difficult trip yet. The next day she and Brooke would return together to Blue Bell; that night she envisioned herself helping her daughter pack and settle up a few loose ends, although she had no idea what Brooke had been through in the last forty-eight hours. She told Mildred she'd practically had to beg the producers for a two-week hiatus to "get her shit together," not to mention the shame she must have suffered being hauled before an L.A. County judge looking like she'd just emerged from an opium den. The sight of her daughter on that entertainment program had kindled in Mildred a maternal call to arms, the kind that could turn any ordinary woman into an action hero.

At first Brooke had told her not to come. She'd been commuting between Blue Bell and her L.A. flat since she was seventeen and didn't need an escort on account of one silly drunk-driving violation. But after speaking to Kenny Zeller who'd coughed up a few details about the arrest that Brooke had conveniently bowdlerized, namely the eighth of Bolivian pearl her little champion of world peace and drug-free schools had quickly stashed beneath the seat of her red Porsche, Mildred knew she had to make the trip.

"Bolivian *what?*"

"Not to worry, Mil, it wasn't even her. You know how things go out there. When in Rome . . . Anyway, get this— she managed to talk the cops out of searching her car. One of them wanted an autograph for his daughter."

"But wait, I don't understand. What did you say she was hiding?"

"Oh, I'm sorry. I shouldn't have said anything. She was holding a little coke. Nothing to worry about, though. She barely touches the stuff. She's a good girl, Mil. A very good girl."

As Kenny spoke, Mildred felt the hands of guilt coil around her neck. *Cocaine?* She couldn't imagine Brooke involved in anything like that. A little too much liquor was one thing, but cocaine! Mildred booked a flight and within hours was California bound.

At the airport car rental, she upgraded from economy to a full-sized sedan and took one of the company's maps to ensure an easy departure. Whenever she made the trip without Tom, that stretch around the car rentals always unnerved her. Navigating the boulevards and highways of Los Angeles had been much easier than friends back home said it would be, what with the special map Brooke had given her. Mildred had a better chance of being stopped by the LAPD for slow driving than floating too far off track, and still those few blocks near the airport, where the scenery resembled a nuclear test site, teased her mercilessly. There were too many lots and too few signs, anxieties complemented by the pressure of her impending visit. Such nervousness always carried Mildred back to the first road test she'd failed almost twenty-five years earlier, running Tom's Dodge through not one but two stop signs and rimming the curb on her parallel park. Vehicles were so weighty back then, Mildred couldn't imagine how anyone passed the first time, yet the thought of telling Tom she'd failed had soured her stomach so badly she couldn't keep down anything but chicken broth and toasted Wonder Bread.

It was Tom who'd given her driving lessons just a couple of months after they'd met, and if she hadn't been in love with him already, it was fair to say she'd left their first class swooning over his wide eyes and angular jaw, a man as sensible as he was handsome, ten years her senior with a degree in chemical engineering from Carnegie Mellon and steady work at Paxton Pharmaceuticals. That first day, Tom kept them sitting in front of the house more than an hour discussing every knob, button, and gauge on the dashboard. Mildred, however, was more interested in their thighs bumping up against each other, the soft cotton of Tom's shirtsleeves against her forearms as he guided her hands in position on the steering wheel. She was close enough to smell the starch in his clean white shirt, a scent conjuring houses with built-in garages, morning kisses before work, all the little tidbits of security. She'd practically had them rearing a happy and healthy brood when Tom pulled her outside for a look underneath the hood. "Most people don't have the first idea how a car works," Tom had said. "But I believe it's important."

Imagine all those hours of lecturing, not to mention the flashcards Tom had designed to test her on the rules of the road, and still she'd failed that menace of a test. The funny thing was, when she finally broke down and told Tom, he simply smiled. Apparently, on his first test he'd mistakenly hit reverse as they were pulling away from the curb and slammed into a motorcycle. The inspector had failed him on the spot. "Practically everyone fails the first time," he'd said, "but not everyone knows how a fan belt works." Mildred was so relieved she actually spit up laughing, a faux pas that knocked them both into long silly giggles. Later, Tom cooked a T-bone steak and string beans, heavenly victuals for a girl who'd spent the past five days on sick food, and eating had never felt so immediate, so pleasurable, so intoxicating, her entire emotional canvas reified in this man feeding her string beans with his fingers.

Thoughts of young love were indeed comforting to a woman pushing fifty in a forest-green rental car, the L.A. freeway spread out in runnels of red and white lights in front of her. And leaving the airport had been a snap. A left turn out of the lot, then a right onto the boulevard, and a few yards later, the freeway. The sheer ease of it, even in the dark, had Mildred chuckling to herself as she pressed the gas pedal closer to the floor, almost delirious with her own success, although that elation soon tumbled into a touch of sadness, as too much of anything eventually bred its opposite. Often the pleasure Mildred took in her solitary victories left her wondering what she might have accomplished had she not jumped straight into marriage.

She turned on the radio and tuned it to the swing jazz station she and Tom loved, bursting in on a Rogers & Hart tune. The name would come to her, though the slash of trombone and snare ushered in thoughts of her husband. Three hours ahead, he was probably flicking the small light in the downstairs bathroom for his father's midnight run before plodding up to an empty bed. The poor man—Tom, that is, not Grampy Harry. If Mildred sometimes found herself wondering where she might have been without him, she was comforted by the fact that he never knew quite what to do with himself at home without her. Once, a few years ago, when she'd returned from a weekend in Milltown visiting her parents, Tom said her absence had thrown him into the kind of fog that accompanied most antihistamines. A romantic notion. To think after all their years together she could still affect her husband as if she were a drug, and that was high praise coming from a man who developed pharmaceuticals for a living. Yet for all her it's-only-fair equations, it still upset her to imagine Tom at home. Alone in a head cloud.

If Cynthia wasn't working she might have kept him company after dinner, then again she wasn't the type to watch TV or play Boggle with them the way Brooke did whenever she was home. Brooke was always more traditional in that way, which is why it was utterly incongruous to imagine her sniffing drugs. Of her two daughters, Cynthia was the one she'd been watching, worrying about the hours she spent alone in her dark room, leaving only for school or the public library, where she volunteered in the adult-literacy program and kept her library card active. Every day she'd come home with another corpulent hardcover Mildred couldn't see behind the shiny University of Pennsylvania book cover Cynthia'd affixed. Mildred had once made the mistake of asking what she was reading. "Just stuff," Cynthia had said.

"What kind of stuff?" Mildred pried.

"History, mostly."

"But why do you hide them?"

"In the public transit system everyone's a social critic," she said, as if her statement were common knowledge, and although it had perplexed Mildred, her daughter's demeanor curtailed further inquiry. Cynthia had a way of making Mildred feel downright invasive at times, an air Mildred couldn't help thinking she and Tom had exacerbated, no matter how determined they'd been not to favor Brooke.

Mildred eased up on the accelerator, lightly tapping the break in tune with Benny Goodman as she exited the highway. At the first red light, she checked memory to map and had no trouble matching the few boulevard blocks and smaller streets that led to Brooke's hacienda. Pulling into the driveway, she saw a few lights behind those blinds like crinkled white construction paper. When Brooke had first moved in Mildred assumed the blinds were temporary. There was no point to transparent blinds, especially for a young woman on television. But Brooke had tossed off Mildred's concerns, saying the blinds were handcrafted in Mexico, as if the aesthetics would ensure her safety. Then she took Mildred's hand and marched her out front to display a network of electronically censored strips, which triggered sirens and dispatched messages to the police station, taped over milky white windows. The closer you got the more opaque the glass. Blinds were irrelevant, Brooke had said, and Mildred could see her point.

She turned off the car and took a deep, damp breath before stepping outside. L.A. was colder than she remembered. Nothing like back home, but she was happy she hadn't tucked her sable into the trunk at the car rental. Normally she wore the coat—a most extravagant twentieth-anniversary gift from Tom—only on special occasions, but that night it was her way of keeping her husband close. She draped the fur over her shoulders in a style reminiscent of old Hollywood and grabbed her overnight bag. If she'd been true Hollywood stock she might have donned her sunglasses, in fact she might have had special sunglasses made for wearing at night when the sun retreated and the soul was caught off guard. But Mildred Harrison had lived her entire life in a place where sunglasses at night signaled blindness, delinquency, or lord knows what other psychological dysfunction, and therefore she was besieged by the stream of flashes like an asteroid shower. Of course, this being Hollywood and her daughter being Brooke Harrison, Mildred quickly realized they were not stars but cameras. Packs of them, or so it seemed. The onslaught of clicks and flickers, the thick lenses in her face, and hands tugging at her overnight bag disabled her. She wanted to turn and give the image-stalkers a piece of her mind. This was private property, not some Hollywood function. How dare they!

At that moment, however, Brooke's door swung open and a young man ducked down the front steps with his arm outstretched. In a quick glance Mildred saw how handsome he was, even by movie star standards. She took his hand and together they barreled into the house, the young man slamming the door shut behind them. "Are you okay?" he asked.

Before Mildred could answer, Brooke threw her arms around her. "Mom, I'm so sorry!" she said, and Mildred felt her throat constrict.

There was so much she wanted to say, yet all she could manage was a teary, "Oh, Brooke!"

"Aw, Mom, don't cry." Brooke leaned back slightly. "I knew you shouldn't have come."

Again, Mildred couldn't speak. She held Brooke tighter, amazed her daughter felt more childlike every time she touched her, as if television had not only stunted her growth but demanded somatic regression. She was getting more and more like women at the soap opera awards: plasticized smile over straight white teeth, and skeletal. *Drugs?* Mildred wondered, overwhelmed by the sudden urge to bare her breast, as if the dehydrated mounds had turned fertile in the presence of her undernourished daughter. It was symbolic, of course. The best Mildred could do was offer to cook dinner as she slowly disentangled her hands from Brooke's bony hips.

"We ordered in," Brooke said. "Is Thai food okay?"

"Thai?"

"It's just like Chinese, only different," the young man said as he handed her a Kleenex.

"Thank you," Mildred nodded. "Thai . . . sure, why not?"

"Sure, why not? That's right." The young man stared at Mildred. She realized she'd seen him in that movie starring all the young actors. And in magazines. "She's terrific, you really are lucky," he said to Brooke, then turned back to Mildred. "Do you realize your daughter is the only person I've ever met who can't say a bad thing about her parents?"

"Really now," Mildred blushed, though she knew it was true. Ever since that first performance at the rec center, the entire Harrison clan had been committed to Brooke's wants and needs, but at times like these Mildred found herself wondering at what cost.

"I keep telling Johnny I had a happy childhood, but he won't believe me," Brooke said.

"I'm so pleased you still remember it that way," Mildred said.

"Why wouldn't I?"

"Well, I don't know . . ." Mildred stopped herself. There had to be some unresolved ache or untended feeling—why else would she seek the approval of millions? Not to mention the drinking, the drugs, and the other fringe benefits of fame that Mildred dared not even consider, especially with the young fellow in front of her smiling so wantonly, as if he were the kind of man who spent his afternoons pleasuring rich older women, a thought that actually made Mildred blush again.

"Wow, Mildred," he said, "you're even better than I imagined . . . and Brooke forgot to mention how beautiful you are."

"Lighten up, Valentino, this is my mother!" Giggling, Brooke shoved her shoulder against his. He put his arm around her and kissed the top of her head, a gesture that comforted Mildred. Had she thought about it, she might have wondered if the presence of the young charmer John Strong had been orchestrated to steer the evening away from her daughter's troubles (*cocaine!?*), but at that moment Mildred was relieved to find Brooke in a zesty mood, and the way the young man had commanded the scoping vermin outside was quite impressive. The result, Mildred would learn over dinner, of his Hollywood upbringing.

John's father was Philip Strong, the actor and B-movie producer; his mother, Gail Vargas, had been a famous costume designer before succumbing to breast cancer a few years back. Both had shared a zealot's tooth for the glamorous life, leaving John to grow up in the shadow of their sundry affairs and addictions as they struggled not to kill each other whenever one of them came crawling back home. They'd managed to stay married ten years, although the way John described it, their coupling seemed the antithesis of anything Mildred had ever called marriage. "I always thought one of them would end up dead before they split, and then one day my father saw the light," John said. He paused to light a cigarette, a pastime Mildred might have prohibited during dinner, but she was captivated by the young man. A sly smile crossed his lips before he exhaled and continued his story. "I'm not just being metaphoric here. My father had this girlfriend who was a Christian Scientist and she started dragging him to services and reading rooms . . . they read a lot, you know? I suppose it's more active than most religions, but anyway, before he could say uncle he was hooked on God and realizing that adultery was sort of problematic. Of course, he couldn't ditch his girlfriend because she was tied into the whole religion thing, so he finally got his balls up to leave my mother. Mind you, I had no idea any of this was going on until much later, but when I was about nine, I guess, I came home from school one day and found my mother in the living room all dressed up and smothered in peanut butter."

"No!" Mildred put down her fork, imagining a second-string movie star: gorgeous, inviting, aging, and insane.

"Yes! And not just any peanut butter, this really expensive flavored stuff she brought back from Spain. It was so bizarre. She had about seven jars open in front of her—chocolate, banana, hazelnut. The room stunk of sweet chemicals and there was peanut butter all over the couch and carpet, in her hair, on her white silk dress with the feather collar, one of her most fantastic designs. She was brilliant, my mother. I'm not kidding, you go anywhere in town and say the name Gail Vargas, people skip a breath before picking up the conversation."

"She designed for Katharine Hepburn," Brooke said.

John beamed. "That's right. And Audrey once, before she fell for Givenchy. Anyway, my mother's standing there covered in gourmet peanut butter and you know what she says to me? She says, 'Johnny, darling, can you get me a cigarette?'"

He snuffed out his own cigarette in his untouched chicken curry and took a sip of wine, eyes wandering between his two reticent dinner companions. "'Johnny, can you get me a cigarette?' Just like that. I can't explain it, but I knew immediately my father wasn't ever coming home again."

"So what did you do?" Mildred asked.

"What did I do? I got her a cigarette. If she could pretend she wasn't covered in peanut butter, so could I. From that day on we were pretty tight, even though I loathed most of her boyfriends. Gruesome parasites. It's tough being a smart woman around here. Your options are totally limited."

"I am never raising kids in this town," Brooke said.

"Sweetheart," John patted Brooke's arm. "That's not the moral. My parents should have had a nice affair and walked away. They both wanted too much to give anything back to each other, let alone to me. It's like, what were these people thinking having a child?"

Silence descended upon the table. Mildred reached for the vegetables smothered in coconut sauce and took a few clumsy spoonfuls. She was already full but eating seemed easier than addressing John's query. Who knew what people thought before coming together and having children? Probably many, like John's parents, weren't thinking at all. Imagining the heights of deprivation and privilege he'd known as a child had spun Mildred into an uncontrollable pathos. He was wise beyond his years, this young man, and the way he strung sentences together like tightly woven petit point bore the mark of someone who'd learned to entertain for survival, unlike her own daughter whose theatrical countenance seemed more of a luxury. Even in her drained and emaciated state, even with her stardom now tottery, Brooke seemed so steadfast and self-assured, as if she could walk away with her identity intact. Still, Mildred wished she'd eat more of the noodles she kept shifting from one side of her plate to the other. Like John, she didn't seem at all interested in food.

"Brooke, you really should eat something," Mildred said, unsure if she'd actually spoken out loud.

"I'm not hungry."

"Honey, listen to your mother," John said, then winked at Mildred. "I've always wanted to say that in real life. That and, 'Do you have a warrant?'"

They all laughed, although Mildred could sense the star-flecked sadness prompting this young man's character, and in that instant fancied herself a detective of the human spirit. For the diamond-cut wrinkles above John's brow reminded her of Cynthia, who'd recently sprouted thick worry lines beneath the scar on her forehead, giving her the same kind of omniscient glare this young man had. Mildred couldn't help thinking of the early years when Cynthia wouldn't speak except to call out Brooke's name, and of course the scar had cemented the two girls further. Only Brooke had the power to soothe her sister, just as her presence seemed a tonic to John's melancholia.

In completing ourselves we look outside ourselves, Mildred thought. Tom was the most rational man she'd ever met while Mildred to this day remained a bundle of nervous ticks. A silent worrier, whenever her husband was more than a half hour late from work she stood at the front window pulling the curtains open and shut until he returned, and if Brooke missed her daily check-in, Mildred chipped the nail polish from her fingernails and methodically picked at her cuticles for hours. Oddly, these fears never materialized into action. Mildred Harrison was not the type to phone hospitals or local police stations, nor to hop on airplanes for that matter. But Kenny Zeller had frightened the daylights out of her, although now that she'd seen Brooke wasn't the strung-out mess she'd expected, Mildred certainly didn't want to burden her beleaguered daughter with her amateur soul-sleuthing. Even if she'd tried explaining her insights, Mildred would have talked herself into a circle. Was it the boy's similarity to Cynthia that bothered her? His brooding presence? The way he couldn't seem to get comfortable in his chair? It was all terribly confusing and the wine had glazed a fog over the room, if not behind her eyes. Mildred reached for her water and took a long sip. Through the glass she saw John Strong's face floating amid the condensed droplets and imagined him drifting into the mist over the Hollywood hills like an image immortalized on a stained glass panel. Only Brooke kept him here on earth.

The wine had obviously eclipsed her brain waves as Mildred's thoughts of heaven and earth were usually confined to the Sunday morning services they'd been skipping more and more unless Brooke was with them; it was one of the family rituals Mildred thought imperative to maintain. She wanted to keep home familiar to Brooke. That night in L.A., however, she determined she would return regularly to church, and she wouldn't drink as much, for she surmised it could have been the alcohol that conferred such ethereal substance on the young heartthrob. After all, he was simply a young man trying to impress his girlfriend's mother, a feat he would have accomplished without clearing the dishes and perking a pot of decaf while the two women sat at the dining room table. "See, he's a good one," Brooke said.

"He seems sad."

"No, he's just really deep."

Mildred squeezed Brooke's wrist and smiled. "I'm so happy for you, honey," she said, deciding that her daughter was riding an eighth of one-hundred-percent-pure love. (It did have a way of killing the appetite.) She remembered years ago telling her parents Tom was the smartest man she'd ever met, despite her family's concerns that he was too old, too set in his ways, but Mildred, secure in the knowledge that Tom was it—her one and only—would not back down. A whiff of nostalgia for the steadfast girl she'd once been circulated, a longing trans-muted into empathy in Brooke's presence. But Kenny's words still nagged, and Mildred felt her chest cave in and breath shorten as she summoned the strength to speak. "Brooke," she said. "There's something I have to ask you . . . about the . . . incident."

"Oh, Mom, it's all lies. I only had a couple of drinks. I was at a party."

"But Kenny said there were drugs."

"Drugs!" Brooke stood up and slammed her chair against the table, and Mildred felt her heart collapse.

She shouldn't have said anything. She'd read about withdrawal, how it could make one irritable and paranoid. "I'm sorry," she said.

"That's the most ridiculous thing I've ever heard!" Brooke shouted.

"What is, my angel?" said John Strong, who'd entered the room with a silver tray.

"Kenny told her I had drugs."

"You? Why, that is preposterous." John put down the tray and, as he set out three mugs and poured the decaf from a glass pot, said, "Listen, Mildred, I can barely even get this one to take an aspirin unless she calls the doctor first. Trust me, one thing we don't have to worry about with our girl here is drugs."

"But Kenny said—"

"Oh, I bet I can tell you exactly what Kenny said. Milk and sugar?"

"A bit of each," Mildred nodded, and he stirred her cup before sliding it in front of her, explaining that the whole thing had been a ploy and he'd like to get his hands on Kenny Zeller for taking it this far.

"This is the cocaine decade," he deadpanned. "Over one hundred billion served . . . But seriously, it's the drug that says you're rich and successful and a little bit daring, but not too much, understand? It's exactly what we need. All of those teen magazines are always talking about how good and wholesome she is, which is really the kiss of death when it comes to a career. There are only so many parts for nuns and virgins, you know what I'm saying?"

Though befuddled, Mildred nodded.

"Mom, you know I've been thinking about my next move." Brooke sat down at the table. John handed her a cup of black decaf. "I don't want to be on a soap forever. I've got too much to give."

"It's a dead-end job," John agreed. "We've got to get her on to the bigger and better, and anyone'll tell you it's all about the next thing. About image. Me, I don't have a problem with that. I've been a bad boy since day one, but come on, look at me. Do I look so *bad* to you?"

Mildred smiled. "I suppose not."

"I suppose not . . . Mildred, you're good. Okay, I admit it, I've got a past, but ever since I met Brooke I can't stop thinking about the future. Right now, the only thing that matters in my life is making her happy."

Reaching over and locking fingers with her beau, her eyes gleaming wet, Brooke said, "See, Mom, he's just the sweetest thing."

For the moment, watching her daughter and John coo affectionately, Mildred forgot all about Kenny and the cocaine. True, she was overwhelmed and still a bit discombobulated from the evening's events, but she was also overjoyed for Brooke and couldn't help imagining the future John had alluded to. There was no taming the pulse of young lovers; nobody knew this better than Mildred Harrison.

Later that night, as she rested her head on the spongy pillow in Brooke's guest room, Mildred hummed the following lines from a Harold Arlen tune, "We might have been meant for each other/To be or not to be, let our hearts discover," before drifting off into a wine-induced slumber. Yet a few hours later she awoke to a soundrack of old-time rock and roll thumping behind the wall next to her, accompanied by a louder, closer kind of keening. Like a woman crying at the top of her lungs, "I'm sorry, baby. I'm so, so sorry!" Or was it all part of a dream? The slurred syntax to her drowsy iconography—John Strong and a blonde (Brooke?) floating panel to panel in a stained glass scenario of Hollywood love.

It would be many months before Mildred remembered that dream, if in fact it had been a dream and not a premonition, for on the next morning she bolted quickly and happily out of bed, eager to sweep Brooke away from Los Angeles for a few weeks of R & R back in Blue Bell, P.A. Puzzling, though, was her insatiable craving for peanut butter.

DREAMS OF THE HOLY LAND

". . . ANOTHER DREARY DAY HERE IN CELL BLOCK 5248, coming to you live from the great city of New York. That's right, New York, New York. So nice they named it twice. I'd like to thank all of my intergalactic travelers for tuning in this morning, we've got a great show for you today, we'll be discussing the shelf life of powdered milk . . . Hey, hey, can you shut the fuck up up there! We're on the air!"

Can't play DJ with the fat lady masturbating. She's been in my empty top bunk since I got back from the laundry. I might have freaked if it had been the only time, if she'd been the first. Instead, I crawled underneath the covers and turned on my radio. I like to talk along, adding my own words.

The fat lady grunts.

"Ladies and gentlemen, pay no attention to the pig-bitch in heat. We have a special guest coming by later. I can't tell you her last name because she's in the 'program' and we're not supposed to say, but her first name is . . . no, let's just call her Anonymous Woman. She's been very busy lately with TV appearances, bene-fits, parties—you don't know the strings I had to pull to get her on the Lily S. Show."

"Spread 'em, lover!" the interloper screams. It's getting harder to ignore her. I pump up the radio.

"First the weather. It's cold today with patchy clouds, a low-pressure system moving over the Atlantic will make it feel like twenty degrees below zero. For all of you nonweatherites out there, that's colder than a witch's tit. Like being caught in the frozen food aisle in shorts and a tank top."

"Oh yeah, yeah! That's it, baby!"

"Hey, fuck off!" I throw off the covers, anger steaming from my nostrils. The pig-bitch groans. This means war.

I stand up, fists tightened at my sides, and there she is. A blob with eyeballs huge and fiery. This demon masturbator. Her arms unfurl like a great ape, the folds of skin jiggling above her pubes. Fascinating, like ridges on a volcano. As much as I want to turn away I'm amazed she can do this in front of me without an ounce of shame. She's a freak of nature; the audience will love it, they're big into freaks. But her screams, her moany stroke-talk and sleepy sort of whimpering, remind me of crybaby Blair. I'm going back in time, an interplanetary leap courtesy of stereophonic sound. "Ladies and gentlemen, we are floating in the arms of unconsciousness . . ."

I fall backwards, my arms curled around my body, traveling Blairward. We're in her house. A head cold makes her cheeks glow and she's got her hair wrapped in a clean white towel. She carries her medicine in a sifter because it's brandy. The only cure for the common cold, she says. I take the glass from her and set it on the side table, turn out the big light so we can see the tiny green Statue of Liberty glowing across the room. Like an ancient queen, Blair leans against the headboard, the two Persians, Grace and Marilyn, at her feet. She pats the bed with her palm and smiles. I dive inside and we're giggling; the sheets so soft, her body so warm. She turns me on my stomach, tickling me, blowing raspberries into the hollow above my cheeks. I'm laughing so hard I can't breathe. I call out for her to stop, which she does, eventually, flipping me over and staring. She takes my right hand in between the two of hers and massages my palm and fingers. *You have such lovely little hands, Lillian.*

The demon screams, "Yeah, fuck, fuck . . . fuck!"

I stay with Blair, feeling the quickness of her heart as she presses my hands above her breasts. She says she needs me. A knot of fear slips down my throat. To be needed is a big responsibility. I move my lovely little hands down to her nipples and squeeze, licking the tips.

"Yesssss, oh yes!"

Someday we'll leave it all behind, she says, just as soon as she quits her job. She's had it with flying. The soul wasn't meant to move so quickly. She says she needs me, says she loves me, says she'll take care of me. Overwhelmed by the warmth, the softness, I nestle my head into her breasts. She says *ahhhhh!* I shut my eyes and suck, suck, suck, feeling her press against me, warm all over, giggling and calling for . . . *díos?* I look up from her spit-soaked nips and she's Mimi.

"Motherfucker, cocksucker . . . oh, yes, yes, yes!!!"

Amplified, the pig-bitch snares my attention. I feel her collapse on my top bunk, a sonic boom that shakes the entire bed. Her leg hangs over the side. I imagine twisting until it unscrews from the rest of her body, then wrapping it around the back of my neck, the flesh of a rare animal. It tugs so tightly I can't breathe. She's strangling me. My obit will read, "Snuffed by the lumpy limb of a pig-woman."

I stand up to get a closer look. She is phenomenal. A mountain of skin upon skin upon skin. I can't stop staring. She flips over on her side, eyebrows fluttering as if she knows the sex sounds get me every time. "Ladies and gentlemen," the mountain laughs, and I shrink so small I can see my entire figure in her eyes like muddy ponds. "Get your spaceships ready," she says, "we're going for a ride in the sky."

Then, abruptly, in a move more cacophonous than swift, this odd woman jumps down from the top bunk and stands in front of me, stalwart on her hefty legs, topped by her barrel of a stomach and too-small head. I want to scream, Get the fuck out of here! It's my room! But when I open my mouth it's as if someone's sliced out my tongue. This woman in front of me with her papier-mâché face and greasy hair is so stereotypical of women in prison I'm sure I've called her to me the way I've gotten used to bringing you and Blair and everyone else inside. My mind has become a transporter. I am the radio.

Loosening up a bit, I let the rage shift to a different part of my body, the part I can't control. The woman kneels in front of me with her hands flat against my stomach. Her touch is gentle though hardly tentative. Before I know what's happening she's unbuttoning my pants, and I'm throwing all of my weight against her shoulders—but I don't usually do it like this. I struggle a bit. She is the biggest fucking woman I've ever seen, and now that we're both standing she's got me pinned against the wall. "What have you got to say for yourself?" she shoves her fist into my face as if she's got a microphone. I turn the other cheek. With her free hand she grabs between my legs, lightly brushing her thumb against me. This is not supposed to happen. Nobody but Mimi touches me there. And not too often. "Your audience is waiting . . ." she whispers, and I am paralyzed. "Not such a big-shot after all, huh?"

She goes down and I bite my cheek, fearing the whole of it: her tongue, my cunt, the electric clash of lips. A complete waste of time. It never works for me, the lovey-dovey cunt worship most girls get off on. Mimi says I need it rough, the way girl cats need to be ambushed and attacked. That was how she took my virgin pussy.

So I stand there pretending because it's easier than explaining. I think of Mimi and the way she holds me with her thumb and first two fingers . . . *hers*; Blair and what I'd like to go back and show her now that I know what is supposed to happen in a double bed, and, of course, you're watching—it's what you do—as I float off in my silver suit and glass helmet.

I am the best disc jockey in outer space. An audience of zillions tunes in for my interview with Anonymous Woman, who's just buzzed into the studio. Images accost me like shooting stars, my cohost announcing them as if we were playing *The $25,000 Pyramid* (in space): screwdrivers, arugula, shiny black cars, men with beards, electrolysis, split-level houses, orange pill vials, French manicures on toenails, big yellow teeth, Bombay martinis, power suits, sunglasses, red onions, dusty pocket mirrors, thick calves, sashimi deluxe, Chanel N° 5, bronze eye shadow, loud belly laughs, tennis skirts, peppermint chewing gum, hair cream, and cigarettes, thousands of cigarettes . . . ultralights.

Ding, ding, ding . . . things that remind me of my mother!

We have a winner.

"Yes!" I shout, and it fools the fat lady, who falls back on the concrete. I pull up my pants and dive into bed, drowning under the sheets, more depressed than before. She's ruined the Lily S. Show. But who cares? Tomorrow is another day. Only I'm stuck in a world of todays. You wrap your arms around me, whispering, *It's okay, Lillian, I'm still here.*

YOU'D BEEN CALLING ME TO THE SILVER SHORES of the Pacific for months before Jack finally contacted a writer friend of his in Los Angeles who'd arranged for Edie and me to visit the set of *World Without End.* Apparently, that was no easy feat. The show had been getting tons of press since your Jaymie Jo Rheinhart started moving things. It began with common objects: pens, notebooks, plates, dishwashing liquid, skateboards, bikes, backpacks. A little concentrated headspace and the right theme music was all it took to lift them, spin them, make them dance, or hurl them against the wall, depending on her mood. Alex Rheinhart thought it was cute until she started levitating people, namely him. Of course, he blamed her boyfriend, calling it some sort of voodoo magic.

Edie said the whole show was racist for making Alex Rheinhart say that on television, but it gave Jaymie Jo the opportunity to reaffirm her love for Max, even though everyone in Foxboro disapproved more than ever, and their anger seemed so real, the way it might happen in any town in America, and I said so. "Of course their racism is real," Edie'd lectured during one of our *World* marathons. We'd watch the whole week in one sitting. She always seemed as into it as I was, but that day she stopped the tape. "Let me tell you something, Lil," she said, "you wouldn't believe the stares I get even when I'm with the Ayatollah. And he's just light brown. People are so racist they don't even know it."

"That's exactly what I'm saying," I argued, quoting a story I'd read in *Soap Opera Digest.* "Maybe if there were more interracial couples on television, people would accept it more. Jaymie Jo's being courageous. She's a role model."

"Jaymie Jo? You say that with a straight face. *Jaymie Jo.* See, this is why everything is so fucked up. Jaymie Jo is not *real*! Her boyfriend's not real. The whole town of Foxboro doesn't even exist, but for some reason this fake person in this fake town is more important than me and the Ayatollah walking into the diner even though everyone's staring like they want to rip our faces off? Like they've got some god-given right. Why is that? Huh . . . why?"

"'Cause this town sucks. At least on *World* people talk about it."

"Voodoo? You call that talking. It's a reference and a stereotype. Please . . . that shit pisses me off."

"So write a letter."

"A letter?" She sprung off my bed. "Hey, that's a friggin' A-number-one idea, Lil. Get out your book. We'll draft a letter."

Of course, we weren't the only ones, although our letter was really cool and had references to Martin Luther King, Nelson Mandela, and the lyrics of Bob Marley (my idea, thank you very much). We knew somebody must have read it when Alex Rheinhart apologized to Max for the voodoo thing, and they joined forces to help find a priest to cure Jaymie Jo from the demons that were making her vomit and speak in tongues, and Edie said, see, you were nothing but a pawn for the producers, and you hated her for it. You were shocked when she wanted to come with me to L.A. You never trusted her, but what could I do after she'd begged and pleaded. "My brother's out there, we'll have a blast," she said. "I hear California guys are really progressive. They don't eat meat and they grow their own dope and shit."

Okay, maybe we had different ideas about the trip, but I had to admit I was happy she wanted to come. It would be fun having someone to hang out with and might make the flight easier. Ever since the space shuttle exploded, I'd been more afraid of flying than ever. You could never be sure they'd checked all the equipment, or what if the pilot hadn't slept for days? And then there were hijackers . . . The more I thought about it, Blair's fear of flying really made sense. I swiped a handful of Valium from Nancy and swallowed one before she dropped us at the airport. Walking through the metal detectors was easier than ever, slower and more dreamy. I kept thinking I saw Blair and kept working up the nerve to say hello, say look, I'm using your book, say why'd you leave, but up close it was just another blonde with wings.

By the time we touched ground in Los Angeles, I could barely remember strapping in and taking off. I think they let us drink screwdrivers. We stumbled out of the gate at LAX and were met by a man in a chauffeur's hat and faded jean jacket who held up a piece of cardboard with our names scratched in magic marker. He was Chuck, he said. Gustave Monde's right hand. We all smiled as he carried our bags out of the airport and into his car, a Lincoln Continental. It was classic—Edie and me sitting like movie stars on the velvety backseat watching Los Angeles saddle up through the smoky windows. I'd been there once before with Jack and Nancy when I was a kid but couldn't remember anything beyond the Chinese theatre and Disneyland. Tourist stuff. This time I had a purpose and Edie was lucky I'd brought her along for the ride. Of course she was too cool to show it, shuffling her cat-eye sunglasses and sighing in her this-is-so-blasé fashion as we traversed the green hills headed for a place called Los Feliz where Gustave's aunt owned a place on a block of palm trees and stucco houses that made me think time had stopped in the early sixties. Just before the hippies descended. Even the cars looked tired and clunky.

I half expected to find Lucy and Ethel sipping coffee in the kitchen after Chuck fit the key into the front door and we dropped our bags on the couch with the plastic covers, careful not to bump into the piano in the center of the room. Chuck walked over to it and flicked a switch. The theme from *The Sting* came out on its own. "That's my favorite thing about this place," Chuck smiled, so goofy, his blond moustache twitching. Edie raised her upper lip, like, You dork. I watched the keys drop up and down, touched by invisible fingers. I'd never seen a player piano in real life. It was like watching colors miraculously appear on a canvas.

Chuck said to make ourselves at home. He had to get back to work, but Gustave would be by soon. Left to ourselves, Edie and I set about inspecting the army of cartoonlike statuettes and odd knickknacks—the marionette in red, white, and blue knickers hanging from the ceiling, an old street lamp next to the original poster from *Snow White and the Seven Dwarfs,* walls lined with African masks and oil paintings with three-dimensional gold frames, shelves crammed with hundreds of tiny colored bottles, small ceramic plates, crystalline animals, frayed black-and-white photos, silver figurines. Gustave's aunt, the legendary French gossip columnist, Filomina Leroux, was keeper of the most bizarre stuff I'd ever seen. The kitchen was awash in sand art sculptures, tiny Civil War soldiers, old appliances, plastic cups from McDonald's, gardening tools, and a supply of packaged seeds to last a lifetime. Edie lifted a white helmet with the nuclear power symbol from the coat rack. "I've never seen so much junk in my life," she said.

"Jack said it was like a museum."

"The museum of junk." She put on the helmet and pointed out the kitchen window. "Hey, look! Frenchie really hooked us up."

In the backyard was a swimming pool the same pale green as the Buick with its top down that I'd spotted in the garage. Edie had seen it, too. She said wouldn't it be great if we found the keys and went cruising, and I faked enthusiasm, but over my dead body was that going to happen. She was trouble in cars.

Outside, Edie kicked off her boots and dipped her feet into the water. I sat back on a rusty lounge chair, its plastic strips so stretched and frayed they must have held more than a few bodies in their day. Maybe even celebrities. Jack said Filomina Leroux had run with the movie star crowd back in the fifties, back when the president himself was a leading man and a liberal. He'd even headed up the actors' union. I imagined him, a handsome guy sipping piña coladas by the pool with the stunning foreign journalist, unaware his journey would one day land him in the Oval Office. Life suddenly seemed long and full of hope.

When Gustave showed up a couple of hours later, Edie and I had barely moved. "You are enjoying Aunt Fifi's house," he said, as if his simply stating the fact made it so. Gustave had a heavy-duty God complex. Jack said this was a good thing for a director, and Gustave did look a little like Jesus before his long brown hair started receding in front. A few months ago, he'd cut it short and started wearing a lot of baseball caps. Now he looked like he played for the Mets.

Gustave rushed us out the door for an early dinner at an

Italian restaurant in Hollywood. "I have less than two hours to spare," he'd said. "I rearranged all things today just to see my favorite girl." He pinched my cheek, and I blushed. For some reason, Gustave liked me.

As soon as we sat down at the restaurant, Gustave ordered for all of us in Italian, then told us about the PSA he was shooting— a national campaign against product tampering starring a famous drug cop from TV. Nice to direct a spot with a mission, Gustave said. For it was as evil as planting a bomb in an airport, this poisoning of random bottles of aspirin. Worse than Russian roulette. Gustave put his forefinger against his head. "If you are putting a gun to your head, you want to know it, eh?"

"What's he like? That TV guy," Edie said.

"Oh, he is a dynamite shithead."

"I hear he's going bald."

"Bald, sure, who isn't? But he has holes in his skin in addition. This is a problem because we are all working for free. The make-up is very bad."

"He has holes in his skin?" Edie practically spit up her water, and Gustave told a story about another famous actress who'd had her lips injected with Vaseline so she could become the spokesperson for a cosmetics company. The executives wanted her lips big and shiny, as if their only purpose was to be kissed. Edie kept shrieking and nudging me, but I couldn't fake interest. All through the meal, I kept thinking of our meeting, you shaking my hand, a knowing twinkle in your baby blues, saying we had so much to talk about now that I'd finally come to the Coast. You tell me about the stress of speaking in tongues on television, problems with your boyfriend, the controversial interview in *People* where you said you were actively looking for the right movie role, the next step. I divulge my latest philosophy of negative space. You say I am wise.

Edie smacked my shoulder and said something about dessert. I ordered tiramisu. She laughed at Gustave's joke: *What kind of wood floats? Natalie Wood.*

You invite me back to your apartment for lunch so we can listen to CDs. The new girl in music-video land sings about love.

You tell me you are tired but must read through next week's scripts. I offer you one of the Valium I swiped from Nancy.

"Earth to Lillian, *dee, dee, dee* . . . Earth to Lillian, come in please," Edie said, her eyes dipping toward my tiramisu with a lone fork print in the custard. "I've never seen you leave dessert. Are you on a diet or something?"

"Hah-hah," I glared. I hated when she interrupted my thinking. Her fork swung toward my plate, and I grabbed her hand. "Don't touch it!"

"You're not eating it."

"Doesn't mean you can have it."

"You are such an only child!" We struggled until she dropped the fork. I sunk my spoon into the tiramisu and shoved a few monster scoops in my mouth, satisfied.

"Piglet!" Edie said.

I grunted.

"I mean it, you're disgusting. No wonder you can't—"

"Shut up!"

Gustave cleared his throat—loudly. We froze. He tugged the sleeve of his linen jacket to check his braided gold watch. "A wonderful meal," Gustave announced, as if he hadn't heard a word we'd said. One last sip of cappuccino before he ushered us out of the restaurant.

On the ride home I saw your face behind the wheel of every passing car. It didn't help that all the girls in California had straight blond hair like yours, and the landscape made me feel as if I'd been here a million times before. Los Angeles had to be the ultimate déjà vu. At a traffic light a Mexican boy was selling oranges. A group of punks flexed in leather and studs, a rainbow of spiked hair. Otherwise the streets were empty. But when Gustave took a deep reverent breath and in between the giant boulevards pointed out the Hollywood sign awakening at twilight, I felt as if I'd reached the promised land. My heart fluttered like a pulsing marquis.

I'd seen this place over and over again in my dreams. Sprawling hills and bright white lights, winding roads and limousines and theatres and movie stars all so close I could feel them rushing into me, cohesive yet abbreviated, like movie previews, but it was better than any film I'd ever seen, any place I'd ever been. It was a living dream.

Back at Aunt Fifi's, Gustave told us Chuck would arrive at nine the next day to take us to the TV studio. "Then you will come to my office," he said. "Or better, you go to Melrose for shopping. I have no more time tomorrow." He kissed Edie and me on both cheeks and I thought we were so lucky it was almost shameful. Gustave noticed and tapped the side of my head. "You carry everything in here, *oui?*" he said, and Edie snorted. As if it were unfathomable I had anything in me she didn't know about. "No, it is not a joke, she has a thousand other lives. A very old soul." He shrugged and kissed my forehead, and although Edie eyed me as if I'd crossed enemy lines, I loved Gustave for making me feel good about being a weirdo.

The minute he left she lifted the coffee can full of keys next to the refrigerator and dumped them out on the counter. All day she'd been dropping hints about driving the Buick so I'd taken precautions. I opened the refrigerator, empty 'cept for a six-pack of Tab, a few packages of coffee, some condiments, and pharmaceutical vials. "What are you looking for?" I played dumb.

"The keys, Einstein. I heard about a place to find guys but we have to drive."

"Neither one of us has a license."

"Your road test's in two weeks."

"Tell that to the California Highway Patrol."

"They're not even real cops, they're too pretty."

"You're thinking of the TV show."

"My brother told me about it . . . it's, like, where all the cool people go. He said he did the best crystal in his life there. The best crystal in his life, Lil. Think about it." She had maybe thirty keys set out on the table in front of her and was dividing them into subcategories by name and size. The table was like something you'd find in an old diner, Formica. Nancy'd had our kitchen counters smothered in it. She said it was good for hiding stains. And it was slippery. The keys slid from side to side as Edie shuffled them. A better friend might have said something, but it was a riot seeing her so determined. She looked up. "Why are you smiling?"

"I'm not."

"Jesus, Lil, what is it with you? You're not even trying. Here we are in the middle of Los Angeles, in a house all by ourselves, and sitting behind fucking door number one is a car! Think of the potential for life experience!"

"Okay, I can't take it," I said. "They're not there."

"What?"

"The keys."

She sighed. "You can sit here all night like a loser if you want, I've got places to go, people to meet, you know?"

"Just stating the facts."

"You are so selfish sometimes. Do you realize how much time I've devoted to you and your *problem*? And what have I gotten out of it? What have I seen? I'll tell you what I've seen: nothing. Absolutely nothing. *Nada*. Zilch. I don't even know why I put up with you."

"If it weren't for me, you wouldn't be here. We wouldn't be going to the TV studio!"

"Oh my god . . . you really came all the way out here to see a stupid soap opera, you really did. You're more fucked-up about this than I thought."

"Shut up!"

"She's not even real."

"Don't talk about her."

"I mean, it's one thing having all those posters up on your wall, but—"

"I'm not kidding, Edie, shut your fucking mouth!"

"Look at you, your cheeks are all red. What's the matter, did I insult your make-believe friend? Your little teen idol? You're such a baby."

The room exploded in colors. Throbbing monsters in front of me, slime oozing from the walls. Before I knew what was happening I'd swiped my arm across the Formica, and the keys flung out in every direction, ringing against appliances, knocking over statuettes, bouncing off the floor. Edie covered her head with both arms. "You fucking psychopath!" she screamed. I felt as if a snake had wrapped itself around my body, cutting off my breath and blood, and the kitchen was about one hundred degrees. I was sweating from every pore.

Air, I thought. I needed air.

I bolted out to the pool and sat down on my torn lounge chair, breathing deeply in the dark, calming myself to the fact that she would never find the car keys. Earlier, I'd seen them dangling in the ignition and nabbed them for safe keeping. No way was I letting anything come between you and me and tomorrow. You were right: bringing Edie along was a big mistake.

A few deep breaths later I jumped to the set tomorrow. You smile at me in the mirror as the woman dabs your cheeks with a cotton ball. Your eyelids flutter shut. Makeup always gets you sleepy . . .

The outdoor lights kicked on and Edie stepped outside sipping from a bottle of gin. She sat down on the lounge chair next to mine, her presence so big it was like sharing a beach towel with an elephant. I wished her away, but as usual she had other plans. She unrolled a plastic bag full of Ayatollah weed and loaded her silver pipe. On the surface of the swimming pool, I traced the movement of her hands, her hair, her face, as if I were creating a stencil. She was a phantom, like your reflection on my window. Somehow out here you seemed closer yet farther away. The elephant woman stood between us.

Edie put the pipe in her mouth and lit up, embers crackling with the scent of burnt chocolate. Marijuana was a sweet sort of high. It made me want to stick my fingers into a jar of honey and lick off every last drop. Laugh at the stupidest things. But making my point required I didn't take the pipe when Edie passed it. "Come on, you won," she said. "And you're a dirty little fighter, too."

Did she know I had the keys buried in the front pocket of my pants? No, she couldn't possibly, but the way she surveyed me when I turned my head I couldn't be sure. I could never be sure of anything with Edie and it drove me nuts. With her, I always felt as if the earth might crack open and suck me down below the way people out here were forever conscious of faultlines and Richter scales, because any minute the ground could start shaking for real. It seemed unfair that a place so magical could go down in a few minutes. Might as well be stoned.

I took the peace pipe from Edie and inhaled, trying to avoid eye contact. "Good girl," she said, her omniscience multiplied in the floodlights. She was larger than life and timeless, as if she'd been here back in the fifties with Aunt Fifi and the president. Of the two of us, I might have had the old soul, but she knew things beyond age and experience. I handed the pipe back and noticed she'd once again slipped on the hard hat with the nuclear power symbol. Settling into a fuzz-buffed mind bubble, I began to formulate a theory: Tough girls like Edie had a way of converting the things they knew into beauty. Like little nuclear reactors. Trouble was, when they went up it was big-time. The world still couldn't get a grip on the fallout from Chernobyl, and that explosion had been a couple of months earlier. On TV we watched people all over Europe say they were afraid to drink milk or eat raw vegetables, unsure how far the radiation had traveled. I imagined cancerous particles like tiny jet planes circling the Colosseum, the Eiffel Tower, and all those foreign boys Edie'd kissed on her trip, wondering which was worse: going up in a nuclear explosion or being sucked through a crack in the earth. Either way it was over immediately, like the space shuttle blowout, or opening the wrong bottle of aspirin and swallowing a poison pill. I felt worse for people living in the fallout, not knowing whether they'd been touched until it was too late. Death was easier sometimes.

Edie handed me the pipe again. It felt like a slab of hot metal in my palm. "Do you ever think about dying?" I said.

"All the time."

"Does it scare you?"

She took the pipe from me and lit up a few times before deciding it was played. Her decision always, when we started and finished anything. Knocking out the residue, she said, "Where I come from death is a beautiful thing."

"In Ohio?"

"How many times do I have to tell you, I'm from—"

"The planet Andromeda. Yeah, yeah . . ."

"See, this is exactly your problem, Lil. You refuse to believe, you won't visualize. If you can't see it, you can't be it. You know?"

She sounded so much like people on talk shows, so California, I burst out laughing. So did she, and within seconds we were hysterical, tears streaming down our cheeks. She turned to me, smiling so big I couldn't believe she was the same person who'd insulted us earlier. "Okay, Lil, now I've got something to show you," she said. "Are you ready for the bonus round?"

I nodded. As long as I had the car keys I was ready for anything. She emptied her pockets, and a cascade of cloudy orange vials and cardboard packages spilled out in front of her. We sifted through the ant hill, identifying what we could—blue capsules, little orange hearts, red dots, big codeine tablets, multicolored dots encased in plastic, but the best was a box that looked like it belonged in an old copy of *Life* magazine and said: *Quaaludes, from the makers of Maalox.* The name was a compression of the words *quiet* and *interlude.* Edie said it was the most beautiful thing she'd ever heard.

She pushed a couple of pills through the silver-and-plastic shield. They were huge and chalky and reminded me of the antacid tablets my grandfather sucked like candy. Edie dropped one in my palm. "I don't know," I said. "They're probably older than we are."

"No problem. I found them in the freezer."

"Okay," I said, and together we swallowed, chasing the pills with the bottle of gin Edie said she'd also discovered in the freezer, and I made a mental note to always check people's freezers as we sat back on our lounge chairs and soaked up the cool breezes of a California springtime. The scent of newly mown grass sifted in and out like a dab of well-placed cologne, soft gusts rustled through the leaves and sent a ripple of waves across the swimming pool. Goosebumps rose up my arms, and my mouth tasted salty, tangy, like blood. I realized I'd been gnawing at my lower lip for who knows how long, as hyped-up inside as the scenery was palmy outside. The damn drug was taking forever. "I don't feel anything," I said.

"Be patient."

"Maybe it's not working."

"Okay, let's eat another one," Edie said, and we swallowed once more, passing the bottle of gin back and forth. It shadowed in obscene shapes and sizes and made us giggle into convulsions out there by the pool in the foggy night and I found myself more content than I'd been just a few minutes before. My legs felt like Jell-O, jiggly but plastered to the chair, and everything inside me heated up, like I had a band of miners drilling inside my veins while outside the winds raised the hair on my limbs.

Everything was fine until you showed up. Floating fully clothed on the surface of the swimming pool, you beckoned me: *How could you, Lillian?*

I asked what's wrong, and your voice came charred with frustration.

You've given over again, and we must not delay. Do you have any idea how busy I am? How much prep time goes into a projectile-vomiting scene? What it takes to speak in tongues?

I said I was sorry.

I can't believe you'd come all the way out here to forsake me for this false god from the planet Andromeda. Somebody's been watching too much Star Trek.

I said it wasn't like that.

"Like what?" Edie said, and I flinched nervously. Turning to the pool I noticed you'd gone under. I looked back to Edie whose face had expanded into a giant balloon, this demonic raccoon with big purple lips, demanding: "What, Lil?" I was paralyzed. In escaping you'd grabbed one of my arms and were trying to pull me into the pool. I turned toward Edie, keeping my arm behind me so she couldn't see you. Didn't want to get her riled again, we'd been getting along so well. I told her I'd drifted off on a cloud, and she said she totally knew what I meant, and slowly, as we settled back into our chairs, I managed to disengage my arm from your grasp. It throbbed with pins and needles—somehow you'd stunned it.

A brittle wind brewed, and I offered to go inside for our jackets. Edie said no. The minute one of us left, she explained, the mood would change. And she was digging our mood even if I kept zoning out. So I sat shivering until we siphoned every last drop of gin through our chattering teeth, and Edie said it was time to go inside where she flicked the switch and hunkered down at the player piano, pretending to play *The Sting*, singing the notes as they rolled out perfectly . . . *da, da, da, da, da-da, da-da* . . . the ghostly marionette smiling over us in the dark shadows. I sat down next to Edie on the bench and watched her fingers move up and down along the keys without touching them.

She stood up in the middle of a line for another roll, a new song, but there was no other song, and she said that was really depressing—a piano that played only one song. She went for the on-off switch but it wouldn't budge and we shared a quick alarming stare before she started fiddling with it again, cursing the damn instrument and finally slamming the cover over the keys. The piano continued . . . *da, da, da, da, da, da* . . . *da, da, da, da, da, da!* . . . and we burst into giggles, writhing next to each other, her body so warm against mine. Every time one of us stopped the other would snort or hiccup and we would be off again until Edie said, look, and pointed to the marionette whose jaw bobbed up and down, laughing with us, controlled by invisible strings. We screamed and ran into Aunt Fifi's bedroom to take cover in the king-sized bed with its insanely bright floral covering.

I pulled back the blankets and dove underneath. Edie followed. Long past the point of communication, our laughter tapered into a few occasional grunts. My brain felt like I'd been shoved head first through a windshield and emerged a palpitating mess. Edie said some more pot would help the coming-down process. She leaned over me to get to the side table where she'd left the works, and I felt her heartbeat against my arm, her skin so warm the heat outside almost matched the burning inside, and I thought, That's love: a matching of inner and outer heat. Moonlight wormed through the window. Sheets rustled, we passed the metal pipe, sprawled across the giant bed the way Los Angeles sprawls through the hills. I wanted to sleep but was suddenly terrified. What if the Quaaludes were too old? Or they'd been tampered with? What if we never woke up?

Edie put a pillow in between her legs and moaned. "This bed makes me want to fuck."

"No shit, Sherlock."

"I don't get you, Lil. Don't you need it? Don't you even want to know what it's like?"

The quiver in her upper lip made me feel insignificant, tiny, static. Cymbals crashed in heavy-metal soundtracks. My body burned like an acid rash. Edie started monologuing about sex, her hips bumping up against that pillow. I burrowed under the covers where it was dark and tomblike. A bed to nurture a million deaths. My vision gone, I felt even smaller, a psychedelic dot trapped inside one of Nancy's diet capsules, playing footsie with my dotty friends until an invisible hand rips open our shield and we spill into a colorful waterfall, like a sequence from a Gustave Monde commercial, all of us struggling to keep afloat before bouncing out of sight, never to fulfill our mission as an appetite suppressant. Alone, away from the other dots, I was useless.

I slithered further inside the bed and stumbled upon Edie's legs. She shaved them almost every day. Her arms, too. Guys were lucky with her, she was so smooth and had big tits. It was an added bonus. One I'd never know. This must be what it's like at the center of the earth, I thought. The air hot and stuffy and you can't have what's lying next to you. On the verge of suffocating, I threw off the covers. Edie's knees clamped the pillow, her hips engulfing its cotton tip. She pushed her kneecaps against my stomach, her skin translucent in the moonlight. It took everything I had not to hug her like I'd hugged Blair in that other big bed, on the other coast, but I sensed she didn't want to hug. I flipped over on my back and stared at the waves in the stucco ceiling. Sleeping with Edie was nothing new, we did it all the time, but something was different in Los Angeles. I could feel the city pumping through her, a Vaseline hypodermic. "Hey Lil," she said. "Can you hear me? You're not even listening, you shit . . . turn around."

I climbed up next to her, and she looked bigger and shinier than all the injected lips in Hollywood. "It's like swimming," she said, and I couldn't recognize her voice. She was starting to sound like Blair, her drunk-talk. "It's like flying through a warm, salty ocean"—her right leg inched over my hip, the other side of the pil-low rubbing against my crotch—"like flying"—with her free hand she pulled the sheets over us again and tightened her body against the pillow, pressing it into me—"or pushing into another world"—her hips bucked—"and if you're stressed or pissed off or something, you just push harder"—she jammed into me, legs moving faster, and it was difficult to breathe, like sucking down smog.

We tightened together, connected by the pillow, and it felt so good, the two of us bumping together in that colossal bed as she whispered words that no longer made sense. Everything around me twitched and throbbed and flashed as I locked onto her rac-coon eyes and shivered, she looked so much like a vampire or witch or Satan lover—all the things I'd heard about her before we'd met, all the things that DID . . . NOT . . . EXIST, no mat-ter how she swallowed me like a psychedelic dot. I buried my face in her sweaty neck. She threw her arms around my shoulders and moaned so loudly it sent me into a flush of convulsions before I drifted into the silvery cotton sea.

That night I dreamed of giant metal hangers sliding up and down mile-long racks of clothing. Opening my eyes to the glittery streams of day I saw a ghostly Edie wearing a sleeveless black dress down to her ankles.

She floated toward me, her hair pinned up and long white neck exposed. I swear I saw vampire marks and blood. No, those were Hollywood thoughts. But there was a blemish on her neck, a small blot that recalled her face in the moonlight. My stomach sank, and I thought I might throw up.

She's still Edie, I reminded myself, still my best friend who at the very worst might be from the planet Andromeda. Before now it had never occurred to me to ask whether she'd come in peace. Mermaidlike, she slithered onto the bed and propped herself next to me. I stretched out my arm to touch her, to make sure I wasn't dreaming, but she flinched as if I might contaminate her. "Rise and shine," she said. "We've got work to do."

Then as quickly as she'd come she slid from the bed into the walk-in closet. I pulled the covers up to my neck and tried to steam the night from my brain. Edie backed out of the closet with a dress in each hand. They were for me to try on. "If we're supposed to be VIPs," she said, "we have to play the part. Now tell me, which dress do you like?" I couldn't answer. My jaw felt as wobbly as the spooky marionette's. Beneath the covers, the fingers of my right hand slipped down my stomach. "Fine, leave it to me—as usual. I like this one." She held up a dress with blue sequins and ostrich feathers. "She's just like my mom, she's got fat clothes and skinny clothes. Of course the skinny clothes are nicer, but you can forget about those, most of them wouldn't even fit me." Fat clothes, skinny clothes, fat clothes, skinny clothes . . . If you repeated anything over and over again it sounded religious. I pushed the back of my head further into the pillow, my fingers dug inside my underwear.

Edie dropped the dresses on the floor and sighed. Hand on her hip, looking like a lost cousin of the Addams Family, she said, "What's the matter *now*?"

"Nothing. Can we get stoned?"

"Not until we're out of wardrobe," she smiled. "Jeez, Lil, when did you become such a burnout? Where was I?"

"My head feels like I spent the night in a boxing ring."

"Poor baby," she said, thighs leaning into the foot of the bed. I pushed my fingers against my crotch, hard. She stood frozen, staring in a way that made me think she knew what I was doing down there. She was smiling, too, as if she were controlling my fingers the way she'd conjured sounds out of the piano I could still hear playing faintly. The same bars over and over again. Like a bad dream. Or insanity.

I threw off the covers and snubbed Edie's dresses for my own trip to the clothing bin. No way was I wearing ostrich feathers! Edie looked forlorn, the end of a long line of salesladies who lost commissions the minute they tried to get me into a dress. Nancy'd grown so weary of explaining that she gave me a credit card. I'd been buying my own clothes for years. "The fat clothes are on the right!" Edie shouted.

"Fuck you very much."

"Just stating the facts," she mocked me.

I plowed my hands through the fancy dresses and jackets. Never in my life had I seen so many different textures, such sheer and shimmering fabrics. The effect when combined with the early morning sun was almost blinding. Apparently Edie wanted me walking into that studio looking like a goddamn Christmas tree, when I knew you would expect me to be sophisticated and worldly and wise. I'd been through practically the entire fat rack before I found a herringbone skirt and matching jacket that belted at the waist like a trench coat. I imagined myself in the outfit, a war correspondent in a foreign country. Someone serious.

I backed out of the closet and held up the jacket for Edie. "Bo-ring!" she sang, but I stepped into the skirt which was a pain to zip up the side. My pink kneecaps poked out like shrunken heads. Edie put the pipe in my mouth and lit up. While I smoked she kneeled over the trunk at the foot of the bed and found a transparent black scarf. She wrapped it around her head and came up behind me in the mirror, her chin peeping over my shoulder and black polished fingernails clinging to my hips. "I wouldn't have thought it but it's okay," she said, although together we were a mixed metaphor, the war correspondent and vampire.

She turned me around, slowly running her index finger down the back of my thigh, and I liked what I saw. Rounded calves heading into an upside down V, the slit saying, *come a little bit closer, not that close; closer, not that close; closer . . .* And in that moment, watching the muscles in my lower legs expand and contract, I felt as if Edie had given me passage to a secret colony. So I trusted her with my bare calves and correspondent's clothing and believed her when she said I looked good in the outfit. She knew about these things; she was a nuclear reactor.

I AM SAD TODAY. Reading about the secret war in Nicaragua. If what they're saying is true, the president and his Contras should be jailed one hundred times over. Only he can't seem to remember any of it and if he doesn't remember it then it couldn't have happened. Memory, imagination, it's a jungle in there.

I feel bad for the Contras, fighting a war nobody will own up to. At least they can congratulate themselves privately. It's okay to kill in the name of freedom, but not for love.

Remember, what I write is *circumspect*. Isn't that a great word? It's one of those SAT words that sounds like the opposite of what it is, bottled-up and overly cautious. I hear a whirlpool of risks and rumors spinning around the *cum* in the middle, and it *should* be in the middle. Everything at its core is about sex.

Ever since I told Mimi about the fat lady in my cell, she's been making me wear a plug up my butt. Two condoms wrapped around the thick stub of a carrot. To get it out I have to yank it by the dental floss she's fixed to the end and left hanging from my body like a wimpy tampon string. I removed it the first day to shower, and while soaping up my ass started burning like crazy, as if it had lost its core. That damn plug had given it life. Without it, I felt abandoned. I ran back to my cell and reinserted the thing with a glob of lard I'd swiped from the kitchen.

She's been waiting for me to mess up, Mimi. Deliciously anticipating the moment she pulls down my pants and finds the string has disappeared. But I won't give in without a fight. Not even at night when she forces me down on the bed, asking whether I've been good or bad, if she'll have to throw me to the she-wolves. Going out, the carrot feels like a big fast dump. Next comes the throbbing, her gloved hand on the back of my thigh, the woolen blanket scratching my neck and chin. One by one she fills me with the fingers of her left hand. Her tattooing hand. It takes everything I have not to scream. I'm too feisty, she says, always repeating her words in Spanish as if we were playing it for a Telemundo soap. As if she's a Contra or something.

She fucks me like she's funded by the CIA.

She fucks me like she's got the whole world in her hands.

She fucks me because she can, whenever she wants, and there's nothing I can do about it.

I have not shit for three days. Nor have I been eating. At meals I take bites and spit the half-chewed particles into tiny rectangular napkins. The thought of swallowing food is repulsive. I don't deserve to eat as long as I'm wearing Mimi's plug. I only allow myself water and orange juice made from concentrate, the kind that's full of pulp and still tastes bitter. Jack used to squeeze oranges in the juicer at our summer house. He would stand over the glossy white sink in his shorts and sneakers, bare ankles peeking above nylon and leather. A casual guy, fun-loving beyond the convention of socks. He always squeezed my glass of orange juice first.

I say this now, circumspect. You of all people should know that one in the flurry of a public *imbroglio* (another kick-ass SAT word, though this one means exactly what it should) cannot be too cautious. I have reason to believe someone's been stealing my notes and smuggling them to the newspapers. How else would they know the things they know? The real question is why should I care? It's not like I have a life anymore, thanks to you. If only you'd listened. Then we wouldn't have to rely so heavily on hypotheticals.

When I see Piper, one of the few women guards, I slip my yellow legal pad into the slit I'd carved in the foam pillow with the sharpened plastic of a Bic. At school I used rollerballs. The better choice for drawing while I was supposed to be taking notes or listening or doing whatever it is regular kids do in school. The art teachers loved me, though the shrinks say they should have discerned my foxy temperament from the way I bent and stretched my women. Picasso had to deal with the same shit. Always slammed for distorting his women, and he never killed one of them. At least not off-canvas.

Piper unlocks my cell and cuffs me, saying I have a visitor. A current hurls through my stomach, bloated from constipation yet growling as if I'd swallowed a rodent. Nerves have a way of loosening my sphincter, but luckily I'm clogged by the stub of a carrot. There is sudden comfort in this thought. I am guarded by Mimi's charms just I was shielded by you.

We make the long walk through the cell blocks, cold today, like a train platform in winter, and quiet as Christmas. I am calm until I see the visitor's list. Nancy's perfect cursive. The room goes blurry. I double over in pain. Anonymous woman has finally come. "You got a problem?" Piper asks.

I can't speak, can't get beyond the slicing through my stomach, though I manage to nod no, no problem. She removes the cuffs and frisks me 'cause I'm still in pants. Not a real criminal yet. I fall forward, blurt out: "I have to use the bathroom!"

"Now?"

I nod.

Piper rolls her eyes. "You better not be messing with me, sugarplum." She flags down another guard to take the group downstairs and leads me to the bathroom. I barely make it inside before vomiting orange pulp and saliva into the sink. My head spins. I run the tap water, flushing my liquids down and out into the river where the gun that killed you still lies. Amazing things can wash away so easily. I try to drink but it's too painful. Instead I stick my nose under the cold water and snort from its stream. At first I can't breathe, then I want to sneeze. Finally, a few soothing drops slip down the back of my throat.

Piper knocks. "Don't you want to see your mother?" I don't respond. "Damn, girl, you are getting on my last nerve today. This is what I get for being the good guy, they take advantage . . ."

I splash a few handfuls of water on my face and walk outside.

"Okay, Cinderella, time for the ball," says the guard, who thinks she's a comedian. All the way to the elevator and down into the visitor's room, she cracks herself up.

The doors open revealing the usual scene in the pit. Family, lovers, friends. I spot Nancy fiddling with a cigarette. Her hair looks shorter, hiked up with mousse and stylish, and she's wearing tinted glasses. Seeing her I am instantly six years old and I've slipped off my grandmother's roof in the Bronx. They have to call an ambulance. I am lying on the grass surrounded by my grandmother, my grandfather, other kids, and a couple of paramedics when Nancy crawls out of her car. She doesn't hug me. She barely even looks at me. As if she's mortified I had the stupidity to fall off a roof. I blank out.

As I approach the table I see my mother's upper lip shake. A vital thing. She lights a cigarette. I sit down across from her and pick up the pack of ultralights. "Can I have one?"

"You smoke?"

"I used to steal them from you."

She nods. "I guess I knew."

A ring of red lipstick clings to her filter making it feel like home, and at home we do not talk to each other. We smoke silently, elbows on the table, cigarettes teetering between the first two fingers of our right hands, our inhale-exhale motions in tandem. It's scary how much we resemble each other. Both small-shouldered with chunky hips and thighs, hers more tethered and toned; both redheads, though I'm the natural right down to my white streak in front, which seems to have gone whiter since I've been in here. In the high fluorescents it even looks gray. Odd for my age, but I've always felt older than the numbers say.

Nancy smashes her cigarette into the gold cardboard ashtray and asks how they're treating me. I say okay and joke that it's probably like rehab only *with* drugs. She doesn't laugh. I guess there's no comparing our incarcerations. She tries to light up again but is too jittery. It's as if she's thumb wrestling with her lighter. "Dammit!" she says, and crushes the cigarette between her fingers. Tobacco shavings fall over the table like soiled confetti. I'll be spending New Year's Eve in jail.

Breathing through my nose, I feel the cold water slip down my throat, no less a talisman than the carrot in my ass. I shift positions to make sure it's still there. Nancy taps her fingers on the table. The lighting is obnoxious. Looking out I can barely see the other faces, each involved in their own thirty-minute dramas, hazy like the city in summertime, when the living was easy and Jack squeezed me fresh orange juice.

I turn back to Nancy and light a cigarette for her. She nods no as if my igniting the damn stick had tainted it, as if it were another damn competition. "Go on," I say. "Take it."

She gives in, sucking once from the filter before setting it down in the ashtray. "I'm drinking too much coffee these days," she says, exhaling deeply. "It's my only addiction—well, that and these. If there's any justice in the world I'll get clean and die of lung cancer. Oh well, everything at its own pace. Its own time. It's eighty-four days I'm clean, Lily; eighty-four long grueling days. What do you think of that? No, don't tell me what you think, I don't know if I can handle it yet. I'm not sure what I'm supposed to do; I mean, we were so young when we got married, so responsible, and let me just say it was like that for everyone around us. I always told you the hippies were a myth, we were the reality. Both of us struggling through school and with a kid, it's like we were born old. We just kept thinking if we did everything before we turned thirty we could relax, slow down a bit, but let me tell you, you get used to things really quickly. Do you know what I mean?"

I nod, a bit uncomfortable with this monologue. Only she won't stop. It's as if she's a talking machine, a jukebox packed with anonymous lingo instead of songs. All of the phrases she's been pumping into her letters these last few months. One day at a time. You only live once. Bottomed out. There but for the grace of god go I. When she says god, she doesn't mean the big G or any of his prophets. In anonymous-land they call it your higher power, but even this dogs Nancy. If there is any such thing, it resides within, she says. Eastern philosophy understands this. She's thinking of checking out Buddhism.

"You can't just become a Buddhist," I say.

"Why not?"

"Because you already have a religion."

"Oh no I don't, I never asked for that one. Nobody ever said to me, 'What religion do you want to be? It's your choice.' You're the one who had the choice."

"Some choice."

"We always wanted you to choose, when you were old enough."

"You said it was all bullshit. What kind of choice is that?"

"This is exactly what I mean, Lily. You have to learn these things for yourself. Took me almost forty years to understand this, but you're lucky, you're still young. And you've got all the time in the world."

"Thanks . . . thanks for reminding me."

"I'm just being honest. All we've got now, Lily, is honesty, right? Do you want to ask me anything? Go ahead, I'll tell you anything. Just ask me."

Why is it whenever anyone says ask me anything I can't think of a single thing?

Nancy waits.

I am anxious, on the spot. Two-dimensional, I could slide right through the space between the chair and table. Slip away. Nancy gives up the wait. She says she and Jack had it all but some-how that wasn't enough. She says she was depressed since child-hood and learned to self-medicate. Who is this woman? I want my snide, sharp-as-manicured-nails mother to joke about the food in rehab, tell me all they served was Wonder Bread, creamed corn, squares of red gelatin. I want to watch her dip into her pill vial, sit down in front of the vanity, and when I tell her I'm going to marry Blair she says okay, sure, whatever, as if the dream of every twelve-year-old girl in America is to marry the drunk stewardess next door. Frame it as question, I tell myself. Ask her why she never once mentioned Blair's name, not even after she'd been erased and we went to barbecues around the swimming pool that used to be her house. But how do you turn all of this into a question? On *Jeopardy* they give you the answers first, and Nancy isn't helping, the way she's going on about herself. Meanwhile, I'm slip-sliding into the cafeteria-like cacophony, the fuzzy smoke-filled edges. I hike up my hips—carrot still there. It burns from my asshole up through my ears. I imagine suiting up in my disc jockey space gear and floating above this woman in her designer jeans and pearls. Her Chanel N° 5 and cigarettes. This woman now dissecting her former life—a, quote, zoned-out, chrome-and-steel existence without core or conscience. Sounds like hippie shit to me. Maybe we're destined to become what we fear most. My fears were more basic: I became a murderer.

Nancy says, "I know you think it's stupid or even cliché, but sometimes clichés are clichés for a reason. We had everything we wanted . . . cars, jewelry, a table at 21. I mean, really, we had more money than a small country, and I was the perfect advertising wife, quick-witted, sexy, up for anything . . . Then I got out there every morning and hustled my ass off. Jack loved that. 'My wife's the big earner around here,' he told anyone who'd listen. And let me tell you, they listened. Jack used to say money talks and bull-shit walks. Remember that? And he was so good at all of it. We both were, and you never want to be too good at anything. I don't know why, but it gets really lonely. The cruelest joke is you can have everything you want and still be miserable. Money cannot buy happiness."

I roll my eyes.

"I'm serious, Lily, I'm not going back. I'm learning how to take care of myself—I never knew how to take care of myself, it's that simple."

"You already told me. In the letters."

"Yes, but my apology must be complete and continual."

"You're apologizing to me?"

"Yes, and you must believe me. I am so sorry."

She removes her glasses and dabs her eyes with a tissue. Make no mistake, she's not crying, but the gesture seems to comfort her. Clouds from her unsmoked cigarette rise above us and I want out of this confessional. A million miles away on Planet Recovery, Nancy can't see I'm still lying on the ground after falling off a roof. Still waiting for a mother who won't touch me or talk to me. A mother who can't see me without seeing herself. Why can't *she* ask *me* something for once?

I shift in my seat for another jab of carrot stub. The pain lets me know I am still here. No way will my mother's rehabilitation nullify my own. Nancy says we can learn from our mistakes and move on. Every day we must be grateful for the simple gift of life. Is she out of it or what? I am in jail awaiting trial for murder. But like the rest of them she believes if she doesn't remember it, then it couldn't have happened. I am worse off than an abandoned freedom fighter.

Piper and the boys start rounding up the troops. Handcuffs on one end, civilians on the other. A few people weep, the volume in the room shoots up a thousand notches. Guards will use force to pry people apart if necessary. There are no real goodbyes in jail.

Before I leave, Nancy grabs my arm. "Lily, there's one more thing . . . about Jack." She takes a deep breath, and my lungs cave in. "The thing is, I'm not sure we're going to make it." Her words burst into quivering lips, and I am paralyzed. As if I've been punched in the stomach. It's the first time today I understand her sentences.

For one second I wonder what it would feel like to really hold my mother, to stretch my arms out and suck her into me, not letting go until the guards with their iron claws tear into us. There is too much commotion, however; faceless people being herded into elevators and hosed down for the long walk to nowhere. This is the worst part of being locked up, the moment when the world splits off into *us* and *them*. Nancy kisses my cheek. I touch her shoulders and her body feels like Styrofoam. I can't figure out what's made her so brittle.

We barely say goodbye before I am shoved into the elevator, its whistles and clinks reminding me I used to be one of them. On the outside. A jolt of longing for the life I'll never have shoots through me. Then I remember my mother's face and understand what few people ever acknowledge: It's not so great out there, either.

AT THE TV STUDIO THEY PASSED US from one person to the next, each saddled with scripts and hooked up to some sort of electronic device. I felt as if we'd infiltrated a giant pod where everyone spoke my father's language and looked as if they hadn't slept in weeks. Only their clothes were impeccable and bright. Edie and I stood out among all the rich pastels.

Away from Aunt Fifi's mirror I looked as if I'd stepped out of a World War II poster, while Edie was a walking corpse in all that transparent black and gothic makeup. At the last minute she'd hung a big silver ankh around her neck making her seem frighteningly spiritual. A messenger from the devil's workshop. No surprise the pastel people stumbled over their words determined not to offend us. At the wrong phrase or gesture we might have gone nuclear on them. Who knew?

One pod led us to a place they called the Green Room. It had beige walls, a blue couch and carpet, blown-up articles from soap magazines on the walls. Nothing green in sight. Steam rose from a Mr. Coffee machine carrying the scent of my kitchen. As far back as I can remember there was always coffee brewing in the morning and I had developed a major craving for it. So much so I couldn't remember a time I didn't drink coffee. It was practically mainlined into my baby bottle.

Coffee stunts your growth, someone had said. I never listened, drinking four or five cups a day, and only at night when I touched my breasts wishing they would expand beneath my fingers did I think maybe it was the coffee keeping them down. Maybe if I'd learned to drink milk I would have grown enormous *Playboy* tits, and guys might have noticed me.

In the Green Room, I poured the steaming liquid into a Styrofoam cup and loaded a plate with miniature muffins and pastries. It was fun being a VIP. Free breakfast. People escorting us around the set. I imagined this was what your days were like, your every whim and desire served up at no cost. I stuffed whole muffins in my mouth as Edie paced back and forth. She said she wasn't hungry and mumbled words to herself. Song lyrics, I think. It was nice to remember songs had words after hearing that damn piano all night long. Chuck had finally shut it off when he showed up. I think he might have broken the switch. "Would you sit down?" I said finally.

"We have to get out of here."

"Relax, okay."

"I can't stay in this room, it's wigging me out. The whole place smells like formaldehyde and the ceilings are too low."

She continued pacing and mumbling. She must have taken some of those red pills to counteract the dope; meanwhile, I'd eaten a couple of Nancy's Valium right before we left the house and had just started feeling dreamy. I grabbed a slice of sugary pastry, picked out the peach filling in the middle and licked it off my fingers. Edie raised her upper lip and grunted at me. "That's all part of the government's conspiracy," she said.

"*Conspiracy,* I like that word." I smashed the dough into a ball and popped it in my mouth. "It sounds like pirates and hidden treasures."

"Seriously, you don't even notice the sugar they put in everything. There's this book my mom has that talks all about how we're being totally controlled by sugar. Do you know how stupid

it makes you? It's, like, the worst drug out there, well, next to cigarettes, but that's a whole 'nother story. Don't get me going . . .
Anyway, it's why nobody gives a shit about anything anymore,
they're all high on sugar. And people, you know, like these television people, they're nothing but pushers. Pushing sugar and stupidity."

"They're sugar-pod people."

Edie turned abruptly from the window. She came toward me
looking like she'd just seen a ghost. Maybe her own reflection,
maybe yours. "Lil, I'm serious, we have to get out of here. We have
to go now!"

The door opened and a pod woman dressed in pink busted
inside. She said she was the show's publicist and told us her name.
It sounded like a gum disease. "So," she said, "which one of you is
Gus's daughter?"

I opened my mouth to speak, but Edie answered. "I am. I've
been dying to come out here for weeks. But don't ask me to speak
French, for some reason Daddy never taught me."

"Liar," I said.

"Wonderful." Pink Pod shook Edie's hand and smiled. "I just
love your father's work. He's a real innovator."

"Yeah, isn't he? And I'll tell you what, he's completely given up
sugar and caffeine."

"Wonderful. How truly wonderful."

"Oh, by the way, this is my friend Lily," Edie said, talking so
fast her lips trembled. "She's Jack's kid, you know Jack, he works
for Daddy. He's a sales guy, and let me tell you, he's the best.
Number one. The guy could sell rocks to the Flintstones, he's such
a babe." Pink Pod turned my way gulping at the sight of me.
Although the Green Room was freezing, I was sweating in that
stupid wool suit. I should have worn my black jeans and T-shirt
and was angry Edie had talked me into dressing up. At least she
looked sexy; I looked like a Communist. I felt moronic and Pink
Pod knew it. When she shook my hand I pressed so hard I cracked
the bones in her fingers. She quickly yanked it away, forcing a
smile. "Don't mind her," Edie said. "Lily's the quiet type, apparently she's got other worlds going on in her head."

"Look who's talking," I grimaced at Edie, but she just laughed.

Pink Pod clapped her hands. "Oh, this is so exciting, are we ready to tour the studio?"

We walked and walked through the spanking-clean hallways and vast rows of closed doors with actors' names written in big cursive letters. As we passed your name my head felt trippy and my body flashed hot and cold like the beginnings of the flu. I was glad we didn't stop, I wasn't ready to see you yet, though I wondered what you were doing behind that door. If you knew I was there. My skin itched in its heavy sheath. I wanted to remove the jacket but had only a tank top underneath; this clothing was holding me captive. Or I wasn't wearing it right. There was no fitting the mold sometimes.

Pink Pod knocked on a few doors, and if they were in, the actors welcomed us with Cokes and questions: what's your name, where are you from, what do you want to be when you grow up, how long have you been watching the show? Edie told them all she only started watching the show when she met me. Where she came from there were no television sets. Poor, deprived girl, their eyes said, although they kept up the chatter. Happily they autographed their faces for us. The chief nurse of Foxboro County Hospital wrote, "Keep on watching," designing the A in the shape of a human eye, while the evil bartender at Flannery's wrote, "We are the *World.*" The guy who played Alex Rheinhart had run out of photos and ended up giving us each a *World Without End* hand towel from his bathroom. He was also the only actor who'd commented indirectly on our clothing, asking if we were extras in one of the scenes that day.

"No," Edie said. "But we're from New York, you know, all the world's a stage."

"Excellent!" he said. "There's plenty of room out here for a highly developed sense of the theatrical."

If we were in New York I would have assumed his words were sarcastic, but out here they all spoke in sugar-pod tape loops, and it was getting on my nerves. I did not risk my life flying across the country for canned comments from soap zombies, those who would pass the rest of their television days in Foxboro. You had other plans: movies, plays, maybe a sitcom. The right role, you told *TV Guide,* was just around the corner.

By then too eager to see you, I asked Pink Pod why we hadn't knocked on your door and was told you were already on the set. "You mean we don't get to see Brooke!" I said.

"Not privately, no."

A knife shot through my gut and I was speechless. Edie stared at me as if I were nuts and I knew it was her fault. She and her connections on Andromeda had disrupted the cosmos. Or maybe the two of you were in on it together. You could have been talking to Edie as well. That had never occurred to me before . . . and she was more interesting than I was. Hot and cold sirens ran through me again.

No, I refused to believe you were talking to Edie. That wasn't logical. Fists planted at my side, I spoke as firmly as I could. "Gustave said we could see Brooke."

"You know how Daddy talks," Edie said.

"Shut the fuck up, he's not even your father."

Edie pulled my hair from behind. "*Don't start,*" she whispered.

"Excuse me, young ladies, do you see this door?" Pink Pod directed us toward the door next to her. "Behind this door, Brooke—or Jaymie Jo as we call her inside—is recovering from her exorcism—"

"Her exorcism?" we both said.

"Yes, yes, you'll see it in a couple of weeks, but that's nothing. Jaymie Jo is on the verge of something even bigger, I won't tell you what just now, but I will say that you are two very lucky girls. Do you know how many fans would kill to see a scene like this? Anyway, if you'd like I can take you into Jaymie Jo's bedroom, I've already received permission, but you must, and I cannot stress this enough, you must promise not to make a sound." The whole time she was talking I couldn't stop looking at her nose. So long and thin it reminded me of a witch's nose. "Do you promise?" she said again.

"Sure," Edie said.

They stared at me, waiting on my response. Funny, now that

I'd come this close to seeing you, I was terrified. A thousand images flashed through my mind. Scenes of our various meetings. Restaurants. Beaches. Airport bars. Maybe you wouldn't recognize me in a skirt. Or I'd say the wrong thing and you'd ditch me forever. Then Edie could take my place. No, that's crazy, you hated Edie, but it wasn't too late for me to walk right out of this studio and preserve what we had. Some doors were never meant to be opened. Simply believing in what existed behind them was enough.

"Come on, Lil," Edie said, a hint of disgust in her voice. "This is your deal."

I remembered what she'd said the night before: Whenever a person leaves a conversation the mood changes. Walking into a scene had to have the same effect: The bond between us might grow stronger or it could snap like a twig. But you would hate me if I chickened out after coming this far. You had no respect for cowards.

So I gave my word not to make a sound, and we slipped through the double doors into the freezing-cold soundstage, my heart pumping as if it were the track to a horror film. Picture it, Brooke. See through my eyes what it was like walking into your world of fake sets and tight costumes. How it pained me to hear the nightie you'd been wearing for weeks had given you hives while I battled my own itchy clothing. I had visions of rubbing down your skin with pink calamine lotion as we traded life philosophies. But there were rumors in the air. Things I would only understand a few months later when your name began to surface in the tabloids, the cameramen whispering that you'd been forgetting your lines and freaking out on the set. That you'd brought in your own makeup lady, a cry for detox if ever there was one. Even that day, when you entered the soundstage, your face looked so thin it was almost skeletal, your eyes incapable of focus. You slipped beneath the sheets, and I swear you pushed your palms together in prayer for a few seconds before the cameras rolled.

Watch now through my eyes. See what I saw when the director called action and you cued into Jaymie Jo as if roused by an electronic current. A surge so radiant its waves ignited the outskirts of the set where I'd been banished behind the cameras. A swell so forceful you clearly dipped deep into your reservoirs to become the corpselike vision we would see for days. Around you the men circulated. Your father, Max, the priest who'd performed the exorcism. It was the perfect setup for flashbacks, but those would be filled in later. Just as we'd see you coughing up green slime and begging Jesus to reunite you with your dead mother. A virtuoso performance that would earn you your second Emmy (the third, of course, would be given posthumously, making soap opera history). But what we saw in the studio that day came after the exorcism, as your father and Max discussed whether to contact the hospital against the priest's wishes and you bolted up in bed. Alex and Max burst into tears. Max tried to hold your hand, but you brushed him off and called to the priest. "Father," you cried. "Oh holy father!" And then something about how you'd been to the other side and returned. And then something about how you'd seen your true destiny: You were going to become a nun!

The director shouted cut! Your body slackened and head slumped over. As if the scene had drained every ounce of energy from your spine. Then you bounced from the bed and walked to the front of the set, making a visor of your right hand against your forehead. I moved out of the shadows. Your eyes found mine and for the brief seconds we connected I felt a series of convulsions charge up my legs as if your spirit had invaded my flesh, and I knew immediately what people meant when they talked about the heart skipping a beat. It was the most peaceful feeling I'd ever experienced. A kind of perfection most people don't get close to in their lives. But like anything perfect, it couldn't last. You winked at me and threw your head back in laughter. My entire body felt exhausted but energized. As if I'd just skied a long, treacherous slope. I closed my eyes and sighed.

It took a few seconds to realize Edie was punching my thigh. "Cut it out!" I said.

"Look." She pointed to the set where you wrapped your arms around a man in a black trench coat. "That's John Strong. He was standing behind us the whole time."

Can you imagine my isolation then, Brooke? The pain I felt upon watching you fall into your boyfriend's arms after what had just transpired between us? It was as if you'd ripped open my chest and poured hydrochloric acid over my heart. I couldn't move, not even when Pink Pod said we had to clear the set. "Really, we must be going," she said. "I promised I'd have you out of here by noon."

"Oh, fuck off, we heard you," Edie snapped, and I burst out laughing. Pink Pod turned to a young woman with headphones wrapped around her neck. "Would you deal with them, please?" she said. "I've been trying, but they are really too much. And Gus is such a wonderful man . . ."

The pod girl nodded, promising to escort us out of the building. Pink Pod stormed off without saying goodbye. Edie shouted, "Goodbye!" then turned to me. "What was her name again?"

"Halitosis, I think."

"Bye, Miss Halitosis!"

The pod girl laughed. She was younger and looked almost normal, like she was passing through TV-land on her way to a rock concert. Maybe she was a friend of yours.

She led us out to the reception area where Chuck was waiting in his silly chauffeur's hat, and Edie and I fell to our knees giggling. In those few seconds it became clear why I'd taken her along on the trip: She was my decoy just as John Strong had been yours. I felt guilty for doubting her and worse for doubting you. What happened on that set between us was too big for the rest of the world. It had to remain between us.

For better or worse, till the end of time, world without end.

AFTER NANCY, I FIND ANGEL LYING ON MY BED, waiting for Chandon to slip her a needle. She can't sit up without chafing the scar from her C-section. Twice, she's ripped open the staples so the wound won't close. It's all she's got left of the boy, she says.

"What's shaking, little Long Island?" Chandon says.

I shrug. Words, phrases, sentences won't coagulate. There's a word for this, a disease. I read it in the medical dictionary.

"It's tattoo day." Chandon smiles at me then looks down at her hands, where she's got the needle filled with clear liquid, not ink. She flicks it with her middle finger, and we, the three of us in my cell, are hypnotized by the few clear drops squeezing through the tip. Seems too small an opening for a drug so powerful, but I know better. I can make the same hole bleed ink into people's skin. We don't go as deep as Chandon'll get inside of Angel—she has to break the vein, once she's done prepping, a task she performs as fastidiously as her laundry duty and for some reason makes me think of a black-and-white cartoon Jack had framed and hung in his office. A group of surgeons hover over a patient with his head cut open and one of them says: "Lighten up guys, we're not making a TV commercial!"

My mother told me there were no dress rehearsals in life. No pain, no gain. If you can't beat them, join them, she said.

Angel holds out her left arm, veins bulging beneath the strip of cotton they'd cut from a pillowcase. Chandon slaps them down with two fingers and the crack of Angel's skin sounds painful. It's probably low-dose next to sinking a needle into your vein or having a baby ripped from your side. Apparently, my birth had been so harsh that Nancy had her entire system shut down afterwards. And she didn't even have a C-section; she kept the scars bottled up inside, self-medicated.

Chandon takes Angel by the elbow and shoves the needle into her arm, carefully depressing the end with her thumb. She wears rubber gloves that stink of bleach and baby powder—Mimi's smells—and has her shirt sleeves folded above the elbow. She knows her turf and is experienced. One of those things everyone always said she did better than most. Silently she removes the needle. Angel shuts her eyes and leans back with her mouth hanging open while Chandon pulls off her gloves and cracks the plastic wrapping on another needle. Mimi would not like this. Their wasting clean needles on drugs. I try and warn Chandon but she laughs. As if Mimi is only Mimi in my imagination.

"She get too damn preachy sometimes," Chandon says. "Got all that Nancy Reagan shit in her head."

"It's not about that."

"Just say this, just say that . . . Who the fuck she think she is?"

"Her little brother OD'd."

"Nope. Sorry. Don't need it from her, don't need it from

nobody, that's why I left the church, praise Allah," she says as she fixes her works on top of the paperback copy of the Koran she carries everywhere. Practicing her Islam, like Nancy's practicing to be a Buddhist. These are dangerous times. Everybody's got something. Chandon wraps the sheet around her upper arm. "Hey, Long Island, grab this for me? I can't get the vein."

I hesitate. She sighs, says come on, she won't tell Mimi or nothing. I sit down next to her on my bed. Angel lies behind us, her legs against my back, warm. I tie the ends of the sheet together and tug hard, staring down at the Koran. "You read any of that yet?" I ask.

Chandon sucks up a thimble full of liquid with another needle. "It's not really what the book says that's interesting," she says, "it's how we interpret it."

"And how do you interpret this?"

"What?"

I nod down at the needle, her thick vein busting through the crook of her elbow.

"Allah forgives," says Chandon, and pushes the needle into her arm.

We are silenced momentarily out of fear—or reverence. It's actually peaceful watching the drug flood into her, witnessing the transcendence. A triumph over all of this gray. If only I could give over that easily. Shoot up. Carry the words of an all-forgiving prophet in paperback. But some things are not forgivable. Chandon pulls the needle from her skin and leans back over Angel's legs with a cozy, satisfied look. The two of them stare at the bedsprings and striped mattress above their heads. I settle in, floating through osmosis.

"What's this?" Mimi's voice startles me.

I jump up. "It's not me, I didn't do anything."

"I give you a little time to yourself and this is what you make of it? You were supposed to be watching them, this is trouble." She turns to Chandon. "And you, you said she wanted a tattoo. You lied to me."

"No I didn't," Chandon says. "She just needed a little muscle relaxer, is all. For preparation. You gonna draw her something nice?"

"His name," Angel says.

"You think I can work on her now? Like this? Forget about it."

"I only want his name."

"Don't be so cold," Chandon says.

"I'm cold? Stupid yunkie shit . . . *mierda.*" Mimi looks at me trying to gauge whether I'm high. She knows I'm not into drugs but hasn't trusted me since the fat lady appeared in my cell. The funny thing is, I can barely remember it and I'm testing the president's psychology: If I can't remember it, then it never happened. Even if it all goes down in my single cell, the one with the empty top bunk. I reach into the pillow, take out my legal pad, and on a fresh page write ALEJANDRO in big block letters. As if Mimi isn't mad enough with Chandon begging her to do Angel's tattoo and Angel mumbling the kid's name over and over, my scribbling is another violation. What's she going to do, shove more carrots up my ass? Stick needles in my eyes? This is supposed to be jail, not some degenerate carnival. I am here for my rehabilitation. To learn to forgive myself and speak in anonymous phrases.

The more Chandon pleads Angel's case for the tattoo, the icier Mimi's words become. She says no way will she touch her when she's so fucked up, bad enough she's got the virus. "It's too much negative energy," Mimi says, "we'll wake the demons."

Angel bursts into tears, still calling out for her son.

"Look what you're doing to her," Chandon says.

"It's not my doing." Mimi shakes Angel by the shoulders. "*Calla . . . calla . . .* shaddup!"

"*Puta!*" Angel spits at Mimi.

Mimi slaps Angel's face, Angel punches her arm, and they're into it. Chandon grabs Mimi by the elbows and hurls her to the floor. Angel cowers against the wall as if she could slip inside it. Her body convulses, reminding me of Nancy's cliché-spouting lips. Mimi calls her a disgusting infected *yunkie,* her pronunciation making it sound much worse than it is. "You have lost all tattooing privileges!" she shouts. Angel wails, younger now, a screaming infant.

A new mission sends me to the shoe box beneath my bed. I retrieve my Walkman and Bic pen, although there are no more needles. I look up at the towering figure that is Mimi, the anger distorting her face worse than the master distorter himself could have envisioned. In her hand, the two drained hypodermics.

"You're not ready yet," she says. "You don't know what you're doing."

"Yes I do, you taught me."

"You know nothing about her energy. This is the worst mistake—you never wondered why there are so many bad tattoos? 'Cause it's not about the picture, it's about the energy, and this is really bad. If you can't see that . . ."

"I don't care."

"So big and strong you are now."

"Give me the needle, Mimi!" I shout, amazed by the force of my own voice. So is everyone else. For the moment it even quiets Angel.

The glaring Mimi crosses herself, then slips a needle into each palm, cupping her fists over them. She holds out her arms, wrists upright, and it's the first time I can see the extent of her suicide tracks. It's crazy but I want to hold her like I wanted to hold Nancy, only she doesn't deserve it. She's got no heart. Angel had tried to warn me, those weeks when she schooled me, stroking my head as she relayed the most disgusting stories I'd ever heard. Tales of human autopsies and digging out people's kneecaps. I'd stopped listening soon after and hummed the *World Without End* opening she loved so much. I never wanted to be street smart, but I really liked the feel of her fingertips in my hair.

Mimi stares down at her fists, then back at me. "You're playing with fire, *chica*."

I hold her gaze.

"Go ahead, then . . . your choice," she says, and because Angel's tattoo has become the most important event in my life, I point to Mimi's left hand. She slowly uncurls her fingers. I take the needle and hook it to the siphoned inner tube of the Bic. Armed with black ink, I sit down next to Angel and touch her shoulder, so smooth and brown it looks like candy. Sweet enough to eat despite the poison lurking below. Like the shiny red apples with razor blades inside that mean people supposedly hand out on

Halloween. As if she's reading my mind, Mimi says, "I'm warning you, she's got the evil blood. This is your last chance."

Her words fuel my determination; I put the needle to Angel's arm and turn on the Walkman. The current surges through my fingers for the first burst of the A. You can etch a tattoo with just a needle and ink, you don't need the motor, but it makes it easier. And there's less blood. Mimi crosses herself again and shouts a few sentences in Spanish. She cannot take me from my work, not with Angel staring at me, her eyes sadder than my grandmother's on the day she walked into the courtroom for my arraignment. Enough to tell me this tattoo, my work, is all that matters. Mimi says I'll be damned to hell. My mother said there is no hell, just endless repetition, and Chandon . . . *Allah forgives!*

Some shouting starts in the other cells. Soon the guards will come. I pick up the speed and by the letter N find my fingers are spotted with ink and blood. Angel shuts her eyes, and I can actually feel her limbs relax. "*Mi hijo,*" she whispers, as if by inscribing his name on her shoulder I am bringing him back to her.

When the banshee calls finally draw the guards, I am on the last curves of the O. There is no explaining this madness: all the banging and wailing, stolen needles, my dirty fingers wiping Angel's shoulder, Mimi and Chandon nowhere to be found. Before I can say anything, Angel is wrested from me. As the guards drag her off, she points to her tattoo and says, "Thank you, Long Island! God bless." My eyes swell, and I'm certain there is no justice in this world.

I hold up my stained fingers begging your forgiveness. Then I smear the bloody remains of Alejandro across my lips.

ANGEL IN MOTION

IN THE BACKYARD OF THEIR LEMON-YELLOW farmhouse was a swing Tom Harrison had built when the girls were young. It hung from the branch of a large sugar maple. A tree as indigenous to the Northeast as the inhabitants of the house it shaded in the summer; a tree no less spectacular for the predictability of its fall colors, the leaves of red and yellow and orange and gold that glistened as if they'd been kissed by the sun. It was a tree with a history predating the couple who'd stumbled upon the house in 1964, a chemical engineer and the bride he'd known barely six months. When Mildred thought of herself back then, she liked the picture that came to mind: an ebullient young woman recently sprung from the dorms of Penn State and deposited into her "real life." She was so plucky then. So much in love. Within a year she gave birth to her first daughter, and although we now know the significance of that event in the annals of daytime television history, the happy parents had nary a clue their baby girl would grow up to be the first in three generations to leave the East Coast.

After Brooke had settled in Los Angeles, she told Mildred that what she missed most about home was the old maple with its swing and coat of many colors. She remembered vividly the day her father had pushed a silver extension ladder against the tree and tucked beneath his arm the piece of wood attached to two thick ropes before beginning his ascent. In her version of the story Tom was a tall, mysterious man who'd disappeared into the leaves and sent down a swing, the object of her youthful contentment. Brooke could sit on that swing for hours, her shins thrusting back and forth, catapulting her into a world normally inhabited by birds, tiny buzzing creatures, and the occasional Frisbee. Brooke recently told Mildred she'd never been as comfortable anywhere in the world as she was on that swing. In motion. Imagining what it was like to fly.

Mildred would have felt less nervous if their conversation had not been predicated on another speeding ticket and failed breath test that landed Brooke in drunk-driving school, where she said she knew practically everyone in her class and viewed it as a de facto networking opportunity. Such flippancy Mildred could not understand. She feared Brooke's drinking was becoming a problem, and her traffic violations from major to minor seemed nothing less than insolent. But the young soap star had a predilection for fast cars. What was the point, she said, of owning a roaring red Porsche if you were going to stay the speed limit? It was speed that made driving fun. Made Brooke feel like she had wings. Besides, the fearful succumbed more frequently to accidents than the carefree, Brooke said, reminding her mother of the time Cynthia had let go of the swing and glided into the neighbor's hedges. Tiny Cynthia, afraid of pumping beyond a forty-five-degree angle with the ground, normally held so tightly to the ropes her knuckles went white. Nobody had imagined she would one day bounce high enough to lose control of the ropes and shoot across the sky. At least that was how it seemed to the eight-year-old Brooke who watched her sister's torso arch peacefully before crashing into the bushes.

The bloody-faced girl came up wailing. Brooke carried her upstairs where she dabbed her face with a hand towel to assess the depth of Cynthia's wound. It was worse than she'd thought. Blood gushed from her sister's forehead, and Brooke could see the white cauliflower that must have been her brain. All the direct pressure in the world wouldn't close a hole that big. She needed help. Calmly, though, she assured Cynthia it was nothing. She said she was going downstairs for Band-Aids and found her mother in the kitchen. "Whatever you do, don't stare," Brooke counseled. "We don't want to scare her." And Mildred had obliged her precocious firstborn, knowing how easily Cynthia frightened and realizing she would not go anywhere—especially not to the hospital—without Brooke by her side.

There had been many days when Mildred worried that Cynthia would someday start resenting Brooke for all of the trials the older girl had put her through, all of the games constructed to test her will and her loyalty. But the accident seemed to further entwine them in each other's identities. Neither girl seemed to have many friends, Cynthia retreating behind her hardcover books and black walls, while Brooke complained of the endless parade of obsequious faces, each willing to do whatever she asked, no matter how rotten she behaved in return. Being on TV could bring out the worst in you, Brooke had confided to Mildred and said she was more grateful than ever for her daily phone calls home. The connection to Blue Bell was the only thing that kept her grounded, the only way she could bring herself to venture out, and she was at a point when making the scene still mattered. For some time she had been auditioning for movies, convinced that elusive part on the big screen would rectify the hardships she'd endured as a daytime ingénue: her second-rate status in Hollywood, the year-round work schedule, and all of those luncheons with screaming fans, benefits for causes she could barely keep straight, and the torturous appearances at shopping malls. She said it was downright degrading at times, and Mildred knew exactly what she meant. They couldn't walk down the street anymore without hoards of people rushing up to Brooke and hugging her tearfully as if they were part of the family. That was the hardest part for Mildred, the lack of separation between her public and private lives. Brooke said it was like that for soap stars. "All of these emotions are, like, bubbling up to the surface," she explained. "People start thinking they really know you." But Mildred couldn't see how a movie career would make things any better. People would still *know* her, even more people. Mildred envisioned nonstop drunk-driving and traffic tickets, additional sleeping pills and skin creams. Since she was a child Brooke had attracted epidermal ailments of biblical proportions. Dermatitis, hives, eczema, boils. It often amazed Mildred how porcelain-smooth her face appeared on television.

Cynthia was lucky, the doctors had said. She could have been blinded. As it was, she needed forty stitches above her right eye, which left behind a birdlike scar that spread its wings whenever she raised her eyebrows. Brooke had said the scar was a wonderful symbol of her flight and told Cynthia she should wear it proudly.

Through the years Mildred found it increasingly ironic that Cynthia trod the earth wearing wings when it was Brooke who had always been enamored with flying; Brooke who was routinely described as "angelic," "cherubic," and "lamblike," and who adored her sister even more for the proof of the heavens she carried on her forehead. What Mildred didn't understand was that Cynthia, too, welcomed her celestial responsibilities. As if the child in her few minutes of flight and its aftermath had made a tacit agreement to bear the weight of her sister's desires. As Brooke slipped further into the world of impulse on the West Coast, Cynthia took on the mission of spiritual cleanup crew. She had already been leading an ascetic life, sleeping on her air mattress and wearing nothing but drawstring cotton pants, generic sneakers, and sweatshirts. Nor did she indulge in any of the usual teenage vices: cigarettes, beer, diet soda, chocolate, potato chips, cheeseburgers, and the like. Since the age of thirteen she had been a strict vegetarian; she wouldn't even eat fish or eggs. Yet she was no proselytizer. The last thing she wanted was to convert anyone else to her lifestyle. It was her crown jewel much like the wings on her forehead, a daily affirmation that she'd broken with the teenage world of stadium concerts and slumber parties in favor of a more cerebral existence. She cultivated her mental prowess by watching over her world-famous sister.

Mildred had heard about twin telepathy, which made sense given their involuntary cohabitation in that most sacred sanctuary—it was hard to imagine each ever developing fully on her own. Cynthia's extrasensory perception, on the other hand, was more phenomenal because she'd chosen it, and Brooke did whatever she could to nurture it as well. Geographically separated though they were, Cynthia swore she knew whenever Brooke was on a bender or fighting a particularly bad strain of insomnia. The minute such warnings came, she called Brooke, often catching her late at night on her car phone as she sped along the highways of Los Angeles. It was her only way of letting off steam, Brooke had said whenever Mildred expressed concern about her driving alone at night. But she wasn't going anywhere, her mother protested, never fully understanding what Brooke had meant when she said she was more at home in her car than she'd ever been in her apartment. She liked being out on the open road. Part of the world, yet insulated from it. Imagining what it was like to fly. She'd graduated from the swing to that car too fast, Mildred said to herself.

One cold autumn day, she was on her way into the kitchen. Outside the windows, crispy leaves barely clung to the old maple and she could not get Brooke on the telephone. It was Saturday so she wasn't on the set, although they had been shooting her scenes at odd hours to accommodate drunk-driving school. Perhaps she was with her boyfriend. The young man from the movies. A star. When Mildred was young they would have called him a matinee idol. And perhaps he wouldn't have had such trouble with the tabloids, something Brooke told her not to preoccupy herself with—there wasn't a truthful word in those pages.

Mildred filled the kettle with tap water to make a cup of tea and turned on the stove. She searched for a task to occupy herself until the water boiled, but the dishwasher was loaded, the counters wiped clean, the stove sparkling. She sighed and was practically ambushed by an unbridled release of emotion. The day had brought a homebound sadness, its mass rising from her abdomen up through her chest and grabbing her by the throat when the sigh came. Although familiar, the feeling was not one Mildred could quantify or qualify, and, as Brooke might have advised, what would be the point of that? If anyone had asked Mildred Harrison what was the matter that day, she would have responded succinctly, "Life weighs." She had long ago accepted the particular isolations of marriage and family life.

Her eyes drifted out the kitchen window where she saw Cynthia standing beneath the old maple pushing the empty swing as if there were a person sitting in the seat. A pinch like an epidural shot through Mildred's spine and she felt as if time had flashed back a few years. After the accident, Cynthia had avoided the swing except to push Brooke back and forth, her own two feet planted firmly on the ground. It suddenly dawned on Mildred that all of Cynthia's "training," from her early years as a hot dog to the day she sat quietly in the backseat of their station wagon after they'd dropped Brooke at the airport to begin her work on the soap, were to help her keep the home front alive for Brooke. Mildred's gloom swelled. She could barely keep her eyes on the forlorn teenager with her short hair and drab clothes without wishing she'd done things differently. If only she had an inkling of what she might have changed.

The kettle bubbled into a whistle, startling Mildred away from the window. She filled her mug with water and watched the tea bag rise to the top. There was no keeping it down despite the battle she waged with her spoon. For some reason this comforted Mildred. She leaned her face into the flowery effluvium and inhaled deeply. The smell of chamomile made her nose twitch. Soon she would remove the tea bag and get on with her day, but first Mildred Harrison did something so out of character she later told Tom she felt as if she'd been possessed by the spirit of the recalcitrant tea bag. For on that blustery fall morning, Mildred Harrison wrapped herself tightly in her lumber jacket, set aside her mug, and walked out back to sit in that swing while her younger daughter pushed.

THE LOVE HOSPITAL

IN A CAR CULTURE, YOU ARE WHAT YOU DRIVE. You knew all
about that living in L.A. Hollywood was like the high school
parking lot magnified for the silver screen. You drove a super-
cool sports car and told *People* magazine you cruised the highways
alone at night. It helped you clear your head. My parents had
given me a new Saab (black—my father thought all cars should be
black), and as soon as I passed my road test I started driving back
and forth on Middle Neck Road, breezing past the manicured
yards and temples and private turnoffs bursting with bushy green
trees, cruising along Northern Boulevard into Queens and stopping at the diner for a grilled cheese and chocolate shake. I got on
the L.I.E. and drove past the airports, Shea Stadium, the globe
from the World's Fair, the old staple factory where worker-trolls
bent metal deep into the night, and sometimes I made it to the
Midtown Tunnel and into Manhattan, where I spent my last summer on the outside working at an ad agency, filing papers, answer-
ing phones, making color Xeroxes of storyboards. They called it an
internship.

All summer long I drove, stopping for long stretches at night
in front of Edie's house, but she wasn't inside. "She's still in Ohio,"
her mother said, when she came to the door in her sweatpants, her
face and eyes puffed out as if she hadn't slept for days, and Ohio
became a mythical place, as far-off as the planet Andromeda.
Where Edie had gone to "rest" after Los Angeles. And every time
I crossed her front lawn, hopping over the revolving sprinkler, my
sneakers slipping through the wet grass, crickets yapping their

heads off, I tried to think of something to tell her mother that didn't sound like I was making excuses.

I went over and over it in my mind, drew storyboard sketches—sometimes I could only get stuff out in my book. Edie'd been giving me shit about it that afternoon. We sat in the window of a touristy bar on Melrose, waiting for Chuck and drinking more coffee since the waitress wouldn't serve us beer. My international student ID card didn't cut it out there; people obeyed the law. Not like New York where you got points for ingenuity. Edie'd opened up the local paper and was reciting all the places we could go later if we had a car. I took out my book and charcoal pencils and started sketching our morning on the set. I wanted to remember your eyes, the way they'd locked onto mine. That old guy Mickey had taught me about faces, but it was harder working from memory than videotape. Maybe I'd have to wait a few weeks to get that scene before finishing. In the top corner of the page, I started outlining big black circles with bright lights inside. Edie grabbed my wrist. "What are you doing?" she asked, and I looked at her like, what the fuck do you think? "Don't give me that face, I know *what* you're doing, but what is it with you? I'm trying to figure out a plan for us and you're not helping at all. I don't get you, you just sit there with that stupid book." She tried to wrangle it from me, but I held on with both hands.

"Let go!" I said.

"You've been carrying that thing around since I met you"— she twisted our hands with the book off the table, huffing—"don't you think it's time I saw it?"

"Get out of here!" I pulled harder, standing up out of my seat for leverage. Edie squinted. A shadow moved up beside her.

"Hey, ladies," said a chubby guy with curly black hair and thick stubble on his cheeks. "What's all this?"

"Depends." Edie spit out her words, not letting up on the book. "Who are you?"

"Just someone who cares."

"You got a car?"

"Of course."

She smiled and let go.

The guy said his name was Rex and he was a consultant for a nightclub. He said he would take us there that night. He said he and his friends would pick us up, and I knew it was pointless to argue when Edie gave him Aunt Fifi's address.

They showed up around ten, three guys in jeans and boots and T-shirts. They smelled of wet newspaper and cigarettes and carried a couple of six-packs. One of them was missing two fingers. Another had skin stretched so thin across his face he looked like a Halloween mask. They could have been anywhere from twenty to forty, and I'm no expert, but they didn't look like consultants. None of this bothered Edie, who invited them in and poured beers into tall glasses. We smoked some and talked about Aunt Fifi's house and the city and how it was so different from New York, though none of them had ever been there. They'd heard about the crime. The skeleton seemed overly interested in me. Edie winked when he sat down and stretched his arm out behind me. He asked what we were doing in L.A. "We came to see a taping of *World Without End*," I said.

"That's not *why* we came!" Edie rolled her eyes at me. "Some TV friends hooked us up. They said, 'If you're going to be in L.A. you have to come to the set.' You know how that is . . . but we really came to party."

"Well, you came to the right place," said Rex. He took a long hit off a joint and held it in. I couldn't believe he was sitting on Aunt Fifi's couch, he looked so out of place among the ancient treasures, like if my father in his designer suits were to find himself working in a coal mine. Something about this felt really wrong.

"So, where are we going tonight?" Edie asked, and they said they had a special place in mind. They said it was the hottest club in the city. They talked about all the movie people who hung out there.

"Have you ever seen Brooke Harrison there?" I asked.

"Who?" said my guy, his hand tightening around the upper part of my shoulder.

"She's on *World Without End*."

"Nope," he said and gripped me harder; my arm felt paralyzed. "Never heard of her."

I inched a few feet back on the couch, thinking, These guys are bullshit. You and John Strong went out all the time. Everyone in Hollywood knew you. I tried backing up a bit more, but the skeleton pressed into me. "There's too many of them, you know?" he said. "And they're all stupid bitches when you get right down to it. Wanna kiss me?"

"Um . . . I can't . . . I have something . . ." Stammering, I managed to get halfway off the couch.

"Come on, baby, just relax," he yanked my arm. "We're gonna have fun tonight, we're going to the club. We can dance. Don't you like to dance?"

"No." I jumped up and saw Edie sitting at the player piano with Rex and the fingerless guy squishing her from both sides. They were pounding the keys, but no sound came out. I ran into Aunt Fifi's bedroom and locked the door behind me.

A few minutes later Edie knocked. "Come on, Lil," she pounded, "we're getting ready to go."

"I'm not going."

"What!? Stop being such a loser and open this door!"

This went on for some time, her demanding I open the door and me saying no. Finally, I relented and let her in, again locking the door behind us. "Don't do this, okay?" she pleaded. "It's too fucked-up. You know, you are so spoiled. You want everything handed to you on a silver platter. You think your dream guy is just going to plop himself down in front of you? Well, let me tell you, that ain't gonna happen. I mean, look at you. You're a total freak!"

"Shut up!"

"No, you shut up! I can't believe how ungrateful you are. Once again I'm practically delivering opportunity to your goddamn doorstep and you're acting like I'm a criminal or something."

"Those guys are jerks. They don't know the first thing about Hollywood."

"They know more than you do, they live here. And they've got connections. Maybe we'll even see your little soap star."

"He didn't know who she was."

"You asked him? Jesus fucking Christ, what did I tell you?

You're going to ruin this thing before it even starts, you always do . . ." I sat down on the bed, crossing my arms in front of me. Edie came up next to me and rested her hand on my thigh. It felt like cement. "Okay, look, I'm sorry," she said, taking another tack. "You're right, these guys are probably idiots, but they're going to take us out. Do you want to go back to New York and say, 'Yeah, I was in L.A. and all I saw was the inside of a TV studio'? Well, I don't want to say that, so please, Lil, just do this one little thing. Is that so much to ask, after all I've done for you?"

"I'm sorry," I said, shaking my head back and forth.

"Please . . ."

"I'm not going."

"Don't make me do this alone," she said, a strain I'd never heard in her voice. Like she was trying to convince me to donate a kidney to save her mother's life or something. Might have worked before that afternoon, before I'd seen you on the set. But we'd really clicked and the last thing I wanted was for you to catch me running around with a bunch of hooligans (that's what my grandmother would have called them). Image was everything in this town.

Edie begged and begged. She offered to get me pot from the Ayatollah when we got home, told me she'd buy me the pants I wanted from Reminiscence, said she'd do anything, and still I wouldn't budge. "God, you're so stubborn!"

"I'm sorry . . . I just can't."

"You mean you won't." She stood up and turned toward me, pointing her finger in my face. "Okay, Lil, if that's the way you want it, fine. But don't come crawling back to me ever again. We're through."

"Oh, come on, Edie."

"I mean it. You and me, we're kaput. Finito."

"It's just one night."

"'Quoth the raven, nevermore!'"

She sauntered off in that tight black evening gown, slamming the door behind her. Outside I could hear her saying she'd be going alone tonight, her friend had come down with something, and one of them, I think it was the skeleton, shouted something about a case of bitchitis. I got up and locked the door. Returned to the bed, steaming mad as I listened to the shuffling of their departure, sounds I'd heard a million times listening from my room at home. The shutting off of this, the picking up of that, one last trip to the bathroom, glasses placed in the sink . . . there was still time. Someone always forgot something, and it took a few minutes to get settled in the car outside. I could unlock the door and make everything all right, but fuck her! I had just as much right to demand she stay home with me. Only the second I heard the car turn over, I felt the blood rush out of me, my stomach an empty valley.

I ran outside and caught a couple of brake lights down the street. "Edie!" I trudged a few more feet, shouting and waving my arms, but the car turned. Shit, I thought . . . shit! I smoked a couple cigs in the wet night, when it finally hit me: I had the keys to the sea-green Buick buried in my jeans, I'd taken driver's ed. I could try and find them.

The car never started, and I slammed my fist against the dashboard the way I'd jabbed my knuckles into the mirror of my parents' bathroom the night I discovered Blair was gone for good. They all left after a while. But knowing that didn't make anything any easier. The bottom of my hand throbbing, I pounded until the glove compartment popped open, and inside it was a gun. Or what looked like a toy gun, almost; I'd never seen a real one up close.

I picked it up, and it wasn't at all weaponlike. Shiny silver with an ivory handle, no bigger than Edie's metal pipe in the palm of my hand, this gun couldn't be real, could it? It was more like the pistols I'd seen saloon girls tuck into their satin underwear in the Old West town, although they could have been real, too. That was all about re-creation, authenticity. I dug further into the glove compartment and discovered a powder-blue Tiffany bag full of bullets. More than fifty of them. I lined up a few on the dashboard like tiny missiles or lipsticks in a department store, the oily, metal-y smell snaking up my nose, then inspected one in my hand. Smaller than my pinkie, it had a gray tip and copper body, and at the base said *norma* and *.38 SPECIAL.* Of course, Norma was Marilyn and

.38 Special a weird country-rock band, and although I had a feeling the bullet had been around before either one of them, I wanted to show Edie how everything connected with everything else, but she was off somewhere in the thick of it, and when she finally did return hours later, so mangled, her eyes puffed up like balloons with makeup smeared all over them, I was thankful I'd tucked the gun inside my belt. I'd first heard a car door slam, footsteps, then the triple ring of the bell out front. Opening the door, I found what was left of Edie: A bloody crack split her lips. Her nose was large and disjointed, big yellow circles under her eyes. Aunt Fifi's dress barely clung to her body. Her hair smelled like cat piss. It made me want to puke. "Are you okay?" I said, and she gazed right through me. "Edie!" I reached for her shoulder, but she brushed me off. "We should go to a hospital or something. You're so . . . I'm calling Gustave, okay?"

"You really missed out tonight," she said, walking right by me like she'd really had the time of her life. The wind blew in after her, then I heard a humanlike rustling in the bushes. I grabbed the gun from my belt and ran outside, scared shitless but no way was I letting anyone fuck with her again. I circled the house, went down the driveway and out to the street, the gun leading the way for me—it was all clear. I ran back inside, bolting the door behind me, and found Edie in the bathroom, wetting a clean white washcloth with hot water and dabbing her face. Within seconds the cloth was stained with blood and makeup. Pink water flushed down the sink. I felt sick to my stomach and suggested again that we call Gustave. "It was so fun." She talked slowly into the mirror, her lower lip so thick she could barely pronounce the consonants. She mumbled something that I swear sounded like "life experience," and then set the washcloth over her face.

"Edie." I put my free hand on her shoulder, and she flinched.

"Get off!" she shouted from underneath the terry-cloth veil.

"But I'm—"

She shook her head back and forth.

"—so sorry."

She pushed her arm into me and the cloth fell off her face. I stood there, my left hand reaching out to her and the Smith &

Wesson in my right, sure she'd say something. But she just turned and picked up the washcloth, then shouted, "Get out!"

"But—"

"OUT! OUT! OUT!"

And they were the last words she spoke to me. Even at the airport she sat motionless, her mouth smothered in lipstick, every inch of her face ghosted with white powder, her eyes doused with mascara and shadow, and every time I remembered how long she'd stayed in that bathroom while I sat by the window clinging to the gun in the palm of my hand, just in case those assholes decided to come back, I shivered imagining how much putting on all that crap must have hurt. When the car service dropped her off, she didn't even say goodbye.

Every time I called, her mom said she's still gone, it's a lot to work through, and I wondered whether she was part of the cover-up, but when school started again, it was Edie who wouldn't come to the door or return my calls. If we passed each other in the hall, she quickly looked the other way. It was terrible. Like I creeped her out or something. I stopped sleeping. Spent entire nights watching reruns and drawing storyboards like the ones I'd Xeroxed at the ad agency, cartoon panels of what might have happened to Edie in L.A. One somehow surfaced in *People*—a joyride ending in a circle of steel-toe boots in Edie's face. The experts said it was so violent for a girl. I think they thought Edie was you.

My eyes swelled up and stung like bug bites. I wore sunglasses all the time, enjoying the dark shadows my world had become. Nancy stopped me in the kitchen one day and pulled up the glasses. She stared directly into my eyes. "What?" I said.

"Nothing."

"I'm not stoned."

"I know." She set the glasses back on my nose and took a few steps back toward the refrigerator, a fart of Chanel lingering behind her. "I wish you were, sometimes."

"What?"

"Maybe it would explain things. Your SATs came back."

"Oh . . ."

"The math is still terrible. I don't know what we're going to do."

"It doesn't matter, I don't want to go to college," I said to her ass. She was bent over the refrigerator, the back of her skirt unzipped so I could see her crack inside her stockings, a backward robber's nose. It was so gross the way she walked around the house in her unbuttoned shirt and stockings, everything just hanging out. I wished she would buy some sweats like the ones Edie's mom wore.

Nancy turned, caressing a carafe of iced coffee. "There's another test in December," she said.

"I'm not taking it."

"Oh for Christ's sake."

"It doesn't matter if I'm not going to college."

"You're going to college. Everyone goes to college."

"For your information, Nancy, *everyone* doesn't go to college." I was thinking of you, how you hadn't even finished high school before you got the role on the soap.

"True." She landed the carafe on the counter between us. It was sweating at the neck. "You want to clean houses or type for a living, they taught you how to type, right? Or you could always work at McDonald's."

Whenever anyone wanted to show you how awful life could be, they mentioned working at McDonald's. What did that say about the hundreds of thousands of people who worked there? They couldn't all have such lousy lives, and it didn't seem worse than any other job as long as I didn't have to work the grill. My skin was bad enough already. Anyway, I was going to do something creative. "Brooke Harrison never went to college," I said.

"Who?"

"You know . . . from *World*."

Nancy burst out laughing. "You're comparing yourself to someone on a soap opera? That's ridiculous. I don't know where you get this stuff sometimes. Brooke Harrison was training for TV while you were still riding your Big Wheel, and look, nobody would ever accuse her of being a good actress, but she's got some talent."

"I have talent. You don't even know."

"Oh come on, Lily, we're talking about real talent here, not your little pictures." Nancy poured herself a tall glass of iced coffee, and we watched the shit-brown liquid roll over the ice cubes, cracking like the synapses in my brain. I thought it was going to explode, an aneurysm of Nancy-hate. She'd be sorry when I was famous and I told the press my mother was dead.

She added skim milk and two packets of Sweet'N Low to her coffee, then pivoted, drink in hand as if she were hosting a cocktail party, before launching into her usual speech: Maybe if I stopped trying to convince myself I was so different from everybody else I could think a little bit about my future, and if I didn't want to take the SATs again, fine, we would work with these scores, at least the verbal was okay, and I had that internship at the ad agency and good references from my art teachers (even without talent). But, she said, I really needed to start thinking about getting into a good school or else I wouldn't have a prayer of grad school and I'd end up working you-know-where. Only the reverse—better scores, better schools, a good job (like hers? she sold houses!)—didn't seem much different.

She left me so bummed out I drove into the dark, waterlogged afternoon. It had been raining on and off for days, turning the fallen leaves into a soggy brown mattress. My wheels splashed through puddle after puddle, but inside I stayed warm and dry, thinking, what crack-up weather, the beginning of a bad story . . . *on a dark and foggy suburban road* . . . good to be in a high-performance vehicle. Jack had said, "Those Swedes make the safest cars in the world. If we were hawking them I'd get that into the spot for sure." I could storyboard it for you to star. I'd been compiling tapes of your scenes on *World,* studying your movements, gestures, and expressions. I knew your kisses, your crying jags, your angst, and, of course, your prayers, now that you'd seen the light and were training to become a nun. We could have made some serious cash from the tapes, you know? There was always someone in *Babbling 'Bout Brooke* pleading for Jaymie Jo montages, that's where I got the idea. But you didn't want me to sell them.

Red lights screamed: *Stop!* I slammed on the brakes, just missing the station wagon in front of me. *Safest car in the world!*

Turning my head, I realized I was on Nirvana Avenue, right by school, and wasn't that the cruelest joke? To build a high school on a path called Nirvana? But it also led to the turnoff for Edie's house, so I figured what the hell, I'd go and see if she might come to the door this time, but when I arrived there was another car in my favorite spot across the street: the old Chevy. Alone, Bobby Davis sat with his elbow folded in the open window, listening to loud music. I nuzzled up my Saab and, from a button by the driver's seat, slid down the other window. "Hey, Bobby," I said.

He leaned a bit further out the window, and boy was he different. About twenty pounds heavier and thicker all over, his blond waves had been cut so short he looked like the guys at the military academy. "Yo, Speck, long time no see," he said, and there was something sweet about how he called me by my last name.

"S'pose you got a message for me," he said.

"For you? I don't think so."

"Then what are you doing here?"

"I . . . I'm just . . . wait, what are you doing here?"

"Waiting for her to break," he said, and his steely gray eyes clouded over. They were red around the edges and bloodshot. He'd always looked like he had pink eye, but that day he was even more teary. "She can't ignore me forever, you know?"

I must have smiled.

"What? What's so fucking funny?"

"That's exactly what I was thinking."

"You want her to talk to me?"

"No, me. She's ignoring me, too."

"You? But I thought—"

"Since Los Angeles."

"What the fuck happened out there?"

"I'm not sure exactly, but it was really bad."

"A'right, follow me. Let's go somewhere else, this feels too weird."

He turned over the Chevy and skidded out into the damp streets. There was nothing for me to do but join him. I hadn't hung out with anyone in months, not even in smokers' corner, which had been overrun by kids who seemed way too young for cigarettes, and I'd been dying to talk to somebody about Edie. So I followed Bobby past the train tracks in the misty, wet twilight, trying to remember an old Middle Eastern saying we'd been hearing a lot of since they discovered the president's men were involved in arms deals over there. It went something like this: The enemy of my enemy is my friend.

Crime is a very slippery slope.

When I was in seventh grade they called us into the auditorium to watch a movie about smoking pot. It was full of creepy music and had all of these reformed junkies, prostitutes, and thieves, dressed up like hippies, telling us how everything bad started after they'd smoked their first joint. The narrator said listen carefully: These people were living proof marijuana led to harder drugs. And some of the girls who'd smoked ended up pregnant.

Everyone laughed at the movie. Like it could never happen to us—but I'd smoked my first joint the year before and had been pinching buds from Jack's drawer ever since. How quickly I'd gone from smoking to stealing. Maybe the hippie addicts had a point. (Note to the president and first lady: If you'd like to use me in your war on drugs, feel free. Just be aware I don't agree with you on anything else.) The way I see it, my theft and possession of a weapon put me in the big league, criminologically speaking. If I hadn't lifted that gun and blue bag full of bullets and rolled each one in a pair of jeans, the way Edie'd packed up her pipe and hid it in her suitcase on the way out, then maybe I'd have no need to scratch these words across endless pages of yellow legal pads. I can't tell you exactly why I took it, but after spending the early morning hours sitting at the windowsill with the gun in my hand, almost wishing those guys'd come back for another round, I wanted that gun. It had become a part of me, the only thing separating me from what happened to Edie out there. I think I knew all along that it wasn't even loaded.

Bobby Davis taught me how to shoot, just like he said in his deposition. He might have been a high school dropout and a pothead, but he was never delusional, just sad. He reminded me of your boyfriend, John Strong. In an interview you said John was like a giant cat, who, missing his mother, kneaded his claws into everything. I guess most guys were like that.

It was always dark with Bobby, past daylight savings and damp and woody. He never called or came by my house, he was just there in the parking lot after school, waiting like all the older guys who dated high school girls. I followed him along the highways and boulevards, driving through parks and shopping malls and cemeteries and golf courses—Long Island had it all and everything looked different in autumn, when the day people stopped coming and the air smelled like a muddy T-shirt. We always took two cars so we weren't really together. But Edie couldn't have missed it, if she'd cared enough to look—the Saab and the Chevy, you couldn't get much different in looks, personality, bod. He always wanted to talk about her and kept asking me to replay the same story like it was a flashback on a soap. It was okay until he started looking for someone to blame.

"How could you just let her go off? What were you thinking?" he asked me again and again, and I had no answer, at least nothing I could put into words. "You say she was your best friend. You were supposed to watch her back, it's an unwritten code, a philosophy."

"She told me we were through," I defended myself. "*She* broke the code."

"Did you ever smell her?"

"No," I lied.

"She always smelled like grape bubble gum."

"Yeah, I guess . . . she was like a funky purple grape."

Her smell was more flowery perfume and antiperspirant, but she did have a grapey aura, and I wanted Bobby to see I was paying attention. Guys liked girls who were fun, funny, and supportive. I'd read that in *Teen* magazine. I bought packs of grape bubble gum and left them on my dashboard. He never noticed. But he liked my tape deck. We used to open the front doors of my car and listen to Frank Zappa while we sat on the hood of his Chevy off the Meadowbrook Parkway, smoking pot and watching the cars stream by in the misty twilight, a net of moist brown pine needles beneath our feet. (Even now, where the only pine scent comes in Mimi's metal bucket, the smell makes me hum Zappa songs.) Bobby loved Zappa; over a couple of afternoons I'd painted his face in oils on the back of Bobby's jacket. He said it looked just like the album. It made him smile. He liked that Zappa sang about Jewish girls and Catholic girls and dancing and screwing and jamming, and he wasn't afraid to curse and lose airplay. We never listened to the radio, except when the World Series started, even though Bobby said baseball was a wussy-ass sport, and that seemed so antisocial, so un-American. I could see why Edie'd had such a crush on him. The thing is, I had no idea he'd liked her so much. He never bought her feather roach clips or made her personalized mix tapes like the Ayatollah did, and always acted like he could take her or leave her. He must have known she had other boyfriends.

My father was at game seven. He'd been calling in favors all over town when it started looking like there would be a game seven. I imagined him sucking down hot dogs and plastic cups of beer as he cheered the team he'd followed since they joined the National League. For weeks, he'd been running around the house with his fist in the air shouting, "The '86 Mets!" They hadn't won a Series since 1969, the year I was born. When I was a kid and we used to go to games, he liked telling me how he'd watched that entire Series on a small color TV with me, a three-month-old baby, in his lap. I didn't cry once, he said. I was never a big crier.

Bobby let the game run at longer intervals that last night, although he wanted to hear the Zappa song about a Jewish princess. It reminded him of Edie. He was about to rewind the tape so we could hear it again, when he leaned out of the passenger seat of my car. "Where the fuck did you get this?" he said, Aunt Fifi's pistol in his hand, looking tinier than ever.

"Be careful, it's an antique." I slid off the hood of his car and went to grab it, but he dangled it over my head. "Come on, give it back."

He laughed. "This can't be yours."

I lunged at him and practically fell over. "Please . . . you're gonna break it!" I said. I'd lugged that gun all the way back from

Los Angeles, took the name tag off my luggage. If it had been discovered I was going to eat the baggage claim check.

Bobby clicked open the barrel, spinning it a few times, a disturbing smile on his face. "It's not loaded. What good's it gonna
do you if it's not loaded?"

Evening made his face whiter, and more eerie. From the car
came the announcer's voice and organ music and thousands of people shouting, "Charge!" Something good was happening at the game.

"Let me guess, it's just for show."

"No," I huffed. He fit the barrel back, took a few steps forward,
and held the gun in front of him like a TV cop about to say, Freeze!

"See, this is exactly why girls and guns don't mix," he said, and
pulled the trigger. It sounded like the click of a seat belt. "Girls are
total pussies. You got no backbone. When God took that rib outta
Adam to make Eve there was nothing to connect it to. He had to
improvise, use sand or something, and as a result you're weak. The
whole lot of you. This is why girls follow guys all over the place."

"I don't see Edie following you anywhere."

He pivoted back and slammed me up against his car, the nose
of the gun at my cheek. "Don't you talk about her like that, you
hear me? You ruined her!" The gun slid down to my neck. Bobby
shoved it under my throat and pushed his body into me, hard. He
smelled stale, like bad cheese. "You understand?"

"Yes."

"Yes what?" he said, the gun practically choking me.

I spit out the words as best as I could: "I understand."

"Understand what?"

"It's all my fault."

"That's better." He backed off, and we were both heaving,
tiny breath clouds sailing between us. "You're lucky," he said. "I'm
in a good mood tonight. Let's see if we can't beat the odds, show
you how to use this thing. You got any bullets?"

I directed him toward the glove compartment and blue
Tiffany bag, then watched as he loaded and unloaded the gun,
explaining about the barrel, the bullets, the safety. He told me the
safety was my personal bodyguard, as long as it was on nothing
bad could happen, and I felt, well, safe. He showed me how to

stand coplike, feet planted directly under my hips, arms extended in front of me, one hand on the gun, the other gripping it from below for extra support on the kickback. It was much heavier when loaded, even with Bobby's hands over mine. He clicked off the safety and whispered, "Ready?"

I pulled the trigger and immediately slid back into Bobby's chest, the shot ringing through my head like a hundred cars back-firing, the scent of fireworks overwhelming the wet leaves and Bobby's boy smells. His hands still guiding mine, he said do it again, and I pulled the trigger, getting better at balancing myself with every shot, although I had no idea what we were shooting at. It was too dark off the parkway, and we'd shut off the interior lights of our cars. Bobby said the noise would attract enough attention. Nobody saw us, but after Bobby'd taken a few shots of his own, a chorus of honks blew through the swish of red and white lights. Someone, somewhere, shouted, "Let's go Mets!" I grabbed the gun from Bobby and emptied the barrel into the cloudy black sky.

"Easy, now." He came up behind me.

"They're winning."

"You happy?"

I turned around and saw the outline of his face, the white of his eyes. "It's about time they won a Series."

"Not that." He nudged the side of my body closest to the gun in my hand.

"Yeah, thanks," I said, more nervous than I'd been shooting. Even in the dark I could feel him looking at me, the kind of look that made me think of people waiting to order food at McDonald's. He took a step closer and his chin almost rested on my head. I leaned back against my car or his, I'd lost my bearings, and he moved into me like we'd been with the gun, only this time we were face to face. When he kissed me I didn't fight it. I pretended I knew what I was doing wrapped up in the softness of his lips and wondered if they were all like this. Loose and wet. Spit kept trickling down my chin. A few times he tried to get his fingers underneath my shirt and each time I pushed them back. I didn't like him touching me. He broke away and exhaled through puffed out cheeks. Like a little boy. Then he traced his right hand along my arm until he came to the gun and pulled it between us. I felt the metal more intensely through his fingers, his eyes mining me for clues the way he'd picked my brains about Edie. He massaged my hands over the gun, and that's when it hit me: I could shoot him if I wanted to, he'd just taught me how. He couldn't fuck with me and he knew it. "You really like it," he said, and I smiled. We were on the same wavelength. "Here, how about this?" he said, and, using both sets of our hands, shoved the gun in the back pocket of my army pants. He let go of me, I heard his belt clink. "Well?" he said.

"Well what?"

"Come here." He took my hands again, and it was okay. I was one move away from the gun in my pocket. He wrapped my fingers around his dick. The skin felt warm and silky and made me think of Edie. She'd said he had a velvet penis, but she'd also insisted she was from a place called Andromeda and told me cigarettes would make my pores swell. Who knew what to believe? But the minute I got my hand on Bobby Davis's dick, all those nights we'd gone out looking for him made sense. It was incredible how smooth the skin felt, even as he got harder.

"Stroke me," he whispered.

I tightened my grip around him, and he flinched. "Ow! Not like that!"

"Sorry." I tried again, grabbing him a bit lighter this time and squeezing.

"No." He put his hand on top of mine again. "Don't grab it, stroke it . . . Have you ever done this before?"

I didn't answer, I was too embarrassed. I'd gotten so carried away in touching him, I never imagined there was a wrong way to give a handjob. I hated that word: *handjob*. It sounded like changing oil. Smelly, wet, greasy, and totally mechanical. This stroking business, nobody had ever mentioned it.

"Damn, I gotta teach you everything," he said, and slowly moved our hands over his dick in a pumping motion, stroking. After a little while we got a rhythm going and he let go, folding his hands back behind his head. I was flying solo. Up and down, up and down, up and down, as he moaned louder and the muscles in my upper arm strained, like I'd been lifting heavy furniture.

I had to stop but stopping wasn't cool, so I channeled all of my energy into my hand. He shouted, "Go!" and I pumped faster out there in the fog, feeling like we'd escaped to an enchanted forest, a place where his penis was a magic wand and my hand the tool of a wizard. He screamed the word *go* over and over, practically in a trance, and I felt good because I could do what Edie had done and also because I was learning something. A skill.

When he came it was what I'd imagined: warm, sticky, and wet. I fell back on the car next to him and wiped my hand on my thigh, slowly, so he wouldn't notice. Guys seemed attached to their stuff. Almost immediately, he hopped into his jeans and headed toward his car. Just like that. No smiles, no kisses, no thanks very much. I stood against my car, sniffling from the chilly wet air. A couple of cars roared by, honking like mad. Someone, a woman's voice, shouted, "Whooo! Mets rule the fuckin' planet!" and she sounded so much like Edie my heart jumped thinking she'd followed us, wishing she cared that much. I felt wet and hollow and thought about lying down in the pine needles to sleep away the winter.

"Hey, Speck, I'm taking off!" Bobby shouted, above the roar of his Chevy.

"Wait!"

"What?"

"Can I follow you out?"

"I guess."

I climbed inside my Saab and quickly turned the keys, my headlights spilling across the blacktop with its dotted white lines, the smoky trees and sheets of steel sky behind it. We were heading into a long, cold winter. Peeling out behind Bobby, I was again thankful for my foreign car with its safety seals, even though I'd already stunk it up with cigarettes and Coke spills and old french fries. I pushed in the lighter and flipped open my cigs, turned on the tape deck and Frank Zappa blared liked an alarm . . . *a nasty little Jewish princess . . . with titanic tits and sand-blasted zits . . .* I had the zits but not the tits—it wasn't fair. And I was only half a Jew. Stuck between two stupid religions and not feeling either one of them. I was such a Gemini. So was John Strong. You really liked Geminis.

Zappa made me too thinky. I switched to the radio, searching for the final score. The lighter popped and I lit up with one hand, tailgating Bobby as we headed north on the Meadowbrook. My speedometer said ninety. Every so often I passed him, and then he'd speed up and pass me, and it was like we were playing a game, seeing who could go faster, until he pulled off at the exit for the racetrack, and I followed him through the off-ramp, a long, silent cavern. We drove a few minutes down a two-lane road flanked by charcoal trees, passing a few lively traffic lights, until we came to a well-lit intersection with a gas station and a 7-Eleven diagonally across from it. I turned into the parking lot behind Bobby and watched him jump out of his car. Girls followed guys all over the place because guys would never wait up.

I ejected Zappa from my tape deck and left my car, slipping the tape into my back pocket. Two guys were hanging out by an old station wagon near the front of the store. Someone hissed as I passed, and I wondered if they could tell I'd just given a handjob. Maybe there was something different about my walk, my face, the way I shoved my hands in my front pockets. I did feel sort of older and tougher with that gun in my pocket. I turned and hissed at them. They burst out laughing. "Come back and tawk t'us!" one of them shouted.

"My boyfriend's inside," I hollered over my shoulder, then walked inside 7-Eleven. I liked the way that sounded, *my boyfriend*. You said it all the time and I could see why. Those two little words said there was someone in the world who cared what happened to you, someone to care about. And have sex with. Must have made you feel pretty normal.

It was so bright inside I wished I had my sunglasses. Light streamed from the ceiling, beamed down on the aisles of reflective packaging, smothering everything in a multicolored shower. That much electricity has a drone to it. You could barely hear the cash register or Muzak. A few people moved through the light in slow motion, not black-and-white, but sepia-toned against the colored stacks. I couldn't find Bobby anywhere.

Walking down an aisle with potato chips, pretzels, corn chips, soaps, dishwashing liquids, bug sprays, I came out at the coffee station. A bearded man in a sport jacket tipped tiny plastic cups of cream into a large Styrofoam container, glancing over his shoulder before adding each cup like he was casing the joint. The kind of thing that happens in convenience stores. I rubbed my hands against my back pockets. Zappa in one, the gun in the other, I was ready for anything. "Hey, slugger," the man said, and I froze. Jack used to call me that whenever I wore my pajamas that said "Slugger" on the front and had Tom Seaver's number on the back.

"Hi, Daddy," a wimpy little voice said, before the kid appeared. He was wearing a shiny blue baseball jacket and Mets cap. The hat was perfectly faded and bent on the left side of the visor, just like my old cap. Where did that kid get my cap?

"What do you have here?" Daddy lifted the king-sized chocolate bar in the kid's hand. "Oh, no way, kiddo, that's way too big. You're mother's already gonna kick my ass for having you out so late. Go and get a smaller one. How about a Chunky?"

"I hate Chunkys."

"How can you hate Chunkys? They've got all those yummy raisins."

"Raisins blow."

The father chuckled, then looked around to see if anyone else had witnessed how cute his kid was, but I was the only one within earshot and I couldn't care less about anything he said, all I wanted was my hat. The father turned back to the kid and told him to get whatever he wanted, but please, buddy, he said, just make it a little smaller, okay? The kid smiled and skipped down the candy aisle. I followed behind him, thinking I hadn't seen my hat in years. At first I thought I'd left it in Scottsdale, but my grandmother couldn't find it, and Nancy had given away tons of my stuff in the big move. I always knew it would turn up somewhere.

The kid put the giant candy bar back on the rack and started picking through the bars and bags. I moved closer behind him so I could grab the hat by the beanie. He kept choosing candy bars, turning and squeezing them, then putting them back. Who was going to want them after he'd battered them like that? Another time I might have alerted the manager. There were rules, you know? But I had a plan. I lowered my thumb and forefinger on the button in the center of the hat and lifted so slowly the kid had no idea. Every time he bent his head toward the chocolate bars I pulled the other way, until I inched the whole thing off his head. Couldn't have been easier. I tucked the hat close to my stomach, took a few steps forward, and smacked into Bobby's stomach.

"What are you doing?" he said, and wrestled the hat from me. The kid turned around and, seeing Bobby with the hat, reached up for the visor. "Hey, that's mine!" he shouted. "Daaaaady!"

His father waddled up, a gargantuan cup of coffee in his hand. "What's going on?"

"He stole my hat!"

"Hey, man, it fell off his head, I was just returning it," Bobby said, handing the hat to the kid, and I felt so stupid. Like I needed him to protect me. I had a gun in my pocket. I could shoot up the whole place if I wanted to, and it was *my* hat. I used to wear it to games when I went with my father.

The kid returned the hat to his head, the father thanked Bobby, and they made their way toward the checkout counter. Bobby stared at me. I was hot as hell and my heart was whizzing like the microwave.

"It was my hat," I said.

"You took it from that kid. I saw you."

"You don't understand."

"Yeah, whatever, I don't give a shit. You're too fuckin' . . . I thought maybe, but . . . you know, you shoulda hooked up with Noz when you had the chance, you're as crazy as he is . . ." A series of tones sounded by the coffee station. "Shit . . . my burrito!" Bobby said, and jumped to the microwave. I followed him.

"What now?" he said, obviously annoyed when I was just doing what he'd said: following. He made a spitting noise between his teeth and grabbed his burrito by the edges of the plastic.

"I have your Zappa tape."

"Keep it, okay. Keep it. Just get off my case."

"But it was my hat. Come back to my house, I'll show you pictures. We can get high . . . c'mon."

"Are you deaf?" He stuck the forefinger of his free hand in my face, his burrito limp in the other like a thick plastic snake. "I said, get out of here. I'm sick of your face."

"Okay, I'll bring the photo album tomorrow. We can—"

"You are fucking pathetic." He brushed past me.

"Why? What did I do? Bobby!"

He turned around and for a second I thought his lips were softening, but his eyes looked meaner than ever. "And if you even think about saying anything to Edie," he said, "I'll kill you."

Then he walked to the cash register, and although I was tempted to follow—we were playing the boy-girl game, right?—I watched him pay for his burrito in the maddening white lights and disappear into the parking lot, thinking he was making a big mistake. Who else was going to buy him six-packs of tall boys and draw Zappa pictures for his dashboard? Give him handjobs along the side of the highway? Listen to his problems? I was the best thing that ever happened to him.

The next time I saw him I was wearing handcuffs, and he was completely shocked, he said. He couldn't believe I'd actually used the gun.

BACK IN COURT AGAIN. Your mother barely cracks a tear she's so poised, as if she's gone way past crying to a much darker place. A holy place. She's been giving interviews saying she prays every day for guidance and the courage to forgive. She has returned to the church and her faith is deep. She doesn't question. Doesn't condemn. She tells reporters you were an angel who mistakenly fell to earth as a human being. An angel who spread love all over the place but was really just burning to get back to heaven.

This blows my mind. I am many things, but not a martyr. The agent who helped you transcend the crystal boundaries of heaven and earth. I acted not out of conviction or philosophy, and on that sweltering day in July, I never set out to kill you. You were everything to me. God, or whoever's out there, please listen: I would do anything to bring you back again. I'd kill myself in a second if I thought it would repay your family for the grief I've caused. If I could extract the pain from your father's eyes. In the halfhearted light of the courtroom his face sags like globs of ashen clay. So does your mother's, despite her tales of angels and long meditative breaths. I want to smack her.

You deserve better. A mother who shouts for justice. Like your fans outside the courthouse holding posters with the years 1965–1987 scrawled across your face. When the police vans roll up they start shouting. Words, some less true than others; words so monotonous they blend into each other: *stalkerbitchdykemurdererwhore!*

I keep my head down, even after the police officers steer me through the crowd and into the noisy courtroom. It's weird, so many people here to see me and I don't know most of them. I'm as famous as you were. But I would never want to be an actress. It's too depressing.

Turns out my mother is the crier. From the moment the judge slaps his gavel, she wails. It is the first time I have ever seen her cry. She used to be a rock. Like me. A woman sitting next to her puts an arm around my mother's shoulder. She is my mother's sponsor. Jack sits in the row behind them, alone. Unshaven, his Italian suit rumpled as if he's been wearing it for days, he rocks back and forth in his seat like an autistic kid. Where's his sponsor? Helplessness pours from him, and it freaks me out. I wish he hadn't come today. It's just another bail hearing, my third since I've been at Rikers. The way I see it, Brickman has one more chance to get me out of here or he's history.

The judge is a Chinese man with a round face and thick glasses he removes to look over my records. He reads silently. Heat steams from the pipes like a clamoring waterfall, making me sleepy.

All I do is sleep since the scene with Angel's tattoo landed me in a new cell. Back on suicide watch, I'm monitored 24/7. I lost my job in the laundry and any chance of growing tomatoes. I have dreams of fiery red tomatoes. Dreams of waking up at dawn and working the fields. Someday I am going to live on a kibbutz. For now I eat hard mealy tomatoes in my cell, and every couple of days they take me to the showers, when nobody else is around. I miss talking to Angel, listening to warnings of the world outside, her world of ice-cold forties and salsa music and infected babies. The weird thing is, I bet Angel's a good mother when she's not too junked out of her head. I try not to remember her stoned, just as in the coldest hours, when death seems easier than living, I try not to long for Mimi. The way her hand doubled on top of mine when I first held the tattoo gun, just like Bobby's hands on the old Smith & Wesson. It's stupid the way people teach you things and then get so surprised when you actually go out and use what you've learned.

I slept through Christmas and New Year's Eve. On January first they let me into the fishbowl. Barely anyone there, the orange chairs and vinyl couches felt oppressive. Streams of light from the window pricked my skin. Better to be in my cold, dark cell, with no reminders of what I'm missing. I made a collect call to my grandmother in the desert and asked her to tell me stories about her childhood. She said the ceilings in her apartment building were so thin she could hear the man upstairs boiling water for his bath every morning before the sun came up. Rats patrolled the hallways as if it was their space and these immigrant people with their pale skin and pushcarts had wormed their way in. The only toilet was at the end of a long hallway with a broken window above it. In the winter it was so cold my grandmother peed through her underpants instead of pulling them down past her thighs.

The worst, she said, was having to share the toilet with so many people. Their smells clung to the air like the flecks of feces hugging the white porcelain basin. "Where do you go to the bathroom?" she asked me.

"In my cell."

"You have your own toilet?"

"Yes."

"See, there's always something to be thankful for."

I had to hang up before I started hating myself. How did I do this to her? This gray-headed woman whose eyelids hung low with the weight of history, a woman who at the age of sixteen had to quit school even though the teacher said she was the brightest in the class and work ten hours a day packaging bottles in a factory to support her family. At night she came home to a smelly shared bathroom.

Now she lives with a man who sometimes can't remember her name, but she won't let them put him in a home. Just as she won't abandon me. She makes long-distance calls to Rikers to see if they're feeding me. She's got the number programmed on her speed dial. The thought of her leafing her swollen knuckles through the instruction manual and learning how to connect to a jailhouse when she pushes my name makes me so sad I'm soggy. My internal organs, beginning with my banged-up heart, are dripping away. In a dream, I scoop up my grandmother, put my hands over her ears, and buzz like a test of the Emergency Broadcasting System, drowning out the noise, the persistent chorus tapping like an old-fashioned telegram: *stalkerbitchdykemurdererwhore!*

When the gavel falls a final time, I am ordered to return to my cell. Brickman has failed once again to prove their holding me without bail is cruel and unusual punishment for a first-time offender whose indictment is clouded with circumstantial evidence. My behavior on the inside has not helped. All of the tattoos and stolen needles. Licking Angel's tainted blood from my lips. If she has the virus, why shouldn't I? One guard testified to confiscating my Walkman and Bic pens. It's not worth going into any more of the proceedings, they do it better on the soaps. Know only that your mother breathes a sigh of relief as they escort me out of the courtroom.

A few days later the A.D.A. gives an interview. I am trying not to be insulted that they've passed my case down to an assistant, a plain-Jane type with an angular Picasso face who from what I can tell wears only gray. She is pleased the judge denied me bail and says it points to the seriousness of my crime. A heinous murder and the worst case of erotomania this city has seen since Mark David Chapman.

She's found a word for loving too much and I am it.

I am an erotomaniac.

I like the sound of it.

The shrink tells me not to think too much about anything

they say. She's never heard of plain-Jane Picasso's word and she's been to grad school. It's the American way to turn the things people do into diseases, she says. I think she was born somewhere else, this shrink, in Europe or Australia. Her accent reminds me of Clay Thompson from *World,* especially when she says the word *darling.* I stopped talking to her briefly last fall when Angel said it was a red flag, like tattooing the word *sicko* on my forehead.

But Angel is in the prison hospital and I am confined to my cell most of the day without anybody to talk to. Without you.

Perhaps I should be in a hospital as well. The love hospital. It has pink walls and heart-shaped hospital beds. Pretty nurses deliver meds in champagne glasses. At the love hospital there is no such thing as loving too much. Everyone is an erotomaniac.

I write the word with my felt-tip pen. No ballpoints for me anymore. They're afraid I might use them to puncture my veins. My sentences look different in felt tip; they're fuzzier, almost crying into the page. Calling out for you the way I can't do otherwise. As hard as I try, I can't make the tears come. At first I had to be tough. Now I am simply blank.

You don't come to me in my new cell. The shrink says this is also normal, there's a word for it, too, probably. Something that means you were never the person I thought you were, meaning I invented the whole thing, meaning . . . I keep remembering the gun and the hole in your chest with smoke coming out of it. It's like it's not real. Like I'm living in the endless middle of *World Without End* (soaps aren't big on endings), but this is real life, where no plot on the planet can ever bring you back. No swindle or cover-up, no "Hah! It was my identical twin you killed!" Even on the show, they left few openings: You were run down by a drunk driver, and everyone in Foxboro mourned for months. It was good for the cast, producers said. A natural outlet for their grief. But it must have been awful watching those episodes knowing the ending was real. At least it gave fans a sense of finality. They could see you were really gone, in life and on television.

And this is the crazy part: I am still here.

Trapped in a world without end, without you.

ICE AND SNOW PILED UP ALL WINTER LONG. Jack tucked his wool slacks into waterproof boots before getting in his car and driving into the city. He'd had a special closet in his office built for his fancy shoes, although he barely touched ground from garage to garage. At home, he hung a bumper sticker on our refrigerator with a picture of a dog lifting his leg to pee. Underneath it said: Just Say No to Yellow Snow.

In February we took a ski trip to Vermont and ate piles of snow with maple syrup on top. Nancy got the flu and was bedridden half the week. I took a lesson every morning. In the afternoons, Jack and I skied black-diamond slopes. At night I watched the sky, first awash in stars, then as the week wore on a sheet of heavy gray clouds that finally dragged in the rain. A skier's worst enemy. People forfeited their weekly tickets and called it quits or spent their final days of vacation driving into town, sipping hot chocolate, playing backgammon and Boggle and Parcheesi in the lodge. We went shopping for new equipment—the sales were fantastic—although Jack said it was the last time he would ski the East Coast; conditions were too unpredictable. I got a new pair of skies I never even tried. The storm had wiped out everything. I swear, you could hear the mountain cry.

One rainy morning, a man in a bright yellow raincoat with matching hat and boots knocked on our door and told Nancy her mother had just called the condo office, and my mother, looking perplexed, said, "I didn't give her that number."

"She says not to worry, but she needs to speak to you immediately. You can call from the office if you'd like."

Nancy grabbed her ski jacket and pointy wool hat that made her look like a woodpecker and stepped quickly into her furry after-ski boots. Jack looked up from the counter and murmured, "Need me?" but she'd already shut the door behind her. He returned to whatever it was he was doing. I walked to the windows and looked out at the gray parking lot. The clouds hung so low you could barely see the mountain. My throat was dry. Back in the kitchenette, Jack sat at the counter.

"What do you think's going on?" I asked, joining him.

"What am I, psychic?" He didn't look up, wasn't even interested. She wasn't his mother.

I opened the refrigerator and grabbed a carton of orange juice. Drank straight from the container. Jack stared at me. I guess I wasn't supposed to, but he did. It tasted better. "Hey," he said, "did you know there's a maple syrup farm near here? I wonder if it's the season. There's only a couple a weeks a year you can bleed the trees . . . You know what they do? They make a hole in the tree and then they tie a bucket underneath to catch the sap. It's wild. I mean, I'd really love to see that. You know, here we are putting a man on the moon and we're still catching maple syrup in metal buckets. Yeah, I'd really like to see that."

"Me too."

He raised his head. "You're humoring the old man?"

"No, really."

"Okay, then let's see if the trees are drooling yet." He hopped off his stool and walked toward the back of the condo, speaking over his shoulder. "And if they're not, we'll come back. We can come back, right? There's nothing stopping us. This shitty little town might be all right in the spring . . ."

He disappeared behind the bathroom door. I sat down at the counter where he'd been sitting. The seat was still warm and felt good. Jack generated a lot of heat. When I was a kid and we used to sit together on my bed, it was always cozy when I got underneath the covers. He'd filled up my room with his body, his words, his maple-y smell. Now he couldn't talk to me without doing a million other things.

Seeking a distraction of my own, I dug up the copy of *Babbling 'Bout Brooke* I had in my backpack. A new woman had taken over your fan club, and for weeks she'd been organizing a letter-writing campaign to an archbishop in the Midwest who had condemned a conflicted and heavily flashbacked kiss between Jaymie Jo and Father Brody. It was a disgrace, the bishop said, a total disparagement of the cloth. He was begging advertisers, in the name of decency, to pull their spots. But this new president of your fan club, a frosted blonde with fat cheeks and red blotches like Gorbachev's on her neck and face, said it was just art imitating life and if the church couldn't deal with having a mirror held up to it then that was its own problem. She was right, even though I hated her guts. The way she said everything was "hunky-Dorito"; her subservient moonbeam of a smile. You couldn't have had anything in common with her.

Anyway, I didn't care much about the church, those bishops were always railing against something, but I was pissed at the writers. They were totally out of touch with your character. Last fall you told *Soap Opera Digest* you'd stopped having sex with your boyfriend to get into Jaymie Jo's head and this had given you strength you never knew you had. I could totally relate. After me and Bobby broke up I decided I was finished with sex. Any idiot could secrete a hormone. It was the opposite that took real work. This is what you'd learned, and now they wanted your Jaymie Jo to give it up because the priest was good-looking, when he wasn't even half as cute as John Strong, and you'd managed to hold him off. Nobody was going to buy it.

I'd crafted these thoughts into a letter to you and cc'd the producers. A response came back, typewritten, so nobody would question it. You wrote (and I quote this from memory): *Dear Lillian G. Speck, I am aware of the problems some people have interpreted in Jaymie Jo's decision. We are working to resolve these very sensitive issues in a way that is satisfactory to everyone without compromising the integrity of the story or anybody's character. I am very thankful for your letter. Without the loyal support of fans like you, the often groundbreaking work we're doing on the show would be impossible. Always, Brooke.*

You scribbled your signature with a prominent *B*, a sign of confidence and complicity, but the letter sounded nothing like you. I knew you were angry about Jaymie Jo's decision, I could read between the lines, but I also knew you had to do what the producers said. In *Babbling* you said you would never intentionally offend the church, and once people saw where the story was going they'd understand. The message was really about "love on the macro scale." And your new fan club president said if anyone knew about macro-love it was you, and I thought, What right did she have to talk about your love? This woman who looked like the leader of the Communists. Who loved *her* so damn much?

I tossed the newsletter and returned to the windows. Mountain still weeping, maples drowning in their tears, drooling. Did the rain help loosen their syrup glands the way my nose always ran in the cold?

Nancy returned, drenched and heavy. Looking at her gave me a chill. The toilet flushed behind the bathroom door and Jack stepped outside. Their eyes met for a quick second, a gray field beaming between them. My throat clamped. Shaking off her hat and coat, Nancy spoke calmly: "My father's in the hospital. He ran the car into the divider and flipped over. He's okay, miraculously. Just a few scratches. But he doesn't remember any of it. He keeps asking why he took the bus to the mall when he has a car, why the driver wasn't more careful. My mother says he's worried about the other passengers, and every time she tells him there were no other passengers, he was driving, he nods, says, 'Oh, that's good,' is quiet for a few seconds, then asks why he took the bus to the mall."

"Okay, that's it, the party's over," Jack said. "The car is history. I told you he shouldn't be driving, he can barely see two feet in front of him on the shuffle board court. What is with motor vehicles out there? Aren't they supposed to test you again when you hit a certain age?"

"This isn't about his driving."

"How many times has he run off the road? Huh? It's always, 'One more time and we'll take the car away.' Well, *one more time* has come."

"He doesn't remember any of it."

"He's too old, let me tell you—"

"Did you hear me? He doesn't remember any of it!" Nancy shouted, and Jack and I both stared at her, so stiff. Like a mannequin. Rain pounded the glass doors, melting the clouds and trees and muddy roads outside. The wind was howling. Nancy walked to the kitchenette, took a glass from the drying rack, and turned on the sink, testing the water with her fingers before filling it. She drank two glasses of water in two long sips, then went for the gin. It wasn't even noon. Jack said he was going out to find the paper, and I asked if I could go with him.

He didn't answer, but I put on my ski jacket and hiking boots and followed him outside. We walked fast, although the rain letting up a bit felt good. Jack talked about the weather, how you don't really notice it until it gets in your way. I noticed it all the time, especially the rain. At home I really liked the rain. Here, it turned this magical wonderland into a scalped mountain. Who'd thought of cutting into it like that? Out there in the rain it didn't seem right.

Jack asked me if I'd met anyone in my lessons, and I shook my head no. "There were a bunch of kids in my class," he said. "We probably got into the wrong groups."

"There were kids in my group, I just didn't talk to them. They were kind of pompous."

"They were all much better than me. Don't say anything. You'll see when you're my age, it's not easy watching people who aren't thinking, If I go too fast I could lose control and break something or wind up dead or paralyzed or worse. One guy literally jumped from mogul to mogul, it was really something."

"A lot of people in my group did that."

"It was like the kid was flying," Jack smiled. We'd reached the general store and went inside.

Jack picked up his newspaper and asked if I wanted anything. I took a few root beer sticks from a glass jar on the counter, he paid, and we left the store. Jack was going over to the lodge to read. "I'll see you back at home," he said, and then must have sensed I wanted to go with him. "You know, one of the guys in my class mentioned a teen center . . . I think it's in the old barn. Why don't you try and find it? I bet there's a lot of kids hanging out. I mean, what else is there to do now, right?"

"Nothing," I said, and feeling the clamp around my neck, barely got out the words, "maybe I'll go," knowing I wouldn't be caught near anything called a teen center. I broke apart from Jack and walked toward the base of the mountain. The chair lift was running without passengers. Every thirty seconds or so one chair disappeared into the clouds as another one emerged from the mist on the other side. I thought it would be cool if we could ride into the clouds together. *I like it down here,* you said. *Let's walk through the woods back to your house. I want to hear more about you.*

No matter what was going on in your life, you always wanted to hear about me. This is exactly why I loved you. And did I have a lot on my mind. I'd been thinking about celibacy. About how sex really wasn't such a big deal. It was one of those things like drinking beer, or root beer for that matter—anybody could do it. Like the song says, birds do it, bees do it, my parents do it . . . You didn't have to be smart or funny or know anything about politics. In fact, you didn't have to know anything at all. It was the lowest common denominator.

And another thing I loved about you was you understood this. Since the bishops had been accusing you of cursing the priesthood, you felt like you had to defend sex, but only when it was tied to love. You said the story line was about a love so strong that—even though it went against all of society—to deny it physically would have been wrong. You said it had nothing to do with sex as we commonly refer to it and I knew exactly what you meant. Sex was everywhere. You'd see it in guys and girls together, holding hands like little commercials for it. Like you're nothing if you're not having sex. I hate to say it, but you were like that with John Strong: Watching you guys together was like looking at sex. But I knew you wanted more.

In *Babbling* you said you were really depressed when you and John broke up. You really loved him, and even though all the tabloids said he was having an affair with the TV star Robyn Carlyle, you swore you never believed them. Publicly, you said you hoped the two of you could work out your difficulties and get back together. But I knew better. There was nothing between you but common everyday sex.

And the breakup was good for your career. Already you were reading through movie scripts and thinking about directing. You didn't need John Strong eating up your time and mental energy. He didn't deserve it.

We'd come to the end of the muddy path that led to the parking lot behind the condo. The drizzling had just about stopped, and it was much colder. If the temperature kept falling, they could maybe turn on the snow machines overnight and fill in some of the grassy patches. We could get in one last day of skiing. I wanted you to stay and ski with me tomorrow but you had to work. It wasn't your fault, it went with the territory, and I was respectful, careful not to throw myself on you like the rest of your desperate fans.

As quickly as you'd come, you were gone. I stood alone in the half-empty lot, feeling as soggy as the barren mountain. People were leaving; they'd had enough. Through the glass doors of the condo, I could see Nancy curled up like a baby on the couch, the empty glass on the table in front of her, and I wished like hell I could have gotten out of there, too.

EACH DAY IS NO DIFFERENT FROM THE NEXT. I wake up to the sounds of the guard depositing my breakfast tray and walk over to the sink. Splash cold water on my face, try to see my reflection in the rusty pipes. Mirrors are taboo. Afraid I'll break the glass and use the pieces to slice up my wrists, they won't even let me keep the compact Nancy gave me.

You don't realize how much you miss your face until you can't see it—or maybe *you* do, Brooke. Is that what being dead is like? No concept of yourself other than your feelings. And nobody to share them with. You're totally alone.

When you think about the word *alone,* what does it look like? A desert with sweeping sand dunes as far as the eye can see? The busiest of streets in the busiest of cities where faces pass at lightning speed and not one is familiar? *Alone.* Say it as if it were an article and a noun: I am *a lone.*

And what does it feel like, that word? *Alone.* Something like nausea, but it breaks the skin in tiny red bumps. Alone is a physical thing.

The water in my sink won't get hot, and the soap barely lathers. It's white with dirty brown grooves in the bar and reminds me of the soap in Edie's bathroom. Her mom bought soap, paper towels, toilet paper, shampoo in bulk for discount prices, and everything seemed distilled, a lesser version of what it was supposed to be. Like Edie after Los Angeles.

Frantic for suds, I rub my fingers and palms over my face, trying to generate some sort of chemical reaction. Spontaneous combustion. If only I could blow myself up like a giant star. Incinerate the person I no longer see. What do I look like in here? What did I look like outside? When I was young I used to think people ignored me because I was so ugly. Jack and Nancy couldn't get too close, fearing the disease might rub off on them. Kids teased me about the white streak in my hair. Whenever strangers looked too closely I assumed they'd never seen a child so disgusting.

You wouldn't understand. Not unless you've ever wrapped your arms so tightly around your neck and shoulders just to know what it feels like to be held. Then you realize you're hugging yourself and it's more lonely than before. No, you couldn't possibly understand what it's like to be *a lone*. Not until you've spent your days and nights in an hourglass. One among thousands, millions, gazillions of granules of sand. Confined yet endless: This is what we mean when we speak of eternity.

Every day I get soap in my eyes, and every day it stings. At least I know my face is there. And you're still lost to me. You've really disappeared this time. Left me to wonder whether it was actually you in the first place, or if they might be right: I never had a chance. But if you weren't you, then how can I be me?

I drink a sip of bleach from the plastic cup the guard slipped onto my breakfast tray. My stomach contracts in rapid buckles. I am going to vomit, but I keep it down. At first I scoured my skin with bleach until it burned, trying to erase myself. It never worked. Sipping again from the cup, I can maybe spit up everything I've kept inside so long. I take out a yellow legal pad and draw a few squiggly lines, but can't concentrate long enough to hold the pen.

There is an interview with your mother in a thick magazine—another gift from my favorite guard, the bleach-carrier. I open the pages to a shock of perfume and find the story I've read and re-read. Your mother says she's happy you were happy in the months before your death. You'd stopped drinking and were thrilled to be onstage again. In such a demanding role, too. What your mother doesn't know and what I've never told a soul is that I smelled the suede flask next to you the day I found you in the stairwell. I knew the truth.

I run my forefinger along the pictures of you. In one you're surrounded by a group of fans at a mall somewhere in America. So accessible, so late in the game. After the haircut, the broken arm, the NAACP benefit where you kept calling it the ASPCA and had to be escorted offstage. The next day you issued an apology, saying your new allergy medication had made you hallucinate. And we bought it, all of us who devoured every issue of *Babbling 'Bout Brooke* and believed you when you said you needed three different pills just so you could breathe. At night I held you in my arms and promised everything would be okay.

But your mother says she knew better. She wanted you to take a break from *World*. Only there you were a few months later on the set they'd created in New York, an action shot, the camera and director visible—who cares? That wasn't the real you. Then you're stepping out of a limo with John Strong, posing at a premiere like you had everything anybody ever wanted: fame, fortune, romance. And you liked your family. Turning the page, I find you sitting on a couch with your sister and that damn happy dog, your father in a chair next to you reading the paper and mother hovering behind him, and it's this one that gets me. The everydayness of it. Like whoever took the shot only had to wait a couple of seconds for you to fall into place: a family.

It hurts so bad I have to cover you with my finger. And still they smile, the dog's tongue like a piece of ham, and I know I can't take you from them, even though you're gone. It's you I've robbed of everything.

Look at me. Listen closely.

I am what it looks like, feels like, this word *alone*.

STARLIGHT, STARBRIGHT

O N A CLEAR AND DEWY SATURDAY IN MAY, the Harrisons—Mildred, Tom, Cynthia, and Grampy Harry—climbed into Tom's new Buick Regal and drove from Blue Bell to New York City. Brooke had invited them up for a dual celebration of Cynthia's nineteenth birthday and the start of her rehearsals for the off-Broadway play *The Roses*. It was her riskiest career move to date, returning to the stage in a controversial new play, one that dealt frankly with early sexual abuse and would require a number of uncomfortable scenes, some nudity and profanity. This was her chance to prove she could really act, Brooke told Mildred, and if reviews were good, it could be her ticket out of daytime. Although Mildred worried that Brooke was setting herself up for yet another disappointment, she managed, as was her way, to sequester those feelings.

The troupe arrived in Manhattan at noon. Brooke met them in the lobby of the Hilton, where she'd booked a suite. There followed the requisite hugs and kisses, then Mildred watched as Brooke clasped her arm through Cynthia's in a proprietary gesture and they giggled all the way to the elevators, as if only Brooke understood the inner workings of her larger younger sister. Compared to Brooke they were all large, Mildred thought, and they really weren't big at all. Even Cynthia, who'd been overdoing it on the whole wheat bread and peanut butter—what else was a vegetarian to do at the university cafeteria?—was not overweight by anyone's standards. She looked like a normal young person in her nondescript cotton clothing and basketball shoes, while the slight and bony Brooke looked alien, almost fossil-like. She wore a tight leather miniskirt that accentuated her protruding hipbones, checkerboard stockings, and tastefully doused her eyes with cobalt-blue shadow, but beneath the trendy clothes and makeup her body seemed barely past puberty. As soon as Mildred saw her, despite receiving the wide-eyed grin she'd been aching for, the one that said, "You are my mother, you gave me life, and for that, no matter how many friends, lovers, and fans pass through my world, you are still my number one," despite even that, she wanted to cry out in bold tabloid fashion: The girl is evaporating!

Of course she did no such thing, afraid of upsetting Brooke upon their arrival, after her daughter had gone to so much trouble planning the weekend. So Mildred bit her lip and followed the family up to the seventeenth floor, where a two-bedroom suite awaited them. Cynthia, of course, would be staying with Brooke in the sublet the *World* producers had arranged for her. While they were not happy about adjusting their most popular story line to accommodate Brooke's "little theatrical diversion," they would do whatever it took to keep her happy. She was a huge audience draw. Yet Mildred wondered whether it was best for them to placate her. Sacrifice was often the wisest of teachers. If she'd had to choose between the play and securing her role on the soap, she might have learned to prioritize and maybe not push herself as hard.

Mildred dropped her jacket on one of the beds and walked into the shared living area, where Grampy Harry was ogling the selection in the mini bar.

"Have whatever you want," Brooke said.

"I say, that'll cost me an arm and a leg. I've heard about these outfits."

"Don't be silly, Grampy." Brooke jumped up and kissed his cheek, laughing. "You're not paying for anything. It'll cost me an arm and a leg, but what the heck? I've got a couple of each."

Grampy Harry took a Coke from the tiny refrigerator and pulled off the top, still looking a bit nervous. He'd never really understood just how successful his grand-daughter had become. To him she was always the little girl who'd climbed in his lap to talk into the wooden spoon they pretended was a microphone, giving dramatic read-ings from his *Popular Mechanics*. He held up the soda can in a toasting gesture before taking a sip. It was a convivial moment, capped by a most convivial afternoon. They had lunch at the Carnegie Deli, Tom's favorite restaurant, then strolled through Central Park, a slight breeze tickling their noses as their shoes squeaked across the damp grass. At four, Brooke took them to tea at the Pierre, quite a scene on Saturdays. The dining room was filled with dignitaries, financiers, a famous white-haired talk show host, and what Brooke called Eurotrash—decadent young Europeans with infinite time and resources at their dis-posal. She said they were revenge for all the rich Americans who flooded into Paris between the two big wars. Grampy Harry told them how eager he'd once been to serve his country, but when he was finally old enough join the U.S. Army in 1918, just as they were shipping off the war ended, and the boat returned to the States without ever touching ground in Europe. A career in civil service would thus be the extent of his public duty, a son who fought in Korea the closest he'd come to any war. Though they'd all heard the story a million times, the Harrison clan sighed with its grand patriarch as they sipped china cups of Earl Gray tea and munched on dry scones and clotted cream. Tom joked that he always gained five pounds whenever he came to New York, while his wife silently charted her daughter's stymied appetite.

Afterwards they had a few hours to rest and prepare for the celebratory dinner that evening. Brooke had made a reservation at a restaurant called Gotham, the sound of which seemed slightly ominous to Mildred. The Harrisons senior and grand patriarch hailed a taxi at the Hilton and arrived at the restaurant before the girls. They were shown to their table and promptly served champagne and black caviar, a delicacy Mildred never would have known herself to favor had it not been for Brooke. The restaurant was quiet and dimly lit. People dressed in evening wear; one man even wore a tuxedo. Mildred wished Tom had worn the tux they'd bought him when Brooke started inviting them to award shows, parties, and various charity events. It was a classic black suit and vest, with a white shirt—no ruffles, as they reminded Mildred too much of wedding musicians—and black bow tie. In it, Tom looked more like Robert Redford than usual, although wherever they went he always got the you-know-who-you-look-like routine from strangers, and it never failed to make him blush.

He didn't say much, her husband, but he looked great in a tuxedo. And he was a pleasant companion, despite his occasional flare-ups, and who didn't have those? Mildred reached her hand across the table and laid it on top of Tom's. He smiled, clasping her fingers between his own, and they stared silently into each other's eyes, satisfied for the moment with what their lives had amounted to.

"Ugh! Gag me with a Swiss army knife," Cynthia said. She stood above them, a sneer crossing her lips.

"So this is what you've been up to without Cyn around?" Brooke winked. Tom let go of his wife, who quickly folded her hands in her lap. Cynthia and Brooke filtered into their seats and it was as if a tidal wave had washed over the table. The smell of perfume emanated from the two girls, as if they'd been accosted by vigilant sample sprayers in a department store, and their faces looked as if they'd ransacked a few makeup counters. More surprising, however, was Cynthia's black cocktail dress that hugged her right shoulder, cutting diagonally down across her breasts to wrap beneath her left armpit. Mildred hadn't seen her younger daughter out of pants since her graduation from high school, and even then it had been a shapeless floor-length skirt and sensible top, but there she was dressed like her sister, although she reminded Mildred more of a field hockey player stuffed into a tutu. "You like it?" Brooke said. "It's Fiorucci. So are the shoes. Cyn, show them the shoes."

Cynthia backed up her chair and raised her right foot in the air. It was covered with a plaid Mary Jane on boxy rubber souls that Mildred thought looked clownish and didn't go with the dress, but when she mentioned that fact, Cynthia huffed, "That's the point!" and Mildred once again felt rebuked as her daughters exchanged a conspiratorial wink.

The girls were quite talkative. Apparently a "scene" had occurred in the cab downtown. Like a rehearsed duet, they took turns telling the story of their driver who'd practically had a coronary when he hit a traffic jam on Broadway and wouldn't stop pounding his fist against the dashboard, crying for God to clear the streets. He slammed the breaks on and off so often his tiny statue of Jesus looked pallid. When Brooke finally suggested he try cutting east, he exclaimed: "You are so selfish!" At that, Brooke and Cynthia jumped out of the cab without paying and walked to the restaurant, giggling and calling each other selfish the entire way. It was too beautiful to be in a cab anyway, Cynthia said, and Mildred wondered where the sentiment had come from. Never before had she heard her youngest daughter call anything beautiful, but she reminded herself she'd never seen her dressed like a misguided debutante either. There was so much she would never know about her children.

A man in vest and bow tie approached to take their dinner orders, and again Brooke reminded Grampy Harry he wasn't paying and could have whatever he wanted. He chose the grilled salmon, the one entrée on the menu he said he recognized, and a lightly creamed portobello mushroom soup, though he confessed the word *portobello* sounded like a public urinal, and they all politely ignored him. Brooke was about to order when her jaw dropped. "Oh shit!" she said, then apologized for the obscenity before popping up from the table. Mildred watched her walk to the bar, where they seemed to be letting her use the telephone. After she returned and they completed their first course, Cynthia excused herself to visit the ladies room and Brooke explained that she'd left Cynthia's birthday cake in the refrigerator, after she'd secured special permission from the restaurant to bring it, no small feat at a new establishment with one of the hottest pastry chefs in the city—"But they know what's good for them," Brooke winked, and Mildred startled at her words, the stroke of venom in her eyes and subtle rise of her back. This was the daughter she rarely saw, the one who thrived on her own publicity folder. It was not a pretty sight.

"Anyway, I caught Johnny, and he's going to bring it down," she said.

"John's in New York?" Mildred asked. "Well, why didn't you say something? We'd love to see him."

"Oh, he had a drinks thing but, actually, it got cancelled, so there you have it. He's on his way." Nodding nervously, she threw her hands in the air and smiled, but there was no fooling Mildred. Brooke was obviously uncomfortable with the situation, and she hadn't mentioned John in weeks. The waiter brought another bottle of champagne, refilling around the table, but when he got to Brooke, she crossed her palms over the glass, flashing an anxious smile. "I'm not drinking during rehearsals," she said, and Mildred was pleased. Perhaps all of those drunk-driving classes were finally paying off, or maybe the play was more difficult than she'd imagined or she and John were experiencing some of the problems the tabloids chronicled or she'd simply had enough. But there was no time for a follow-up question as Cynthia had just returned, and their main courses were being served.

Mildred once again held her tongue when she saw that Brooke had ordered only a bowl of tomato bisque to follow her mixed-greens salad. Even Cynthia had indulged in an entire plate of grilled vegetables, some of which Mildred had never even heard of, let alone seen, with a strange assortment of purées. Brooke said she'd spoken to the chef about making sure there were vegetarian options for Cynthia on her birthday. It was sweet the way they took care of each other, and nobody could accuse them of not eating their vegetables! Besides, Mildred's roast duck smelled too delectable not to warrant her full attention. She looked down at the sliced fowl doused with a rainbow of colorful peppers and orange peels, resting on a bed of some sort of grain, and before sticking her fork and knife into the meat, softly said, "I'm all yours." A tiny snicker rose through her radiated cheeks. Alrighty, she thought, no more champagne, although it was difficult to stop with those waiters refilling her glass every few minutes, but at least everyone except Brooke received the same treatment and therefore, as far as she knew, they were all equally impaired and probably hadn't heard her flirting with her food.

They ate fiercely and happily, chatting mostly about (rather than directly addressing) the food in rich adjectives and making mellifluous lip-smacking noises. They reminisced about the day's events—they couldn't have had nicer weather! In May, New York became the most wondrous city in the world, Brooke said. And so much closer to home than Los Angeles, they all agreed.

A waiter approached the table but stood off to the side as two busboys cleared their dinner plates, stepping up only after they'd finished to skim the table with his silver crumber. He handed out dessert menus, and just as they settled in to read them, a boisterous current overtook the restaurant and seemed to sweep all heads toward the front door, even the disaffected waiter proffering a sideways glance, as John Strong and two tall women with short dark hair entered the restaurant. Brooke grimaced, "Oh god, I can't believe he brought them!"

They all stared as John Strong approached the table

looking every bit the screen idol, his face illuminated by the twenty candles in the big chocolate cake, and a stunning girl on each side of him. "It's the Gargolye twins," Brooke whispered loud enough so they'd all hear. "Anna's okay, but a bit weird, and Paulina . . . she's another story entirely."

"Which is which?" Cynthia asked, and was quickly informed that Anna had the rounder, sweeter face, although Mildred thought they both looked like the somber women she remembered from her parents' union magazines in the fifties: dark hair and eyes, milky-white skin and prominent jaws, as if they'd been trained forward by years of sloganeering. Only these girls were much, much taller than she'd envisioned.

"Who are the Gargle twins?" Grampy Harry asked.

Brooke laughed. "Don't call them that, Grampy. Paulina loves throwing things. They're models, from somewhere in Eastern Europe."

"Eurotrash!" Mildred exclaimed merrily.

"No, Mother," Brooke rolled her eyes, but it was Cynthia who scoffed worse than when she'd seen Mildred and Tom holding hands earlier. As if Mildred were the most ridiculous creature she'd ever set eyes on. Why did Cynthia have such a problem with her? Or was it Mildred's problem? Was she acting that badly? Nobody else seemed to notice. Perhaps the champagne was making her paranoid. She remembered then that she wasn't supposed to drink so much. Easier adhering to this precept at home, of course.

"Mom, Eurotrash is like if you're from Italy or France, the real Europe," Brooke explained. "They're from the Communist bloc. Anyway, they've been on the cover of practically every magazine. Now they're trying to do movies, but I've seen their reel—"

The trio reached the table and John Strong set down the cake, throwing his fingers in the air with a resounding "one-two-three," and, as they all launched into a honeysuckle-sweet version of "Happy Birthday to You," Mildred was charmed the Eastern European models knew all the words, surmising they must have let them celebrate birthdays behind the Iron Curtain, a thought that for the moment brought her closer to the vast melting pot of humanity. She sang out at the top of her lungs. By the time they reached the climactic "Happy birthday, dear Cynthia!" Mildred's eyes were clouded with tears.

Cynthia smiled and blew out her candles. The maître d' whisked away the cake and had three more chairs brought to the table. John Strong put his hands on Brooke's shoulders and kissed her forehead, then sat down next to Grampy Harry, who seemed nonplussed by the sudden boost in star power at the table. He proudly announced he was feeling a bit of indigestion, and everyone laughed. Mildred was mortified. "Fantastic! You are the real thing, sir," John Strong clucked with more charm than ought to be allowed. He had the kind of smile any car salesman would have bargained away his mother for. Turning to Brooke, he said, "He's special, isn't he?" Brooke smiled and said of course he was. "I'm going to call you Sir Special," John Strong said. He put his arm around the old man and handed him a cigar. Cuban, he said. Smuggled in from Havana that very morning. John Strong offered one to Tom as well but he declined, and thus the famous young actor and wanna-be war hero knighted Sir Special shared a smoke, accompanied by a few serious words about cigars.

A Gargoyle reached for the bottle of champagne, filled the empty glasses all around, then shouted for the waiter to bring another bottle. "How old are you today?" she asked Cynthia.

"Nineteen."

"Ah, nineteen," she said, and her accent sounded exactly the way Mildred had imagined it from the magazines. "I think always of nineteen. It is like another lifetime to go."

"How old are you now?" Mildred asked her.

"A true woman must not reveal her age," she sighed.

"We're twenty-three," the other one said.

"Anna!"

Mildred giggled. "That's hardly old."

"In Europe, no, but in America, we are spoiled," said the first one, Paulina, Mildred thought. "Over here, past twenty, nobody wants to hear from you nothing. And in America is where the money is. It is the difference between gray and black, right, Anna?"

Okay, she was definitely Paulina, Mildred registered, and made a mental note to remember that she was seated between John Strong and the sweeter-looking one, Anna. Yet as soon as she thought she had it straight, the two of them started tumbling like gymnasts out of their seats and gliding to the bathroom, the public telephone, or whispering together by the bar. Once John Strong had to get up and fetch them from the front of the restaurant. Another time Brooke dragged one of them out of the bathroom, and she came back with the same dour expression, though her eyeballs flared like fireflies. She told them all she was a student of soap, and nobody thought to ask how she'd embarked upon such an endeavor nor what it entailed.

John Strong tried to move things along, proposing toasts to Brooke for her work on the play, to Cynthia for her birthday and for making it through her freshman year, and finally to Mildred and Tom. "These people are *parents*," he said, and chugged an entire glass of champagne.

Mildred wasn't surprised to see Tom's cheeks redden, yet she was practically knocked from her chair when he stood up and raised his glass. "I'd like to say a few words," he said. The Gargoyle girls whispered heatedly to each other. Anna, the sweet one who studied soap—Mildred was getting good—looked distraught; Paulina angry. "Hey, hey, the man is speaking!" John Strong shouted. Paulina bolted from the table. "Don't worry about her, she's got a social disease. Go ahead, Tom."

John Strong picked up his glass for the toast. Tom curled his tongue against his upper lip, and for a second Mildred worried he'd lost his train of thought and felt embarrassed, but thankfully he recovered, taking a deep breath and slowly beginning to speak: "Well, of course, this isn't really my thing, so I hope you'll all indulge my sloppiness and forgive the inarticulate moments—"

"Hear, hear!" John cheered, then put his arm around Brooke, and she fidgeted as if the limb were a heavy satchel she would be glad to relinquish at the soonest possible occasion. Mildred remembered the night she'd first met the young actor, how Brooke had nestled into his shoulder as if they were the two missing pieces of a puzzle, how much in love they'd seemed. Watching them, Mildred couldn't help reminiscing about her own first love, who happened to be her husband. Funny, she thought, how infectious love is and how off-putting its disintegration. Mildred studied her husband as he stood, cheeks flushed and glass in hand, and wondered if she was still the one he thought of when he thought about love.

"The truth is," Tom continued, "I just wanted to take this opportunity on behalf of Mildred and myself to say what we find ourselves mostly writing in greeting cards these days—it's not easy watching your children leave home, right Dad?" Tom raised his glass to his father, who nodded politely. "Anyway, seeing these two girls go off into the world and make their mark, each in her very own and very dynamic way, has really been the highlight of our lives. We are so proud of you both, so moved by your creativity and inspired by your generosity, and we are just pleased as punch to be here tonight. So . . . cheers!"

Mildred's cheeks radiated, her heart swelled. She was floored by Tom's eloquence: a man of few words but he made each one count. John Strong bounced up with a champagne bottle in his hand, took a long sip, and passed it on to Grampy Harry who stood and did the same. Like this they passed around champagne bottles and cheered. Mildred glanced over at Brooke and her face seemed peculiarly void of emotion. Or was Mildred being paranoid again? Now that she thought of it, she was a bit self-conscious standing and guzzling hundred-dollar champagne in the middle of one of the finest restaurants in town, but nobody seemed to mind them causing such a ruckus—fringe benefits, again. Sometimes Mildred could hardly believe the things they got away with.

The waiter returned with slices of birthday cake and they all sat down to their final course. Mildred, though relieved to be off her feet, felt a bit wistful. If she required a few moments of introspection, however, they were robbed by Paulina Gargoyle, who returned to the table and dropped a black patent-leather handbag in front of her sister. "You are the most luckiest girl in the planet," she said.

"Where did you find it?"

"In the telephone box. This was the one thing I ask you, I ask you can you take the big bag and you say, 'Yes, yes, yes.' You idiot! You will not lay your fingers near it anymore. Understand?"

She looked crestfallen. "I'm sorry."

"Oh, don't cry, you are simply lazy."

"My mind is no good."

"It's finished . . . don't go down on yourself."

"Sometimes I think there is always a PA to follow me and picking up things and everything."

"Anna, I said stop. Enough!"

"I totally get that," Brooke nudged Anna.

"You too!" Paulina shouted. "Enough."

Brooke ignored her. "I leave things all over the place, too."

"Shut up, will you!" Paulina picked up a champagne flute by the stem and slammed it against the table. Tiny flecks of glass shattered to the floor like crystals in a snowglobe. Mildred covered her eyes.

"If you even knew what she did!" Paulina shouted at Brooke. "She is so stupid, and you, you are even more horrible encouraging her."

"How dare you, like, come in here and insult me in

front of my family!" Brooke shouted. "You weren't even invited."

"That's what you think—you are so stupid!"

"Me! Have you looked in a mirror recently?"

"Okay, I think we'd better be going," said John Strong, and grabbed Paulina by the arm. "Anna, you too," he said, and they all looked at the sweet one who caressed a small piece of soap between her hands, as if she were washing. A look of panic crossed the leading man's face. Mildred glanced over at Tom, who cut the air with his outstretched hand, a sign they shouldn't get involved. This sort of trouble was out of their league.

Grampy Harry reached into his pocket and pulled out a tiny wrapped bar of soap. "I collect the little ones," he said. "Got a whole jar of 'em back home. Here, take it."

"I couldn't."

"Now, don't stand on ceremony, miss. They leave more than ought to be allowed in our room. I insist."

Anna took the tiny bar from Grampy Harry, unwrapped it, and held it under her nose. "Ah, but it is not milled," she said. "There is an exclusive pleasure in milled soaps, and they are only sometimes found in restaurants."

"You stupid girl!" Paulina shouted, struggling to free herself from John's grip. "I am going to break you off your head."

Still restraining Paulina, John nudged Anna up out of her seat with his free hand. "Give me the soap," he said, and she held them tighter into her stomach. John turned his head to the table. "Nice seeing you all but we've got another party to go to."

"Let go of me!" shouted Paulina.

"Young man," Grampy Harry addressed John. "If you'll allow me to offer one final word of advice."

"What's that, sir?" John Strong said through gritted teeth, a Gargoyle clamped in each arm.

"You are going to be so sorry only one hour from now!" Paulina shouted at Brooke. She twisted under John

Strong's shoulder but couldn't break free. "Remember the thing you ask from me, well, you will come and cry to my feet!"

"When hell freezes over." Brooke stood up in front of Paulina and was so dwarfed by the stealth bomber of a fashion model that Mildred found herself rising to move behind her daughter, despite her husband's silent warning.

"Never serve only yourself," Grampy Harry advised John Strong. "And always find the right man for the job."

John smiled. "Thank you, Sir Special. I'll send you a box of Havanas, but we really gotta go now."

"Thank you for gifting me," said Anna to Grampy Harry.

"Now hands off!" Paulina shouted. She shoved her elbow back into John Strong's stomach. He heaved forward. The irate Gargoyle glared down at Brooke, who held her stare. For one second, they were all stilled. Mildred could hear the fizzle of champagne bubbles coming from the table, a soundtrack too elegant for Paulina as she turned and stormed out the front door. John Strong took Anna under his arm and followed, flipping his head slightly to call out a name that must have meant something to Brooke.

She picked up a champagne flute and emptied its contents into her mouth. "It's medicinal," she said, upon catching her mother's worried eye. Mildred drained her own glass, hoping it might quell the pounding behind her forehead or drown out the obnoxious silence left by the glamorous, if not a bit off-color, trio.

"What a fine boy," Grampy Harry said.

"Yeah," Cynthia agreed. "But those models are a little creepy."

"I know, totally," Brooke said, then almost immediately her face collapsed as it had when she realized she'd forgotten Cynthia's cake, and Mildred knew she remembered something, perhaps the "thing" Paulina had said she'd be crying for, and this set Mildred's mind racing at a roadrunner's pace. She wondered if the Gargoyle girls were some kind of front, if perhaps they were Russian spies, the kind Mildred had read about in thick bestsellers, or maybe they were drug runners, a more troublesome equation given their proximity to her daughter. America was presently embroiled in a war on drugs. Mildred remembered the Reagans appearing together on TV last fall, pleading with Americans to swing into action just as they'd done during the Second World War, as this, too, was a fight for freedom. Talk to your children about drugs, the first lady had said. But where did you start? And what if they told you it wasn't what you thought, if you'd let them convince you it was all about image and not based the slightest in reality? Mildred shuddered, thinking again of that night in Brooke's apartment and wondering whether she'd been hoodwinked. Such suspicions would have to wait, however, as everyone had rebounded from the previous scene, and Brooke suggested that Cynthia open her birthday present. She handed her sister a rather large box with a big red bow. Cynthia ripped it open and pulled out a thick chain and padlock, then discovered a Polaroid of the ten-speed bicycle Brooke had purchased for her. Cynthia wailed, gleefully jumping up from her seat and throwing her arms around her sister.

The two girls hugged and cried and told each other they were the best, as Mildred and Tom looked on, if not exactly upstaged (they'd given their daughter a few of the books she'd requested and a small tent she'd once admired in the sporting-goods store), then a bit perplexed. Cynthia had never expressed any interest in a bicycle, always a stalwart proponent of public transportation. She wouldn't even let Mildred and Tom pick her up at school, preferring instead to store her few belongings on campus and ride the bus home from Philly, and as far as Mildred knew Cynthia had never even sat stationary on one of Brooke's old bikes, all of which were still kept in the garage. Mildred glanced across the table at her husband, who shrugged and raised his eyebrows as if to say, Who knew? and by way of agree-ment Mildred shook her head back and forth slightly.

When the waiter passed, Tom made certain to ask that the check be delivered to him and not Brooke. If Brooke had heard him, she decided not to argue or was simply too overwhelmed by her own generosity and its effects upon her sister that she simply didn't care. Watching Brooke run her fingers through Cynthia's hair as the young girl giggled, the two of them shivering with delight, Mildred softened slightly and couldn't help thinking how blessed they all were, really, and at that moment she made a silent vow to talk to each one of the girls about drugs. She would find a way. Tom yawned loudly, calling Mildred from her silent crusade, and she smiled at the dashing man aglow in the warm light of the candles, the man who'd managed to artic-ulate so stunningly everything they'd been feeling these past few months though they hadn't once confessed their thoughts on the subject, reminding Mildred, much like his hand between her breasts at night, that they were together in this—married—and it was more romantic than ever. She couldn't wait to feel his body beneath the quilted covers of their king-sized bed back at the Hilton. Tom gave his wife a quick wink, then took out his money clip, and she purred silently, slathered in their connubial transference.

"What a day!" he cried.

"A wonderful day," Brooke agreed.

And they gathered up their belongings and left the restaurant, Brooke promising outside in the breezy spring night that she and Cynthia would go directly home, and even if Mildred had suspected anything different she kept her mouth shut, heeding instead to her own agenda. There would be plenty of time for her children, she thought, plenty of time for the family. The rest of the night in the city belonged to her and her husband.

SUPERNOVA

I FIRST READ ABOUT YOUR OFF-BROADWAY SHOW in *Babbling 'Bout Brooke*. The article said you were playing a college student coming to terms with your sexually abusive father. There would be a confrontation scene where you remove your shirt and bra in front of him. Everyone would soon be talking about it, some of your fans balking, How dare you break the wall around your character! Jaymie Jo would never do anything that aggressive! They were so ridiculous.

The play was set to begin previews at a theatre on the first of June, two days before my eighteenth birthday, and would run through the middle of July. Six weeks plus rehearsal time was all the *World* producers would give you in New York. They'd constructed a special set and geared the plot toward your joining the conflicted Father Brody in the monastery. The controlled environment would save you both from animal passion. If that didn't work, Father Brody was going to leave the priesthood.

As soon as I could I ordered a ticket to the first performance with my credit card and went into the city to check out the theatre, hoping I might run into you. There was another play up, and the lady at the box office told me nobody rehearsed in the same place they were going to perform. Bad luck or something. The night of the show, I drove into the city and parked my car in a garage across the street from the theatre. Having an hour to kill, I dropped into a diner with pink neon stars in the window, sat down at the counter, and ordered a cup of coffee, which tasted like motor oil. I opened four packs of sugar and mixed them with the grainy liquid. An old man next to me dribbled pea soup down his chin and mumbled into his bowl, ". . . It's a hoax . . . blah, blah, romantic love, who cares? . . . Nothing to be so damn proud of . . ." I turned away from him, trying to concentrate on the specials scrawled on a blackboard in front of me. But it was hard. He was loud and, from what I could tell, drunk. He'd had it up to here with love. I brushed the side of my parachute pants, the pair I always wore into the city, checking for my gun.

A few years earlier, there was a man who carried a gun when he rode the subways. One day he shot four boys who he said were trying to rob him. A boy was partially paralyzed. The man was white, the boys black. The media took the man's side, saying we had to be aware of menacing urban youth. People started talking about rising crime and violence. They were frustrated and afraid. Jack wanted Nancy to take a self-defense class. She came into the city a lot on her own and should be able to protect herself.

When I met Edie, about a year later, she said my father's response had been racist. She said we had to beware of white people with guns. Before she got the life knocked out of her in Los Angeles. Nobody was safe anymore.

I remembered a joke Jack liked to tell:

What's the difference between a Republican and a Democrat?
A Republican's a Democrat who's been mugged.

I put a dollar on the counter for my coffee and jumped off the stool. The old man grabbed my arm. I grunted and flinched away, my heart speeding. Fucking lunatic was lucky. I was armed and so far still a Democrat, even though I hadn't voted.

"Hey!" the man called out. "Hey you! I'm talking to you." I turned and he stared right at me, crusty green soup caught in his stubbled chin. "You can't have real love if you don't have children!"

"Settle down, Jimmy," pleaded the woman behind the counter.

I got out of there as quickly as I could and ran to the theatre. A young woman led me to my seat and handed me a *Playbill*. I read and reread your bio until the lights dimmed and the curtain opened. You were the last of the cast to be introduced, although everyone had been talking about your character before you got onstage. There were all kinds of little plots involving friends and lovers. I was bored to tears until the second act when you confronted your father. Removing your shirt was a big mistake. A few people gasped. A man stood up and his chair creaked loudly. Everyone turned toward him, a few people said *shush*. He stormed out. You kept up your monologue. Crying like the biggest crybaby in the world. I can see how you got the part, having been through all those teary-eyed scenes on *World,* but I was sorry you'd taken it. How could you stand there half naked in public? I knew you were acting, I wasn't that naïve, but it was your body, your silken flesh and nipples glaring like pink neon stars before hundreds of prying eyes. My *Playbill* slipped from my lap, and I bent down to get it, incurring the wrath of the shushers. "I dropped my *Playbill,*" I whispered.

"SHUSH!"

I didn't make another sound until you came out for two curtain calls and I screamed my lungs out. Despite the nudity, I was so proud of you. I decided to hang around and wait after the show. The lobby was clearing out, so I asked a man in a blue velvet vest where I could find your dressing room. "Behind the stage," he said. "But you can't go back there."

"I'd like to see Brooke."

"You and half the city."

"But . . ." I wanted to explain who I was but suddenly thought better of it; he'd never understand.

"If you go around the building and turn up Ninth Avenue, you'll see an alley that leads to the stage door. That's as close as you're gonna get to Brooke Harrison."

"Thanks," I said. Maybe he understood more than I knew.

I left the theatre and followed his directions. Ninth Avenue was bustling with skanky restaurants, homeless men with grimy faces begging for quarters, heavy foot traffic heading for Port Authority. Ever since I was a kid I'd heard stories of girls stepping off buses from places like Iowa and being forced into prostitution. There was even a TV movie about it. But it never seemed that dangerous to me. Just dirty. I passed a couple of theatres, a steakhouse that bled a smoked-meat scent into the streets, then came to the alley, where I turned and saw a group of people, mostly young girls, women, and a few men who looked like fathers, waiting by the stage door. A few weeks ago, in a TV interview you'd said it was difficult always meeting the demands of your fans. "Don't get me wrong, I love my fans, but sometimes it's a bit of a strain," you said. "I mean, John walks down the street and he's John Strong, but me, I'm Jaymie Jo Rheinhart." You said when you were in Italy last summer with your family, a busload of American girls chased you around the Vatican. They wanted to take pictures and hug you. You said people always put their arms around you because they see all these crazy things happen to you every day and they feel bad, which you could understand but it wasn't too cool. So in Italy, you were like, "Can't you see I'm on vacation? I'm with my family." But it didn't matter. Because to them you were just Jaymie Jo in a foreign country.

You were not going to be happy with this scene. I tried to break through the crowd and get closer to the stage door to warn you, but it was no use. Nobody would budge, not even the fathers who clutched their rolled *Playbill*s and looked up at the electrified sky, trying to pretend they weren't standing in an alley waiting for a soap star. I turned and bolted down Ninth Avenue to the parking lot, where I paid the attendant, and he brought me my Saab. Windows open, I chain-smoked as I sped home along the L.I.E. in the warm June night, thinking I would return in a few days and see if the crowds outside had died down.

Any theatre lover will tell you that you can often catch the second act of a show for free since the ushers never check tickets after intermission. I'd learned this from my mother, who once pointed to a lady sitting next to me at *Grease,* where the seat had been empty during the first act. Nancy was appalled. She said if you didn't have the money for a ticket you had no business being at the theatre. Your show had a sold-out run, thanks to reviews as good as the producers had anticipated. There was even talk about extending a few weeks. But I still managed to sneak in a couple of times after intermission and find a seat, Nancy be damned. Once,

I got as far up as the second row, where I could see the beige make-up running down your temples and noticed your arms were full of bruises. They must have come from all of the thrashing around you did on stage. The role was just as physically demanding as your exorcism had been.

Two weeks into the run, I cut my last classes on Wednesday to see if I could scalp a ticket for the matinee or at least second-act it. I thought I might have better luck catching you afterwards on a weekday. I took the train in to avoid rush hour coming back and arrived at the theatre a bit early. There was nobody at the box office, but the front doors were open so I walked inside. I went to the bathroom and pumped sweet-smelling soap into my palms, then ran it through my hair to tame the waves. Outside, a man was setting up the small bar, and I could hear rustling coming from the box office. I needed a cigarette, but didn't want to leave the building. I thought maybe I could first-act the play. Sneak inside and shirk the ushers until the curtain went up. I was already in the building, why leave and have to buy a ticket?

I ducked behind the bar, toward the side of the balcony. There was a red Exit sign hanging above a door, which was open slightly and seemed to lead to a stairwell. I walked to the door and pushed it slowly. The spring creaked, and it sounded menacing, like an Abbott and Costello movie. I imagined a mummy on the other side. My breath came faster, ghoulish faces flashed through my mind. Only the gun in the side pocket of my pants calmed me as I pushed the door all the way back and walked into the gray cement stairwell. The walls were dark and floors dotted with cigarette butts. I'd stumbled upon the right place. I turned my head and there you were, sitting on the grated metal stairs with your head folded between your legs.

I gasped.

You looked up, barely registering me, then put your head back in between your legs and stared down at the step beneath you. Sweat poured from my armpits, down my back, between my legs, and I felt as if my head might explode from the pounding. I didn't know what to say, wasn't prepared, and could not for the life of me move. You picked through your hair with your fingertips, as if you were braiding, and when you got down to one single strand you yanked it from your head with a snap. There were stray hairs around you. I stood, fascinated you could do this in front of me as easily as you could take off your bra on stage. At least it was me who found you and not someone who wouldn't understand. My pulse slowed and I stopped sweating, but my neck and lungs felt heavier than normal. It's stupid but I wanted to weep. I'm not sure how long we stayed, you weaving and picking, and me watching, before the man in the blue vest who'd led me to the stage door the other night came through the stairwell and saw you sitting there. "Ms. Harrison, Sampson's been looking all over for you," he said, bending down in front of you. "He's got your notes from last night." You didn't respond, not even to ask what notes, which is what I wanted to know, but when he offered you a hand, you shoved it away and slowly leaned up against the wall. "I'm sorry," he said, then pivoted closer to me. "And what are you doing in here?" He sniffed the air. "Ugh! You were smoking. How many times do we have to talk about this? Smoking in the back office only. Now go on in and get your vest from Tabitha, and we'll forget it this time."

I was too flummoxed to ask what vest and couldn't take my eyes off you. You held one palm against the wall and swayed toward what must have been your dressing room. I was about to turn around and run from the building before this guy realized I wasn't who he thought I was, when I saw the suede flask on the stairs where you'd been sitting. I kneeled down and picked it up. It reeked of alcohol. "Give me that!" The man yanked it from my hand. "Now, go on, go. I know we don't pay you, but that doesn't mean you can break any rule you want. Tabitha's already opened the house."

"Okay," I said, and followed him out. But before we left the stairwell, I swept my hands over the step where you'd been sitting and grabbed a few strands of your hair.

In the lobby, a couple of people stood by the bar, waiting for someone to appear behind it. Others clustered in small groups. We tracked down Tabitha, a bleach-blond woman with a waxy yellow face who must have been about Nancy's age, and when the man in the vest went to introduce me, he apologized for forgetting my name.

"It's Edie," I said.

"Of course, Edie," he said. "We had you here a couple of weeks ago."

I nodded.

"Must'uv missed you." Tabitha grabbed my hand and shook it hard. "A blessing you're here today, though. Two other girls canceled. I'll have to take the balcony myself. Follow me."

A bunch of keys hung from her belt loop, jingling as she waddled toward a musty room with a cluttered desk and stacks and stacks of *Playbills* on the floor. There were a few shelves on the wall, separated into little boxes. Some were empty, some had blue vests, T-shirts, and other clothes. "Do you remember what size we gave you?" Tabitha asked.

"Large," I said. It had to be big enough to fit over the blue Oxford I was wearing. She reached up and grabbed a vest. "Do you need a T-shirt?"

"I don't think so."

She looked me over. "Oh yes you do. Only white under blue, sweetheart."

"Oh," I looked down at my clothes, "I remember."

She handed me the vest and T-shirt, which was wrapped in plastic, and pointed to a stack of *Playbills*. "Grab a batch after you change, put your clothes in a cubby, and don't forget to shut the door behind you. Lotta sticky fingers around here, if you catch my drift." She whispered the last line with her head down, as if she were confiding in me.

I nodded and started unbuttoning my shirt, thinking how funny it was to be removing my clothes in this theatre the same way you did every night. Tabitha left. I finished undressing and ripped the T-shirt out of its wrapping. It smelled like new cotton and was stiff against my skin. When I lifted the blue vest, I noticed a cigarette burn near the left shoulder. That, I would report immediately. I wasn't about to get falsely accused of smoking twice on my first day of work.

THE GUARDS HAVE BEEN SLACKENING WITH ME, allowing me a few hours a day to go to the library, use the rowing machine in the gym, watch TV in the fishbowl, usually during meals when nobody else is around. They've also let me outside a few times since the weather started warming up. Keeping a watchful eye on me, of course. They don't want me picking fights I'll lose and end up in the hospital or worse. Their job is to keep me alive for my trial, which seems further off than ever since that last bail hearing.

"Not to worry," Brickman said, a week later. "The longer we go, the less impact they'll have. Time is on our side."

"I don't care, I can't take it anymore. I'm going crazy."

"You have to trust me. We have a damn good shot of getting you off free and clear. How'd you like that? You can walk outta this place and never look back . . . and even if you are convicted, I'd be surprised if they can get anything more than manslaughter."

"That's not what Miss A.D.A. says."

"Let her talk. What does it matter? She's just stalling. They've got no case and she knows it. So just sit tight. Every hour inside is time served. And believe me, you're better off here than Upstate. At least they're watching you."

"I want to go Upstate. I think it's time."

"You don't know what you want."

"I have an appointment with destiny."

"Send my regards."

"I'm serious. You don't know what it's like in here, and besides, I'm a fucking murderer. Does that mean anything to you? I did it. I killed her. I killed Brooke Harrison!"

"Shut up! You're delusional, you didn't kill anybody!" he shouted, and my shoulders caved inward. "I'm sorry, but how many times do we have to go through this. I can't help you if you don't do what I tell you."

"I want to be a normal prisoner."

"You want to be back out there with those psychopaths?"

"I'm one of them."

"No, you're not. You're different."

"I want to be normal. Please let me be normal or . . ."

"Or what?"

I looked down. He approached the table where I was sitting and shoved his oily nose up next to mine, like he was one of Blair's cats. An effective tactic. You'd say anything when you're staring up into a guy's hairy nostrils. "Or what, Lillian?" he said, drawing out every syllable so it was the ugliest name.

"I don't know." I turned my head away from him. He pushed himself backwards and rolled up his sleeves. Another one of his talks was coming. Would he appeal to my guilt about my father? How he's lost everything on the trial, including his wife, and all he ever tried to do was make me happy. Didn't I have anything I ever wanted? Wasn't I lucky? Or maybe he'd talk more about the D.A.'s case. How plain-Jane Picasso still couldn't find one person who'd seen me at the theatre the day you were shot, and even worse, she couldn't dig up the missing weapon. The only person who'd claimed to see a gun was a drug-addicted high school dropout with a criminal record; Edie'd said she had no knowledge of it at all.

But Brickman didn't give a speech that day. He just sighed and said, "Remember, there's no law in the state of New York against being a soap fan."

"But that's not the whole truth. And I wasn't even a soap fan, don't say that. I hate soap fans."

"All right, all right, I'll make you a deal: I won't call you a soap fan if you forget about the truth. There is no such thing as truth in a courtroom. It all boils down to how we show it versus how they do, and they've got the burden of proof, you must have learned this by now . . . All we've gotta do is put the slightest bit of doubt in one person's head. Persuasion, Lily, that's what it's all about. Giving people a scenario they want to believe and, believe me, they want to believe you."

"Why?"

"Because you're a girl."

"Huh?"

"Let me put it to you this way: Girls are sugar and spice and everything nice. Understand? It may sound stupid and old-fashioned, but people cling to this stuff. It's all they've got. The minute they start thinking a girl could be snakes and snails and . . ."

"Puppy dog tails."

"Is that really it?"

"Think so."

"All right, so you've got boys running around with puppy dog tails in their pockets and where do you think they got them? They cut them off the puppy. And that's the bottom line here: Boys do things like that, girls don't."

"But that's not the—"

He held out his hand. "Eh-eh-eh . . . remember our deal."

"It's just a dumb saying. Nobody believes it the way you're talking."

"Oh, yes they do . . . it's cultural mythology. You look confused. What the hell are they teaching you these days? Anyway, if you don't believe me, ask your father. I bet he can tell you all of it." He took an accordion file from his briefcase and set it down on the table. "Or better yet, read the depositions. That might settle your mind a bit."

The depositions do nothing to settle my mind. I've been reading them in the library, the only place I can bear it, surrounded by books and wooden tables with names and numbers and curses carved into the top. The room is familiar yet detached. Like the set of a play. I read the words of people I know and try to pretend they're actors on stage. Today I'm watching Edie. She seems frightened and a bit sorry for me despite the one letter I received from her early on saying she'd hired a lawyer and that I had no right to impersonate her at the theatre. I thought she'd get a kick out of that. I wrote her back and am still waiting for a response.

Now she tells her story to the D.A.'s people, and I'm surprised how sympathetic she sounds. She said I was a putz and a freak and really awkward around other people, but I made her laugh. And no, she never thought my relationship with you was too weird.

E.S.: You have to remember, everyone was watching World *back then. Lil taped it every day. We'd get high and laugh our asses off. It was fun watching Jaymie Jo and Max fall in and out of love. They were totally romantic. But then when all of that religious stuff started and Jaymie Jo became celibate . . . please! I don't know what those writers are thinking sometimes. Anyway, that's when I stopped watching. In my opinion the show went totally downhill after that. Lil said it was because Brooke was more interested in getting a movie career going.*

A.D.A.: How did she know?

E.S.: She read it somewhere. She was always reading and cutting out articles.

A.D.A.: And you didn't think that was odd?

E.S.: A little bit, but like I said, everyone was into World *back then. All the girls talked about it in gym class. Lil did go a bit overboard with the posters and making her own videotapes, but I went with her to a fan thing once and you should have seen some of the whacked-out shit . . . I'm sorry, can I say that?*

A.D.A.: You can say whatever you want.

E.S.: Okay, you should have seen it. One girl brought this photograph of her room and every part of the wall was covered with a picture of Brooke Harrison. Lil never did anything that bad. We were totally cracking up. See, Lil thought they were as ridiculous as I did.

A.D.A.: When she was around you, perhaps. What about when she was alone? Did you ever think of that?

E.S.: Sure, of course I did. But it's not what you think. See, I have this theory about her. I think Lil really liked girls and didn't know how to show it, even though I tried to be there for her. I'm very liberal that way, whatever floats your boat, you know, but I don't think she was ready to say it, which is weird 'cause her parents were so cool. Anyway, I guess it was just easier having a crush on a TV star.

A.D.A: That's all you think it was? A crush?

E.S.: Yeah. Why, what do you think?

A.D.A: I think—

MR. BRICKMAN: Objection! Move to strike.

A.D.A.: Were you aware that Miss Speck stalked Miss Harrison in the last few weeks before her death?

MR. BRICKMAN: *Objection! Move to strike the word* stalked *from the transcript. There is absolutely no evidence of this.*

A.D.A.: *She was at the theatre three times a week.*

MR. BRICKMAN: *It was her job! . . . Off the record.*

OFF THE RECORD CONVERSATION

A.D.A.: *Miss Sharpe, did you have any interaction with Miss Speck in the week before Miss Harrison's death? The week of your high school graduation?*

E.S.: *To be honest, Lil and I weren't speaking then. I mean, she tried, but . . . I don't know, and anyway, I just find it hard to imagine any of this. I'm telling you, she was a total putz. She couldn't even keep her shoelaces tied.*

A.D.A.: *She used your name to get a job as an usher.*

E.S.: *I know.*

A.D.A.: *What if the police had come after you?*

E.S.: *Okay, no offense, but be serious!* [Laughter] *She only used my first name. There's more than one Edie in New York. And we played the name game a lot. Besides, she never did anything wrong at the theatre. In the papers, they all said she was the nicest girl. And a really good usher.*

A.D.A.: *Why were you and Ms. Speck not speaking then?*

E.S.: *People grow apart, you know what I mean? I had a new boyfriend, was in heavy-duty therapy, stopped smoking dope, I don't know.*

A.D.A.: *When did that happen?*

E.S.: *Senior year.*

A.D.A.: *After Los Angeles?*

E.S.: *Yes.*

A.D.A.: *What happened between the two of you in Los Angeles?*

E.S.: *Nothing happened. I mean, it's like I really don't remember. You know how sometimes you've got a place in your head but you're not sure if you were really there or you dreamed it? That's what I think about L.A.*

A.D.A.: You did go to the set of World Without End, *didn't you?*

E.S.: Yeah, yeah.

A.D.A.: And nothing happened there?

E.S.: Nah, we just stood and watched them tape a scene. It was kind of boring.

A.D.A.: You watched Brooke Harrison tape a scene?

E.S.: Yeah, but to be honest, we were more interested in her boyfriend, John Strong. He was so much cooler. We couldn't believe he was there. They must have had plans that day or something.

A.D.A.: And after the taping . . . what happened then?

E.S.: I don't really remember. We were smoking a lot and we found a whole bunch of pills at the house we were staying at, so like I said, the entire thing is sort of a blur.

A.D.A.: Thank you, Miss Sharpe. We'll finish up after lunch.

I throw down the deposition and push my fingers into my eyes, rubbing them furiously until they burn. I wish I could gouge them out and never have to read anything again. But it wouldn't stop the voices. Edie. Everyone at the theatre. At school. They're all protecting me. *Because I'm a girl?*

Removing my hands from my eyes, I see tiny circles of light, then a figure coming toward me . . . Edie? When I focus harder I see it's Chandon. She comes by sometimes when I'm in here and we play Hangman. Her face is so drained she looks whiter than me. Her lower lip trembles, and she's hyperventilating. I take her hand, and my stomach drops.

"Mimi's dead," she says, and wails at the top of her lungs. My body springs to attention. Chandon collapses next to me in a fit of tears.

"What?!" I grab her shoulders and shake her. "Chandon, what are you talking about? You mean Angel, right? Chandon!"

I say her name a few more times and beg her not to cry, but she can't stop and I suddenly feel like a jerk for trying to make her. *Mimi's dead?* Can't be. It doesn't make sense. And I don't know what to do for Chandon. I hear myself saying words I've never said before, things like *it's okay* and *don't worry,* as I gently rock her in my arms. She smells like sweat and cooking oil, and I imagine her in the kitchen of a small apartment frying chicken cutlets. Hours later you can still sniff the scent in her hair when she's watching TV.

"It's okay, baby," I say, and it's not my voice I hear but Blair's, the way she'd soothed and smothered me with caresses. The memory strikes me so vividly I feel it course through my body. I stroke Chandon's hair, tell her everything's going to be okay, even though it's a lie. Her shoulders buckle beneath me, her breaths growing deeper and deeper, and I stay with her as if I were a blanket, our shoulders rising and falling together.

We pass a few minutes like this before she fidgets beneath me. I pull back. She pivots until we're face-to-face, our arms loosely connected. "It was so fucked-up, Long Island," she says, "so fucked-up."

I rub her back with my left hand, ask what happened.

"She was coming around with her pail last night, and a bunch of Stella's bitches caught her. Gave her a massive blanket party."

"Stella!"

"No, no, don't think that way . . . it wasn't you. They thought she was messing with one of their girls or something. Anyway, she was all alone 'cause a bunch of us was in the fishbowl playing cards and we didn't hear nothing . . ." Her shoulders start shaking again, and I grip her tighter. "It was the worst thing you ever seen. They stabbed her forty-eight times. She lost too much blood, and we were fucking playing cards!" She wails, and I can only hug her, while inside I'm churning. *Forty-eight times!* Girls aren't supposed to do things like that.

"We were playing cards," Chandon cries again and again. There was nobody around to protect Mimi. Someone would pay for this. If not now, then later. On the outside. Chandon promises she'll get revenge, and I hold her.

A guard bursts into the library and breaks us apart. The girl on duty must have freaked out and called. He is a hulky man I've seen only a few times before. He shoves my wrists into a pair of cuffs and says it's time to take me home. I try and resist. "Don't fuck with me," he says.

"Fuck you!"

He yanks my cuffed arms up my back, and I scream. It feels like he's torn off my shoulders. Pain shoots between them.

"Don't you do nothin' crazy, Long Island!" Chandon shouts.

"She is fucking crazy, you don't know that by now?" the guard says. He shoves me into a freestanding shelf. A few books tumble to the floor. "One more word out of you and you're going back in the cage. You understand?"

I nod my head, and he shoves me toward the door. As he drags me out of the library, Chandon cries, and all I can think is, it should have been me. Why am I not dead yet?

We reach my cell and he throws me down on my bed. I'm wondering what's coming next, what he'll do to me. I wrap my arms around my pillow, just as I'd had them around Chandon's body, and with the guard watching I squeeze as hard as I can. The sheet and lining rip. A big chunk of foam pops up like a piece of toast. The guard says I'm fucking crazy, and you know what happens to crazy girls inside. "Please," I look at him, "I need your help."

He moves closer to the bed. "Say it isn't so."

"I need to use the phone."

His face contorts as if he can't believe I'm asking what I'm asking. My back throbs like it's been stabbed forty-eight times.

"Please!" I beg.

A smile crosses his lips, and he says I'm lucky he doesn't beat the shit out of me. Such a lucky girl, he teases. I don't tell him that's what they all say. He says maybe there's something we can do to get me to the phone. I know what he wants, I've done it before, though not with this one. From where I sit on the bed it's an easy reach for his hips. I put my hands around him and rub my face against his crotch. The material is course. My cheek bristles. He pretends he's shocked, but I have other evidence. I unzip his pants and take him in my mouth. He is silent. Then, a final gasp like he's stubbed his toe.

He turns around and wipes himself on my sheet before zipping up. Without a word, he cuffs me again. We walk silently to the telephone in the fishbowl. He removes the cuffs. "You got five minutes," he says, and sits down in a folding chair where he can keep an eye on me. I remove a folded-up letter from my sock and punch the number on top into the telephone. Someone accepts my collect call and tells me to hold.

"Davina Moore," comes a voice so smooth it makes me think of sleeping on satin sheets at Blair's. So long ago.

"Ms. Moore, I need . . ." I stammer, and suddenly can't breathe. The air won't get through my nose and throat. Like I'm breathing through semen.

"Are you okay?" asks the voice so sweet I almost want to hang up. I don't know where to go with it.

"I'm sorry, I'm bothering you."

"Not at all. I contacted you first, remember. Tell me what's going on, Lillian. Why are you calling me now?"

"Can you come here?"

"Are you looking for a new lawyer?"

"No . . . I mean, I don't know what I'm . . . Are you a feminist? The articles all say you're a feminist."

Through the phone I hear her chuckle. "Depends," she says. "Is that good or bad?"

"I don't know."

"Well, that's a start. I'll come by tomorrow."

"No! That's no good . . . it's no good!" My voice is so shaky I'm going to lose it with that guard staring at me and I can't believe I just had his dick in my mouth, surely no feminist would approve, but Mimi's dead and Chandon's a mess and I have to do something.

"Did you hear me?" she says. "I'll be there first thing."

"No, please . . ."

"What is it? Has something happened to you?"

"I've been drinking bleach," I say, but my words are gobbled up in a giant hiccup.

"You're what?"

"I'm not supposed to be here."

"Lillian," she says, and it's the way she says my name, whole, the complete opposite of Brickman's syllabic contortion, that makes me feel like I'm melting into the milky air, and for the first time since I've been at Rikers, I cry. "Lillian, please, you have to try and tell me what's going on."

The guard stands up and slowly walks to the phone. "I can't. He's coming. He's gonna hang up." Leaning his arm on top of the pay phone, he says time's up. I whimper into the phone. "Please, Davina!"

"Hang on," she says. "I'll be right there."

He clicks his forefinger down on the metal tongue and smiles. Tears roll down my cheeks. He removes his finger and the dial tone kicks my eardrum. I hang up the phone and hold out my hands to be cuffed.

EVERY COUPLE OF DAYS I CHECKED IN WITH TABITHA to see if she needed me to work. It wasn't as easy as it seemed that first night. She said she had a new pool of ushers. Apparently, some of your fans had gotten the idea I'd stumbled upon. They were a crafty bunch.

I managed to get in a couple of times the third week, arriving early to check for you in the stairwell. But you were never there, and after the show you ducked out early or left through the front door to avoid the scene in the alley. You needed your sleep since you had to be at the TV studio at dawn. You were exhausted. That day in the stairwell you could barely keep your eyes open. I thought you needed a vacation and wanted to take you to my house in Southampton, early in the week while Jack and Nancy were at work and the theatre was dark. I was worried about you, afraid you might collapse one night from exhaustion or sip too heavily from your flask and slur your lines. And you were literally pulling your hair out. That was so weird. I tried writing you a letter expressing my fears, but couldn't find the words. Instead, I sketched scenes in my book with a few swatches of dialogue, then transferred the best ones to pieces of oak tag the way I'd seen them do at the ad agency. They were like public service announcements, only private. Between the two of us.

Next time I worked, I would slip the boards under your dressing room door, only I couldn't figure out when that might be. There was the small matter of graduation. I didn't want to go, but my grandparents had flown in for the ceremony, and Jack and Nancy were planning a little party afterwards. Nancy had asked me if I wanted to invite Edie, and I was sure she was tormenting me. She must have known we weren't friends anymore; Edie hadn't been over in a year. I told Nancy I'd get back to her, but never did. She never mentioned it again, either.

On the morning of my graduation from high school, I woke up and found the kitchen smelling like a campfire. My grandmother was toasting her English muffin. She liked to burn the bottoms and drip honey on top. Grandpa sat at the kitchen table in his pajamas and a felt cowboy hat, munching on a bowl of Fruit Loops. It was the only cereal he would eat, which was fitting, according to my father. Watching him pulp those red, green, and yellow Os between his dentures made me sad. I poured a cup of coffee and loaded it with sugar. "Is that all your having?" Grandma asked.

"Yeah. I can't eat in the morning."

"Have a little breakfast. An English muffin, some cereal."

"I'm really not hungry."

"Nobody in this house eats breakfast. I never heard of such a thing," she said. "So, you ready for the big day?"

"I guess."

Grandpa looked up from his cereal. "What's this all about?"

"Lily's graduating from high school."

"Really." He turned to me. "What grade are you in?"

"Twelfth."

"The twelfth grade! How did that happen so fast?"

"She's growing up," Grandma said, then to me: "Are you nervous?"

"Not really."

"It's okay to be nervous," she said, and I realized I was looking down at her thinning scalp. Either I'd grown or she'd shrunk or it was all a matter of perspective anyway.

She was so happy to be there for my graduation, I pretended it mattered. "Maybe I'm a little anxious."

"Why are you anxious?" Grandpa said.

"I'm excited about the ceremony."

"What ceremony?"

"Hog, it's her high school graduation."

"Really? What grade are you in?"

I looked at Grandma, her brow furrowed and eyelids heavy. She nodded, as if it was okay to answer. "Twelfth," I said.

"The twelfth grade! How did that happen so fast?"

"Believe me, Grandpa, it wasn't that fast," I said.

The toaster oven popped open with a loud ring. Grandma slid out both sides of her muffin with a fork, dropped them on a plate, and drizzled a tablespoon of honey on top of each piece, watching the sweet liquid fall as if its presence rooted her in the world. Something she could count on. She must have gone through so many jars of honey in her life. If you lined them up, they would probably connect New York to Scottsdale. She sat down at the counter and took a crunchy bite. "Mmmm, just the way I like it," she said.

I put my coffee cup in the sink and said I was going up to change. As I walked upstairs I could hear Grandpa asking why I was changing and Grandma explaining that it was my graduation. I wondered what would happen if she answered differently every time. Would he still forget the questions?

In my room, I put on the new U2 album I'd been listening to nonstop. They took their name from an old U.S. warplane, the kind we used to spy on the Russians, when we were still spying on Russians. But they were antiwar. It reminded me of something Edie had said: We could be both pacifists and revolutionaries. The lead singer was both, and his voice ached with fury, the best kind of protest. My grandfather had taught me that, years ago in Scottsdale, when he played me the song about the man who never returned.

I forced myself to the closet to figure out what to wear. Inspired by the music, I selected a pair of army pants cut just below the knee, shiny new combat boots, and a tie-dyed T-shirt. Mixing images of war and peace. At the last minute, I stuck my gun into the back seam of my underwear. They were Hanes briefs like my father's. I liked the fit, and the waistband was thick enough to hold the gun in place. Suited up, I felt like a Sandinista or Contra, whoever the revolutionaries were. I'd just about finished when Nancy called my name. It was time to go. I grabbed my blue cap and gown, which happened to highlight the blue I'd dyed my white streak the week before to match the vests at the theatre.

Grandpa was still wearing his hat and pajama top, only it was tucked into a pair of gray slacks that looked like plastic. He saluted me as if I were in the army, and my stomach dropped. Did he know I was armed? No, I was just paranoid, unless there were spy cameras in my room. It was something Jack might do, then keep the control panel in his walk-in closet. He watched everything else on video, why not me? My thoughts were getting really strange. I made a mental note to grab a couple of Nancy's Valium before we left the house. Grandpa beat a drumroll with his fingers on the counter, and I heard the sad-mad singer's voice. Looking at the old guy wasn't easy. If I were a different kind of girl, the kind who walked around unarmed, a target, I might have cried. Grandma Rose came in and kissed my forehead. "I thought maybe you'd wear a dress. You don't have any dresses?" she asked, and I said no.

"I lost that battle years ago," Nancy said. I hadn't realized she was in the kitchen. She was so sneaky.

"A girl should wear a dress to her own graduation."

"Ma, forget it, okay?"

"What's all this about?" Grandpa said.

"They want me to wear a dress," I said. "What do you think, Grandpa?"

"Dresses are nice. Where are you going?"

"To my graduation."

"Graduation? What grade are you in?"

"Twelfth."

"The twelfth grade! How did that happen so fast?"

"Magic," I said, liking my answer better each time. "But what do you think? Should I wear a dress?"

"Where did you say you were going?"

"To my graduation."

"Graduation? What grade are you in?"

"Twelfth. Happened so fast, didn't it?"

"Okay, enough already, it's time to get going," Grandma said, glaring at me, and I felt terrible. "We'll wait in the car."

I ran after them. "Wait! Grandma, I'm sorry."

"When I was a girl I begged my mother for a dress. 'A dress?' she said. 'Where do you think you're going in a dress?' I had no graduation to go to. You don't realize what a privilege that is, you should show some respect."

"Grandma, I swear if I had a dress I'd wear one, but I don't own any. I look totally gross in them. My knees are all knobby." I had no idea what that word meant, but I'd heard other girls use it when they talked about their knees. Better she thought I had ugly knees than knew how really wrong I looked in dresses. Like if Nancy started wearing jeans and flannel shirts and packing a pistol above her crack, it would just be wrong.

"Such a different world," Grandma said, and looked over at my grandfather. He'd sat down cross-legged on the lawn. We walked over to him.

"I'm really sorry," I said again.

"Forget it, pumpkin, I can't stay mad at you on your graduation day, can I? Now, give me a hand."

Together, we lifted my grandfather up and put him in the backseat of my car. They would ride with me to the ceremony; Jack and Nancy could deal with everyone else.

On the way to school, still feeling like shit, I asked Grandma to tell me about Nancy's graduation. A million times I'd heard how Nancy had to return for it since she had already finished classes and enrolled in City College, where she met Jack. They fell in love, and within a year, had married and moved into their own apartment in the Bronx. They'd spent most of the sixties there. Grandma loved telling that story. Somehow it meant she'd raised her daughter right.

At school, I helped them out of the car, and we waited for Jack to pull into the parking lot. Grandma said it was a lovely day. Grandpa took out a wad of chewing tobacco, placed it against his cheek, then tipped up his felt cowboy hat. Since he stopped remembering things he'd been acting more and more like a cowboy. Grandma went along with it so he'd be comfortable. She rented videos of old Westerns and wore silk rodeo shirts. Called him Hog. It was like they'd created a whole new life. You could do that in the West, she said.

When my parents showed up, I split for the picnic tables to have a cigarette before the walk. A few little kids laughed on the swings behind the fence. I watched them kick their legs in the air and flutter, looking like they might catapult into a sky bluer than Nancy's eye shadow. They couldn't have been more than five or six years old, so young it wasn't even clear whether they were boys or girls, and no parents in sight. I wanted one of them to fall, then felt guilty about it. I could always shoot their parents. I sat down and lit a cigarette, looking across the parking lot at the red-brick compound. After today I'd never have to come back again. It didn't matter. I was headed for buildings just as ugly. We'd visited Syracuse a couple of months earlier, and the dorms reminded me of projects. Inside everyone wore argyle socks.

I put out my cigarette and quickly stood, feeling queasy and light-headed. I didn't want to go to graduation, didn't have to, but what else could I do? If Edie'd been with me things might have been different. But in almost a year she hadn't said one word to me. Of course she was the first person I spotted by the auditorium, where we were lining up for the march outside. She wore sunglasses and red lipstick. My pulse increased as I approached her, the entire senior class plastered against the wall around us. She turned her head toward me, and my heart raced. I smiled. She looked away. A teacher screamed through a megaphone: "Two minutes and counting! Everyone get in line."

"Edie," I said.

She didn't move. There was another amplified sound I barely registered. More people rushed into place. My feet were stuck in plaster, my skin falling off with each silent second. I said her name again. She was about to turn when Belgrave came by. "What are you doing out here? Get back in line."

He led me back between Gavin Solomon and Donna Streeter, then shuffled away. I was self-combusting beneath my gown, so wet I hoped the gun didn't slide down my leg. It would suck getting caught with a gun just before graduation, but it was the only thing separating me from the rest of them: part of the who that made me. *There goes Lillian G. Speck and she's armed so don't fuck with her.* I once heard a song about a homecoming queen with a gun who shoots up the school and embarrasses her friends. Bunch of wimps. But before I could remember the words, we started moving like a giant snake toward the side doors and outside to the bleachers. I spotted Gustave in the audience standing next to Jack with a small video camera in front of his eye and tried to motion for him to stop. He just smiled as we filed into the bleachers. I kept wishing I could disappear before I had to stomp down and pick up my diploma. And it was a long wait. There were speeches by a couple of teachers and two classmates I'd never seen before, and I couldn't help wondering what would happen if I jumped up and started shooting like the girl in the song, though you lose points if you're not homecoming queen or valedictorian or voted most likely to succeed by the yearbook staff. Where is the irony in the "class nobody" shooting up graduation? So I stayed put, baking in the sun and counting the passing cars on the road behind the football field, until, finally, one of the teachers told our row to stand and walk slowly down the bleachers so we'd be there when the principal said our names. A few people whispered, and I hoped I wouldn't pass out or trip when I got to the principal. She called Edie's name and my spine tingled watching her flip Edie's tassel and smile. A lot of kids screamed and swung their diplomas in the air. Edie just grimaced at hers, as if she were wondering what to do with it. I wished she would tear it to pieces. The old Edie might have.

When I made it to the principal, I heard Jack scream my name. He wanted me to smile for the camera. It was mortifying. I couldn't imagine how you dealt with it all the time. Maybe that's why you were pulling your hair out. We were going to have a lot to discuss later. Somehow I managed to get back to my seat without falling, and before I knew it, the ceremony was over, and I was a high school graduate. Everyone threw their hats in the air and headed toward their families. I found mine, which had grown to encompass Gustave, Pamela, and a couple other friends of my parents from the city. They were all talking to one another and barely even noticed I'd come up. I tore off my cap and gown and sat down next to my grandfather on the grass. His hands were covered in dirt, and the ground next to him looked like it had been attacked by cows with frenzied eating habits. "Want some chew?" he said, and held out a handful of grass. His shirt stunk of fertilizer.

"Oh, Grandpa."

"Hog, what are you doing? That's not your tobacco!" Grandma lifted him up.

"I'm just sharing the field with this lovely lass." He put his hand on my shoulder. "My granddaughter . . . what grade are you in?"

"Twelfth."

"The twelfth grade! How did that happen so fast?"

"I know, she is so grown up," Gustave said, camera in hand. "Stand with your grandpapa and wave . . . say cheeseburger . . ."

"Peace," I said, but made a gunlike shape with my thumb and forefinger: revolutionary and pacifist.

Nancy burst in next to me. "Hey, Lily, guess who I just saw."

"Turn to me, Nancy, over this way."

"Hi, Gus," Nancy waved. "Welcome, everyone, to Lily's graduation. At first we were afraid it might rain, and we've got the backyard set up for a party, so that was upsetting, but it's turning into the most beautiful day. And I just ran into Lily's friend, Edie."

"You what?"

"She was with her mother and her boyfriend, I think his name is Robert. He's going to Harvard in the fall."

"I know who he is!" I snapped at her, although I didn't. I couldn't believe Edie had a whole other life.

"I invited them to the party, but they were all having lunch in the city. Edie said to say hi and congratulations. Gussy, can you follow me? I see the Huberts over there. I'm trying to get them to list their house with me. Let's see what they have to say on tape."

Gustave took his camera and followed my mother over to another group of people chatting away beneath a bursting green tree. I was steaming mad at her for talking to Edie about me. But she'd said to say hi. She probably wanted to talk before the ceremony, probably wanted to tell me about the new guy, and I would tell her all about Bobby, even though he'd warned me not to. She had to know about him; he turned out to be such a jerk. We had the whole summer ahead of us.

"I'm hungry," Grandpa said.

"There's tons of food at home," I said.

"Let's get a move on then, young lass."

I wrapped my arm through his, and with my grandmother next to us, steered him toward my car, promising steak and champagne for lunch.

"Yee-haw!" said Grandpa Hog, and we laughed, excited for the party, although I'd already received the best graduation present I could have asked for: Edie and I were going to be friends again.

My entire family left for the Hamptons the next day without me. I'd told Nancy that Tabitha had called and wanted me to work. Nancy said she was proud of me for ushering at the theatre, and I assumed she was zonked on Valium or some of the other pills I'd been snatching from her hiding place, most of the soothing, calming variety. She was queen of the quiet interlude. "It's nice to see you actually doing something," she said. I never told her you were in the play. That was between the two of us. Instead I dropped a few stories about the theatre people with their quirks and superstitions. The last time I ushered, Tabitha had me pace three times around the lobby, holding the director's dirty socks. She said it was an offering to the theatre gods. If we circled before every show, they would extend the run through the end of July. Jack sneered and said it was bunch of B.S., but I wasn't sure. I liked that they created their own beliefs, no matter how silly they seemed to other people.

As soon as my family hit the highway, I called Edie and left a message on her machine. I told her it was great seeing her at graduation and said I wanted to hang out this weekend, then set about waiting for her to call me back. There was plenty to keep me busy. I had two weeks of *World* taped and had barely seen any of it. Since the play started it was hard watching you on screen when I could see you in real life, although we all saw too much. The more I sat through that second act, the more convinced I was you shouldn't have agreed to take your shirt off. How could anyone take you seriously after that? I decided to draft another Brooke Harrison PSA, this one about your career.

I took my colored markers, charcoal pencils, chunky eraser, sketchbook, and a stack of empty storyboard panels, and spread everything out on the kitchen table. I was hungry but sick of eating. There was so much food in the house since my graduation party, I couldn't go five minutes without someone, usually my grandmother, asking if I wanted a piece of chicken, mozzarella and tomato salad, white asparagus spears, goose-liver pâté, and if I said I wasn't hungry she complained I didn't eat. "Grandma, look at me." I bunched up a couple of rolls of stomach skin. "Does this look someone who doesn't eat?"

"You need protein," she said. "And a banana for potassium. If you promise to eat a banana a day I'll be happy."

"Okay, I promise."

A bunch of almost-ripe bananas beckoned from the counter, but I couldn't bring myself to eat one. Food had a way of settling me down and I needed to keep my energy up for Edie's call. The coffee pot was still plugged in, so I poured a cup of *jojo*—Jack's word for coffee. It was cold and stale. I added some water and reheated it in the microwave. Five tablespoons of sugar made it almost tasty. I took the mug to the kitchen table. Lying in front of me was my sketchbook, its covers expanded so it looked like the mouth of a whale; over the years I'd jammed it with newspaper clippings, stickers, pieces of loose-leaf paper with drawings I'd done in class, pages of heavier paper with charcoal drawings, stuff from your fan club, the trip to L.A., and, early on, anything I could find about Delta Airlines. Blair had said, *Whenever you draw you'll think of me,* but the more I filled the book the less I remembered. I ran my fingers over the cover. What used to be hard and shiny as brand-new asphalt was cracked and faded like the neglected streets around the theatre. It barely had any heft to it as I turned the cover and the first page, the one that said Lillian Ginger Speck in bubble letters, popped up on its own. I hadn't looked this far back in a while. The drawings were terrible: airplanes and stewardesses and pencil sketches of the boarded-up guest house, all before I'd met Mickey and learned about color.

There were even a couple of pages of pressed leaves from the oak in front of Blair's, the one that came down with the house to build the swimming pool hardly anybody ever used. Flipping the pages, my throat felt bitter and pasty, and the coffee raged through me. I had a sudden urge to tear out the beginning, erase everything about her. She'd deserted me, why should I be stuck with the memories? I reached around my back, checking for the gun. Still there. Nobody could fuck me. If I ever saw her again I'd pretend I didn't know her. I nuked another cup of jojo, then turned to the empty section in the back and started thinking.

I always began with the book. Talking to you on paper. "Brooke, you've made a disastrous career move, flashing your tits like some tacky bimbo. I've got to get you back on track, show you what's important."

Okay, but I'm not sure I want to see it.

"What am I supposed to do? Stand by and watch you ruin your life? I don't think so."

I don't know what you can do at this point.

"Let me show you." I broke down the page into four panels and drafted a moral: no more nudity.

Okay, that's the easy part.

"Be patient."

Drawing was a long, revolving conversation. The only time I could lose myself (other than when I was watching *World*). Forget the rumblings in my stomach, my runny nose, the burst of cold air streaming from the vent above my head, why Edie wasn't calling. She was probably with him, Robert Whatever who's going to Harvard. It didn't matter. I had my own stuff to do. By the time I looked up it was 9:14. She really should have called. I tried her house again, but nobody picked up. We could have ordered a pizza and hung out watching *World* like we used to. With everyone gone, this damn house felt like an empty theatre. You could hear the wind rattling beyond the windows. I went upstairs and took a couple of Nancy's quiet pills from the tissue holder in the bathroom. Waiting again, now for the pills to take effect, I turned on the makeup mirror and smoked a cigarette in the different shades of light. One switch had me in a bar, the next outside, another in an office. Each was somebody I might be, in the future maybe. I liked me best in dark lighting. It hid the tiny red veins and made me sort of tan. This was how we should meet.

After a few more cigarettes, I decided to drive by Edie's. It was a balmy night. Everything looked the same but softer, and slightly twisted. Like those mirrors at carnivals where I looked like myself but really tall or skinny or stumpy. I made it to Edie's in no time and sat for a while listening to the tape I'd made the day before: one song recorded a few times in a row—a ballad that reminded me of Edie. I was going to play it for her, before we talked about guys. I closed my eyes and sang along. My shoulders shook with the singer's words. He repeated a line . . . *and you give yourself away, and you give yourself away* . . . and I felt it so deeply I realized it wasn't Edie he was singing about, but you. You had to stop giving yourself away, Brooke. I was trying to help you. The whir of a passing car jolted me, but it didn't matter. Edie wouldn't understand. I turned on the ignition and headed home as fast as I could.

FOUR OF US SIT AROUND A METAL CARD TABLE: me, Jack, Nancy, and my new lawyer, Ms. Davina Moore. A big piece of granite hangs from a silver chain over the black V-neck sweater, exposing her soft caramel skin, and her dreadlocks are carefully bunched on top of her head. I see her through my parents' eyes, not what lawyers are supposed to look like, and wonder if she's got half of Brickman's killer instinct. Whether that matters. The thing is, I had no idea she'd be black but now I know it couldn't have been any other way.

She's explaining to Jack and Nancy what happens if I change my plea. Very calmly she tells them there's a new kind of defense, something like insanity but you're still guilty. It was invented after the guy who shot the president got off on insanity. People said it's not fair, this guy's guilty as sin, who cares if he's nuts? Enough people that they changed the law. The thing is—and I said this to Davina at our first meeting—I'm not crazy. Have a look at my loony tests: The shrinks declared me to be of exceptional intelli-

gence, hyperaware of my environment and my actions. Davina
said don't worry, she'll order new tests. You can make people say
whatever you need them to say. But I'm not crazy, I repeated, and
she said, "I know."

Now she tells my parents it's all a game. Our job is to determine the best way to play.

"This is a waste of time," Jack says. "Brickman's got all of this
figured out already."

He's upset about losing Jonathan Brickman. The shark. He
can't understand why I'd fire his guy in favor of the woman with
big jewelry and dreadlocks. "Why don't you tell me how this is
supposed to work, then?" she challenges my father.

"It's simple. She says she didn't do it and there's not enough
evidence to prove otherwise."

"What about the confession?"

"I don't know, what about it? She was confused . . . she's a bit
of dreamer, you know? Most kids are. Believe me, I'm in the business of dreams. She was all wrapped up in her head. You see it
every day."

"That kids confess to murder?"

"Happens all the time, talk to the cops. They all want to do
something big. They want to feel important, be a bit rebellious.
Cigarette companies understand this, but here's what they don't
say: You grab a kid at twelve and he's yours for life. Me, I'd never
work for a cigarette company, but what I'm saying is—"

"Jesus Christ!" Nancy snaps. "Would you cut the bullshit?"

They stare at each other, the first time since they walked
inside, so much pain between them you can see particles of suffering jump like Coke bubbles when you first pour the glass. Their
faces fall. People say those bubbles'll rip the enamel off your teeth.
Nancy sighs achingly, like she's seen more of this world than she
ever wanted to. "For god's sake, Jack," she says. "This isn't a market study, she's your child."

Jack lowers his head, and I'm melting in scathing Coke bubbles, that word hanging out there: *child*. I never felt like one.

Nancy talks. She says they wanted me to be happy. That's all
they ever wanted. But nobody'd taught them how. The drinking,

the drugs, it helped for a while, she says, and I step out of my body and watch like it's a movie, the worst kind of melodrama. Nancy wallows in it, the most emotion I've ever seen in her. The scary kind. It envelops her like the big explosion at Chernobyl, gaseous and invisible, a deadly aura that colors everything within a hundred-mile radius. She's living in the fallout, and they wouldn't even let her bring in her sponsor. The woman waits outside in the car, warming her antiradiation blanket.

Davina pushes her chair back and it caws obnoxiously, calling me back to the table. She puts a hand on my mother's arm. "I know this is difficult," she says.

"Difficult?" Nancy says, her eyes like glowing green ponds. Toxic. I swear they were never that bright. And beautiful. I have never seen my mother look so good. She stands up and, leaning her palms on the table, says, "Of course it's difficult, but this is where we live now. The rest is just padding. We were great at the padding, weren't we, Jack?"

Grumbling, my father runs his hand through his hair, then buries his head in his elbow.

"See, he doesn't like difficult."

"What the fuck do you want from me!" He raises his head and there's a storm in him. Anyone can see. I'm sorry we asked for this meeting, but Davina said it was important. From the moment we met I'd felt a balm in her satiny voice and wanted her to be my mother. But that's usually trouble: when I start wishing. Davina stands up now and walks around the table over to where my real mother is hyperventilating. Jack digs his thumbnail into the scrappy metal and it makes a wailing sound; Nancy breathes. Every movement seems miked like that day on the set when you were still mine. Breaking the silence, one of her best skills, my mother tells my father he can start by being honest with himself, being honest with her, with me.

Annoyed, amplified, he grouses. "Oh, yeah, you're one to talk."

"Meaning?"

"This is not good. Not one bit of it. And you're getting on my case? You sound like Betty Ford, or, no, more like a bad *Saturday Night Live* imitation of Betty Ford. Wake up!"

"Oh, I'm up. More than you'll ever know."

"We've got things to take care of here."

"I am taking care of *things*. For the first time in my life. And it's not like I'm getting any support . . . from either of you."

Her radioactive gaze falls my way, and I want to rip her apart. She's in pain, I tell myself, but so is my father. They're gagging on it.

"Whoa, whoa!" Davina holds her open palm in front of Nancy but lowers her head toward Jack. "We're getting way off the subject here. Can we please just stick to the case?"

"Right." Nancy takes another long, loud inhalation.

"Are you okay?" Davina says.

Nancy nods, deflating, and it's like all the light in the room shifts her way. She says she's doing what she has to do, says she's trying to experience emotions as they come, says right now she feels terrible, just terrible, then bursts into tears. Jack eases out of his chair. "Aw, shit, Nance . . ." He inches forward but she flags him off, sobbing.

"Maybe we've had enough for today," Davina says, either nervous or frustrated, and I'm afraid she might bail. It's too much. Me.

"No!" Nancy shouts. "I have to talk to Lily. Lily?"

I stare at the watery streams of mascara running down her cheeks, like soot. And she's still gorgeous. "Come over here, please," she sniffles. At her right stands my father, petting the almost-full beard on his chin, oblivious at first, then he realizes I'm looking at him. And he doesn't turn away. His face breaks and for the first time in months he smiles, not his million-dollar J.F.K. but like he means it.

"Lily . . ." says my mother, and Jack tips slightly in her direction, nodding okay.

The last one up, I walk to my mother. She takes both of my hands in hers and says, "I'm so sorry. Can you ever forgive me? I need to know you forgive me."

"This isn't your fault."

"No, no, that's not what I mean. About the stewardess, we have to talk about that. We have to unravel the puzzle, seek out the source. Otherwise we're doomed to endless repetition."

"What stewardess?" Jack hinges forward. "What are you talking about?"

"It's nothing." I let go of Nancy's hands, way too uncomfortable.

"The girl next door."

"What?"

"That blonde. Remember, when we first moved in . . ."

"The blonde?" He squints, then turns to me. "Oh my god, did she—is that what's going on here?"

"No, no," I say. "It's not what you think."

"We've definitely had enough for now," Davina says.

"If she laid a finger on you, I'll—"

"No . . . not like that. She told me things . . . and gave me my book . . ."

"What book?" Jack says.

"Stop it!" I shout. "I don't want to talk about it."

"We have to, Lily. It's important."

"What do you mean, book?"

"Shut up! Both of you . . . shut up! Shut up! Shut up!" I shout, swinging my fists in front of me, not far from where they're all standing, staring, and I know exactly what they're thinking, looking at me like I'm a fucking nut WHEN I'M NOT! Just read my loony tests. You'll see. I take a deep breath, let it out with a big, windy *whew!* and say: "I'm sorry, but you guys are really on my nerves."

Davina steps toward me. "I can finish up alone if you want."

"Forget it, we don't need you," Jack says. "I still don't get why you're here."

"Because I asked her," I say, firmly. "Because she's my lawyer."

"You've already got a lawyer."

"I picked her."

"Oh," he exaggerates, slapping his forehead. *"You picked her!* Why didn't you say so? Now I'll sleep better tonight." Pushing backwards, he trips over a chair. "Fuck!" he says, and kicks it over. His face is pink, eyes monstrously engorged. I imagine him pummeling the chair into scrap metal. But he crosses his arms in front of him and crumbles into the cement, falling in on himself like a perfectly blown-up building, a pile of bricks, white smoke and drywall, into nothing. So much destruction he can't face it but he won't walk away, and I think maybe that's love, sticking around when everything you know turns to dust, and remember that day in the diner with pink neon stars? The old man had said, "You can't have real love without children," and like it or not, I'm his child.

I look over at Nancy, standing quietly, hands bunched into the pockets of her blazer, not a hair out of place, but her water-logged eyes tell a different story. And she's not running from it either; not anymore.

MONDAY THE THEATRE WAS DARK. Tuesday I had to drive my grandparents to the airport, which left me half loopy by the time I finally made it to the city on Wednesday. I took the train in early and sat in the diner, drinking cups of coffee dark and sweet, and looking over my storyboards one last time. Even better than I remembered, each had its own little message but wasn't too preachy, and I'd given the cartoon-you heart-shaped cheeks and big, round eyes to capture your range of emotions. They were ready. I carefully edged them into a large manila envelope upon which I'd written, "The Brooke Harrison PSAs: A Guide to Your Resurrection." My plan was to slide the envelope under your door; I didn't want to bother you before a matinee. But when I arrived at the theatre the front doors were locked. Panicked, I checked my watch and realized it was even earlier than I thought. I retraced my steps down the street and up along Ninth Avenue. It was one of those tropical days, where dog-breath air slouched against your shoulders and the whole city steamed up through its pores. I walked slowly, not a good idea during lunch hour. People scurried down the street, keeping their eyes forward and hands tucked against their sides. I dodged in and out of bodies, bouncing off shoulders like a silver pinball, and all around blared the *bing-bing-bong* of trucks and taxicabs and buses. People shouted to each other, taking up half the sidewalk and walking on the wrong side. You were supposed to keep to the right just like driving, but groups of suits and tourists always crowded to the left. "Stay to the right," I shouted, but nobody ever listened. As if on instinct, I ducked into the alley behind the theatre.

Leaning back against a grimy brick wall, I searched my side pockets for a cigarette and rubbed my fingertips against the silver gun. I could pick off the tourists who swayed flagrantly to the left but that seemed a stupid use of it. And too risky. Three and a half years after he shot the four black boys, the white man—this urban cowboy—was found guilty of illegal weapons possession. Not assault or battery or shooting to kill, just possession. If the gun had been licensed he would have walked. For some reason, that frightened me more than anything else.

Finally, I found the pack of ultralights I'd pinched from Nancy in the front pocket of my backpack and lit up. Smoking in the summer was so great. Your hands stayed warm, and the smoke killed the stink of the streets. It was also time-consuming. I probably smoked more than anything, except maybe watching TV or drawing, and they were all connected anyway. Everything was. Like the way we ended up working together.

I finished my cigarette and was about to leave the alley, maybe bing over to Blimpie's for a ham and Swiss, when I noticed the stage door was off its hinges. Moving a few feet closer, I realized it was a mirage. The door was merely propped open, so I walked inside. My eyes took a few minutes adjusting to the darkness, and even then I was disoriented. I'd never been this far back before. It felt like a cave, cool and shadowy, and somewhere close by I could make out the whir of machinery which must have been the air-conditioning. I walked a few steps along a narrow hallway and came to a row of doors, all painted black with name plates hanging on them. In all the time I'd been ushering I hadn't seen the dressing rooms: Your name etched on the door made my ears pound, like in L.A. It was easier when you came to me. I thought about hightailing it out of there but figured I could slip the drawings under your door and then come back in an hour or so to see if Tabitha needed me to work.

I slithered my backpack from my shoulder, unzipped it, and removed the Brooke Harrison PSAs. Before shoving the envelope under your door, I held it in my hand and blew on the opening for good luck, the way I always did with your letters. I bent down in front of the door and smelled something funky, that burnt-sugar crack smell. Maybe the boiler. I set about pushing the envelope underneath the door, but the groove was so tight it took a bit of effort. Holding each side between my fingers, I inched it slowly. About halfway through it got a bit easier, and I thought I must have hit that moment of inertia we'd talked about it physics. "I caught you, you bastard," came a voice from behind the door. Then the rest of the envelope disappeared and the door swung open. I rolled forward onto the floor, looking up at you. Disappointed or maybe confused, you said, "Who are you?"

The fall had me completely tongue-tied, caught unprepared as I was. It wasn't supposed to happen like that. Now how was I going to explain myself without sounding like a stupid fan? "Listen, message boy," you said, "I'm in no mood for this today. Tell me what he wants and make it fast."

You didn't recognize me. But maybe I wouldn't have recognized me, so gnatty and sweating like a maniac. You asked again who I was, and again, and the more you asked, the quieter I became. You were supposed to know. The world started closing in, walls bending forward, air constricting, your face an engorged balloon. How you'd look in the Macy's Thanksgiving Day parade.

Overwhelmed by the chug of my heart, terrified of you standing over me, I imagined you bringing your foot down and crushing me, splattering my insides all over the walls. But you stepped back and said the name, *Johnny*. I struggled to my feet, still without speaking a word. "Oh, Johnny, Johnny, you're never going to learn," you smiled, and up close your teeth were even whiter and more perfect than they seemed onstage, and boy were you skinny. I felt like if I blew on you for good luck you'd fall right over.

"So tell me, what's it this time? Is he dropping the Czech? Going back to meetings? Or does that sick bastard really expect me to go home with him?"

Having no answer, I turned away. The room had more of the funked-up science-lab smell, and it was dark and messy. There were clothes flung over the chair in front of your vanity and more scattered across the couch. Your dressing table was brimming with all kinds of cosmetics. A rainbow of lipsticks and eye shadows in various stages of use. Next to it was a small table with matchbooks, an ashtray, and what might have been a glass pipe. I couldn't tell, you rushed to cover it so fast. "Wait a minute, what am I doing?" you said, gnawing your lower lip, and I realized you needed me more than you knew. I remembered Blair, the way she'd put her arms around me late at night. "He's not going to win this time," you said. "He's the one who fucked everything up."

"I know," I said, the way I talked when you needed support.

"You do? Who are you?"

I was too distraught to answer. *You were supposed to know.*

"Okay, fine, I can't take it anymore," you said, almost in tears. "Why is he tormenting me like this?"

I stepped forward. "It's okay, Brooke . . ."

"No! I won't go back!" you shouted, and shook the manila envelope up high, for the first time noticing what it said. "'A Guide to Your Resurrection'? Wow, is he Catholic! But no, I've had it. I already told him . . . and I don't care what you've got in here!"

"It's just a few drawings."

"Drawings?"

I nodded yes. You looked at me as if I'd sprouted a third eye. "I made them for you," I said.

"*You?*"

"Yeah."

"Are you an artist?"

"No. Not yet anyway. I'm going to school in the fall. Syracuse University. I'm taking some art classes, but I'm going to major in communications. Maybe work in an ad agency."

"How did you get in here? The theatre's closed."

"The stage door was open, so I thought I'd leave my drawings."

"Are you a fan?" you said, as if you already knew the answer and did not like it one bit. I shook my head no, again unable to compose a sentence. This whole episode was degenerating into the most horrible experience of my life.

"I'm an usher here," I blurted out.

"For this play?"

I nodded affirmatively. "You can ask Tabitha."

"So you're an usher, but not a fan."

"I guess."

"With drawings for me?"

"Yes."

"That's it?"

I nodded again. You sort of smiled and asked, "What's your name?"

"Li—umn . . ." Everyone at the theatre knew me as Edie, but I'd signed the drawings with my own name. It was more important to protect my cover or you'd never believe anything else I said. If you ever asked I'd say I used a different name for my art. Lots of people did.

"I'm sorry," you said.

"Edie. My name is Edie."

"Cool name. So do you want an autograph or something, Edie? A picture?"

"No."

"That's right, you're not a fan," you smiled. "It's okay, I've heard it all before. A lot of people don't want to say the F-word. Come on, we'll get you a picture."

"No, really, I don't want one . . . I just wanted to give you the drawings."

"Thanks." You glanced at the envelope again. "But what's all this about resurrection? That's a little weird . . . a little scary."

I laughed.

"What's so funny?"

"Well, I mean, you've had an exorcism, been lost in the South American jungle . . . and you kissed a priest last week!"

"That was on TV," you said, looking at me like I was an idiot or something. My brain or whatever was between my ears started throbbing. "I know that," I said. "I told you, I'm not a fan. You know I'm not like that."

"Okay, okay." You backed up a couple of feet, hugging the envelope against your stomach, and a bell went off in my head: You weren't ready for the drawings, you were too far gone. You didn't even recognize me. You just stood there biting your lower lip and then said, "So listen, Edie, I'll take a look at the drawings and let you know what I think, okay?" A tiny piece of flesh hung over the edge of your lower lip and you picked it off with two fingers. Blood pooled in the groove, and watching it I was instantly calmed, like I'd taken one of Nancy's quiet pills. I'd imagined this moment a million times and never would have thrown in the lip picking. People were so bizarre.

You sucked your lip through your teeth, and looked a little bit like my grandmother before she put in her dentures. For some reason I felt really sad.

"Are you sure you don't want a photo?" you said, and jutted your face out like the balloon-you again. "I have new publicity shots from the play. I could write a message just for you."

"Don't worry about it," I said, regaining my composure somewhat. "I really didn't want to bother you. Actually, I'll even take back the drawings. It's just a few scribbles."

"No, I'd really like to see them. It's not every day someone draws something for you, right?" You stared at me, your eyes and lips softening, and for the first time since I'd fallen into your dressing room, we connected, just like the day on the set when you'd sought me out in the darkness and winked in my direction. We were together in this. You put the envelope down on the table and grabbed a pen and a shot of you onstage, your eyebrows squinted in confrontation though you hadn't yet removed your shirt. On it you wrote: "To Edie the usher, Thanks for the drawings! Always, Brooke," and then handed it to me.

"Thanks," I said.

"No problem." You led me closer to the door. "Maybe I'll see you around the theatre."

I nodded and couldn't believe this was the meeting I'd been anticipating for years. A quick exchange of drawings for a photo. And everything I'd said was so stupid, of course you didn't know it was me. We needed to sit down together, we needed to have lunch, but my tongue-tiedness was back. Unable to formulate a sentence, I got hotter under my skin. It's okay, I calmed myself. You'd promised to look at the drawings. Soon you'd understand. There was plenty of time. With all the strength in my body, I stepped my right foot out, then my left, and it was an easy path to the door.

"Take it easy, Edie," you said as I exited.

I turned slightly and waved. You went back into your dressing room, and I ran to the stage door. Out in the alley, I stumbled against the wall and fell to the ground. It was covered with muddy garbage and cigarette butts, but I didn't care. I was breathing like I'd just sprinted a quarter-mile dash and dying for a cigarette. Instinctively, I dipped my shoulder, but nothing came forward. "Fuck!" I shouted, a thousand buses screeching inside in my head. I left my bag outside your dressing room! *Stupid idiot! Idiot, idiot, idiot!* I screamed a few more obscenities, banged my head against the bricks. All of my money was in that bag! My house key, car keys, an expensive Syracuse sweatshirt—Nancy had been shocked: "Thirty dollars for a piece of cotton!" As if she had anything in her closet that cost less than thirty dollars. She was such a hypocrite. Jack had bought it for me anyway—a copy of *People* magazine, and my sketchbook! I had to go back.

It took a little while to psych myself up. It's okay, I repeated, just slip inside and grab the bag. It had to be right outside your door. I could get in and out without disturbing you. And if you saw me I'd just say I left my bag. I was allowed to come back for my own bag. Besides, I'd missed the chance to ask if you wanted to have lunch. This could actually be a good thing, I thought, as I walked back through the long hallway a second time. It was foggier than before and smelled like smoke. A few steamy clouds drifted from your dressing room, and my backpack was nowhere in sight. As I came closer, I saw you kneeling down next to the table, a pile of papers burning in a metal bucket in front of you. My backpack was next to the fire, its contents spilled out on the floor. In your left hand was one of the Brooke Harrison PSAs. You were dipping it into the flames.

"What are you doing?!" I shouted.

You looked up and it was your exorcism face I saw. "You didn't fool me for one minute," you said.

There was a jolt in my chest, a pounding in my head, my heart, through the walls. Like my entire body had been turned inside out.

"Those are my drawings!"

"He put you up to this. Nobody else is that psychotic. Well, you can tell him where his precious warnings are now."

I lunged at you trying to grab the drawing, but you dropped it on the burning pile. A flame brushed against my arm. "Ow!" It scorched. I could smell the hairs burning. "Stop it!" I screamed.

"I can't believe they let you work here . . . or was that just a story, too?"

A couple of storyboards were still on the couch. I reached for them, but you slapped your hand over the pile. "Not on your miserable life," you said, and tossed them into the flames. "I'm getting rid of him for good this time, getting rid of everything . . ."

"Hey, that's my book!" Pounding was everywhere, my book in your hands, flames the color of my mother's hair roaring in front of you, illuminating your glowing white skin, your blond hair, those blue demon eyes, looking really disjointed like they were turned toward a car wreck, as you opened my book and started thumbing the pages, smirking with naked contempt, the way you'd looked at those people in Foxboro when they wouldn't accept your black boyfriend, only this time you were laughing at me, and my book, the one thing that was really mine, the one thing Blair had given me, and there it was hanging over a bucketful of flames.

I reached into my pocket and pulled out the gun.

You laughed out loud. "Are you going to shoot me? Are those your orders? He is really desperate this time. Okay, go ahead, do me a favor."

You flayed your arms out in front of you, almost knocking the gun from me, but I steadied my wrist with my left hand, then moved it underneath for support like Bobby Davis had shown me, and if I could just scare you off and get my book, before you—

"Hey!" I shouted. You were ripping the pages one by one like that day I'd spotted you pulling the hairs from your scalp, crazy, focused, only the hair was yours, you could do whatever with it, but that was my book you were tearing, throwing the pages of my life into the smoke and flames, kicking up the heat a few more notches, frying my brain so hot I was afraid I'd faint, but it was mine and how could you leave after you'd given it to me and said whenever I draw I'll think of you and there you were destroying it. "Please . . ." I begged.

"Stupid fans!"

"I'm not a fan. Don't call me a fan."

"You're pathetic." You ripped another page.

"I'm warning you, don't make me shoot, I don't really know how . . . just give me back my book!" Through the fiery light I saw the melting blue and red Grateful Dead skeleton on the front cover. You'd once said they were your favorite band, and I'd listened, going out and buying all of their albums, and when you said the albums sucked compared to bootlegs I went to a concert and before the show in the parking lot bought a couple of tapes, and you were right, they were better, you were right and I'd listened. I heard everything you said and you were destroying me . . . I lunged forward and with my underneath hand reached for the book, but missed. You laughed. "Stop it!" I shouted. "Give me my book!" I reached out again and grabbed the edge of the cover but couldn't get a good grip, and you yanked back, still laughing, like it was some bizarro game, only I didn't know the rules, maybe you had to be famous, but all I wanted was my book and you wouldn't let go and more flames engulfed us and someone, it couldn't have been you, screamed, "I hate you!" and then the loudest noise I ever heard rang through my ears, knocking me back toward the wall and searing my eyes shut, though my arm and chest throbbed, and I opened my eyes but couldn't see a thing through all the smoke.

Slowly, I balanced upward and realized I was still holding the gun. Only it was scorching hot and vibrating in my palm. I pulled the trigger! But the safety was on. Through the roar of the fire I heard you whimpering. NO, THERE'S NO WAY . . .

I shoved the gun back in my pants and turned over the table. You were lying on the charred floor, a hole the size of a quarter in your chest with smoke coming out of it. I touched your shoulders. "Brooke!"

Your eyes were wide open, the bluest blue I'd ever seen. "Why?" you said.

"Oh my god! I'm so sorry . . . Can you move?"

"Why?"

Your head slouched to the left, and your eyes fluttered. I thought when you shot people they fell over and died like in movies. But you were still alive, watching me now. You said it again: "Why?"

"I'm so so sorry, I didn't mean to—the safety was on, I swear . . ."

You shut your eyes.

"Brooke!" I shook your arms. "Brooke! I love you!"

Opening your eyes again, you looked horrified. "Shhhh," I whispered, and sat down beside you. I pulled you up slightly, held you, stroked your hair. "You're going to be okay . . . hang in there."

You sunk into me, and I felt your body relax slightly. "It's okay, I'm here," I said softly, and we melded together for a couple of beats and I thought if I kept breathing, kept my heart pumping, it'd be enough. And it was. For a while. And in those few beautiful minutes there was nothing but you and me and I felt closer to you than ever, felt as if everything in my life had led to this. Then you edged up slightly, twisting your shoulders and trying to speak. "Don't," I said. "You have to save your strength . . ." But you pushed forward and your neck gave out. I held your head. Your eyeballs rolled up in their sockets, lids clamping over them. You went totally limp and suddenly I was alone. "No, don't leave . . ." I hugged you. Smoke filled the room, flames drifting to the couch. I stood up and saw my shirt was drenched in blood. Smelly, metallic red. A horror. People used that word too lightly. I wanted to throw up but held it back. I had to go but didn't want to but had to or else . . . I dug my burned-out book from the embers and dumped it in my backpack. Then I took off my shirt, shoved it in the bag, and put on the Syracuse sweatshirt.

I bent over and, grabbing you by the armpits—they were still warm, a good sign—pulled you out of your dressing room and into the hallway. For a second, I thought about dragging you all the way to the hospital, but I smelled like a firecracker and was splattered with blood. You were a star; I was nothing. They wouldn't believe a word I said. I set you down next to the wall, gently, like I imagined you'd put a baby to sleep, and I remember thinking distinctly, *Now there's something I'll never do.* You looked so graceful, like a blond china doll. My eyes filled with tears.

"I'm going to get help," I said, and turned and ran out the stage door. Pushing my way through the crowds on Forty-second Street, I was terrified each person I passed was going to stop me: *Bing! You're under arrest.* After running a couple of blocks, I called 911 from a pay phone. When the operator answered, I said there was a fire, gave the name of the theatre, and quickly hung up. The rest is all a blur. I know I moved fast, probably not staying to the right, as I ran all the way to the West Side Highway. A helicopter flew overhead, and I was convinced they were coming for me. I felt like a wild animal. Hunted. And I deserved it. My heart was beating so fast I thought I'd have a heart attack and I kept repeating, "Please be alive, Brooke, please be alive." I could barely get down the sickly air, so thick it obscured the yellow dot of sun, its heat pressing down on me. Sweating, pulsating, I crossed the highway and crawled onto a grimy wooden pier. It stank of piss and oil and seaweed. I leaned over and vomited, then, catching my breath, reached into my pants and took out the gun. The metal still felt hot. Holding it between my palms, I shut my eyes and blew on the side for good luck, thinking, What are you, crazy? I lifted it above my head and with a loud scream hurled the gun into the river.

ASTEROIDS

T HEY SCATTERED HER ASHES underneath the old sugar maple. In a small ceremony restricted to family and a few close friends. There had been a funeral in Blue Bell, their tiny church overrun by more than two thousand mourners, many forced to remain outside listening through stereo speakers. At least it was summer and a glorious day for it. If one didn't know any better—although it would have been a stretch to find some such person in town—the scene might have resembled the annual church picnic, minus a few punch bowls and barbecue tables, or one of those outdoor rock concerts Brooke had always loved. Closer, though, the tone was unmistakable: not a steady jaw among the masses who'd politely set out blankets, rising with the omnipotent vibrato coming from the speakers and bursting forth in tearful funeral hymns. Watching segments of it later on the local news, Mildred thought Brooke would have been pleased. Above all, she'd wanted to be adored.

It was Cynthia who'd insisted on having her sister cremated, and in the absence of a will or any other written direction, they listened as she told them about a night she and Brooke had driven down to Tijuana, and while drinking shots of tequila underneath a net of twinkling constellations, promised never to let the other one be buried, each terrified of being caged in the earth, if perhaps for different reasons, and spooked by the prospect of having one's life reduced to an inscription on a grave. "She never under-stood how people talked to tombstones, you know? She thought it would make much more sense to, you know, stand under a tree and say, 'Oh, hey, here you are. I've got something to tell you . . .'" Cynthia choked up, which got Mildred going, imagining her daughters, after only two decades of life, barely old enough to vote or drink or drive, talking about death and dying in a way Mildred had never examined herself. Now that she thought about it, she'd just assumed they'd all end up together in one of the family plots. How remarkable that these two had discussed alter-native plans, and how tragic that their world, so different from Mildred's own, had warranted such a conversation . . . and yet they were right, Mildred thought, besieged by a deeper sadness than she'd ever known, waves of hopeless-ness infected with a clenching anger and resentment. *She wanted the girl to die!*

Quickly, she pushed the thought aside—though in all her years she couldn't remember ever having such trouble with repression. Festering over the next few days of out-stretched arms, phone calls, pity casseroles, that feeling seeped into everything, morning and night, coloring her actions so that even an innocuous act like preparing her cup of tea brought visions of pouring the one-hundred-eighty-degree water over the girl, and then, of course, scalding herself for the evil act. Why couldn't she be more like her husband? Her rock. So far he'd only cried one time that she knew of, that first day in the hospital when he pounded his fist through three layers of drywall and plas-ter in the operating room and shouted, "Goddamn you!" He was sedated and, a few hours later, had ten stitches knitted into his hand, which seemed to strengthen his lean-on-me shoulder. He was never far from Mildred when she needed a hug or a few soothing words, though the two of them often passed each other like soldiers in war films, moving slow-motion through a haze of useless opulence, everything couched in absurdity. Everything except the details. Tom had taken charge there, concentrating on the minutiae, perhaps to avoid the very feelings that Mildred herself couldn't contain.

She went to see the pastor. Ralph Rickett had baptized both of her daughters. He'd married Mildred and Tom, and in his heartfelt eulogy for Brooke had spoken about her in terms of the small-town girl they all knew, the one who'd visited Blue Bell Nursing Home since she was a child and who came back every year to see the play at the rec center, the young woman who above all honored and cherished her family. She believed the world was a wondrous, loving place, he'd said, and in her optimism she elevated us all. But Mildred was having trouble ascending. She wanted answers. She wanted justice. She wanted revenge. Ralph Rickett, if anyone, had to understand that.

In his study, he took Mildred's hands in his and explained that everything she was experiencing was indeed normal, and together they prayed, although Mildred couldn't see what good it would do. God had obviously deserted their house. Still, she returned a few times more and, one day in an uncharacteristic display of emotion, confessed the anger, the guilt, her inability to occupy herself for longer than a minute, and again they prayed, Ralph guiding her with soft, easy words, at this point merely asking for guidance.

"It's not enough," Mildred blurted out, springing from her seat.

"Be patient, Mildred. Only through understanding will you be able to forgive."

"I don't want to forgive!" she shouted. "My daughter is gone. Don't you see? She took her from me. She took away my baby . . ." Mildred cried, and Ralph Rickett came out from behind his desk and wrapped his arms around her, perhaps reasoning that she needed a friend more than a man of the cloth, and Mildred took comfort in his light off-duty clasp, so different from her husband's fervent clinging, a reminder of the agony they might never be able to squeeze from each other. How did anyone ever get through this? She cried deeply, wholeheartedly, as if it were the first time she'd shed a tear, and Ralph told her to embrace the grief, to let it flow, and soon her focus shifted to him. What a good man, she thought, living his life through the heightened moments, good and bad, of others, and for one second she could see how a pastor might take advantage of this situation—the priest who'd played opposite Brooke's character on *World Without End,* for instance—and with that thought, she trembled, fearing something in her own composition had been permanently altered. "I'm becoming a bad person," she said softly.

"No, Mildred," Ralph said, leading her back to her chair and kneeling in front of her. "You've suffered gravely. Whatever you're feeling is entirely reasonable and true, and nobody will judge you for it, least of all God. He knows exactly what He's handed you and how much and why."

"Do you expect me to believe there's a reason for this?"

Ralph sighed, "I think there is. Perhaps it's something you and I will never know, but you've got to believe. Have faith in God, and He will take care of you."

"And if it were your daughter, Ralph?" Mildred spit out the words, ambushed by the bile in her own voice. She tried to lighten the tone. "Would you be sitting here telling me the same thing?"

From the pastor came another meaty sigh, then he backed up and walked to the window. Sun splashed through the trees outside, casting sinister shadows onto the opposite wall. He lowered the blinds and turned to the grieving mother, his eyes ragged and cavernous, as if all the suffering he'd seen throughout the years had suddenly laid claim to his face, and Mildred had to fight the desire to soothe him, saying something nice or lighthearted to temper the mood, but she was tired of keeping things together. Defiantly, she said, "That's what I thought."

"Oh, Mildred," Ralph turned to her, merely a sliver of

his long-suffering self. "What can I say? This is an unspeakable tragedy . . . it just sucks!"

"Ralph!" she blushed, half angry, half amused.

"Forgive me, but I'm at a loss and I've known you too long to play it any different," he said, his voice recovering a bit of bounce. "The only thing I can assure you is that I have an unshakable faith in God, and mine is a Christian God, remember? A God who sacrificed His own son for the good of mankind. So if I were looking for answers, I couldn't think of a better place to start."

"You're only saying what you're supposed to say."

"I'm telling you what I believe."

"Well, at the moment, 'it sucks' is a little more restorative."

"I understand, I truly do, but you have to trust that these feelings will pass and you'll be whole again. And this is where faith comes in. Look, if you're too angry at God, try talking to Brooke." Mildred eyed him as if he'd gone mad. "She's still here, Mildred. Maybe you can't see it now, and this is why you must be patient, but Brooke is with you. She'll be there whenever you're ready."

In the weeks that followed, Mildred in zombielike wanderings found herself drawn to the old maple. Many hours did she spend, barefoot, circling in the shade, or from the swing dangling her toes over the just-shorn grass, its tentacles prickly and stinking of summer, deep green leaves swaying in the breeze above her head. It wasn't even their true color. That would come in a month or two when the chlorophyll drained into a gorgeous burst of yellow and orange, which every year reminded Mildred that Brooke's birthday would be coming soon. It was impossible to believe there wouldn't be another one, ridiculous to think she was here and her daughter wasn't. Those colors were going to be difficult. She still couldn't stand too long in the green before thoughts of sawing down the tree surfaced. Sometimes it was just too painful to look, let alone to begin a conversation.

Then one day from the kitchen window, Mildred spotted Cynthia idling in the swing, which in high summer seemed to drop straight out of the sky, its strings were so absorbed by the thick leaves. John Strong sat at her feet, his legs outstretched, hands planted casually behind his back, staring up at her with what Mildred could only describe as stars in his eyes, and she knew immediately that he'd never gazed upon Brooke with such intensity, and something in their easygoing yet intimate body language informed Mildred that this was no fly-by-night union. The two had been cavorting excitedly, hatching a plan to start an organization for families who'd been affected by violent crime, and they'd even appeared onstage together at the memorial in L.A.—another event attended by thousands, only this time it was held in an old Hollywood theatre, featuring a list of speakers any young actress would have been thrilled to number as friends. For her part, Mildred was numbed by the service, everyone saying essentially the same thing, some speaking with performer-like grace while others couldn't get through their remarks, but all of it was too much.

Worse was the trip to clean out Brooke's apartment. How difficult to assess which of a person's belongings had merit or meaning, what to cart home or divvy up or hand out. And there were too many hands in the pot. Friends and neighbors and colleagues they'd never met before . . . Why were they all here? It felt like a tag sale, a bargain-basement free-for-all—who wants the Cabbage Patch doll? Brooke's videotape collection? The Russell Wright dishes? After bunching a pile of old birthday cards and photographs and *Playbills*, Mildred felt dizzy. John led her to the couch they'd labeled for the Salvation Army and said he'd return with a glass of water. Mildred watched him take a few steps then pivot abruptly toward the bedroom. "What the fuck are you doing?!" he shouted. Some of the mumbling and sorting ceased, attention turning toward the inflamed voice. Mildred saw John jump a few feet into the room, his finger pointed, screaming, "Get your grubby hands out of there . . . !" Despite her headache, Mildred stood and ambled to the bedroom, where she came upon John Strong and a young woman engaged in a tug-of-war over a pink cotton robe. Mildred felt sick to her stomach. "Let go!" John shouted, face contorted, veins the size of earthworms in his forehead, and still she pulled. "You stupid fucking cunt, let go or I'll smack your fucking head into the wall!"

"John, no!" Mildred covered her mouth.

Ignoring the plea from his girlfriend's mother, he twisted the young woman's arm up toward her face. "Ow!" she said, yanking back and tearing the robe. They scrutinized the severed garment.

"You ruined it," she said. "And it's Gita Moonsa."

John grunted incomprehensibly as the woman, prize thwarted, turned and left the room. He watched her through the rictus mask of shock then tipped back against the wall, Brooke's torn robe cradled in his palms. Slowly raising his head he caught Mildred's doleful stare and frowned. "It's her bathrobe," he said softly.

"Oh, honey." She went to him, arm curling around his shoulder, and every bone in his body seemed to collapse. She sat him down on the floor. He was hyperventilating so deeply his limbs shook. Tears streaming, he burrowed into Mildred's embrace, and though she, too, was infuriated, she tabled her aggression and rocked him with all the compassion and succor she could muster, gently assuring him that nobody was going to take anything else. Not while she was there. And in her ability to afford a bit of relief to the grief-stricken boy, Mildred felt the bubble around her beginning to crack.

They took more, of course. Smuggled out things they thought they could collect or trade or sell. And why shouldn't they? Once Brooke had become Jaymie Jo Rheinhart she belonged to her fans as much as to her family, and this is what Mildred, no matter how she reasoned it, could not forgive, even as she watched Cynthia and John gregariously plotting away underneath the old sugar maple as if they were on a mission guided by Brooke herself. And while it made sense that these two, so similar really, would dedicate themselves to Brooke's memory, Mildred was besieged by a familiar worry about her younger daughter: that she would remain forever in the shadow of her sister, and with that came a certain solace that she was again fearing for Cynthia, although she knew there was not one thing she could do about it. As a mother you want to give your children the world, she thought, but in the end you give them to the world.

At dusk she walked to the tree. A misty pink glow on the horizon, smell of the earth rising up through the air. Mildred Harrison kicked off her sandals and raised her head to the leaves. "Hello, sweetheart," she said, and told Brooke what she did that day.

APRIL 15, 1988: POSTSCRIPT

I OFTEN THINK ABOUT MY LAST NIGHT OUTSIDE. How I'd struggled and stowed away for hours, changing trains three times, to make it as far east as I could. It was cooler by the shore. And from a distance the water twinkled spectacularly, a muddy blue-green in the last gasp of twilight, and I hoped you were recovering in a hospital bed.

Then I heard the news. In the drugstore. It was channel 9, I think, and the anchorwoman was visibly shaken. She said you had been fatally shot in your dressing room. She said police had arrived at the theatre after a 911 call about a fire and found the slain actress. She said they'd rushed you to the hospital but it was too late. They were now questioning your friends, family, and boyfriend, John Strong, and if anyone else had any information about the crime they were asked to come forward.

I bolted from the store, running straight down to the beach, my sneakers crunching into the sand, packed hard from the previous days of rain. Heavy black clouds moved through creamy orange streaks of sky, air so damp it clammed my clothes. But I was sweating bullets: what a demented thing to say.

At the ocean's lip, I dropped my backpack and walked into the waves splashing over on themselves in tiny whitecaps, paddling me at the waist. I thought about going deeper, setting myself out to sea, where I'd be reunited with Blair in the undersea world and maybe you'd be there, that look in your eyes, the one I'd first seen at my grandparents' condo, it was there in those last few seconds, I swear. You had the look.

Cold suddenly in the black black water, I shivered. A couple of sea gulls fluttered nearby, one craning its neck sideways to jostle something on its back. It had a glowing pink glob caught in its feathers. Bubble gum. That stuff could take years to wash off. And it soiled with age. I imagined the old gull with a blacktop scar on its back. Anything good or sweet or brightly colored could eventually become damaging. I felt sadder than ever, out there waist-deep in the bay, and wished I had someone to talk to, but everyone was gone.

I slouched up out of the water and sat down on the beach. A jogger passed, the first person I'd seen in a while, and I watched him disintegrate into a black shadow as he ran down the beach and it looked like a fade-out, like dying, which slayed me all over. Wind bustling, I smoked a cigarette with my hands cupped, then emptied the contents of my backpack out on the sand. There was my bloody shirt, the copy of *People,* my half-destroyed, charcoal-edged book. It smelled like a neglected campfire and felt lighter than ever. Flipping the frayed pages turned my stomach. You were everywhere—in sketches, cartoons, clips from magazines . . . I tore out a page and the wind lifted it up and carried it down the dark beach like the cloudy trail of an airplane, and I stood up and screamed into the rumbling bay, screamed, "Why? Why? WHY?!"

First I burned the magazine. Then the shirt. And, finally, the book, warming my hands over the flames as my life went up in smoke. Then I lay back and dozed for a while. When I awoke the clouds had edged out slightly, making way for a few intrepid stars, and I remembered I was still part of the world; in fact, I'd never felt so aligned with it—sand, water, and the great galaxy of emptiness above, I matched it molecule for molecule, as if my body were disassembling like people in the teleportation machine on *Star Trek*—and it made me think of a prayer I'd once heard on the radio out in Arizona: "You are a child of the universe, no less than the trees and the stars; you have a right to be here."

Understand, I had to believe something. Why not proclaim myself part of an infinite universe, where you might return someday in a supernova of love and forgiveness? I was a bit like your mother in that respect, demanding you be bigger than this world.

To this day, she maintains you got where you needed to be. As much as I try to believe her—and it's taken awhile—I can't. My heart is as dusty black and empty as that last night sky.

I still love you, Brooke, and I always will. For that I won't apologize. The rest I offer up to the lawyers, judges, shrinks, and reporters, to all of your fans who hate my guts, to your family and friends and boyfriend, John Strong, although I recently heard he's married your sister and, I'm sorry, that makes me mad. Seems like they'd have more respect for your memory, but who am I to say? We're all supposed to be healing. So maybe this'll help. All I ask is that you clean up the punctuation a bit and please be kind.

Also from **AKASHIC BOOKS**

KAMIKAZE LUST BY LAUREN SANDERS
*WINNER OF A LAMBDA LITERARY AWARD
287 PAGES, A TRADE PAPERBACK ORIGINAL, $14.95, ISBN: 1-888451-08-4

"Great courage must account for such complete disregard of political correctness, and great sensitivity for such sadness."
—Amanda Filipacchi, author of *Vapor* and *Nude Men*

"Lauren Sanders's novel *Kamikaze Lust* makes a connection between unrealized lives, sexual repression, and the fear of death. In her hands, what is usually clichéd or gratuitous is hot."
—Amy Ray of the Indigo Girls

SOUTHLAND BY NINA REVOYR
*WINNER OF A LAMBDA LITERARY AWARD AND A FERRO-GRUMLEY AWARD
348 PAGES, A TRADE PAPERBACK ORIGINAL, $15.95, ISBN: 1-888451-41-6

"What makes a book like *Southland* resonate is that it merges elements of literature and social history with the propulsive drive of a mystery, while evoking Southern California as a character, a key player in the tale. Such aesthetics have motivated other Southland writers, most notably Walter Mosley."
—*Los Angeles Times*

"If Oprah still had her book club, this novel likely would be at the top of her list . . . With prose that is beautiful, precise, but never pretentious . . ."
—*Booklist* (starred review)

SOME OF THE PARTS BY T COOPER
*A BARNES & NOBLE DISCOVER GREAT NEW WRITERS PROGRAM SELECTION
264 PAGES, A TRADE PAPERBACK ORIGINAL, $14.95, ISBN: 1-888451-36-X

The novel that's changing the way we define "family." The Osbournes, Sopranos, and Eminem are only "some of the parts" that make up the whole story of the new American family.

"A wholly original novel that's both discomforting and compelling to read . . . questing characters."
—*San Francisco Chronicle*

MANHATTAN LOVERBOY BY ARTHUR NERSESIAN
*FROM THE AUTHOR OF THE BESTSELLING CULT-CLASSIC *THE FUCK-UP*
203 PAGES, A TRADE PAPERBACK ORIGINAL, $13.95, ISBN: 1-888451-09-2

"*Manhattan Loverboy* is paranoid fantasy and fantastic comedy in the service of social realism, using the methods of L. Frank Baum's *Wizard of Oz* or Kafka's *The Trial* to update the picaresque urban chronicles of Augie March, with a far darker edge . . ."
—*Downtown* magazine

HAIRSTYLES OF THE DAMNED BY JOE MENO
*THE DEBUT NOVEL OF THE PUNK PLANET BOOKS IMPRINT
*A BARNES & NOBLE DISCOVER GREAT NEW WRITERS PROGRAM SELECTION
290 PAGES, A TRADE PAPERBACK ORIGINAL, $13.95, ISBN: 1-888451-70-X

"Joe Meno writes with the energy, honesty, and emotional impact of the best punk rock. From the opening sentence to the very last word, *Hairstyles of the Damned* held me in his grip."
—Jim DeRogatis, pop music critic, *Chicago Sun-Times*

"*Hairstyles of the Damned* is observational comedy of the best kind, each glittering small detail offering up a wave of memories for anyone alive in the latter part of the previous century . . . Beware: Joe Meno can make you remember."
—Bee Lavender, *HipMama* magazine

THE FALL OF HEARTLESS HORSE
BY MARTHA KINNEY
*A SELECTION OF DENNIS COOPER'S LITTLE HOUSE ON THE BOWERY SERIES
100 PAGES, A TRADE PAPERBACK; $11.95, ISBN: 1-888451-73-4

"I love this book. How Martha Kinney created this utterly unique and powerful piece of writing . . . is beyond me. As a grateful and admiring reader I can only thank her for this work and eagerly await more."
—Amy Gerstler, author of *Ghost Girl*